The Ace

——— A Novel ———

Jack D. Hunter

Blue River Press
Indianapolis

The Ace is a work of historical fiction. Apart from the well-known actual people, events and locales that figure in the narrative, all names, characters, places and incidents are the products of the author's imagination and are used fictitiously. Any resemblance to current events or locales, or to living persons, is entirely coincidental.

The Ace © 2008 Jack D. Hunter

All rights reserved under International and Pan-American Copyright Conventions

No part of this book may be reproduced, stored in a database or other retrieval system, or transmitted in any form, by any means, including mechanical, photocopy, recording or otherwise, without the prior written permission of the publisher.

Cover designed by Phil Velikan and Jonni Anderson
Packaged by Wish Publishing

Graphics courtesy of National Archives and Records Administration

ISBN: 9780979924064
Printed in the United States of America
10 9 8 7 6 5 4 3 2 1

Distributed in the United States by
Cardinal Publishers Group
www.cardinalpub.com

BOOKS BY JACK D. HUNTER

The Blue Max
The Blood Order
The Tin Cravat
The Expendable Spy
One of Us Works for Them
Spies, Inc.
The Terror Alliance
Florida is Closed Today
Judgment in Blood
The Flying Cross
The Potsdam Bluff
Tailspin
Sweeney's Run
Slingshot
The Cure
Addie (under pen name Lee Thompson)

TELEGRAM RECEIVED.

FROM 2nd from London # 5747.

"We intend to begin on the first of February unrestricted submarine warfare. We shall endeavor in spite of this to keep the United States of America neutral. In the event of this not succeeding, we make Mexico a proposal of alliance on the following basis: make war together, make peace together, generous financial support and an understanding on our part that Mexico is to reconquer the lost territory in Texas, New Mexico, and Arizona. The settlement in detail is left to you. You will inform the President of the above most secretly as soon as the outbreak of war with the United States of America is certain and add the suggestion that he should, on his own initiative, invite Japan to immediate adherence and at the same time mediate between Japan and ourselves. Please call the President's attention to the fact that the ruthless employment of our submarines now offers the prospect of compelling England in a few months to make peace." Signed, ZIMMERMANN.

Chapter 1

The Curtiss guy made it clear that he knew more about the Jenny than anybody alive. Along with that, he elevated his chin and looked down his long nose while he talked, condescending, implying that Carpenter was wasting company time by asking his stupid questions.

Three minutes of this, and Carpenter set military courtesy aside. "Tell me, Randall, do you want to sell this thing to the Army or don't you? If you do, knock off the haughty crap and let me fly it. If you don't, just say so, and I'm on my way back to Mineola."

Randall's jaw muscles clenched. "Well, now, I'm not used to being talked to like that."

"And I'm not used to some self-satisfied pencil pusher treating me like a grade-schooler looking at his very first flying machine. See these wings on my collar? They mean I'm one of very few U.S. of A. Signal Corps guys who knows how to get one of these crates into the air. So quit the schoolteacher shit and let me put this one up there."

"Why are you so...testy...Lieutenant?"

"I just spent four hundred million hours on the New York goddamn Central Railroad, eating cinders and rattling my brains out on a seat that was made out of marble. I haven't had a good sleep for three days, I haven't had a good meal for longer, and I'm in no frigging mood to go through flight school again, especially when the teacher is a salesclerk with a celluloid collar, a long nose, and bad breath."

"Well..."

Carpenter turned, shoved his boot into the fuselage stirrup, swung into the Jenny's rear cockpit, and settled in the bucket seat, fastening the lap belt in two impatient tugs. Lowering the goggles over his eyes, he nodded over the cockpit rim at the mechanic, who had been standing by, struggling to hide a grin.

"Switch off."

The mechanic hung his weight on one of the propeller blades and moved it through an arc, a soft sucking sound coming from the engine.

"Switch on."

After giving the propeller a hearty tug, the mechanic stepped back, and the barking and roaring began. Carpenter worked the throttle and rudder to goose the machine across the snowy turf and into a turn to the wind. He sat there for a time, feeling the airplane coming alive, moving the ailerons and elevators through their full travel, smelling the warming oil and rich exhaust. Satisfied finally, he eased the throttle into full power and waited watchfully as the Jenny skittered and bounced across the snowy ruts and lifted him into the winter sky.

This time there was no magic. Ordinarily, takeoffs cured anything—hangovers, guilt trips, heartburn, warts. The farther away the earth, the stronger and cleaner the body and soul. But now he couldn't throw off the dark self-contempt inherited from last night's tumble with the cellist's wife. Her old man, somebody big in music, was on his way to a Chicago recital, and while he was in the parlor car playing gin with some people, she was driven by what she claimed to be insane boredom to lead William the Conqueror to drinks in her Pullman bedroom suite, where she permitted him to "take advantage." Truth was, she was ugly, over-perfumed, and altogether inept, feeding her pretense of being led astray by insisting on a prissy missionary position.

He had left her early, feeling this rotten self-loathing, and so this morning he had taken it out on Randall, the Curtiss salesman. Disgust. Guilt. Grubbiness he couldn't wash away. A hungover perception of himself as a rich man's brat being led through life by his dingus. Randall, clean, starched, dapper, stuffy, and supercilious, was precisely the worst kind to confront when climbing out of a cesspool.

The engine sputtered, and Carpenter sat up straight, his brooding shattered instantly by the sound of danger.

The altimeter gave him only eleven hundred feet, and a quick glance showed him nothing below but Lackawanna, a vast, smoky smear of steel mills, rooftops, and a forest of chimneys and poles tracing grimy, narrow streets.

The engine quit altogether, its racket leaving the evening to the soft sighing of wires, and the Jenny began to sink.

"Damn, damn, damn."

※※※

John King set a pot of coffee to perking on the kitchen stove, then went into the tiny living room and dropped into its only easy chair. He looked about him as if seeing the place for the first time.

A prison it was.

Had been. Would be.

Here he had spent his boyhood, a mishmash of incongruities and anxious suspicions endured in unremitting poverty. From boyhood through puberty into this—what was it now, tentative manhood? Tentative was the word, whatever it was. All of it suffered in this two-story box on a patch of threadbare grass at No. 15 Factory Street.

As he had progressed from shorts and knee socks through knickers to long pants, the house had remained a bittersweet In-Here surrounded by a malevolent Out-There. The In-Here was a cosmos of subtle change and contradiction, in which Father somehow became Dad and Mother became Mom, a place where Dad's consistently dreamy indifference provided mere background to Mom's more gaudy center-stage seesawing between cheeriness and despondency. Dad, dozing away his days among piles of books and newspapers, filling the room with the stink of his ill-tended meerschaum pipe, had contributed only fluency in German and an appreciation of the literary classics to John's education. The rest had been left to Mom. She had seemed gratified by this and along the way had risen above her own biases and personal demons to caution her son that—contrary to what he heard in the schoolyard—all Italians weren't crooks, all black people weren't shiftless, all Jews weren't greedy, all Irishmen weren't drunks, all Poles weren't stupid, and all Frenchmen weren't sneaky, even though all of them were guaranteed to call John's family, the Königs-Kings, "Krauts" and other obnoxious and stereotypical labels. "That's the way people are," she had said, "trying to make themselves feel superior by making others feel inferior. Well, by golly, you and Dad and I are above all that, understand, darlin'?"

Despite Mom's assurances of his clean-cut features, his well-proportioned body, and his gentle manner, his mirror told him he was a rawboned *Klotz* with acne and unruly hair. He had all the standard masculine attributes, including mechanical aptitude, but mechanics and the applied sciences were boring. For him, the good stuff was art and music and the musty smell of libraries. He was pained by circuses and zoos because of what they did to animals; he disliked football because he was too skinny to play it; he disliked baseball unless he could pitch; he disliked girls, except those whose tits were swelling, a phenomenon he found mildly interesting. But he also learned his strengths: he had a sense of humor; he learned quickly, even those subjects that bored him; he was capable of quick decisions, most of them turning out to be valid; and he perceived the orderliness of music so clearly he taught himself to play popular tunes on the decrepit upright piano some former owner had left in the basement. He loved books and libraries because they helped to satisfy his huge curiosity; he played a mean game of ice hockey, had a great marble collection, could run like a sumbish, could hang head down from a tree branch for ten straight minutes, could burp on purpose, and would go up in hot, tight spirals over any form of unfairness.

The Out-There was like the moon, with a lighted side and a dark side. The one, while not thoroughly understandable, he could see directly; he was only dimly aware of the other by way of schoolyard scuttlebutt and the guarded conversations of his parents. Both sides were scary. The visible side contained puzzling polarities: mansions and hovels, dew-covered farms and coal-blackened factories, crystal lakes and garbage-choked harbors, sparkling limousines and rusty Fords, Lake Erie's sweet breezes and Lackawanna's choking soot. For a boy, the visible contradictions were beyond comprehension.

The dark side he couldn't see was even worse, because it was built mainly of whisperings and his own imagination.

Late at night, when they were getting ready for bed and thought he was sound asleep in the bedroom across the hall, his parents would whisper of weird or ominous things, such as that poor dear Mabel Somebody down the street whose husband, crippled and unemployable after a steel mill accident, had stuck his head in the gas oven and left her with two kids and no way to support them. Or how the daddy of Natalie, a pert, long-haired school chum, had mysteriously drowned in a lake during a family vacation in Canada. Lots of death and misery were in those whispered conversations, and he had frequently gone to sleep with a sense of impending doom.

The coffee's smell broke into his ruminations, tantalizing, but he decided he would rid the front walk of its ice patch first, making the coffee taste all the better later on.

❋❋❋

He had just finished chipping the glaze from the cracked cement walk when a glissando of whispering, clacking, and barking came out of the wintry twilight sky. The sound had risen so quickly, so insistently in the dinnertime silence, he had instinctively flinched. Blinking, he saw the biplane rushing past, a khaki shadow barely clearing the power poles and street lamps aligning the narrow strip of Factory Street. It continued in a peculiar wobbling, as if it were a living creature struggling to put off its approaching doom. King watched, mouth open, eyes wide, as the machine took out the trolley wires at the Benson Street turnaround then slammed to the pavement, careening through the St. Benedict Parochial School's playground fence, slewing, scattering wheels and wings and motor parts, coming to a convulsive halt in a cloud of dirty snow and a jumble of seesaws and swings.

King was only vaguely aware of running, slipping, and stumbling down the rutted street, and of vaulting the playground fence and plunging into the wreckage, where he clawed away at the tangle. His first clear thought was that beneath the pile was a man who was going to be incinerated if the gasoline and oil staining the air caught a spark.

"Hi, pard." The voice, deep and groggy, came out of somewhere. "Sure nice of you to stop by."

"Where are you?"

"Down here between the carburetor and the tailskid, just east of the exhaust pipe."

"I can't see you—"

"I can see you. Lift that aileron right in front of you. I'd help, but my legs are crammed in by something and I think my arm's busted."

"I smell gas. Is this thing going to blow up?"

"Maybe. Wasn't a lot of gas in the tank, but enough to worry about. Those wires I took down might have some juice left in 'em."

King felt panic gathering, and he tugged and kicked at the snarl of fabric and splintered wood with no apparent success. "We need some help." He cast an anxious glance around and was cheered to see that a small crowd had gathered along what remained of the fence line.

"Hey, will some of you lend a hand here? The aviator's hurt, and he's trapped."

The knot of people stood silent. Then a man he recognized as Mr. Adams, the plumber who lived at No. 33, pulled up his collar against the chill wind that had begun to stir. "Think again, Kraut. That there's a bomb waitin' ta go off."

"You're just going to stand there and do nothing?"

"Why should I risk my butt just because some snot-nosed Kraut kid wants to play hero?"

The little crowd murmured agreement, and King stared in angry disbelief. "There's a man in here. He's hurt. He could die, for Pete's sake."

"I ain't gonna die with him."

The deep voice came up from the junk.

"Take it easy. We'll just wait until the cops or the trolley car people or the electric company guys come to see what the hell happened. Meantime, do yourself a favor and clear out while you got the chance."

King's anger had triggered his stubbornness. "I'm not going to leave you alone, mister. I'll get you out somehow."

"Then easy does it. One piece of junk at a time. Slow and easy. Okay?"

King grasped the aileron and pulled it toward him a few inches. He was aware that he was holding his breath, and the idea that his breathing might ignite the fumes stirred a mad need to laugh. Something gave, and with a shift of a shoulder he opened a kind of tunnel, at the bottom of which he could see the top of the man's helmet, a glittering of goggles and a patch of leather flying suit. Turning feet first, he lowered himself into the stinking jumble and was able to seize the flier's right shoulder.

"You got me. But try to stay away from the other shoulder. That's the one that hurts like sin."

"Are both your feet caught?"

"Mainly the right one. Pull me up a bit and release my safety belt catch. You do that, and I think I can get some purchase that'll untangle them both."

They struggled, and eventually they rolled out of the wreck and onto the stained snow, gasping.

"Hey, Kraut, want a cigarette? I'll throw you a light." There was a scattering of laughter.

"Nice neighbors you got, kid." The flier's voice was heavy with pain.

"They don't matter."

"Help me to my feet. I want to see if I can stand."

King placed his hands under the flier's arms and hauled him erect. He was big, and there followed an interval in which he clung to King, a dazed bear, wobbling, searching for equilibrium. Holding each other, they sidled away from the wreck and the patch of oil-soaked snow, shuffling toward the fence and the street beyond.

"That's a piss-poor dance," a voice called. "You two sweeties need practice." The laughter was louder now.

The aviator moved away from King and turned his head slowly to regard the crowd. "Who said that?"

A chunky man wearing a knit cap and a checkered lumberjack stepped forward. "I did, sweetie. Got somethin' on your mind?"

"Yeah. I get a kick out of your sense of humor. I think you ought to, too."

With surprising speed, the aviator's right boot left the ground and, arcing, landed with a thud squarely in the chunky man's groin.

A sound came up from the knot of people, a kind of protracted gasp, and the man, groaning, squirmed in the snow, feet pulled up in the fetal position. King's astonishment mixed with a surge of actual alarm when he saw anger and vengefulness stirring along the fence. He knelt quickly and brought up a piece of broken wing strut. Stepping to the aviator's side, he said, "My house is that yellow one up the street, mister. The door's unlocked. Get there as fast as you can." He turned toward the crowd, swinging the length of splintered ash in savage arcs. "Hurry. I'll cover you."

The impending battle ended at once when, in a soft whoomp, the airplane wreckage erupted in a roiling fireball that sent an evil orange glare racing through the twilight. The crowd scattered like beads from a broken string.

"You okay, mister?"

"Yep. Let's get to the house."

"You go ahead. I'll be there in a minute."

King, feeling the heat, slipped and slid to where the man in the lumberjack still lay, abandoned in his agony, his wide, glassy eyes fixed on the fire racing its way across the fuel-sodden slush. Clutching the checkered wool, King dragged the man to the street.

"You'll be safe here until your friends come to get you."

"You son-of-a-bitchin Kraut," the man gasped.

"You're welcome."

❖❖❖

King found the aviator standing in the middle of the living room, a huge, bedraggled teddy bear, bloody here and there and looking lost and confused. He took the man's elbow and steered him into Mom's old sewing room, which he had been using as a first-floor bedroom since Dad had entered the hospital.

"Lie on the bed. I'll get some things and clean up some of those cuts on your hands and face."

"I'm a mess. I don't want to dirty up that nice clean bed."

"Lie down. I don't want you falling down and dirtying up my nice clean living room rug, either. Blankets and sheets I can wash. A ten-by-twelve fake Oriental, that's something else."

The aviator rolled onto the bed, which sagged and squeaked under his weight. King went to the kitchen and gathered bandages, tape, and iodine from the cupboard.

When King returned, the aviator's eyes were closed, and he was breathing with effort. King felt for a wrist pulse the way the clinic had taught him to do with Dad, and it seemed strong enough, so he opened the fur collar, shoved the sleeves higher on the forearms, and began to swab the cuts and bruises with clean water.

"What's your name?"

"John King."

"Bill Carpenter here. Second Lieutenant William J. Carpenter."

King felt the right arm, and there was no suggestion of a broken bone. "I think you have a bad sprain, not a break. I'll wrap it up good until the emergency people get here."

When he was finished, King realized that Carpenter had fallen into a deep doze, so he gathered the supplies and took them to the kitchen. Then he returned to the easy chair and listened to the hooting and clanging of the arriving firefighting crews. He knew the police would be here soon, but a lethargy had settled over him, and he found he didn't really care.

Carpenter stirred, then stood, surprisingly steady, at the hallway mirror, examining the adhesives covering the cuts on his forehead and chin. "I owe you, John King. If ever there was the right guy at the right place, you're it."

King made a minimizing sound. "You'd have done the same for me. People have to watch out for each other."

Carpenter turned, gave him an amused stare, then broke into open laughter. King marveled at the display of beautiful, even teeth.

"I said something funny?"

"People don't say things like that much these days."

Carpenter crossed the room and dropped onto the settee beside the fireplace. He sighed again and yawned. "Do you want something to eat?"

"No thanks. That coffee smells good, though."

King fetched a mug from the pantry, and the hot dark drink crackled as it poured. He was aware of Carpenter's scrutiny, and to camouflage the awkward bashfulness this brought on, he asked a question. "What happened to your plane, Lieutenant?"

"Bill. I'll always be Bill to a guy who saved my life." Carpenter pursed his lips and blew away the steam rising from the mug. "I'm based at the Signal Corps air field in Mineola, out on Long Island. They sent me here to visit the Curtiss factory and try out a Jenny with some new fittings and give a recommendation as to whether they show military promise. I'd just taken off from the Curtiss factory strip north of here when the engine went on the fritz. It gave up somewhere over your house."

"You were lucky."

"Yep."

"The cops'll be here any time now."

"Been wondering what's taking them so long." Carpenter took a long pull at his coffee, then pushed himself to his feet. "Gotta wee-wee." He waddled off to the bathroom.

King realized that the house was getting cold, so he went to the basement, rattled the furnace grate, and when the fire had shown some vigor, placed four shovels of new coal in the strategic hot spots, and opened the living room flue to its limit. Satisfied, he returned upstairs to find Carpenter standing at the window, looking up the street at an approaching phalanx of blue-coat policemen.

"Sorry to stink up your place. But these duds are all I got. If I took 'em off I'd be going downtown with my wienie dangling in the breeze."

The image amused King, and he chuckled. "That would sure put some headlines on the headlines, wouldn't it?"

Carpenter traced a line in the air with a forefinger. "I can see it now: 'Intrepid flying ace, questioned about plane crash, waves his joystick at admiring crowds.'"

They broke into outright laughter and were nearing hysteria when the doorbell rang.

The police were loudly upset.

They pushed their way through the door and, like a small surf surge, carried King down the hall and into the living room, waving papers and smelling of stale tobacco and old whiskey. The leader, a squat sorehead with sergeant's chevrons on his coat, barked, "You own this place?"

"My father owns it. He's in the hospital."

The sergeant pointed angrily at Carpenter. "Did you grab this flyin' machine driver and force him to come here? Have you been hidin' him out—principal in a major accident?"

"Hiding him out? No. He needed attention. His cuts and bruises—"

The cop broke in. "Why dint you let us know he was here? We had to ask a jillion people before they allowed as how you forced this flyin' machine driver into this house. Hidin' a principal in a major accident can put you in the slammer—ya know that?"

King was dealing with his confusion when Carpenter pulled himself up from the settee, swaying, his eyes hot, to loom over the sergeant. "Listen to me, Porky. I'm a commissioned officer in the United States Army, and I'm under special orders, which means I won't put up one more freakin' minute with your Keystone Kop bullying. That crowd of assholes thought it would be entertaining to watch me roast alive in the wreck. This boy held them off until I could get to his daddy's house, where I could wait for you to take me to a military hospital. You give that kid any more bad mouth and I'll have you up to your ass in a federal prosecution. Understand?"

Even King, in his confusion and anxiety, knew that Carpenter's speech was a huge pile of horse manure. But the sergeant wasn't all that sure, and with this mountainous, bunged-up flyin' machine driver bending over him, he was obviously unlikely to carry things further.

"All right," the sergeant snapped at his crew, "let's get this principal to the emergency ward. We'll sort out the charges later."

Chapter 2

The restaurant was on a fashionable tree-lined street just off Capitol Hill. Standing in the foyer, Otto von Dietrich suggested a beer keg topped by an artillery shell, an effect created by his portly body, to which his bald, almost conical head seemed attached without benefit of a neck. His suiting was of the most expensive and well-tailored serge; his oxfords gleamed from incalculable swipes of a polishing cloth; his foulard was obviously worth a small fortune. But the whole effect was made ludicrous thanks to the starched white collar, rising high in the current fashion, which reached virtually to his ears. Thaddeus Slater, shaking the man's fat hand perfunctorily, privately marveled at the German's stoic indifference to what simply had to be exquisite torture.

"Ah, Congressman Slater," von Dietrich murmured unctuously in faintly accented English, "I have been looking forward with much pleasure to this occasion."

Slater's glance swept the restaurant, taking in the wall-sized mirrors, the rococo ceiling, the fluted columns, the velvet drapes at the tall windows, the glittering chandeliers. "I, too."

"I've arranged a private dining room."

Von Dietrich nodded at the maître d', who led them through the potted palms to an ornate archway below the balcony, upon which a string quartet dealt busily with Vivaldi.

The room was small but elegant, and they sat at a table whose faultless white cloth seemed to make the silver and crystal settings all the more brilliant. With the door closed, the music became muted, a development for which Slater was profoundly grateful; Vivaldi's chattering style always made him nervous and irritable.

"I'll leave the wine selection to you, Congressman."

"Thank you. But I never take alcohol at lunch."

The German appeared to be disappointed, but he recovered quickly with his pouty smile. "You won't mind if I have some Riesling?"

"Please do. But I might mention, too, that we in the Congress, thanks to the press of current business, rarely have time to enjoy prolonged Washington lunches."

The German waved a gesture of assent. "I understand, sir. But it's a pity, because we Germans are very fond of food and drink. As a matter of fact, it's quite common among the more prosperous Berliners to have seven meals a day. Breakfast upon arising, a second breakfast of beer and sandwiches around eleven, a main lunch of four or five courses with wine and beer, cakes and coffee at three, sandwiches and beer around five, a main dinner with several kinds of wines at seven, and a substantial supper before going to bed. There's an old drollery, 'It's not true that Germans eat all the time. They eat only during those periods of the day that separate their seven regular meals.'"

Von Dietrich paused, his heavy-lidded gray eyes twinkling with challenge. Then he pressed, "Are you sure you won't indulge me? Allow me to give you a small demonstration of our noontime folkways?"

Slater smiled politely. "I'm truly sorry, sir, but I really must run soon. A salad, coffee, and I'll be off."

"As you wish, Congressman."

They watched wordlessly as the waiter served them. When they were alone again, Von Dietrich cleared his throat and, assuming a confidential manner, said, "My duties as a lobbyist for the Imperial German government require me to ingratiate myself with the well-placed, important members of the Wilson administration and the Congress. And you, sir, are among the most well-placed and important of all."

Slater recognized this as pure baloney, but it was gratifying nonetheless. If the German chose to lay it on, he must have a good reason, and whatever the ulterior motive and no matter how brazen the blarney, it was good to find that he was considered worthy of Berlin's attention. *A man is known by the flattery he gets, eh?*

Hiding his amusement at the German's imprecise and revealing word choice, he asked, "So just how do you propose to ingratiate yourself with me, Herr von Dietrich?"

"Ah. You come directly to the point, Congressman. I like that in a man. It saves time and unnecessary sparring."

Here Slater put into play rule No. 1 of *The Politician's Guide to the Intimidation of Bullshitters:* Stare at them and say nothing.

They took a moment to sip coffee, during which the quartet dropped Vivaldi for a more restful Strauss. The German broke the pause with a question. "Is it true, Congressman Slater, that you are extremely opposed to the current agitation here in the States for war against Germany? The press would have us believe this, and my government has asked me to sound you out directly."

Slater shrugged. "The only people here who want war with Germany are business tycoons and large-scale international shippers who are angry at the kaiser for sinking our ships on the high seas. I am with the common folk, who do not want to fight and die simply to make things easier for the plutocrats. As I see it, Germany has a right to plug up traffic carrying war supplies to its enemies. Any country would do the same."

"Ah. Well said."

Von Dietrich toyed with the stem of his wine glass, seemingly deep in thought. After a time, he said, "I shall come right to the point. My government feels there aren't enough well-placed Americans who think as you do. And we fear that our highly necessary U-boat interdiction of shipping will alienate even more of your people. Therefore, we would like to, ah, enlist you as a persuader, an opinion leader, who will subtly sway your congressional colleagues into supporting President Wilson's reluctance to chastise the kaiser."

"You mean you want me to be a paid lobbyist for the German government?"

Von Dietrich held up a pudgy finger. "Not exactly. We realize that as a member of Congress it's not possible for you to lobby openly on behalf of any cause. But—"

"So you're talking under the table, is that it?"

"So to speak."

Slater pretended annoyance. "I'm not for sale."

The German smiled slyly. "Of course not. But we also know that you are very deeply in debt. Especially to the Universal Finance Combine, which holds the rather sizeable mortgage on your farm and residence in your home district. And which, by the way, is a company owned by Donner Gesellschaft of Berlin. And which, I understand, is preparing to foreclose on your mortgage."

"You guys play dirty, don't you?"

The German shrugged again. "In war, one does what one must."

"So what's the deal?"

"Your mortgage will be paid in full and you will receive fifty thousand dollars in cash to start. An additional fifty thousand will be placed in any bank account of your choosing each year in which the United States Congress remains neutral in the current conflict."

Slater went into the thoughtful mode again, then said, "Hand me my mortgage, signed paid in full, and seventy-five thousand dollars in cash bills. As soon as you do that, we'll be in business. Otherwise, no."

Von Dietrich smiled, took an envelope from his jacket pocket, and slid it across the table. "Here is your mortgage, as specified. The cash will be hand delivered in a plain package to your office in the morning. You must, of course, sign for it."

"I'll be there."

"Excellent.

Chapter 3

The school grounds were already under reconstruction, and the electrical wires had been restored by the following noon. After watching some of the to-do from the upstairs bedroom window, King had a lunch of sausage, cheese, and tea. Then he dressed in his brown suit and starched white shirt with the celluloid collar, tied his red knit necktie, pulled on his tatty overcoat and fedora, and left to board a trolley that would, with three transfers, take him to the Southside charity hospital. As he rode, he closed his eyes against the snow glare and let his body sway with the car's squealing rockabye, which eventually brought on a half-doze.

He tried and failed to remember the last time he had laughed so openly, so explosively. The tears in his eyes, the shaking of his shoulders, the heaving of his belly had together produced something of the quality of an orgasm. When the police had crowded into the living room, barking questions, the amusement had melted in the heat of his own fluster. But it returned as he watched the almost comedic interplay among the self-important bluecoats, caught up in a confusion of their own, and wavering while Carpenter roared down at them in theatrical, cockamamie outrage.

As the cops shoved him out the door, Carpenter had called back over their heads, "Thanks a lot, pardner. Keep the faith. I'll see you sometime."

Swaying in his trolley seat, King smiled again, then, feeling a flash of guilt over the contradiction between yesterday's goofy melodrama and today's grim mission, he forced himself to think of his father, dying by inches in a grubby bed in a grubby hospital and muttering hypocritical prayers to a God he never believed in, filled with tearful self-justification.

Ludwig König, as King now knew and hated himself for knowing, had gone through his whole life as a sponger, born in Munich to an upper-middle-class family whose indulgent members had forever seen him as a dreamy, studious child to be protected against reality. When they had died in a fire that consumed their opulent home, Ludwig, the sole survivor, became a professional houseguest, ignoring his degree in architecture to trade his undeniable charm and wit for the gracious quarters and fine cuisine of rich family friends. Eventually he had fallen for the lure of America, where, he believed, there would be marvelous opportunities for even richer associations. His sponsor, a Buffalo realtor, had treated him well at first, but then that sole support vanished when the realtor, a dedicated toper, smashed his Cadillac against an unforgiving elm in Delaware Park. With no important connections and no friends, Ludwig's few architectural commissions amounted to nothing more than garden trellises and room additions. To escape abject poverty, he'd married Molly McGavin, a delicious first-generation colleen who had a steady job cleaning bank buildings and a blind passion for the culture exuded by "this fine, Continental gentleman."

All of this King had learned by way of his mother's letters and diaries he'd found hidden in a chest behind the chimney in the attic. These had lifted some guilt from him, since he'd long seen his father as a loafer infuriatingly willing to let others slave through the years to support his lazy ways, and Mom's papers were absolute confirmation.

It might have gone better if his mother had been more open and vocal about her spooky and mostly guarded Irish convictions about God. Spiritual she was; churchy she was not. Because he loved her so much, King had accepted her teachings and admonitions without question. If, then, she had assured him early on—

flat-out, and with no equivocation—of God's existence, he might have been able to avoid much of the torment in his later life. As it was, and as if hedging her bets, she would hie him off to a Protestant church on Easter and Christmas, would lead him through his now-I-lay-me's at bedtime, and, on special occasions, would make his embarrassed dad say grace at dinner. Other than that, he had been on his own.

Thinking about all this now, he was surprised they did even those things, since Mom had suffered terribly as a child in a church-run home for children in Chicago. Her father died when she was a tot, and her mother was virtually forced into working as a charwoman. The poverty was so great Nanny couldn't afford to keep Mom and her sister Aunt Hazel living with her in her Southside tenement, so she put Mom in the orphanage, mainly because she wasn't old enough to work and Hazel was. But Mom never got over what she saw as an abandonment, and after years of enduring humiliations and sexual abuse in church-operated institutions, she couldn't bear to look at a clergyman or a nun. (King learned this when Aunt Hazel blurted it all out in a fit of weeping guilt and sorrow after Mom's funeral. Mom and Hazel loved each other very much, and Hazel shared Mom's rage over those early injustices.) King himself had developed a kind of stand-off, wait-and-see attitude about religion because of the unexplainable early memories that continued to haunt him until this day.

The total of what he remembered began with an ice-cold butt and a fleeting but intense nostalgia. Family lore said a doctor named Barden had delivered him, decided he was stillborn, tossed him onto a tin table, and turned his full attention to Mom.

In those days (he'd since been told), the infant mortality rate was generally considered to be just another melancholy reality to be expected and endured, like bad weather and false teeth. Most babies made it, but many didn't, and that was that. So from society's point of view, it was entirely reasonable for Doc Barden to ignore the silent little lump and battle to save the endangered mother.

And—here was the weird part—as the lump in question, he actually remembered the scene. The evening light beyond the tall windows, the medicinal smell, the cold metal against his nates, the scurrying, the clattering, had remained undiminished in his mind. He'd been aware of his own aliveness, and he was in no way surprised when a tall, indistinct figure appeared beside him and somehow induced the nurse, a small form in white, to come to the table, bend over him, then snatch him up and run with him to the big form in white, who (Mom had told him years later) was the doctor, trying to calm her spectacular distress.

He also still recalled with great clarity lying in Mom's arms and feeling a deep sadness, a poignant yearning for something wonderful that had been left behind.

With all this, and absent any real parental direction, he had developed his own religion—a potpourri of Golden Book feel-good adages and credos intermixed with a strong dose of the mysticism exuded by Mom, who, he suspected, had something of the medium about her. She'd been incredibly intuitive, often bordering on the clairvoyant, the prescient. She would speculate on the nature of God, extol the "wisdom" of the Bible, and was a firm believer in predestination and reincarnation. Dad viewed all religions with bland indifference, and for himself had clung to the idea that he'd rather live his life believing there is a God and finding out there is none when he died than live his life as if there isn't a God and, dying, finding out that there is one. Now, at death's door, Dad seemed to find his late wife's Irish spookiness uncomfortable and depressing. He had implied as much during his son's last visit, confiding in a croaking voice that all through their marriage "Molly was *sonderbar*, Johann—weird. Those big eyes, seeing things that weren't there. *Unheimlich.*"

Under his breath, King, now uneasy and unhappy, said, "She sure didn't have much on me."

When he arrived at the hospital, the receptionist, a tiny woman with a face that told of decades endured as a loser, said, "Mr. King, the ward supervisor wants to talk to you before you visit your father."

"Is something wrong?"

"I have no idea, sir."

"All right. Thanks."

The supervisor was in his office, feet on his desk, glasses on his forehead, and a huge sandwich in his right fist. His jaw moved lazily from side to side as he chewed, slowly grinding, like a cow's.

"You wanted to see me, Mr. Bolinski?"

"Mmm. Yeah." Bolinski took a moment to brush crumbs from his white lab coat and wash down his chew with a gulp of coffee. When all was in order he said, "Your pappy is inta dementia. He prolly won't make much sense, maybe won't even reckanize you. I thought ya oughta know."

"Dementia? Is that temporary, or what?"

"Well, put it this way: Your whole pappy is temporary. He won't be with us long. I just dint want you to have kittens when he tells you he's seein' Jesus and starts pickin' invisible feathers outa the air. I wanted to tip ya off, save you some shock. That sorta stuff."

"Can I see him now?"

Bolinski waved his sandwich at the ward entrance. "Sure. He ain't busy with nothin', I can tell you that."

❋❋❋

He looks smaller every time I see him, King thought.

Hat in hand, he stood beside the sagging bed, where a splinter of winter sunlight illuminated the waxen face, the closed, fluttering eyelids and sunken cheeks. The body under the blankets seemed narrow, diminished, the hands folded above them spidery and translucent.

"Hi, Dad. Came by to see how you are."

The lids parted, revealing eyes that suggested wet agates. There was no recognition in them. *"Wer bist du? Was willst du?"*

"John. I'm your son, come to visit."

"Unmöglich. Ich hab' kein' Sohn...."

"Whoa. You got me. All five foot seven of me."

The old face remained impassive, the old voice trailed off in an indecipherable rattling. King suddenly had a clear vision of his own loneliness and aloneness. The withered caricature on the bed was the only person in the world with a direct link to him, and now even this tenuous connection was unraveling. Ludwig König was, in effect, already dead. The understanding of this was now complete, and he felt himself giving way to a dreary self-mourning edged with panic. The Earth was twenty-five thousand miles around, peopled by umpteen million souls doing things, making things, hoping for things, achieving things, struggling with love and hate and triumph and failure. But now, with the passing of the befuddled little dreamer on the bed, none among them knew or cared anything about Johann König, AKA John King. He despised the tears he felt forming, because he knew they were for himself.

He leaned over the bed rail and, brushing away a wisp of white hair, kissed the clammy forehead for what he knew to be the last time, and whispered, *"Wiederseh'n, Vati. Gute Reise. Und kuss Mutti für mich. Erinnere sie, dass ich sie liebe."*

Blinking and choking, he pushed past Bolinski, who was standing at a file cabinet in the outer office, flipping through folders.

"Well, that dint take long," Bolinski said.

"You have the papers that say I'll pay for the burial and headstone, right?"

"Wouldn't let ya outa here without 'em."

"They also have my neighbor's phone number. Call me on that when it's over." *Damn this tight throat. Makes me squeak like a schoolgirl.*

Something in Bolinski's face softened. "Take it from me, kid: You feel like cryin', cry like hell. Get it outa your system in one big bunch. I know what I'm talkin' about."

"Men don't cry."

"Ya wanna bet?"

King slapped on his hat and went down the corridor to the stairway leading to the building's main entrance, hurrying, as if trying to outrun the tears that rushed his eyes, the sobs that prepared to explode. He virtually careened down the steps and burst out the door into the pale sunlight, gulping the cold air and relishing a sense of escape. At the curb he paused, breathing hard, forcing back the grief with a deliberate, mechanical checking of his change purse for the trolley tokens that would return him to Factory Street.

"Hi, pard."

He turned quickly, surprised, dabbing at the water on his cheeks and feeling a kind of warmth, to confirm that the voice was that of 2nd Lt. William J. Carpenter, standing tall and crisp in his tailored military topcoat and glistening boots and visored cap, grinning and holding out his hand.

"Well...I...Bill. What in the world are you doing here?"

"Chasing you down. Your neighbor told me where you'd gone."

King made no effort to hide his pleasure. "Well...why? Can I do something for you?"

"Nope. It's what I gotta do for you. Two things. First, I'm going to introduce you to the angels. Next I'm going to buy you a steak by way of thanks for everything." He pointed to a Model T parked across the street. "So get in the car."

"Angels?"

"I'm taking delivery on a replacement Jenny. I want to test it locally before I risk taking the damned thing over the Alleghenies. For that, I need ballast—some weight in the front cockpit. I also need ballast in the front cockpit that I can talk with by way of a new phone system the engineers have come up with. I could take along any one of the Curtiss guys, but I want to take you. You're a guy who needs some heavenly air in his soul. And you're a guy I need to thank special."

"Well—"

"No arguments. Let's go."

❋❋❋

The machine was larger than he expected it to be, with its two wings spreading widely and held together by a spider web of wires and turnbuckles and struts and woodwork so polished and smooth it looked like furniture. A taut, olive-hued fabric covered everything, glistening in the sunlight and smelling of banana oil; and the engine, ticka-tacking in a lazy idling, seeded the air with an aromatic mixture of hot oil and spent gasoline.

"You all set, kid?" Carpenter's voice crackled in the helmet's earphones.

King spoke carefully into the mouthpiece affixed to the chest of his borrowed flight suit. "I think so."

"I didn't tighten your belt too tight, did I? Gotta keep the blood circulating in the cold up where we're going."

"Seems fine."

"Lift your goggles now and then to keep them from steaming."

"All right."

"Remember: Wherever you go I'll be right behind you." Carpenter laughed loudly at his own joke.

The idling propeller dissolved in a mahogany-hued blur as the engine erupted in a deep, busy roaring. The rutted ground began to move beneath them, slowly at first, then more quickly as the machine asserted itself. The motion became a racing, and King felt a lightness, a lifting under the seat cushion, and the bouncing and gentle swaying ceased as the snowy turf fell away.

Oh, my God. Look at me. I'm up here. I'm...Oh, my God.

Below, the earth was a great gray platter dotted with swatches of white and etched by the lacework of roads and tree lines and agriculture. Off to the left Lake Erie sprawled, cold and spooky under a drifting of low-lying clouds. Around him, the machine trembled and made little squeakings, and he was simultaneously excited and appalled by the realization that the only thing between him and a fall of thousands of feet was that floorboard under his shoes.

"How you doin', kid?"

"I...It's great..."

"Ain't it so. Myself, I never get used to the feeling."

They flew with no further comment for a time. Then Carpenter asked, "You don't get motion-sick, do you, kid?"

"I don't think so. Why?"

"I'm gonna try a couple twists and turns. If you start getting sick, let me know. And don't even think about tossing your cookies over the side. If you gotta throw up, let it go on the floor. You heave over the side, it'll just blow back into my face, and I'll be most displeased, as the saying goes."

King was thinking about this when the horizon abruptly tilted, and he was being pressed into his seat. The turn was tight and to the left, and as it steepened his head sank into his shoulders and he felt his cheeks sag. Then suddenly the turn was to the right, and after a brief moment suggesting pause and the sensation of floating, the phenomena returned. Involuntarily he seized the leather-padded cockpit rim, and he felt a dampness in his gloves.

"You okay, kid?"

"You're scaring the hell out of me."

"If you can say that, then you're okay. Just relax. I'm going to do a stall and a couple of revolutions of a spin to see how well this critter recovers. Nothing to fear. Remember, I'm right behind you." Carpenter laughed again.

At first, nothing but sky appeared beyond the nose, and the propeller slowed, its blattering falling off to a kind of rhythmic whoosh. The machine began to tremble, and strange noises broke the relative quiet. Then the bottom fell out of everything. King's stomach felt as if it were about to push its way out of his mouth, only to rush back to his groin when the mad twisting began. The Earth was straight ahead, but it was a whirling kaleidoscope of dark, wintry colors. The sensation of falling increased.

"Holy shit!" He could barely hear his own voice.

"Sorry, sir. We don't allow uncouth language aboard this here vessel. Please refrain from using the word 'holy.'" Carpenter's laugh accelerated. "Now grab your balls, unless you want them to squeeze out your ass. I'm now about to shove this puddle jumper into recovery."

The whirling steadied, became a straight dive, then eased into level flight. And later, as the airplane descended, engine idling, wheels kissing the frozen turf, John King understood that he would never again be the same. He remembered the poem about aviators he had read in the Sunday supplement, and now it applied to him—personally. He had soared through the high blue and had been as one with the angels.

Chapter 4

Carpenter took him to a restaurant in a brownstone in the ritzy section of Delaware Avenue, north of Niagara Square in downtown Buffalo. King had been in this part of the city only twice in his life, once as a boy while passing through on a trolley bound for Kenmore, where one of Mom's old friends was having her funeral, and the other when trying unsuccessfully for a job at the DuPont plant on Riverside. Melancholy had prevailed at both events, and so he wasn't overjoyed when Carpenter pulled in, gave the Ford over to the brass-buttoned door people, and, waving toward the regal entrance, said, "In you go, Jonathan. Chow time."

"This will cost us a bunch, Bill. I'm not sure—"

"Just because you're a little guy doesn't mean you have to think and act little. *Au contraire.* Take Napoleon: He was twice as short as you are, and look where it got him."

"Exile on Elba, that's where."

"Yeah, but he didn't have William J. Carpenter on his side. You do, and William J. Carpenter is going to buy you a steak only a teeny bit larger than Texas. Stop worrying, li'l feller."

King stopped at the doorway, suddenly annoyed. "I'll appreciate your cutting out the remarks about my size. I'm not big, I'm not little. I'm average. So cut it the hell out."

Carpenter grinned, took him by the elbow, and swept him into the wake of the maître d', who led them to a candlelit table beside a corner fireplace. "Everybody looks tiny to me, Tim. Besides, I was waiting to see how long it would take you to tell me off. I was even wondering if you ever cussed."

They sat and were immediately fussed over by a pair of dandies in white coats. King secretly marveled at how Carpenter bossed them around without seeming to be bossy. An eyebrow lifted here, a finger waved there, and they filled the water glasses, noted down his murmured wine order, lit his cigarette, and unfolded the menus in elegant, fawning sweeps.

"You've been here before, seems like," King said, amused.

"No, but I'm good with a phone. They think I'm scouting for a place to hold the Officer's Club annual party."

King sighed and shook his head. "You not only have a size fixation, you're also an aspiring carnival promoter."

Carpenter laughed. "Now I know why I like you. You're a little squirt just into shaving, and yet you talk snooty, like a college professor. Fixation? Aspiring carnival promoter? Shit. Where'd you learn to talk like that anyhow?"

"I read a lot. And I do everything I can to avoid sounding like a Kraut."

"Can you talk Kraut?"

"Live with something for twenty years, it sort of sticks."

"Which means yes?"

King nodded. "And some of the best books I've ever read were among those in my dad's German collection. But these days it doesn't pay to let something like that get around."

Carpenter's grin faded, and he took a thoughtful drag at his cigarette. "Ah, yes. The impending war against the kaiser. The president's trying to keep us out of it, but we're going to be up to our asses in that scrap before we know it."

"You really think so?"

"Well, hell yes. Don't you? The kaiser's sinking our ships, killing our people, tying up our sea trade with submarine blockades, and our politicians and business guys are raising holy hell about it. They want the kaiser's scalp, and Wilson's gotta listen or he'll be outa his job, believest thou me."

The soup appeared before them in another obsequious swirling, and they set about spooning it up, almost to the rhythm established by the string quartet that fussed its way through a Straussian cliché.

"You say you're twenty, Johnny?"

"Mmm."

"They call you Kraut because of your daddy?"

"He was born and raised in Munich. My real name is Johann König. A first generation American. Since everybody got so mad at the kaiser, people with German names have been really catching it. Windows broken, tires slashed, pets killed, turn-downs on jobs—the whole thing. So I weaseled out and Anglicized my name. It was too late, though."

"But, hell, you're an American by birth."

"Who makes that distinction? It's the name that counts."

"The U.S. of A. damn-old Army makes that distinction, buddy. If you're a citizen by any description, the Army'll take you in. You want out of Factory Street and all that Kraut malarkey? Then join the freakin' Army."

They sat for a time, Carpenter smoking and looking around at the others in the dimly lit room, King making a business of sampling the crusty rolls and onion soup. He welcomed the interval, because it gave him the chance to consider, then reject, Carpenter's bizarre suggestion. Instinct told him that the Army would only intensify the prejudice. He was drawing up a mental list of reasons when Carpenter said, "See that guy at the table by the window over there? The chubby guy with the bald spot. Bow tie."

"So?"

"Congressman Thaddeus Slater."

King sent a covert glance toward the table beside the high window. "I've read about him in the papers."

"Damn right, you have. An important guy."

"I'm supposed to be impressed?"

Carpenter nodded toward the window table again. "Be more impressed by the guy who just showed up."

Despite his resolve not to gawk, King gave in to another glance. Across the table from the congressman, a waiter was sliding a chair under a reedy man in an expensively tailored pinstriped suit.

"Looks familiar. Who is he?"

"None other than Hobart Fontaine, famous aeronaut and aircraft manufacturer. He took what the Wright brothers did and ran with it. He's right up there with Curtiss and Martin these days. The newspapers gave him a lot of attention last year when he flew one of his planes under the bridge crossing the Niagara Gorge. Veddy, veddy famous fella." Carpenter paused, his eyes narrowed in speculation. "Now why would those two heavyweights be chowing down together? In this eatery. In Buffalo, of all places."

"Maybe the congressman wants to buy an airplane."

Carpenter's thoughtful gaze came around to regard King with mixed amusement and surprise. "Hey, Professor, you're not so young and dumb after all." He laughed softly.

"Look who's talking," King deadpanned.

Carpenter's gorgeous teeth glistened in a broad, candlelit grin. "I'm liking you more and more, Yo-han Kernik. For a little kid, you show promise. Yes, that's exactly what I was thinking, and you know what? I'm thinking Slater doesn't want to buy an airplane. He wants to buy lots of airplanes. Yep. That's it."

"Where are you getting that stuff, Bill?"

"Slater is chairman of the House Military Oversight Committee. He has a big bunch to say about the federal money, the resources, that get assigned to the Army and Navy. And let me remind you, you promising little ex-Kraut, the U.S. of A. just ain't got many military flyin' machines. We got no more than one squadron of training planes, and you just had a ride in the heap that ranks as our newest and best. We got—count 'em—sixty-five regular and National Guard officers, me among them, and a thousand enlisted men assigned to aviation duty. We're lumped together in a kind of auxiliary to the Signal Corps. None of us knows Bean One about aerial gunnery, bombing, or photography, and what little we do know was picked up in '13 when Black Jack Pershing took us down to the Mexican border to observe while he and his so-called punitive expedition kicked the Mexican bandits outa our Texas towns. Well, maybe our chubby little congressman over there is out to change things, eh?"

King watched the waiter replace his soup dish with a steak that formed a sizzling centrality for an encampment of baked potato and garnished mixed vegetables. He sipped his wine, thinking, dredging through things recently read.

"Why Buffalo? This isn't Slater's turf. And Fontaine's factory is in Texas. Seems sort of unlikely."

"My question exactly, Yo-han. They're plotting. They don't want to be seen talking. So Washington and Dallas are out. Buffalo's an airplane town that's so cold nobody looks at anything for fear their eyes might freeze. Nyah-ha-ha." He made his laugh sound like the villain's in a melodrama.

King attacked his steak and found it to be superior. Chewing in slow enjoyment, he weighed Carpenter's theory and found it to be unlikely and a bore. He dabbed his lips with the napkin. "Maybe. But they might just be old friends, here to visit other old friends. Or any one of a thousand other possibilities."

"Take it from me, child: Guys of that horsepower don't have any old friends. They're both ruthless, cast-iron loners—self-centered sons-of-bitches who want only money and the power it buys. Sure, they're surrounded by people, up to their asses in people. But they use those people. They don't make friends of them."

King said, honestly curious, "All due respect, but why are you so worked up over this kind of stuff, Bill?"

Carpenter, his face given suddenly to a dark frown, forked his steak and took off a corner with fierce little slashes of his knife. "My old man was a four-term congressman from a nowhere district in the Dakotas. Turned out he was a ruthless son-of-a-bitch who wanted only money and the power it buys. He used everybody. Even his family."

Despite the string quartet, the dining room clatter, and the outside traffic, a heavy silence seemed to gather around them. King wavered between mortification and sympathy, simultaneously embarrassed by his having triggered this rotten confession and moved by compassion for the confessor.

"Bill, I'm sorry. I didn't mean to upset you—"

"I know you didn't, you dumb shit," Carpenter rasped. "But you just plain goddamn well better learn how to ask questions.

Which questions. You're gonna stay a dumb ex-Kraut shit unless you do."

King, dealing with shock and anger now, asked softly, "Just why do you care if I remain a dumb-ass ex-Kraut? Who the hell are you to tell me what I better do or not do? I happened to drag you out of a wreck, and you've thanked me with an airplane ride and a steak. So what do you care about what happens to me from now on?"

Carpenter's frown deepened. "That's another question I've been asking myself, pardner. As you'd say, 'Why indeed?' And I come up with only one nutty, sentimental goddamn answer. What is it about you? I'll tell you what it is about you. You remind me of what I once was. The kinda kid I was. A straight arrow. All filled with good will and good intentions and good-guy stuff. A serious kid with a head full of school learning and Horatio Alger bullshit. And the only thing I can say is that I don't want you to lose it, like I did."

King felt a sudden, inexplicable guilt. Its force compelled him to ask, "You didn't like your father, Bill?"

The big man sent an angry glare at the embers in the fireplace. "He never gave me a chance to."

"You mean he didn't like you?"

"He only liked us when a camera was around. Only on whistle stops. Only when people were watching. Those times, he'd put his arms around Mother and me and give us that big politician's grin. Other times, he didn't think about us one way or the other."

In the interval, and because he could think of nothing else to say, King said, "I'm sorry, Bill."

Carpenter pushed back his chair and waved at the waiter. "C'mon, pard, I gotta get you home and me back to the flying machine business."

"I haven't finished my meal—"

"Yes you have. C'mon."

Chapter 5

Slater made his opening move. He leaned a bit forward, elbows on the table, and made his face show open frankness. "Given the proper circumstances, Mr. Fontaine, I could arrange a very lucrative federal contract for aviation studies vis-à-vis U.S. national defense."

"Studies, sir? What kind of studies?" Fontaine asked warily.

"There's little doubt that America's active participation in the European war against German expansion is only a matter of time. We are today the only major nation that has no significant military capability in the air. Studies must begin at once to determine what is needed to correct that condition—how best to proceed if we are to make the United States the premier air power. Who would be more qualified to undertake such studies than the man whose name is synonymous with aeronautics?"

"You flatter me. Surely the Wrights, Glenn Curtiss..."

"Gifted, capable individuals, to be sure, Mr. Fontaine. But heavily anchored to existing locations, established factories, and that kind of thing. They are very well-equipped to build airplanes, certainly. But I'm talking research—military studies in collaboration with the War Department, a look, not at what's possible today, but at what we should be doing for the American aviators who'll be shooting at Germans in, say, 1920."

"And, if I understand you correctly, we're talking about a new location, a location in—"

"In my congressional district, Mr. Fontaine."

"Ah, yes. I see."

"A new facility employing hundreds, with manufacturing costs and profits guaranteed by government contracts."

"I already have a rather large plant in Texas—"

"Indeed you do. But it's also a plant that currently stands idle. Your airplanes have not been selling well."

"The market's lean. Aviation is still in its infancy—"

"Not for long, Mr. Fontaine. Not for long. England, France, Germany—even Italy—have large military air organizations, flying machines of advanced design and capability. We'll have to charge ahead hard if we're to catch up, to assure our fair share of what most certainly will soon be an enormous industry with an enormous international market."

"This is all rather overwhelming, Congressman. I haven't the foggiest notion as to how I might obtain a federal government contract for a kind of work I've never done in a facility I can't yet visualize."

Slater smiled. "That's where I come in, Mr. Fontaine."

"What do you need from me?"

"Simply your agreement. Your agreement to do what I ask you to do, when I ask you to do it."

"Well, I can't say that I feel comfortable with—"

"You stand to make millions, you know."

"I have to ask this, Congressman: What will you be getting out of the arrangement? Besides a new research facility in your district, that is."

"The satisfaction of knowing that I've served my country well, Mr. Fontaine."

"Ah, yes. Of course."

Slater cleared his throat and moved on to his next step in the plan to become rich. "Tell me, Mr. Fontaine, if you were asked to name the single most important raw material in the manufacture of flying machines, how would you answer? I mean, whatever the machine and its purpose, what single material must it have?"

Fontaine thought about this, then replied, "You say 'raw material.' By that I assume you are not talking about manufactured goods—steel, fabrics, acetate dopes, rubber products, and so on."

"Right. A single raw material. Absolutely critical to aircraft manufacture."

"Then I'd have to name ash. The wood. Ash lumber. It's vital to the construction of a strong, lightweight, flexible aircraft framework. Even the Germans, who are using welded steel tubing in some aircraft fuselage frames, still require ash for wings and control surfaces. In short, no airplane today can be built without an ample supply of ash lumber." Fontaine paused. "Your question is curious. Why do you ask?"

"In my committee responsibilities, it's important that I stay up on various raw material availabilities."

"Ash isn't all that available, Congressman. The richest and most expansive source in the continental United States lies in the Pacific Northwest. Vast acres of ash forest up there. Not all that much elsewhere."

"Mmm. Interesting."

❋❋❋

After Fontaine left, Slater turned to the man seated at the next table—Ned Raymond, his executive secretary, campaign manager, speech writer, and dirty linen chaser.

"You heard all that, Ned?"

"It went well, I think. I'm betting you'll hear from Fontaine before the week is out. He's hurting."

"Of course. But we now have a greater priority. I want you to have George Mason set up a real estate company as a cover for me. I want its proceeds, but I want no direct linkage with it. George is a savvy lawyer. He'll know what to do."

"Let me guess, Congressman: You want to buy some ash timberland."

Slater chuckled. "As much as we can get. Tell George to figure the financing. As soon as possible, because all hell will break loose after I reveal the contents of Zimmermann's message."

"I still think you ought to go easy there, Congressman. The State Department, even the president, have got that under heavy wraps until they can figure how to handle it."

"Well, they'll be relieved of that responsibility after tonight's speech. The people will explode, and Wilson and his cabinet will have no choice but to declare war."

"I'm afraid that'll make you a pariah, Congressman. The whole administration and much of Congress will want your scalp."

"To be sure. And that will make me famous, a man to be reckoned with in national and international affairs. When Slater speaks, people will listen, eh? After all, he's the one who exposed Imperial Germany's treachery, eh?" He laughed.

❋❋❋

Slater loved being a congressman. His youth and early manhood had been bleak, lonely, rootless, and belabored by the resentment of a world that failed to recognize the special qualities beneath the bland mediocrity he presented to it. He'd always been stubby, always cursed by a round face that seemed caught in a perpetual pout, always thin of hair and fat of belly. But he had also always been curious, and his curiosity had driven him to books, and books, in turn, had led him to government, which had at last placed him as the home district administrative assistant to U.S. Representative Roscoe T. Harvey. And with Harvey's death in Kearney after five terms in the House, and with no potent contender to be found by the opposition, Slater cashed in on the favors he'd personally set up for Harvey constituents—ranging from destitute widows to fat-cat bankers—and he succeeded his boss almost by default. Now, in his own third term, his ambition and fear of obscurity were driven by barely concealed power-hunger, envy, and greed—cardinal sins to which he happily confessed (only to vulnerable or equally sinful insiders, of course).

"God, I love this job!" he erupted, laughing. "Even when it brings me to Buffalo, of all places."

Raymond, dourly steering their rented Cadillac through the frozen slush on Humboldt Parkway, sniffed. "The next time you come to Buffalo, I hope you leave me home."

"Ned, my lad, you should be delighted to be here. It means I like you. It means I'm getting you ready for bigger things. After all, how many admin assistants get to travel first class with their bosses? Eh?" He laughed again.

Raymond shivered. "Can't you get me ready in Bermuda?"

"Patience, Ned. Patience. You haven't seen anything yet."

They rode for a time, saying nothing, swaying with the sedan's patrician negotiation of the ruts.

Raymond broke the pause. "All due respect, Congressman, I still think it's a mistake, your springing the secret cable thing on this audience tonight. The State Department people, the president himself, for crissake, will hang you out to dry."

Slater nodded, smiling. "Oh, they'll try, Neddie boy. Indeed they will. But the stink will be so big, the public outrage will be so huge, they'll be kept in their cages. And I'll be the center of international attention from here to hell and gone. Yessiree."

"Well, I wish I felt better about it."

"See, Neddie? That's why you need more training. This is a square-driven nail, and when you run into opportunities like this you've got to recognize them for their career-advancing potential. You see a nail, you smack it hard, direct, and nobody'll be able to crowbar it out without tearing up everything around it."

They eventually arrived at the elegant porte cochère of the academy and were welcomed by the managing director and his staff, all dressed in swallowtail coats and looking like frozen butlers. They surrounded Slater, gabbling Etonian pleasantries, and virtually carried him by the elbows into the marble interior and along imposing corridors to what they called "the meeting room," which was in truth a decent-sized amphitheater filled with a throng of politely attentive young men.

Raymond, suddenly uncomfortable in his plebeian brown tweeds, was shown to a seat among the celluloid-collared, bowtied students forming a prim black line in the front row. He looked around the room and finally spotted an alcove in which several equally tweedy men were making notes on rumpled wads of paper. He smiled wryly. Just as Slater had predicted: The press was here.

The meeting was called to order, the introductions were made, and Slater finally stood at the lectern, sending his stock smile around the room and acknowledging what an absolutely wonderful honor it was to have been invited to address so many of tomorrow's leaders. Then, after giving five minutes to a fawning recital of the academy's history and just why the hell it had been located in Buffalo during the Civil War, he lowered his brows severely and, in somber tones, swung into action on just why the hell he was now located in Buffalo on the brink of another war.

"I'm here to tell you fine young men that we are today facing the most difficult—even terrifying—crisis ever to engulf our great nation. Everything we stand for, believe in and cherish, lies now, incredibly vulnerable, in the path of one of history's greatest despots, the German emperor. He has been killing our fellow citizens, destroying our hard-won properties, interdicting our life-supporting trades. And through it all, our own president," he seemed to spit the name, "Thomas Woodrow Wilson, has stood by doing nothing, openly fearing anything that might possibly further aggravate the German kaiser. His cowardice in the face of a demonstrated enemy is beyond understanding, beyond, indeed, contempt. I call it treason!"

Slater sipped from the water glass provided him, enjoying the rumbling that traveled around the room.

Here it comes, Raymond told himself.

Slater leaned forward on his elbows, let his somber glance roam through the audience, then lowered his voice in the manner of one about to share a confidence. "And tonight, I have the duty to reveal to you the shocking breadth of the kaiser's conspiracy to overthrow the government of the United States."

The room was now in electric silence, waiting.

"Washington has intercepted a most secret cable from Berlin to Mexico City. Washington is reluctant to reveal its contents to us, the American people. Why? Because President Wilson fears it might bring us into a war against Germany. Well, my dear young leaders of tomorrow, his fears are not mine. Nor, I suspect, will they be yours when you are privy to what the cable is all about."

Slater paused theatrically, relishing the gathering suspense.

"The cable, literally designated 'most secret' by the German government, is an attempt to enlist the Mexicans as German allies—allies whose primary duty would be to invade the United States and seize Texas as the first step in forcing the American government to bend to the German will!"

Slater paused again, and the silent shock in the room was almost palpable. Then a challenge came out of the audience. "How do you know all this, Congressman?"

Slater drew an envelope from the pocket of his suit coat, his eyes, glaring now, sweeping the room. "For any of you who might doubt my announcement, let me read to you the exact text of the intercepted telegram sent by Arthur Zimmermann, Germany's foreign minister, to the German ambassador in Mexico City."

More silence as he took a paper from the envelope, unfolded it, sipped some water, and then began to read aloud:

Berlin, January nineteen, nineteen seventeen.

On the first of February we intend to begin submarine warfare unrestricted. In spite of this, it is our intention to endeavor to keep neutral the United States of America. If this attempt is not successful, we propose an alliance on the following basis with Mexico: that we shall make war together and together make peace. We shall give general financial support, and it is understood that Mexico is to reconquer the lost territory in New Mexico, Texas, and Arizona. The details are left to you for settlement.

You are instructed to inform the president of Mexico of the above in the greatest confidence as soon as it is certain that there will be an outbreak of war with the United States and suggest that the president of Mexico, on his own initiative, should communicate with Japan suggesting adherence at once to this plan; at the same time, offer to mediate between Germany and Japan.

Please call to the attention of the president of Mexico that the employment of ruthless submarine warfare now promises to compel England to make peace in a few months.

              Zimmermann.

As Slater refolded the paper, the room rocked in pandemonium. The prim, black-suited students arose from their seats, shouting and shaking their fists, and they began a tidelike movement for the exits. The chancellor nudged Slater aside and began hammering the lectern with a gavel and demanding things in an unintelligible parade- ground roar. The butlers had gathered in an agitated knot, faces close, voices strident. The rumpled press reporters were in the adjacent corridor, struggling over possession of the public telephone there.

Raymond sidled up to Slater, who stood on the dais, looking profoundly pleased with himself.

"Well, you did it, Congressman," Raymond shouted over the din. "One way or another, you've got yourself into an A-1 type prairieland tornado."

"Yes," Slater beamed. "And I've also stiffed the Germans for a mortgage and a potful of moola."

"I don't get it. How so?"

"Never mind. Meanwhile, I'm going to stand right here until the last question has been asked. This is my debut on the stage of international fame, and I'm going to wring it for every drop it holds."

Chapter 6

On April 6, 1917, the United States declared war on Imperial Germany.

On April 7, John King was notified by the county that, on April 30, the property at 15 Factory Street would be auctioned off for delinquent taxes.

On April 8, 2nd Lieutenant William J. Carpenter, U.S. Army Signal Corps, was jumped two grades to captain and was ordered to London, where he would serve as aviation technical advisor to the U.S. War Matériel Acquisition Mission.

On April 11, John King sat beside his suitcase on the front steps of the Factory Street house, watching the "We Buy Used Things" truck grinding off with the three beds, two chests of drawers, two easy chairs, dining room table, four straight-back chairs, three mirrors, two end tables, three carpets, five boxes of clothes and shoes, gas oven, ice box, and six lamps that were his parents' total legacy. The piano had been left in the cellar because the moving crew decided it was too heavy and bulky for four guys to handle on those dark and zigzag wooden stairs. Besides, King rationalized, it hadn't belonged to the family in the first place, and it should remain where they'd found it.

He turned his face to the breeze, feeling in it the passing of winter and the promise of spring and breathing deeply of it in a fruitless effort to fill the void in his chest. Panic was at the edge of his mind, too, and he sought to counter it with a pad and a pencil and decisions as to how to use the $326 the truck crew boss had paid him.

The sound of boots in the snow intruded. He looked up. She was standing in the sidewalk slush, chunky in her winter coat, her wool cap pulled low so that it seemed of a piece with the roll of scarf around her neck. Her large blue eyes regarded him somberly.

"Hello, Tillie."

"I came to tell you I'm sorry."

"Thanks. But I just didn't have the money to pay the taxes."

"That's not what I mean," she said. "I'm sorry that my daddy was so nasty to you, calling you those names, throwing you out of the house."

"He didn't throw me out. He just told me to leave and not come back."

"He's known you for years. We went all the way through school together, for Pete's sake, and he never minded your being around. Sorta liked you. And then, all of a sudden...I don't know what happened."

"The war, Tillie. It's the war thing. The neighborhood thinks I'm a German, and your dad didn't want to be seen being nice to me. The neighborhood would get on his back for that."

Her lower lip trembled. "He didn't have to call you a Kraut, a Hun. A Heinie. You're as American as he is. As I am."

"He was talking for the benefit of Mrs. Halloran. She was brooming her porch and could hear the whole thing. What Mrs. Halloran hears, everybody hears."

"It isn't fair."

"It's what's going on today."

She looked off down the street, as if considering a thought and groping for its words. He studied her profile, suddenly touched by the realization that the little girl she'd always been was now a handsome young woman. She had always been in his life, a fixture of the school years whose background hovering had become as much a part of his day as the classroom itself. And, despite her taciturnity and his own boyish preoccupations, there had been a subtle bonding due to their shared interest in books and music, discovered during her tenth birthday party at her house on A Street. On each of her birthdays, her parents would invite her classmates and pals for a big shindig, complete with favors and paper hats and cakes and homemade ice cream, and almost always, to his embarrassment, Mrs. Connell would get him to play some folk songs the kids could sing. So he would sit at the spinet in the parlor, red-faced and self-conscious, and plunk out the old clichés, while the others, equally uncomfortable, would dutifully sound off. It was a pain, and Tillie tried to make up for it by taking him into the library and showing him the glass cases in which her daddy kept his collection of rare, antique sheet music. Sometimes Mr. Connell would be there, behind his desk, puffing his pipe and quietly correcting Tillie when her explanations were off the mark. He was a tall, thin man, and his gray eyes were watery and sad. It was easy to see that he was crazy about his little girl, and Tillie would always give him a kiss on the cheek before leaving the room.

"Did they take away your piano, John? The one in the cellar?"

"No. They didn't think they could get it up the stairs."

"So will you play for me? One last time?"

He sighed. "I don't think so, Tillie. The neighbors are probably watching us, and I don't want them getting any wrong ideas. For your own sake, you really ought to leave right now."

"I want to kiss you goodbye, John."

"No. For the same reason."

"I've wanted to kiss you ever since fourth grade."

"I know."

"You knew, but didn't do anything about it?" There was accusation in her question.

"You were like my sister."

"I love you, John."

"No you don't. You're just being sentimental. I'm honest-to-Pete grateful for your friendship, Tillie, but don't sell yourself any wrong ideas. I'm too risky."

Her large eyes were brimming now, and she turned quickly and trotted up the street.

King sat in the twilight after she'd left, thinking of everything and nothing. After a time he stood, stretched, and went into the empty house for what he knew would be the last time. As he moved about in the gloom, he realized that the encounter with Tillie had cost him more than he'd thought. She'd been his best friend, and his cruel rejection, for all the hurt it had caused her, had left him actually sick in the belly.

More disturbing, though, was the creeping suspicion that something was fundamentally wrong inside him, and what he was feeling was more than nausea. It was indefinable, ephemeral, a whispering in the back of his mind. There were times, like now, when the whispering came through as distant voices, muted and conspiratorial, and the corner-of-the-eye impression that something—or somebody—had crossed the room behind him brought a chill. And then suddenly, standing in the drab little living room, considering ghosts, he felt the full weight of his aloneness. No parents, no family, no friends, nowhere to go. This, the house he'd grown up in and knew by every board and nail, along with all the innards lovingly accumulated by his mother, were gone for all time now.

He wandered to the cellar and sat at the old piano, letting his fingers run over the yellowed keys, evoking rich seventh chords, diminished ninths, augmenteds, walking-bass jazz runs, and upper-register trills. From these he segued into some of Mom's favorites. First her signature hymn, "How Great Thou Art." Then a thoughtful rendition of "Charmaine," followed by a rollicking "Bill Bailey," with which she would always sing along.

He was halfway through a dreamy "Second-Hand Rose" when the sadness in him suddenly became grief of such intensity that its sigh became a sob, and the sob became an uncontrollable weeping that turned him from the bench and sent him wailing to his knees, a boy once again, wringing his hands, rocking back and forth, and crying for his *Mutti*.

Chapter 7

The leftenant was obviously nervous about entrusting one of Britain's finest aircraft to the likes of this "Yankee." He danced beside Carpenter's loping stride with mincing little steps, some forward, some sideways, some rather like hopping up and down, waving his clipboard, chattering through his buck teeth about the vast difference between training planes and service machines. "And I might remind the captain that, while the Curtiss JN-4 he is accustomed to flying is a most stable and forgiving machine, the SE-5, with its superior, high-horsepower engine and slimmed-down fuselage, is not one to tolerate inexperienced handling. It is a machine to be respected."

Carpenter said, not looking at him, "That's what I'm here to find out, wouldn't you say?"

"Well..."

"How can I respect something before I find out if it's respectable?"

The leftenant said nothing more, choosing instead to make a business of jotting something on the clipboard. To make him feel better, Carpenter strode up to the machine, eyes squinted solemnly in the manner of a rancher considering a horse, then went around it, pulling a brace wire here, tapping the satiny finish there, even kicking a tire and running a hand along the curve of the propeller. Posturing done, he placed a boot in the boarding stirrup and swung easily into the cockpit, where he settled in, pulled the seat belt across his lap, and began to familiarize himself with the instrument layout—magnetic compass, oil and temperature gauges, tachometer, air speed indicator— and inspected the Vickers machine-gun mounting, the stick-mounted trigger, the wing-mounted Lewis gun and its reloading track. Eventually satisfied, he nodded at the mechanic standing by the propeller in polite alertness.

"Okay, son. Pull her through. I'm off to see the Wizard."

※※※※

The machine lifted away in a no-nonsense, businesslike climb, and at three thousand feet he leveled off to feel its personality. The engine, a 200 horsepower Wolseley Viper, rumbled in an even, reassuring way, and a few quick turns, left and right, told him there was great stability here. A nice airplane. He glanced down at the Farnborough airfield below, orienting himself, then, settling into the seat cushion, he gave himself over to flying for the pure pleasure of flying.

Some slow rolls, two to the right, two to the left, followed by a brace of snap rolls, told him right away that this airplane's integrity could be its largest problem in combat. It was too honest, too leisurely in its basic maneuverability. The mock dogfights in which he'd flown a Sopwith Camel two days ago were almost breathtaking adventures, because the Camel—dubbed "the fierce little rasper" by the factory people—was so quick and nimble it seemed gymnastic. Make a right turn and, poof, it would be over and done almost before he could keep from going into another. Entering a spiral, he'd had to fight to keep from dropping into a spin. A split S would get him out of an opponent's cone of fire and into a power dive in five seconds. The Camel worked him into a sweat. This sweetheart, the SE-5, was a Lorelei, luring him into dangerous complacency when white knuckles were preferable. Yet it went dutifully to its rated service ceiling of seventeen thousand feet without a whimper and only mushed and fell off when he tried to push it beyond. It was a fine craft to dive, too, gaining speed and maintaining full controllability in the plunge.

"Okay, sweetheart, all in all, I'd say you're a nice girl, and I'll be recommending you to the high command in London. So let's go down and get me a drink."

A glance over the side gave him a surprise. The day had been bright and cheerful, with the beaming sun making the vast spread of Hampshire a spectacular in green, gold, and purple. He'd been so preoccupied with the workout that his airman's sense of the weather had been lulled by the day's initial beauty, so he'd given virtually no attention to the gathering of haze off to the southeast. Now, though, the haze had become a substantial blanket of fog, a chalky smear obscuring everything below all the way to the horizon. If the Farnborough air station was someplace down there, he couldn't even guess where.

"Damn!"

The fuel gauge registered near-empty, too, which precluded any sustained cruise-and-search pattern even if ground detail had been apparent. He reduced the throttle setting and adjusted the mixture control to lean, allowing the ship to descend in a gentle power glide, resigned to the fact that—at best—he would be making a blind landing among a scattering of rural villages in territory known to him only by this morning's cursory study of the charts. At worst, he could be over some significant population, and it would be Lackawanna, New York, all over again, with trolley wires and no John King standing by.

He felt the pounding of his heart and the moisture collecting in his gloves.

"Keep cool, Willie. Don't piss in your pants."

Oddly, the thought of John King had brought a wisp of reassurance. Certainly, in all of Hampshire, England, there would be at least one man cut of King's cloth. And there was no reason why, if coincidence had provided King once, it couldn't dish up his counterpart here in this corner of Blighty.

"That's right, Willie. Hold on to that idea. And remember: Under no circumstances will you wet your pants. You will not—repeat not—let any Englishman see that you've wet your pants."

As the plane's long nose sank steadily toward the fog, propeller windmilling, wire rigging sighing softly, his gaze swept from side to side, then straight down, from side to side, then straight down. On one of the sweeps to starboard he saw what appeared to be a dark spot in the white. He sat erect, eyes wide and staring.

"There you are, goddammit! A hole. And here I come, you beautiful sumbish."

He added power and went into a hard diving turn, and the dark spot turned green and purple, and there was even a suggestion of a tiny house. With the mist just sitting there like that, he had no need to consider wind direction, so he guided the ship through the hole and prepared for a straight-on landing no matter what lay ahead.

He broke into open laughter.

"Well, I'll be go-to-hell. Looka that gorgeous, wide- open pasture. Smack dab in front of me. With the sun shining on it, for crissake!"

The SE settled easily, its wheels kissing the grass, then, after a long, gentle rumbling, came to a halt a few yards from a stone wall and a line of oaks. He cut the switch and, after the propeller ticka-tacked to a halt, sat there for a time, eyes shut, feeling the blessed silence. When he looked around again, the fog had settled in anew, the sunlight had disappeared, and he could barely see the lane beyond the tree line.

He laughed again, shaking his head. Unbuckling the belt, he swung out of the cockpit and stood tentatively on the damp sod, testing his equilibrium. Satisfied, he went to the wall, opened his flight suit, and, sighing, relieved himself.

"Perishin' poor manners to show a girl, I'd say."

Carpenter looked up, his hands adjusting his suit in quick, panicky motions. "My God. I didn't see you. I'm really sorry."

She was on a donkey cart, a dim form under the trees, the reins looped casually in her lap. Carpenter heard her soft laugh. The animal snuffled and looked bored.

"Ain't the first I seen."

"Well..."

"The way you talk, you must be one a them Yanks over at Farnborough."

"Right." *And it's been quite a while since you were a girl. I put you at about thirty.* "Tell me, ma'am, is there a telephone around here somewhere? I need to call my people and let them know where I am."

"Hop on beside. I'm with the Red Slipper Pub and Inn down at the crossroads. The pub has a phone. Charlie'll charge you for usin' it, though."

"I can handle that. Lead on, fair lady."

❋❋❋

Carpenter finally got through to the factory's main office and, after some snaps and crackles, to Leftenant Smathers himself.

"You'll have to come and get your SE-5."

"Where've you been? Is the aircraft..."

"You won't be happy about it."

"Where is it?"

"It's in a pasture, next to a wall, under some trees. A place called Thorpe."

"Dear Lord! Will we need a lorry, a wreckage crew?"

"What you'll need is gas and someone to top its radiator, brush some weeds and mud from its tires, and then fly the damn thing out of here."

"Thank heaven." Pause. "Why can't you fly it out, Captain?"

"Because I'm due back in London, and I'm taking a train. Besides, I plan to stay a little drunk for a day or two."

Carpenter hung up, returned the phone to its niche beside the bar, and grinned widely at Bernice. "Now, then: Any more scotch under that handle thingy you pull there?"

"Right-o, Yank."

❋❋❋

Consciousness returned behind the darkness of Carpenter's eyelids, and he lay, silent, motionless, seeking to gather a defense against the aching that emanated from his nape and savaged its way to his soles. Eventually he opened an eye, then the other, to consider the slanted wooden ceiling, dimly lit by the dawn beyond the leaded panes of a dormer, which spoke of ancient times and unspecific loneliness.

He became aware of her presence beside him, and he ventured a glance. She was on her back, legs spread, naked, snoring, arms flung outward, face partially hidden by the dark tangle of her hair. He considered her for a time, dealing with remorse and pain and wondering how in God's name he could have drunk enough—lowered himself enough—to couple with this cow. As he eased himself off the bed without awakening her, he caught her scent, a mixture of kitchen grease and old sweat, and he feared he'd be overcome by nausea. Somehow he was able to silently retrieve his uniform and flight gear from the corner where they had been flung and make it to the lavatory off the landing below. There he washed his face and hands and dressed, avoiding the mirror hanging on the wall. He crept down the remaining stairs, moved stealthily across the sleeping pub, and, lifting the latch, let himself out the door and into the misty daybreak.

He walked numbly along the road for what seemed to be hours before the driver of a lorry laden with vegetables agreed to take him to the nearest bus line to London, some forty-five miles away.

CHAPTER 8

For King, a geography buff, it was unsettling to admit that he wasn't at all sure just where Camp Dix was located. New Jersey, yes. Somewhere between New York City and Philadelphia, he'd been told. But having made most of the trip from Buffalo on a long, stinking, cinder-spewing train overcrowded with bad-smelling draftees, with only an occasional view out a grimy window, he'd become disoriented. Upon detraining on a rainy midnight and marching to a tent city surrounding miles of wooden clapboard barracks under construction, he could have been on the far side of Mars.

All he knew for certain was that it was thousands of acres of gritty land that had been cleared for the establishment of a basic training and staging area for the Army, and now, during his sixth week here, he was lost in a vast conglomeration of pyramidal tents, clapboard-and-tarpaper buildings, gravel roads, forests of power and telephone poles, and broad flatlands over which he marched—*ten hut, right shoulder harms, squads right, harch, hup, twup, threep, fourp, close it up in the ranks, hup, twup, threep, fourp, colyum layuft, harch, hup, twup, threep, fourp, stop bobbin' in ranks*—on and on and on. And when he wasn't marching, he crawled and dug holes and fired shots from a rifle at paper targets and stuck bayonets into straw dummies and took showers among legions of naked men and ate greasy, lukewarm food in mess halls teeming with flies and cockroaches. The nights in the ten-man tent were dark ordeals of heat and cold and snoring and whimpering and lonely, whispered prayers and curses, where the only sleep was fainting from exhaustion.

He hated all of it, but mostly he hated weekly KP duty —those seemingly endless dawn-to-dusk relegations to the kitchen serving Company C, Third Training Battalion. Hard work he was used to. Even hard work in hot, humid, closed-in places, thanks to the part-time job he'd had at Finkel's Delicatessen while waiting for admission to trade school. But here, tyrannized by the all-seeing and sadistic Mess Sergeant Amos Tucker, he was unrelievedly consigned to the pots and pans sink after morning, noon, and evening chow, a duty climaxed at nightfall by the hand-cleaning and scouring of twenty garbage cans.

Tucker was a rangy, craggy-faced backwoodsman who had found a home in the Army. The mind behind the ever-present scowl seemed filled with suspicion and viciousness, both capped by a prevailing, loud-mouthed lewdness. King became wary of this last quality early on, when in the gang shower one evening he caught Tucker staring lasciviously at his behind and muttering foul appraisals of it to Corporal Widman, himself no model of propriety.

The next day being a day off for him, King went to a novelty store he'd seen on a Bordentown side street and for thirty-nine cents bought himself some protection—a paste-on sore, a theatrical prop that was all red and green and purple and oozing and about as disgusting a display as any he'd seen outside the medical books in the Lackawanna municipal library.

On the following KP night, he had completed the last garbage can, coiled and hung the hose on its rack behind the mess hall, and draped the cleaning cloths on the rail there when Sergeant Tucker, Corporal Widman and PFC Dalonzo appeared out of the gloom.

"Well, now. There he is," Tucker said, shifting his wet cigar stub to the other corner of his mouth. "Li'l Lord Fauntleroy. The smartsy who talks so hoity-toity."

"Never struck me as smartsy," Widman said. "Just a pain in the ass."

King stood, tense and wary, as they closed around him.

"Speakin' of ass," Tucker said, "this Li'l Lord Fauntleroy has a real nice one. You ever seen him in the shower, you guys?"

"Yeah," Widman said. "Nice and round and firm. Like a little kid's."

Tucker made a sighing sound. "I'd like to take a closer look at that little rounder." He unbuckled his belt. "Grab him, guys."

King turned to run, but they were on him, and he was bent cruelly over the drying rack. He squirmed and kicked and tried to shout, but a hand was over his mouth and another hand was pulling down his fatigue pants. At the edge of panic, he saw what he must do: He bit the hand.

"Ow! You little son of a bitch," Widman snarled. "You made me bleed."

Over his shoulder King improvised quickly, "Something you ought to know, Widman. I've got a case of *Bramstokerus draculitis*."

There was a suspenseful pause.

"Oh, yeah? What the hell is that?"

"Rare disease. You break out in sores and keep losing blood. The medics don't know what to do about it. No known treatment. They're talking about giving me a medical discharge."

"You're bullshittin' us," Tucker snarled. "Get those pants down, Dalonzo. I'm gettin' me a piece of this bullshittin' Fauntleroy."

King felt the cold night air on his rump.

"Hey, wait. What the hell is that?" Dalonzo said.

"What's what?" Tucker was impatient.

"It's a sore on his ass..."

There followed a protracted pause.

It was broken when Tucker announced, "Aw, the hell with it. Come on, you guys, let's go. He ain't all that round anyhow."

They left, and, after pulling himself together, King went to his tent, which was unoccupied because the other nine guys were shooting pool in the battalion dayroom or eating doughnuts at the Red Cross hut. He pulled a pencil and schoolboy pad from his barracks bag and began to write under the pale light of the bulb suspended from the center pole. It didn't go so well at first because his hand was trembling and he kept wanting to run home to a home he didn't have.

July 18, 1917

Dear Bill:

I'm sending this to the last APO you gave me for your London assignment. I hope it reaches you, because I really need your help. As you see from the address, I'm currently at Camp Dix, a large cantonment being built in New Jersey to train troops for eventual shipment to France.

I saw a note in the *New York Times* that listed you among the American delegation seeking info and advice from the British on the kinds of planes our Army should have, so I assume that the censors won't mind my writing directly to you about my earnest desire to transfer into the Air Service, where I might serve our country ever so much more effectively than I am now.

Understand, please, that I am not in any way trying to shirk the duty to which I've been assigned. I am a soldier, and a soldier serves where those who have a larger picture of the many needs of warfare place him. But I want very much to face the enemy, not spend my days peeling potatoes and cleaning garbage cans and shooting at paper targets.

Recalling the wonderful experience you gave me that day in Buffalo, when you used me as "ballast" in your testing of the Jenny, I'm convinced that my future, both military and eventual civilian, lies in aviation. I have little doubt that I could learn the fine art of flying, and I have less doubt that I would be a first-class flying warrior. I score very high in mathematics, physics, geography, and the other sciences and arts that are obvious considerations in aviation. But more than that, I have a keen desire—make that a determination—to excel at whatever I do, and this could hardly be listed among my weaknesses as a candidate for military flying.

If you can, if it's at all possible, will you take the time to advise me on how best to proceed in obtaining a transfer to the aviation section? Will you please put me in contact with the appropriate offices and/or individuals? I'll be more grateful than mere words express.

Congratulations on your promotion to captain and please accept my very best wishes for continued good health and accomplishment.

Your devoted friend,

John King

He folded the note, slipped it into his remaining envelope, and took it down the dark company street to the headquarters' outgoing mailbox. Before Lights Out and Taps, he was back to the tent and on his cot, ignoring the noisy arrival and bedding down of the others, lying motionless and staring at nothing.

Sleep was slow in coming, because that damned inner voice kept telling him that he had made a dreadful mistake. The Army was said to be very hard on those who violated the chain of command, who went over the heads of their superiors, who violated the strict protocols of military organizational procedures.

Was a letter to a friend such a violation?

If so, who would accuse him? The censor who first saw the letter and weighed its content and obvious request for favoritism? Or would Bill himself, now located in the heart of supreme military machinations, forget the old days and take offense at being asked to abet an impropriety?

The voice said, *You are a fool, John King....*

Chapter 9

Bill Carpenter was a consultant-at-large with nobody to consult. Adrift in the ungodly labyrinth of London and its seeming thousands of headquarters and bureaus and missions and amalgamated pomposities, he found his days and nights to be an endless procession of dreary hours given to boredom and loneliness and an unnamable anxiety, and tonight, lying beside some sleeping woman he knew only as Cynthia, he'd seen himself as an occupant of one of those long Texas cattle trains, car after car crammed with benumbed animals, rattling off to a fate they did not know. Restless and depressed by the image, he slipped out of the bed, went naked to the casement overlooking the snoozing city, and stood there, smoking a cigarette and listening to the predawn stillness. After a time, he felt a chill and turned to the darkened room in search of his robe.

Warmer now, he picked up the half-empty bottle of scotch that stood among the glasses and knickknacks on the sideboard, considered pouring himself some, then decided against it. He'd been drinking far too much in the past weeks, and the day before yesterday he'd made a little vow: no booze at any time other than those off-duty occasions demanding association with unredeemable assholes.

The problem: He was himself the most unredeemable of them all, and there was no escaping him. So the vow was quickly and rationally set aside, since alcohol was forsooth, forthwith, and for crissake, basic to any endurance of himself. There in the darkness, accepting the unassailable logic of this, he opened the bottle, lifted it high, and swallowed three large, fiery gulps.

He sank into the easy chair beside the dormant gas-log fireplace, eyes watering, throat stinging in a glorious sting.

"Hoo...."

Four gulps later, his blurring gaze wandered to the letter from John King, lying pale and somehow forlorn on the desk.

Stupid son of a bitch. Doesn't he know when he has it good, for crissake?

※•※•※

In the dawn twilight he stirred, and the empty bottle rolled from his lap to the floor. He opened his aching eyes and saw that Cynthia had departed. *Thank God for little favors.*

He sat for a time, watching the daylight brighten, listening to the doves cooing on the eaves and to a delivery man somewhere whistling "It's Long Way to Tipperary."

He reached for King's letter and read it again, squinting. Maybe the sumbish wasn't so dumb after all.

He went to the desk, sank into the chair, and, after opening his stationery pad, raised the pen like a baton, a maestro summoning the muse. With an exaggerated flourish, he began to write, *Took care of you, Yo-han. Now I'm takin' care of me.*

Chapter 10

The committee hearing room was warm and stuffy, thanks to the advancing summer outside. Electric fans were humming, and those windows that were operable had been opened wide in the hope of enticing a breeze, yet the primary result was an influx of insects borne on the sounds of traffic below. Low-lying Washington was often described as a frying pan designed by the founding fathers to keep an even heat under the governmental fatback. If so, Slater thought now in a testy moment, they'd done a helluva job, and the high ceilings and marble halls subsequently built by a defensive Congress did little to compensate.

The focal point of today's hearings was William Mitchell, a sharp-faced lieutenant-colonel freshly arrived from Paris, where he was serving as the ranking American air officer in Europe. Slater had taken an immediate disliking to the man, knowing, as he'd found in his research, that Mitchell was a scion of big, important railroad money, highly educated in all the right schools here and abroad and considered rather widely in the military set as an arrogant self-promoter and single-minded airpower advocate and just too goddamn hotsy-totsy to spend time in congressional hearings. Slater was no stranger to self-promotion, of course, but he resented it when he saw it lurking in someone like Mitchell, who already had everything.

"It's nice to have you here with us, Colonel Mitchell, and the committee appreciates your making a sea voyage to satisfy some of the questions we have regarding the establishment of an American aerial combat force."

"My pleasure and honor, Mr. Chairman," Mitchell said, somewhat condescendingly.

Slater consulted a sheaf of papers on the table before him. "I see that you are yourself a military aviator, Colonel."

"Yes, sir, I am."

"Where did you take your training?"

"I was here in Washington last year as a member of the general staff. I felt it was important to have direct knowledge of aviation, so on weekends—on my own time—I would take a boat to Newport News, where I spent all day each Sunday taking flight lessons. I completed the course satisfactorily, and so I'm now ranked as a military pilot."

"I see. Commendable. And, I dare say, expensive." Slater paused, rattling some papers. "Rather unusual, isn't it, for an officer as young as you, a mere thirty-seven years old, to have been assigned to the general staff?"

Mitchell's thin lips hinted at the onset of irritability. "I assume that my superiors had their reasons to appoint me to that post, sir."

"To be sure."

Slater took a moment to turn toward Ned Raymond, seated to his right rear and armed with a stack of files. Behind a hand held carefully so as to screen his mouth from the press table and public seating, he whispered, "This jasper promises to be a pain in the ass. Any special vulnerabilities? Anything I can rattle him with?"

"No," Raymond whispered from behind a file folder held next to his cheek. "He comes from a rich, socially prominent family and is said to be a stiff but straight arrow all the way. A lot of professional jealousy around him, but no skeletons. But I'll keep looking."

Slater returned his attention to Mitchell, who was sitting ruler straight and exuding wary watchfulness.

"So then, Colonel, I'd like to invite a general statement from you. Your official assessment of the situation vis-à-vis the proposed American aviation venture."

Mitchell, flanked by a captain and a first lieutenant, suggested the chairman of a school board unaccustomed to back talk from uneasy parents. He ignored his colleagues and the notebook lying open before him, readjusted himself in his chair, and gave Slater a level, uncompromising stare.

"First of all, Congressman, our activities in Paris and London can hardly be described as a venture. They are a hard-driving, concentrated effort to determine the best and quickest way for the American military forces to acquire the aircraft and equipment that will drive the enemy, first, out of the sky and second, out of the war. There is nothing venturesome about our goal and the means to attain it."

Slater felt the heat rise below his celluloid collar. "Seems to me you're splitting hairs, Colonel. You're being preciously semantical. Venture implies risk, and even you will have to admit that there are certain risks in deciding what's best for our nation. So please forgo the linguistics and give us your statement."

The captain whispered in Mitchell's ear, and it was a moment of reappraisal. The colonel, Slater saw, had just been warned by his legal counselor to play nice, that it would do no good to antagonize a congressman who had a heavy grip on the purse strings.

"My apologies, sir. I did not intend to wander from the subject. It's simply that we—those of us composing the American missions in Paris and London—are deeply immersed and try earnestly to minimize whatever risks are inherent in any of our recommendations."

"Of course, Colonel. Tell us about it. The floor is yours."

Truce acknowledged, Mitchell finally opened his notebook. "Congressman Slater, other members of the committee, I appreciate this opportunity to lay before you some of the basic conclusions arrived at by the American Aviation Office at 49 Boulevard Hausemann in Paris. We have had extensive talks with the French Aeronautic Office, as well as with the Royal Aircraft Establishment in London, and I personally have interviewed aviation leaders in Italy. From these discussions, our office has developed a list of needs to be met if the United States is to participate effectively in the air war against Germany.

"Our primary conclusion is that the only defense against aircraft is other aircraft. And we have additionally concluded that the ground war will remain in a stalemate indefinitely and can end only when one or both antagonists succumb to pure exhaustion. Therefore, to bring about an end of hostilities favorable to the Allies in general and the United States in particular, the war must move aloft. Key to winning the military struggle is the airplane—"

Slater broke in. "Excuse me, Colonel. You are saying that this is your personal conclusion?"

"Yes. But it is also widely shared among air planners in England and Italy, Congressman."

"Not France?"

"Well, the French see military aviation as a special weapon to be used in support of the ground effort, the ground armies. Tactical support. Reconnaissance. Photography and the like. Those activities which assist ground troops in their mission. London—and, as I say, my office as well—believe that aircraft are better used in long-range, strategic attacks on the enemy's infrastructure, his rear echelons of support. Cut off their supplies, and ground armies will collapse. This view is held quite strongly, I might note here, by Major General Hugh M. Trenchard, commander of the Royal Flying Corps, as well as Mssrs. Caproni and Douhet in Italy."

"What you're saying, then, is that it would behoove us to concentrate on amassing a fleet of bombing aeroplanes?"

"Yes, sir, but not to the exclusion of other types. Pursuit planes must be copiously on hand if the bombers are to be protected. Photoreconnaissance planes must show the bombers where to bomb. The Air Service must be large enough, broad enough in capability, to ensure complete efficiency and success."

"Where will we get these aircraft, Colonel?"

Mitchell consulted his notes then replied, "Our analysis of the situation tells us, sir, that there is simply no way for the United States aircraft industry to expand and provide aircraft in sufficient numbers before 1919, perhaps spring of 1920. Therefore, it's imperative that we acquire existing designs from our allies, from France, England, and Italy."

"But I'm told that it would be very difficult for those countries to supply us. I understand that they are hard put to build enough machines to meet their own needs."

"I'm suggesting licensing, Congressman. We can license the right to build machines already flying effectively for the British, French, and Italians. Using the official blueprints from those nations, our aircraft manufacturers can build Spads, Nieuports, Sopwiths, De Havillands, Breguets, Capronis, Handley-Pages. Moreover, we can improve on those designs. The Germans have been using with great effect aircraft whose construction utilizes welded steel tubing in place of ash, which is in very short supply worldwide. There is no reason why American ingenuity and technology can't build, say, a De Havilland with steel tubing, or a Spad, or a Sopwith—"

"Excuse me again, Colonel, but you are aware, aren't you, that we have just nationalized the ash lumbering industry in this country? That vast acreages have been reserved specifically for the aircraft industry?"

"I am, sir. But I'm speaking of technological improvement, of the idea that the status can't remain quo if an industry is to constantly move forward—that, if you'll pardon the pun, the aircraft industry can't just rest on its ash."

A tittering raced through the room and quickly became open laughter in the spectator section. Annoyed, Slater pounded his gavel. "Order. Order." To Mitchell he said, "This is a serious matter, Colonel. There'll be no more of that kind of thing."

"Of course, sir."

"The Congress went to great lengths to save this vital raw material for your exclusive use."

"I understand, sir. My point was simply that we, as a nation, must be innovative."

"We got your point, Colonel Mitchell," Slater said peevishly.

Ned Raymond tapped Slater on the shoulder and, moving his head close, whispered his own wry pun, "Go carefully with this. Mason hasn't got your ash completely covered yet."

Slater gave Raymond a reproving glare. He rattled some papers and said to no one in particular, "All right, then, let's move on."

※※※

The remainder of the morning and much of the afternoon were given to a ranging discussion of current capacities of the American aircraft industry, the theories of tactical versus strategic airpower, availability of manpower and resources, the advantages and disadvantages of placing manufacturing orders on a cost-plus-ten-percent basis. It wound up with Mitchell's strong recommendation that the Americans should at first concentrate on building vast numbers of training planes and acquiring as many frontline combat machines as could be spared by England, France, and Italy. Advance combat training for air crews could be undertaken in Europe until such time as the American effort hit full stride. But Mitchell proved to be a bulldog on the matter of long-range bombing, strategic attacks by large explosives-carrying aircraft that would destroy enemy infrastructure, population centers, and their factories and armament centers, making it difficult to impossible for the enemy to supply his frontline troops. The big bombers—the British Handley-Page and the Italian Caproni—should be the first order of business, should be built in great numbers under license, leaving the production of most pursuit and observation craft to the Allied nations already supplying them. He eventually became so fixated on the subject that his commentary ballooned into repetitious oratory, so Slater adjourned the hearing at 2:35 p.m. for resumption the next morning at nine o'clock.

※※※

That evening, alone in his office, a glass of bourbon in hand, Slater stood at the tall window and regarded the city beyond.

Washington was large and energetic in the way of politics-oriented cities, seeming always to be in motion and noisy with commerce. But all the urban bustling had a counterpoint, a dreamy rhythm that spoke of the small town—of hitching posts, of kids playing tag after supper, of quiet gossip on shadowy porches, of mingling smells of kerosene and stables and rose gardens and pot roast and dad's pipe tobacco. For Slater, a man who had never had a real home, evening walks along the tranquil residential streets were a pleasure that hurt too much. Every lamplit window, every sound of soft laughter, every tinkling piano, fed his vision of belonging to someone someday, of owning a big white house like that one there and whiling away the evenings with the tender sharing of ideas and memories and creature comforts. But in immediate contradiction, he'd recognize the truth. He would never belong. To anyone. To anything. He was cursed by a need for insularity, for the time and space demanded by the search for money and power, and the cost would most surely be a lifetime of walking lonely streets, always outside, looking in.

Ah, what the hell....

The New York Times.

PRESIDENT CALLS THE NATION TO ARMS; DRAFT BILL SIGNED; REGISTRATION ON JUNE 5; REGULARS UNDER PERSHING TO GO TO FRANCE

 A Proclamation by the President of the United States

Chapter 11

The day was mercilessly hot, with no breeze and a fine alkaline dust rising from the roads and fields far down range from the firing line. Some of it, seeming to have a life of its own, drifted lazily across the distant tree line, complicating King's attempt to qualify as a marksman. Lying on his belly, squinting along the barrel of his Springfield rifle, he sought to focus on the black circle on the white target sheet a hundred yards away. But thanks to the dust, the sweat in his eyes, and his preoccupation with maintaining the proper position, his first three measured shots each drew a waving of "Maggie's Drawers," the infuriating red flag signaling a complete miss.

Corporal Spitzer, the coach lying beside him, snuggled closer and told him, "Yer not keepin' the butt close in on yer shoulder. The butt's wanderin' around, and I'm guessin' ya just put three new holes in the moon. An' keep them legs flat and spread, and yer ass down, and yer elbows dug in. Shee-it, man: think of yerself as a tripod. Two elbows dug in the dirt, yer ass pressin' the dirt hard, like yer shovin' inta a dame."

"You sure have a way with language, Spitzer."

"Well, if ya jes' listen to me, maybe you'd hit somethin', fer crissake."

"Why can't I just aim the damned rifle and shoot? Why do I have to think about all this other crap?"

"Because the Army says ya hafta, tha's why."

"You mean it's not as important to shoot Germans as it is to look good when I'm shooting at Germans, is that it?"

"Now don't get smart-assy on me, King, goddammit. Jes' do what I friggin' tell ya."

Defiantly, King slid the bolt, reloading the chamber, then pointed the rifle at the dot, and squeezed off a shot.

The pitman signaled a bull's-eye. King and Spitzer traded surprised glances and began to laugh together.

"Shee-it," Spitzer said.

The range officer called a cease-fire, and the troops rolled from the prone to sit in the dust and stretch and bitch and wave angry hands at circling insects.

A PFC wearing a messenger brassard hopped off his bicycle, strode up to the range officer, saluted, said something, then remounted and rode off, bowlegs pumping.

"Private King!" the range officer called. "Report."

King looked at Spitzer, who showed his bad teeth in a grin. "Oh-oh. Ya musta done somethin' re-e-el bad, pal. Bein' called outa line by a captain, no less."

King stood up and trotted toward the range officer post. *Damn, damn, damn. I knew it, I knew it. That letter to Bill put my ass in a real crack. King, how could you have been so absolutely stupid?*

The captain stood tall and straight in the shade of the parasol covering the post lectern. His eyes were steely gray slits below his broad-brimmed "Boy Scout" hat.

King stood at attention and saluted. "Private King reporting, sir."

"You're wanted at regimental headquarters G-1, King," the baritone voice advised.

"Now, sir?"

"Certainly not next Christmas. Get going."

"That's a two-mile walk, sir—"

"Gracious. So it is. Would you like me to order a limousine?" The captain sighed. "On your way, soldier. Double time."

"I mean, sir, if they want me right away, I can't get there right away."

The captain pointed theatrically toward the main camp. He dropped his voice to whisper in exasperated sarcasm, "*If* you'd be so kind, please."

❊❊❊

By the time King arrived at the regimental headquarters building, his dark blue fatigues were ashen gray from the coating of dust his two-mile trot had stirred up, his eyes were bleary with sunblindness, and he had to go to the latrine so badly he thought he might explode.

He stood in the relatively cool gloom of the big clapboard building, blinking at all the signs and arrows and self-conscious in the dishevelment he exhibited to the brisk, crisply uniformed noncoms and officers bustling about with papers in their hands.

He followed the arrow labeled "Regimental Personnel Officer," and at the end of the corridor a buck sergeant at a desk said, "What's your business, soldier?"

King swept off his floppy hat. "I'm supposed to report to G-1. Name's King."

"You're reporting in that god-awful rig? Don't you know that when reporting to Regiment you have to be all shiny in Class A's?"

"I was on the firing line. The captain there said I should report here at once. I was given no time to change my uniform."

A balding head appeared around the jamb of the inner door. "The captain was right. Come in here, Private King."

"Yes, sir." *Oh, God, I'm in for it. Sure as hell.*

King hurried through the door. A major stood by the window, peering out at the parade ground. He wore faultlessly pressed summer tans and glistening cavalry boots that boasted silver spurs. The bald spot was freckled, and the dark hair around it shone with pomade. He was a real dandy.

"Tell me, King," the major said, gaze still fixed on the outside distance, "what makes you so important?"

"Sir?"

"You don't look like much. A little squirt in altogether disreputable fatigues. What's behind all that?"

"I don't understand, sir."

The major turned from the window and gave King a solemn inspection. He waved at what looked to be a cablegram lying in a patch of sunlight on his desk. "Who are you, to be subject of an urgent wire from the Office of Chief of Aviation in London, England?"

Holy shit! Bill actually did something....

King gave two full seconds to consider an answer. Much against his better sense, he kept the soldierly seriousness on his face, but an inexplicable rush of zaniness drove him to give a Carpenter-like answer. "I'm not sure, sir. But it might have something to do with my friendship with General Pershing's family. Would the major be kind enough to tell me the subject of the cablegram? Perhaps then I could give a more satisfactory answer."

The major's eyes revealed a hint of awe. "General Pershing? Black Jack Pershing?"

"Yes, sir."

"The cable is signed by a Captain William Carpenter, per Lt. Col. William Mitchell, chief of the aviation research team in Paris. It instructs me to have you transferred at once to the Army Air Service center at Mineola for certification as a military pilot."

"I see, sir. Thank you, sir. Captain Carpenter, a flier himself, is not only a highly skilled staff officer but is also very well connected, socially speaking."

"You know him?"

"Very well, sir. We've flown together. Lived through a couple of narrow escapes together, actually."

The major sank into his swivel chair. "I see. Well, I'm afraid there's a problem, King. Mineola tells me they have no room for another student at this time. So I've taken the liberty of having you assigned to the nearest air training station with a vacancy. I hope Captain Carpenter will understand. I mean, I'd hate to have him think I'm playing loose with Colonel Mitchell's order."

"Not at all, sir. Captain Carpenter, like Colonel Mitchell, is an altogether reasonable man. He'd be the first to realize that you're doing the very best you can, given an unforeseen obstacle like this."

The major nodded, relief on his face. "Good." He paused. "You speak like a well-educated man, King. How come you're only a private at a draftee training camp?"

"I plan to make the Army my career, sir. I allowed myself to be drafted so that I will have direct knowledge of the Army and its ways from the bottom up."

"You want to be an officer?"

"Of course, sir. An aviation officer. Aviation is where all the opportunities lie."

"Your willingness to start at the bottom is commendable."

"Thank you, sir."

The major pulled himself together, assumed a military expression, and announced briskly, "The best I could do was to cut your orders for the Air Service auxiliary training field outside Malvern, Pennsylvania, near Philadelphia. You will report next Monday, with no delay en route. Transportation by Pennsy Railroad to Philly, transfer to the Pittsburgh Express, with a drop-off at Malvern." He added, somewhat unctuously, King thought, "That's on the Philadelphia Main Line, you know. The west and northwest, where all the very wealthy live. Perhaps you have friends there..."

My God, how lies do build. "Yes, sir. A few."

The major handed an order packet across the desk and said, "That will be all, Private King. Good luck."

"Thank you, sir." King gave a snappy salute, did an about face, and strode for the door as best he could with his bursting bladder.

"King?"

He paused at the door. "Sir?"

"I plan to visit the Malvern aviation center some weekend soon. An informal inspection, so to speak. Perhaps you will show me around."

"It would be my great pleasure, Major."

"Good. You are dismissed."

King virtually dashed to the end of the hallway, where a door bore a latrine sign. He almost didn't make it, he was laughing so hard.

Bill Carpenter, you'll be the death of me yet!

Chapter 12

Agnes Hogan's apartment was large and lavish, placed in an elegant cul-de-sac off DuPont Circle. Raymond had visited it twice before, not as a client, of course, because his salary would barely accommodate a voyeur's admission, let alone services. She was a friend of Slater's, and Raymond had been sent there by the congressman to deliver small but somewhat hefty packages, wrapped tightly and sealed with wax. Tonight, though, his mission was more complex, and this pleased him because it was proof that Slater was trusting him more and more with delicate business. Agnes was reputed among the cognoscenti to be the capital's queen of illicit sex and publisher of an array of pornographic magazines and photo folders. Raymond doubted that Slater himself had the virility to patronize Agnes on a personal basis—he had been watching closely for more than a year and had yet to see Slater show the slightest carnal interest in any, literally any, of the throngs of women within his daily rounds—but he appeared most capable of using Agnes's fringe activities.

Agnes, tall, willowy, with auburn hair and penetrating blue eyes, welcomed him to the dimly lit, heavily perfumed inner drawing room and wasted no time getting to the point. She waved him to an overstuffed chair and asked, "Am I to understand, Mr.

Raymond, that Congressman Slater sent you here this evening rather than come himself? Am I to take that as an insult?"

Slater had prepared him for this question. "Not at all, Miss Hogan. It's an expression of his confidence in you, in your trustworthiness in delicate matters. As he says, 'I love that woman. She has never once let me down.' And I must add that he's long wanted me to have the great experience of getting to know you, as part of his dedication to my longterm training as his understudy."

"You look too intelligent to ever want to be a congressman, Mr.—" She waved a hand. "I'm terrible with names. Pardon me."

He doubted the truth of this, but went along with the fiction. "Raymond. Ned Raymond. And I really don't want to be a congressman. I'm learning how to get around Congress, how to handle congressmen, so to speak." He paused and gave her a conspiratorial smile. "Naturally, I'd rather not have Mr. Slater find that out."

She smiled back, showing him her gorgeous teeth. "Well, he won't learn that from me, Mr. Raymond. And let me add that you have just gone up a thousand percent in my estimation."

"That's good news indeed, Miss Hogan."

"Agnes. Call me Agnes, Ned."

"Thank you. Agnes."

She chose a slender holder from the coffee table, inserted a long, flat, Russian-type cigarette, ignited it, and took a leisurely, deeply inhaled pull. In the subdued light, her blue eyes looked almost black. "So what's on Slater's mind this time?"

"I see no reason to beat around the bush. The congressman is prepared to pay you one thousand dollars to set up credible evidence of Senator Francis X. Murray's rumored pederasty. The congressman wants to own Murray."

She laughed, a soft, low sound. "I'd say that's getting right to the point all right, Neddie, my boy. I predict you'll have a great career. Directness is so rare in Washington. Directness is something to be cherished, to pay handsomely for."

"I'm really not very good at the diplomatic doubletalk thing."

"As I say, a fine asset these days." She sank back on the sofa, her expression turning thoughtful, serious. After another pull at the cigarette, she blew a cloud of smoke at the ceiling and said, "A thousand isn't enough, Ned. Sorry."

"It's twice what a new Ford costs."

"So now you're a statistician. I don't care a fig about the cost of a Ford. Anyhow, I'm a Pierce Arrow gal."

"So then, what's your price?"

"Fifteen hundred and expenses."

"Like what kind of expenses?"

"Whatever. They'd be properly invoiced."

"All right. I think I can handle that."

She held out a hand. "You have the money with you?"

"Of course." He drew his wallet from a jacket pocket and counted out three five hundred dollar bills. "Here you are."

She took the money, folded it, and placed it in a side table drawer beside her. She smiled. "You can tell your boss he's already got his bug on a pin. I've supplied the senator with two boys, and I've got photos of the action."

"Photos can be faked. Can you authenticate these?"

"What's in it for me?"

"Another five hundred."

"My partner Sam and I pretended to be mommy and daddy constituents taking the boys to meet their senator on a quiet Sunday afternoon. Senator Murray told us to wait in the outer office. But he got so busy with the kids he didn't realize Sam was getting some nice Kodak exposures through the connecting door. Sam used to work for Eastman in Rochester, and he processed the rolls in the little lab he has. The prints are fuzzy, but they show a lot of detail of Murray's Capitol Hill office. Including a daily calendar on the wall above the big leather couch where all the action was taking place."

"Sam sounds like a right handy fellow."

"Yep. And since we were setting Murray up for some blackmail, we also made sure the building guards signed us in when we arrived. Witnesses, you know."

"Have you shown him the pictures yet?"

"Not yet."

"All in all, the senator's more of a fool than I thought."

"Ain't it so."

"The five hundred will be waiting when you bring me the

Kodak stuff tomorrow at noon. The Willow Café. You know it?"

"Of course."

※※※

When Raymond arrived at Slater's apartment, the congressman was steeping in the bathtub, head nestled in a pillow, face to the ceiling, eyes closed in deep comfort, with a tabletop Victrola sitting on a chair beside the tub, filling the room with the rich tenor of Enrico Caruso.

"Back already, Neddie?"

"Yes, sir. It didn't take long."

"Take a chair. And turn that thing off."

Raymond flipped the off lever, admiring the machine. "When did you get this?"

"The Victor people delivered it yesterday. In gratitude for my arranging to have aircraft wings built in their sluggish, inflation-belabored factories."

Raymond chuckled and shook his head. "You are really a prize, Congressman. You didn't have anything to do with that. The Aircraft Production Board set that up."

"Mmm. But the Victor people in Camden thought I persuaded the board to make the move. I didn't affirm or deny. If that is their perception, so be it. In our business perception is everything."

"Yep, you're a real prize."

"Indeed I am, Neddie. So how did things go with the gorgeous redhead?"

"She was already setting up Murray for blackmail. She had pictures of him sporting with a couple of boys. I paid her fifteen hundred dollars for them."

Slater feigned shock. "My God, man. For fifteen hundred dollars I can buy the Mississippi River."

"Sure. It would go well with that thousand-acre tract of ash timber your little company now owns. But it could never do you favors the way a senior senator can."

Slater ran a washcloth over his bald spot. "You do have a way of getting to the core of things."

Raymond sat on the chair next to the washstand and took a moment to regard himself in the hand mirror there. "Have you looked at the mail I brought you this afternoon?"

"Not yet. It's out on the hall table. Fetch it, and we'll go over it together."

"There's one letter that's a real lulu."

"Irate constituent?"

"Not a constituent. But irate? Oh my, yes."

Raymond rose, went into the hall and returned with a handful of envelopes. "Want me to read it to you? I think you need a laugh or two."

"Read away."

Raymond rummaged through the small stack and selected a rumpled envelope that looked as if it had made a round trip to the Gobi Desert. He opened the letter, held it to the light, and cleared his throat.

"It's from a guy posted to the Aviation Mission in London. This is what he says:

```
Dear Congressman Slater:

It is with the utmost respect that I address you,
the premier congressional authority on military
aviation matters. I am aware of your great work
in establishing practically overnight the
Bensonville Center for Aeronautical Research, an
achievement that has been much applauded here in
London, both by our country's representatives and
our British allies as well. Since I am a fully
qualified flying officer, and since your research
place could probably use a man of my skill, and
since I'm bored out of my goddamn eyes with this
shitty assignment, I respectfully request that
you use your good offices to get me the hell out
of this asshole place and put me to work in a
goddamn airplane, where I belong.

With sincere best wishes for continued success in
your most honorable service to our great nation,
I remain,

Captain William J. "Stuck in England" Carpenter,
Spiritual Leader of the 201ˢᵗ Horse's Ass Bri-
gade.'"
```

Slater laughed, a soft hissing sound that shook his shoulders and sent little waves racing around the bath water.

Raymond laughed, too, but loudly.

"Now that," Slater eventually managed, "is an absolutely enchanting letter. Charming." He broke into renewed laughter, then asked, "What's the man's name again?"

"Captain William J. 'Stuck in England' Carpenter, Spiritual Leader of the 201st Horse's Ass Brigade."

They laughed some more, and Slater said, "Know what? I think a man like that could serve me well. First in that need I feel forming at Bensonville. I'm not too happy with the way Fontaine is setting up his operation there. Taking over the old Rickman Tractor Company buildings and refitting them with his airplane stuff. It's not what he agreed to do. Building an entirely new plant calls for a lot more people—jobs. The vacant tractor plant is more like redecorating, if you know what I mean."

"Sure. But it's a helluva lot faster. He'll be building airplanes by next winter. Putting up a new building would push him into the fall of 1918. And we need planes as fast as we can get them."

Slater thought about that. "Well, I just get a bit uneasy about Fontaine now and then. I don't trust him altogether."

"So you want to plant a spy, right?"

"Yeah. Somebody who knows a lot about planes who would be so grateful to me he'd never sleep. And then I want to plant him on the staff of that bigmouth, Billy Mitchell. I want to use Carpenter as the pipeline into Mitchell's intentions."

"That's where he's been working, Congressman. He'd have a hemorrhage if we sent him back to Mitchell's operation."

"Correction. He's never been on Mitchell's staff. He's been an ant in the Mitchell bureaucracy."

"Still, Mitchell's no dummy. He'll see at once that Carpenter's your spy."

"Nope. Not if we have Carpenter promoted to major and have him assigned by our good friend and patsy, Senator Murray. Senator Murray has as much interest in the plant at Bensonville—and what Fontaine's doing there—as I do. So Murray pulls some of his own strings in the Army and arranges, most indirectly, to have the Army appoint Carpenter to Mitchell's headquarters staff. Carpenter is, after all, an experienced airman, and no doubt Mitchell would be delighted to have him aboard instead of being wasted in some basement office in London the way he has been."

Raymond cupped a hand and examined his nails. "So how do we let Carpenter know he's to serve as your spy?"

"I tell him."

"And if he refuses?"

"I will arrange to have him transferred to the infantry and made military attaché to our legation in Tierra del Fuego."

"Do we have a legation in Tierra del Fuego?"

Slater shrugged. "How the hell do I know? I'm not sure they even have flush toilets down there."

Raymond showed the obligatory smile. "So I'll get him over here for an interview."

Slater nodded his decision. "Yep. He's the one. Get him on the next ship and make sure it's a fast one."

Chapter 13

There was something surreal about King's arrival in Malvern. First, when he detrained, a barracks bag over his shoulder and his order packet under the other arm, bewildered by the apparent affluence of the surroundings and excited by the sense of adventure, he heard his name being called by a page. It was like a hobo in Rome being summoned by the Vatican. Second, the page turned out to be a PFC standing trackside in Class A uniform, with a visored cap, perfectly wrapped leggins, and shoes so polished they seemed to have been dipped in caramel sauce. And third, there was something spookily familiar about the man. King knew he had seen him before, but where and when, he had no idea. Worse, a peculiar something about the man's lips suggested that a sullen, knowing smile lurked behind the military stiffness.

"I'm King, here as ordered. Now what happens?"

"I drive you to the post."

"And you are...?"

"Pratt. The post C.O.'s driver and gofer."

"Oh." The name meant nothing. In the pause, King felt he was expected to ask, "How come the C.O. is giving me this royalty treatment?"

"Beats the hell outa me, soldier. I just do what he tells me to do."

Sullen. That was the word for this guy. "What's his name?"

"Bascomb. Captain Aubrey T. Bascomb the Third."

"Sounds sort of snooty."

"You ask me, if there was two more like him before he came along, I hope somebody slams the gate before a fourth one shows up."

King humphed, appreciating the bizarre construction. "Hard to work for, is he?"

"Not if you don't mind being treated like a friggin' coolie every day."

"Is he a pilot?"

"Yeah. He's the chief instructor. Teaches the cadets that show promise, he likes to say. Other times he just walks around, pokin' things with his ridin' crop and lookin' like he smells somethin' bad."

King said, "I know the type."

The vehicle was a big olive-drab Hupmobile touring car with the top folded back, open to the bright blue sky. King threw his gear into the cavernous backseat, then climbed into the front passenger seat beside Pratt. He held out a pack of Lucky Strikes. "Want a root?"

Pratt shook his head. "Against captain's orders. He says it doesn't look dignified when I smoke while driving."

"Sheee."

"Yeah."

They headed west from the railroad on a winding concrete road shaded by rows of towering trees and bordered by miles of tidy stone fences.

"Good Lord. Look at that place," King said, craning for a better look at a Tudor home that spread like a sundae topping over a range of small, wooded hills.

"That's one a the smaller ones."

"Smaller? It's got to have forty rooms."

"Hell, Penshurst, down the way from here in Penn Valley, has seventy-five rooms. A whole damn wing just for the servants."

King sat back in his seat, bemused. "Where do people get money like that?"

"Railroads, shipping, oil, steel. That's on the surface. Beneath the surface they steal people blind, con people, shaft people, and sometimes kill 'em."

King gave Pratt a sidelong glance. "You sound like one of those Bolsheviks."

"I'd be one if I knew how to spell it."

"You look familiar. Have we met somewhere before?"

"We never met."

"But you act like we have. And you don't like me. Is it because the C.O. is treating me nice?"

"I don't give a damn about you one way or the other."

King gave that a moment of thought, then said "Okay. From here on it's mutual. Stay out of my life, Pratt. I don't have time for self-satisfied shits who can't spell."

❋❋❋

The airfield was a broad expanse of clover bordered by carefully cropped trees and rolling farmland that would have made a nice calendar picture. Along the north border was a line of buildings—four hangars, a machine shop, and what appeared to be the headquarters shack, which was hardly a shack, being constructed as it was of carefully pointed fieldstone and white-painted colonial trim. King counted seven yellow Jennies lined up in front of the hangars, with a gaggle of trucks and oil servers parked in the blue shadows. A dozen olive-drab pyramidal tents formed a neat rectangle behind the stone house. To one side of this, a squad of shirtless men was leaping and waving its arms in response to the shouts of a phys ed sergeant, and farther on, another squad, this one in full field gear—with steel helmets, no less—was doing the manual of arms under the direction of an exasperated second-looey. For all the summer heat, the activity seemed to be in frenzied fast-motion, like some of those comical Mack Sennett pie-throwing picture shows at the old Bijou.

Pratt pulled the Hupmobile up to the front door of the house and waited silently as King pulled his gear and dropped it to the grass. When Pratt drove off, an orderly came briskly down the stone steps.

"You're Private King?"

"That's right."

"Leave your gear there. Somebody'll take it to your tent. Captain Bascomb wants to see you, toot sweet."

The stone walls, shuttered windows, and ancient timber created an inner coolness, and there was the smell of polish and soap and gun oil intermixed. King jerked his tunic into adjustment, brushed some dust from the sleeves, and rubbed his shoes, one at a time, against the woolen nap of his leggins. He pulled off his cap, ran his fingers through his hair, then followed the orderly into an office whose door carried a sign proclaiming that it belonged to Captain A. T. Bascomb III, Commanding Officer, 33rd Auxiliary Training Company, Aeronautics Section, U.S. Army Signal Corps, Knock Before Entering.

The orderly rapped on the door, opened it slightly, and said through the crack, "Private King is here, sir."

"Have him enter."

The orderly's nod told King to do as ordered. The man disappeared down the hallway, and King stepped into what was clearly hallowed territory.

He stood the proper three paces from the desk, clicked his heels, and threw a manual-perfect salute at the man seated in the government-issue swivel chair.

"Private King reporting as ordered, sir!"

The captain was, like the installation around him, the picture of military perfection. The creases in his uniform were sharp enough to whittle hickory, and the insignia on his collar glistened, as if it carried an inner light of its own. His black hair was carefully oiled and parted in the middle and, with his matching mustache, suggested the groom on a wedding cake.

"At ease," the captain said, returning the salute with an indolent wave. "How was your trip, King?"

Surprised by the very unmilitary nature of the question, King blinked. "Ah...fine, sir. Fine, thank you, sir."

"I won't keep you long. The company clerk will sign you in and show you to your tent. But I wanted to...ah...fill you in a bit on what we're doing here."

King blinked again. "That's very nice of you, sir."

"I understand you're a personal friend of General Pershing."

William T. Carpenter, I sure as hell am going to kill you. That's a frigging promise. Kill you!

"Well, sir, I'd certainly not lay claim to that—"

"I understand. You'd rather not have that information get around. Your peers might think you'll be using that fact as a means of receiving preferential treatment. I assure you, King, your secret is safe with me."

"Ah...very kind of you, sir."

"We're glad to have you with us. This would appear to be a very modest ancillary operation, but there's more to it than meets the eye. The land we're using is quite historical—once part of the estate of William Penn himself and now owned by Silas G. Whiting, whose great-grandfather was an associate of Ben Franklin and founder of a publishing empire second to none. Mr. Whiting, who still lives with his wife and daughter in Farview Manor, one of the Main Line's most elegant mansions not too far from here, is himself an aviation enthusiast and has invested importantly in the work of Glenn Curtiss and the Wrights, in Dayton. When he learned that the Air Service training facilities in Mineola and Essington were bulging at the seams, he volunteered the loan of this land for development by the Army. He and his family have actually visited us here on two occasions, I'm happy to say, and he remains one of our staunchest supporters."

There was a pause, and King sensed he was expected to say something. "I'm most impressed, sir. And, I might add, I'm proud to have been assigned to your unit."

Bascomb nodded, showed a prim, self-satisfied little smile, and said, "Good. Good. Now, off you go to the orderly room, King. You are dismissed."

King saluted again. "Thank you, sir."

"And in your next letter to General Pershing, please tell him I wish him the very best."

"Yes, sir. Thank you, sir."

Chapter 14

For all its country club atmosphere, Camp Silas G. Whiting evinced an undertone of grim seriousness and a need to hurry. Captain Bascomb was indeed a foppish sort, all taken up with himself and ready at any time to let it be known in his New England drawl that he was in absolute, don't-dare-question-me command. Yet behind this air of effete tyranny he seemed determined to make something of the gaggle of nondescripts that had fallen into his purview. He made it clear that the pleasant surroundings were not to be simply enjoyed; they were to be seen as the arena in which lazy incompetence would be transformed into zealous skill, which, in turn, would perhaps make one iota of difference in the outcome of the war. This was the way he actually talked, and the weird part was that he really seemed to mean it.

To King, it came through at first as sheer melodrama calculated to deify Bascomb and denigrate the peons. But then a pattern formed, and subtly he began to welcome its rigors and impositions. Every day he became physically tougher and mentally more alert, and every day he learned at least one more trick in the art of staying alive. And toward this end there'd be a daily lecture from Bascomb or his staff officers reminding "the cadets" that they were in the first of three phases of enlightenment: here they would undergo six weeks of ground school—the study of aircraft engines, the machine gun, map reading, aircraft rigging, meteorology, navigation, and instruments—and to be sure they had no moments of unproductive idleness, there would be basic close-order drill and physical fitness programs. Once all of this was out of the way, they'd move into the second phase: primary flight training in the JN-4s under the supervision of Bascomb and his instructor pilots. The third phase, advanced flight training, would come at flying schools in Britain, France, and Italy because there were no planes in the United States suitable for advanced training and no pilots qualified to give such instruction.

So the camp was becoming ever more crowded with the formation of three distinct groups: the training cadre, those in ground school, and those learning to fly. As soon as the rookie pilots shipped out and the ground school "grinders" took their place in the air, a new, always larger batch of educated idiots would reoccupy the ground school part of "Tent Town." The beautiful valley's serenity had been forever lost to the rumble of engines, the thumping of machine guns, the cadenced shouts of men dashing about in their underwear, and bugled formation calls blaring from sunup to sunset.

Those few free moments he had he gave to the dayroom piano, a fairly decent Aeolian baby grand Mrs. Whiting had sent over from Farview Manor for use by those cadets who played. There were three: Vance, a gaunt Harvard man who was really very good with classical stuff; Kappel, a Cornell grad who liked to compose bawdy lyrics for iconic folk songs; and King, whose repertoire was any tune that could be whistled, thanks to his unerring ear and perfect pitch. In fact it was he who compelled Andy Rawlings, another ground schooler from 130 Tent, to tell listeners the same old joke any time King was at the keyboard: A piano player in a saloon has a pet monkey. A patron orders a beer. The monkey hops down from the piano, saunters along the bar, and stops to eat a peanut. The monkey's tail drops into the patron's beer. The annoyed patron snarls at the piano player: "Hey, Mack! Do you know your monkey's got his tail in my beer?" Piano player replies, "No, but hum a few bars of the chorus and I'll fake it."

It was all in good fun, but invariably it made King uneasy. In private moments he recognized that he had an ongoing problem with his view of himself. No matter how well he did in navigational math, field-stripping the Vickers machine gun, tracing the OX-5's oil lines, the 100-yard dash, artillery spotting exercises—whatever—he was nagged by a voice that reminded him of his personal inadequacy. No matter how hard he tried, how good he became at something, there was always a hitch. And the piano epitomized this. He could have taken lessons. He could have learned to read music. But he was more interested in articulating the music in his soul, or whatever it is in a man that drives him to express the inexpressible and to take great gobs of time, expend huge amounts of effort, to reproduce precisely the music that other souls had written down on paper seemed never to equate. *Still, the voice would tell him, you're not a musician, you're an impostor and therefore contemptible.*

This was not helped at all the evening when he'd been doodling on the keyboard, groping for a satisfactory melding of diminished sevenths to serve in his new composition as a segue from the second-chorus release to the coda.

Vance appeared in the doorway. "I've been watching and listening, King. You've got a problem."

"Oh?"

"Mmm. You'll never be a musician."

"Is that so? How come?"

"You make sophisticated noises on the piano, all right. But that's what they are. Noises."

King felt a mixture of annoyance and defensiveness. "That's what all music is. Noises. Satisfying noises."

"No. Intonations. Agreement of sounds. Soulful protocols. Order and form."

"And, according to your prescription, semantics."

"You tend to defy or ignore order and form. The stuff you put out is, more often than not, cacophonous. Unmindful of the established. Arrogant. Rebellious."

"Wait'll you hear what I've done to 'Twinkle, Twinkle, Little Star.'"

"You make a joke of this. But I'm serious. You're not a musician. You are a noise-making impostor."

King sighed. "Well, you're right, of course. But what I don't understand is why you take it so big. I am, after all, merely amusing myself."

"Not so. You are abusing those of us who have worked and studied, worked and studied for years, to learn how to make the right moves. You treat our art, our skills, as if they are parlor games. And we resent it."

"Well, I'm sorry, Vance. I really am. I have a great talent for making people resent me. And I'm sorry that my noise-making has added you to the list. Ironically, I think you're a splendid piano player. A bit mechanical at times, but overall, great technique."

Vance gave him a lingering stare. "You picked up on that 'mechanical' thing, eh? I've heard that from critics over the years. I don't know what to do about it."

"Do what I do. Relax. Have fun. Stop making such a big thing out of proper form, protocol, precision. Make music. Your own music. Nine times out of ten, even the guy who wrote the piece expects you to do that, to use his written-down dots as a road map for enjoyment." King chuckled, remembering. "Know what? I once saw the piano music for an orchestral arrangement to be played New Orleans- jazz style. The piece opened with a 32-measure piano solo in 4/4 time. As written, the score began with a single measure with the number 32 in it. Above the 32 were these instructions to the pianist," he drew a line in the air with his forefinger, "'Hit everything in sight.'"

Vance laughed, a single explosive "Hah!"

"Funny, eh?"

"Droll. Quite droll."

King said quietly, "Relax, Vance. There's room for everybody in the music world."

✳✳✳

A simple announcement on the orderly room bulletin board listed King among seven who would next report to the flight line at 0800 hours for primary flight training. Uniform of the day: fatigues, helmet and goggles waiting in plane. King's instructor: A.T. Bascomb, Capt. Inf.

No transition of any kind. No graduation ceremony with flat

hats and tassels. No dress parade. Just the government's way of saying enough of this shit, on with the next. King wanted to whoop and dance, but he confined his exuberance to a nod of satisfaction and the celebratory gulping down of a Hershey bar.

It was a beautiful morning, warm, and redolent of dewy grass and distant pines. Captain Bascomb managed to look natty even in his dark blue fatigues, an effect augmented by his helmet and goggles. They traded salutes, and Bascomb said, "Rear cockpit, King."

King swung aboard and settled in, fastening his helmet strap and trying to hide his excitement. Bascomb stood on the fuselage stirrup and began pointing in that way of his. "Ground school covered most of this, but we'll go over it again. Fuel gauge there. Altimeter there. Air speed there. Oil pressure there. Throttle. Clock. This is an early model, so there's no compass, no tachometer. I have an altimeter in the front cockpit, switch, throttle, stick, rudder bar, some map racks. And that's it. Now check your controls."

King moved his feet, and the rudder waggled obediently. The stick pulled, elevators up, pushed, elevators down. Stick right and left, and ailerons reply. "Controls working properly," he said.

Bascomb nodded. "I'll take us up, then let you follow through with me on the stick and rudder to give you a feel for things. You'll notice that when we pick up speed on the take-off, the nose tends to pull to the left. That's torque at work, and you'll see how I compensate with a bit of rudder to keep the nose pointing straight ahead. And the touch is always light. Over-controlling or ham-handedness can turn into trouble. After gaining headway, I'll raise the tail enough to keep the plane on the ground until it is well past its minimum flying speed, maintaining course with the rudder. When maximum ground speed is reached, then very easily and smoothly, I'll take it off the ground. Any questions?"

"No, sir."

"If you need to talk, tap on the coaming behind me, and I'll throttle down so you can be heard."

The captain stepped on the lower wing and eased himself into the front cockpit. He lowered his goggles and nodded at the mechanic standing by the propeller. "Contact."

The prop was swung, the OX-5 barked into life, and they sat

there for a time, immersed in the rich exhaust smell, as the engine warmed to its task. Then Bascomb's helmeted head nodded, the mechanic pulled aside the wheel chocks, and, engine bellowing, the Jenny began its waddling dance across the turf. Lift-off was easy, smooth, and when the altimeter registered a thousand feet, the Jenny tilted into a gentle leftward turn.

King grinned in the sunlight and wind. "Oh, boy!"

They flew for half an hour. At the outset, Bascomb throttled down and shouted over his shoulder, "Keep your feet on the rudder bar and your hand on the stick! Try to feel what I do! But if I tap myself on the head, get clear of everything! It means I want full control!"

King was fascinated by the way he could actually sense what Bascomb was doing and was about to do. There was something almost mediumistic about it.

Bascomb surprised him halfway through the flight. He raised his hands in the air. "Take over, King!"

It was then, in that magical moment on a bright summer morning, that John King began to fly. He was tightly wound, but in a good way, excited, awed, delighted, and yes, damn it, thrilled to feel the machine respond so readily, even to his slightest touch.

Bascomb pointed upward, so King instinctively knew that more power would be needed. He eased the throttle forward, brought the stick back slightly, and let the plane fly them to fifteen hundred feet, where he leveled off and awaited further instructions. Bascomb drew a figure eight in the air with his forefinger, and King made a full turn to the right, then to the left. Early in the maneuver, Bascomb shouted, "Keep the nose on the horizon, damn it! You're letting it sink! Give us some top rudder!"

King made three more eights.

"All right, King! Give me the plane! We're going home!"

King sat back, folded his hands on his lap, and watched, filled with an emotion that had no name, as Bascomb brought them in low over the deep green trees and set the ship down without a bounce.

Back at the flight line, standing beside the Jenny and making notes on a clipboard, Bascomb, without looking at him, said, "You did well, King. Don't get all swollen up over it, but I think you're a natural. Naturals come along now and then. And I think you're one of them. Time will tell."

He couldn't hold it in. "God, Captain, that was the most wonderful experience I've ever had!"

"Wait'll you solo. That's better yet. But in the meantime, just play it cool, King. Keep it cool. In this business, excitement and overconfidence kill."

Chapter 15

As King and Bascomb made their way to the headquarters building, a glistening black-and-cream Packard touring car came up the road and pulled to a halt across their path. The girl at the wheel smiled in the shade of her broad-brimmed straw hat and waved a hand.

"Hello there, Captain Bascomb! May I have a minute?"

King marveled at the transformation. From the somber conqueror of military skies filled with the sense of God-how-great-I-am, Bascomb turned instantly into something akin to a wriggling puppy. He swiped the helmet and goggles from his head in a swift, almost panicky motion, and he seemed unable to decide whether to dance, bow, or curtsy.

"Miss Whiting! What a delightful surprise! I'm so very glad to see you again!"

"Thank you, Captain," she said in a soft contralto. "I realize I'm intruding on your very full day, but I come on a mission that requires an early response. That's why I drove over, rather than send you a formal note."

"I couldn't be more pleased. What can I do to be of help?"

King felt himself caught in a social situation that called for his quick withdrawal, but, lacking as he was in the social niceties, he wasn't sure how to manage it. And there was something embarrassing about the way Bascomb was laying it on, his ornate, Victorian mannerisms, and the oh-dear-me lah-di-dah high society crap dished out by the girl. It made him wonder what price he might have to pay later on when Bascomb had time to think about how a cadet had caught him in an uncharacteristically silly moment.

Damn it, it had been a great day up to now.

"Excuse me, sir, but I'll be in the orderly room, filling out my flight form."

It was only then that Bascomb seemed to remember King's presence and his own need to demonstrate good manners. True to form, he went swiftly to his passé protocols. "Oh, yes, of course. Miss Whiting, may I present Cadet John King, who has just returned from his first flight lesson. Cadet King, meet Miss Mary Lou Whiting, whose family has graciously given us permission to use this land."

Because he didn't know what else to do, King clicked his heels and made a stiff, Prussian-type bow. "Delighted, miss."

She grinned easily and extended her hand. "How do you do, Cadet King. Tell me, are you German?"

He touched her hand, flustered. "Ah, no, miss. What makes you ask?"

"That funny little bow. I've spent a couple of summers in Berlin, and all the men there were forever clicking their heels and bowing in that stiff, funny little way."

"Oh." He felt the warmth of his blush. "To tell you the truth, miss, I have no idea why I bowed like that. It just sort of happened."

She laughed, genuinely amused. Then, with barely a pause, she dismissed him, turning her full attention to Bascomb. "I must talk to you about something, Captain. Would you mind if we went into your office?"

Without looking at him, Bascomb said, "Carry on, King."

King had completed the paperwork on his flight lesson and was heading for the canteen when Captain Bascomb leaned out his office door. "Oh, King. I'm glad you're still here. Miss Whiting has asked to speak with you."

"With me, sir?"

"Come in. Right now, please."

King stepped into the office, surprised and confused. Miss Whiting obviously saw this and moved to put him at ease.

"I won't keep you but a moment, Cadet King. Captain Bascomb has very graciously agreed to attend a patriotic tea dance to be held at Farview in support of the Red Cross and under the auspices of the Main Line Junior League. And, better yet, he's promised to extend the invitation to the officers and cadets serving here and to provide the transportation between the base and my home."

She paused and gave the captain a warm smile. It was another interval in which King felt he was expected to say something. But why was thoroughly beyond guessing.

"That's nice, miss."

She laughed that soft little laugh of hers. "And I'm afraid that you, my dear, have been singled out for special duty that afternoon."

Again he was at a loss. "Tend bar? Wash dishes?"

And again she laughed, this time openly, and Bascomb, because he was still in a massive throe of fawning, joined in, although King could see he was embarrassed and displeased by the way he'd answered Miss Whiting's overture.

"Nothing like that, dear boy. Captain Bascomb tells me you play a really fine piano, and I'm wondering if you'd be willing to play a little for us during the dance intermission. Please say you will. It will provide a sense of mutual participation—the Junior League and the Army in cahoots on behalf of the Red Cross, so to speak. You know what I mean, I'm sure."

✸✸✸✸

Through all this nicey-nicey palaver, Mary Lou's mind had been dealing with an exasperating preoccupation with King's nose. Outside fashion magazine illustrations and the Franklin Museum's statuary rooms, she'd never seen a man with a perfect, classic, sculpted nose—not too long, not too short, straight, and with well-shaped nostrils.

Until this one. This John King.

He was certainly not handsome, in the manner of those regal

men in the haberdashery illustrations. But he had this great nose, and a jawline that spoke of masculinity, and a level blue gaze which, when combined with that curling at the corner of his mouth, suggested that here was a youngster who had seen the world and forgave it anyhow. She speculated he was on the cusp: callow teenager, moving into manhood. So what kind of man will he be? Behind the eyes and in the chest under those shapeless blue fatigues, what forces were at work?

Not that it would make any difference. Her record with men of any age was dismal. She liked them in general, and they were almost always nice to her because her father was so very rich. But nothing ever developed. The last time anybody had made a pass at her was at the country club Halloween dance, when a drunken George Beaumont IV had squeezed her behind during a waltz. And she couldn't remember the time before that. It was something to do with the way she looked, according to her father. Once, when she was complaining at breakfast that men just never seemed to be interested in her, Father said it was because she was *too* good-looking, adding, with poorly concealed satisfaction, that her looks were so great they convinced men she was unattainable.

She knew that her father was rich and powerful enough to afford the truth—he never lied, he once said, because he just didn't have to. Lies, he said, were for the weak, the penurious, the socially insecure. So if he was telling the truth (as he saw it) vis-à-vis her looks, then he was probably right, and she was condemned to a lifetime of gorgeous celibacy. She was a good girl and wanted to remain a good girl, but imagination and libido frequently gave her fits of frustration and envy. Envy, by happening upon Gladys Richman and Timmy Randall making torrid love during a weekend at the Rehoboth Beach house. After peeking through a partially open door, her mind had been forever stained by the images of beautiful naked bodies busily seeking new ways to become entwined. She was only fourteen at the time, a year younger than Gladys, two years younger than Timmy, and it was a long time before she could look at either of them without feeling jealous awe. God, if that drab little mouse could land a hot number like Timmy, what in hell was wrong with Father's smug analysis? Certainly there was someone out there who wouldn't be intimidated by "good looks."

"Well," King was saying diffidently, "there are piano players a lot better by far." He gave Bascomb a desperate glance. "You've heard Gil Vance, I'm sure, sir. He's studied piano all his life, and nobody can do the classics any better than he can."

"Vance is very good," Bascomb said carefully, not willing to fully commit himself until he knew just what kind of music Miss Whiting was looking for. "But—"

"Classics? Oh no, dear man. The intermission crowd likes fast and lively and modern. You do handle those, don't you?"

King smiled, feeling himself to be on more solid ground now. "Sure."

"Fast, lively, and modern is his specialty," Bascomb put in helpfully.

King had an absolutely marvelous smile, she decided. Lopsided, yes. But that was its charm. And his eyes, an astonishing blue, crinkled at the corners when it was in full play.

"All right, then it's agreed. The party, Cadet King, will be from four to seven on Saturday next. And I'm delighted that you and Captain Bascomb are willing to aid and abet. The party is a benefit, with the Junior League and guests contributing the proceeds to the American Red Cross in France. We thought it altogether appropriate for the young men serving at the field here to be our special guests."

"I'll be there," King said, feeling much better about everything.

※※※

Later in the tent, after a long shower uncomplicated by the presence of anyone else, King sat on his cot and went over ideas for the musicale. He was simultaneously pleased and frightened by the whole idea. With no effort on his part, with no strenuous exercises of social rigmarole, he had been handed a significant compliment. But with every advantage comes a liability, and in this case his ego had been well nourished by, not only the invitation, but also the electricity sent his way by the beautiful Mary Lou Whiting. All in all, women interested him. The liability part here was that this woman interested him in a curiously frightening way.

Make that a curiously libidinous way.

✳✳✳

Dear Bill:

I've been thinking about you a lot lately and realizing over and over how much I owe you for having arranged my assignment here. Things have been going surprisingly well, and the satisfaction is almost as deep as my gratitude to you.

As you've probably discerned by now, I'm a rather odd duck. I march to a drum very few others seem to hear, and I, myself, am often made aware of this by way of strange, unexpected, and often disturbing mental images that seem totally unrelated to the reality I'm living. Like earlier this evening, after chow, when I was taking a walk in the twilight.

In the sky there were marvelous gatherings of altocumuli, those huge piles of creamy white cotton-like clouds in the evening blue, and I had a sudden, crystal perception of being in a beautiful city that covered a mountaintop and glittered in the sunlight. There were tall columns, broad plazas, whispering trees, splashing fountains, a soft breeze. And I felt a great happiness. It was precisely the vision I'd had as a baby when I was less than a year old. And all this still in my mind, decades later, as clear and sweet as it was that day. Where does something like this come from? How is it possible that a tiny kid can see and be thrilled by a scene so incredibly beautiful, so filled with concepts and detail that can only be appreciated in an adult mode?

Later, when I was in second grade, I was walking home from school one fall afternoon, and again I had a sudden, indescribably poignant view of myself as the youngster I was, lying on my back on a gentle hill blanketed by wild flowers. (Impossibly, I distinctly remember what I was wearing—Lederhosen and knee socks, an attire totally alien to a six-year-old kicking leaves in a suburb of 1904 Buffalo, New York.) And lying beside me, dressed in what I recognize today as a dirndl and wearing a flower in her golden hair, was a beautiful little girl who seemed to glow in the sunlight. She was holding my hand, and, keeping her gaze on the sky, she said gently and clearly, "I love you, John."

Was she speaking English? I can't say. All I know is that I understood her and was happy. Was my name in that other place also John? Or was I hearing the name, whatever it was, and understanding it as John? Who's to say? That scene—so deep, so grown-up, so mysteriously beyond my capabilities then—never left me, and today still touches me, moves me, unaccountably makes me want to weep.

There were other incidents strangely outside the old déjà vu concept. One of my favorites is the vision I had at Camp Dix. I was scrubbing garbage cans and had taken a moment to catch my breath. As I stared out across the plain, I was suddenly elsewhere. I was standing at an ornate balustrade edging a wide piazza, and I was gazing out at a broad sweep of sunlit sea. There were splendid gardens all around, and I was luxuriating in the gorgeous day. (Again, I swear, I was conscious that I was wearing the short tunic and sandals affected by the Caesarian elite.) Behind me, a voice called softly. When I turned, there was this beautiful woman—again, seeming to be aglow in sunlight—lying on a chaise, smiling, and holding out a hand to me. And still again, I had that consuming sense of happiness and belonging.

Then, ingloriously, exquisitely disappointed, I was plunged back into the world of sweat and stinking cans.

Where do these haunting flashbacks come from, old friend? Surely somebody must know. They're just not telling us, right?

Well, I didn't mean to belabor you with all this nutty stuff, but you're the only person in the world I can talk to, it seems, and these things weigh heavily on me sometimes, and I feel the need to share them with someone who has shown that he understands me and likes me anyhow.

So thanks again for everything, Bill. I know you find little time for personal correspondence, so I won't expect any answer soon. But do write when you can. You're my only true friend in this world.

Good night from John.

Chapter 16

For Carpenter, Washington had always been an evil, melancholy place. In his boyhood, when his father had been in Congress, he'd been allowed to visit only twice. It cost too much to maintain two households, one in the District and one in the capital, his father had complained, and it certainly cost too much for mother and son to ride railroads across two-thirds of the country just to say hello, when Father was busy passing laws and conferring with important people and wouldn't have much time for them anyhow. The boy's impression of the nation's capital derived from one visit, calculated to have him and Mother appear with Father in a rotogravure, and from another given to a "family day" picnic for members at the White House. So young Carpenter's impression was one of huge, forbidding buildings, scary broad avenues, brooding monuments, and loud, overly effusive people—all working together to present a spooky, unhappy mosaic. Both times it made Mother cry a lot and Father angry and defensive in the face of her hurt anger over being left alone in a hotel so much.

As for him, the boy, he cried, too, and was never sure why. Looking for answers, staring at the high, nighttime ceiling of some hotel, it occurred to him early on that Father and Mother should never have married. She had been a good wife and mother, clean and neat and properly efficient in the kitchen and other domestic venues. She was tall and stiffly dour, with a throaty voice that turned shrill whenever she felt she was being "put upon," and it seemed she was always more put upon than anything else, because his dominant memory of her was one of high-voiced complaint and accusation—railing at the housemaids or cooks or Bert, the gardener, when she wasn't tearing into Father.

So on this day, stepping from a cab in his sparkly, shiny, creased and beribboned Class A's and mounting the steps of the House Office Building in a kind of trot, he was determined not to give in to the sadness that seemed to follow several paces behind. He was no longer a boy, and Mother and Father were long gone, and this was just another rotten town filled with the usual rotten people, and he was just as good, if not better, than any of these sons of bitches. By the time he entered Congressman Slater's anteroom and presented his credentials to a pudgy receptionist, who regarded him coolly over her pince-nez, the adrenalin was flowing and he was on full alert.

Relax, Carpenter. He's just another friggin' pol.

"Congressman Slater is in conference. He'll be with you soon, Captain..." her eyes flicked to his card, "...Carpenter."

"Good, because I can't give him too much time. I've got some important military people to see."

She looked at him severely, the eyeglasses glinting. "There aren't many people more important than the congressman," she said. Nodding at a row of straight-back chairs along the wall, she added, "Take a seat."

He ignored her and went to one of the tall windows. There was a heavy overcast, and everything was gray, even the lawns and foliage. After a time he said, "Look out there, and you'd never know there's a war on."

It was her turn to ignore him. He gave an ostentatious glance at the wall clock and said, "Well, I'll be getting on. He said three o'clock. It's now three-fifteen. Tell Slater I said hello."

He was making for the hallway door and she was sputtering when an inner office door opened, and a round, bald little man in an alpaca jacket peered out. "Ho there. Are you Captain Carpenter?"

"Yes, sir. And you're...?"

The woman gasped, and the round man grinned and said, "Slater. Come on in." To the pince-nez he said, "Milly, no more phone calls or visitors for awhile."

Carpenter said, "That goes for me, too, Milly."

Her pudgy little cheeks puffed outward in exasperation, and the spectacles fell to hang on their ribbon. Then suddenly, after a suspended moment, all three of them began to laugh, and the earlier pompousness fell into outright hilarity. "Captain Carpenter," Milly said, laughing and shaking her head, "you are truly prime."

"And you, Milly, are a cute little bird. Especially when your glasses aren't hiding those pretty peepers."

"Enough of this romance," Slater said. "Come on in and set your valise in one of these overstuffed jobs. Whiskey?"

"Whiskey would be mighty welcome about now."

❋❋❋

"That was quite a letter you wrote me, Carpenter."

"Sorry if I was overly ragtail. But, believe me, I was—am—one frustrated soldier boy."

"What's the major problem?"

"Nobody knows his pecker from a pink pompom over there in London. We're presumably trying to build an air force, yet hardly anybody over there has even ridden in a plane, let alone figured out how to buy a good one."

Slater got right to it: "What option do you recommend?"

"We don't have any options. It'll take at least a year to get our domestic factories turning out planes of any worth, while the Germans keep introducing new ones by the month, it seems—each one better than the last. The only thing left for us to do is to buy whatever equipment the Limeys and Frogs can spare and teach our guys to fly and maintain them."

Slater nodded, took in an ounce of whiskey from his glass, and rolled it around in his mouth, a real drinker appreciating a real drink. He swallowed slowly and sighed contentedly. "As you know, I'm trying to set up an aviation research facility in Bensonville, in my district. We'll be looking for new ways to speed up production, new ways to make better planes. If we don't, we'll be fighting the Germans in 1921, maybe 1922, with 1917 airplanes. And that's what we'll be doing if we buy today's European leftovers."

"You're preaching to the choir, Congressman. I just finished three months of wringing out every type of aircraft the Allies have, and, take it from me, most of them are plain shit. If they're this bad now, guess what they'll be like in 1920. Meanwhile, the Krauts have renovated their most reliable types and are in the process of bringing out a brand new Fokker fighter. The D-7 type. And right behind that is the D-8 type, an upper-wing monoplane that's got the British air intelligence people jumping around with their balls tied in knots."

"Fokker's not a German, he's a Dutchman, right?"

"Right. And he tried to sell his planes to the Brits as far back as 1914, and the idiots turned him down. So he took his goods to the Krauts, and they've been burning our asses ever since. I had a chance to fly a captured Fokker Dr-1 triplane while I was at Farnborough, and that's nothing more than a three-wing kite with a motor up front. But you know what? That little devil flies rings around anything the Brits and Frenchies can put in the air. No fooling. I found that you can turn it a hundred and eighty degrees, flat, without even banking the wings. Like it's a pinwheel. Like it's a puck skidding around on ice. Somebody can be chasing it, staring straight at its tail, when *foop*, he's suddenly looking straight at its engine and machine-gun muzzles. You give me a plane that can do that, and I'll be a triple ace in twenty minutes."

Slater took another drink and thought about all this. "I wonder," he said finally, "if we could buy Fokker away from the Germans."

Carpenter gave him a lingering, surprised stare. "You're joking, aren't you, Congressman?"

"Why would I be joking? Everybody has his price. And I'm willing to bet that Fokker could be bought out from under the kaiser. Germany's bank accounts are already at dipstick zero, and we've only begun to tap our treasury. We could outbid the Krauts with our lunch money."

"Fokker would never do it. He's a man of principle, and he's made a deal with Berlin, and he'll honor it."

"I don't understand people like that. But anyway, it was a thought..."

Carpenter polished off his drink and, holding out the glass for a refill, said, "So then, you have something I can do out Bensonville-way?"

Slater picked up the bottle and poured a liberal splash. "As a matter of fact, I do." He took a moment to refill his own glass, lips pursed, thinking. Then he said, "I'm a little goosey about Hobart Fontaine and what he's really doing out there. First of all, he's refurbishing an existing factory that's been idle for some time, instead of building a new one, as agreed. That's edgy enough, but what truly upset me are the reports that he's trying to emulate Tony Fokker by building airplane framework with welded steel tubing."

Carpenter humphed. "Nothing wrong with that. In fact, I'd call it a big fat plus. Welded tubing is pretty damned strong."

"You don't get the point. Our aircraft industry is very heavily committed to ash—ash lumber. So why would he be going against the flow?"

"Research. I thought you said the Bensonville plant is to be dedicated to finding new ways to make airplanes."

"Yes. But within the existing parameters. Within the bounds of what is practical in light of the materials and capabilities already at hand. Speed is what we're after—speed in getting good airplanes into the European skies. We can't afford to screw around with theoreticals when our people are waiting, tongues out, for superior planes made faster and in better ways with the stuff we now have and are familiar with."

"But I just told you, Congressman: The Germans are already using welded tubing to great effect. Welded tubing is something we Americans are pretty goddamn good at, too. We don't have to prove anything in that department. And take it from me: A fuselage built with tubing is just as light and a helluva lot stronger and less complex than one built of ash."

This time Slater didn't savor his whiskey. He just put it down in a noisy gulp. "You keep that up, Captain, and you'll be talking your way out of an extremely lucrative job."

"Job? I can't take a job. I'm already employed full time by the U.S. of A. Army. Which, by the way, frowns on moonlighting by its people."

Slater smiled. "Let me be blunt. I'm suggesting private payment. Money placed in a bank account or even in a coffee can, neither of them traceable to you and your military association."

Carpenter gave him a puzzled look. "How in hell would that work?"

"Senator Murray, senior senator from my state, working completely and separately from me, will pull some of his strings at the War Department and have you promoted to major. He will see to it that the Army assigns you to Bensonville as a quality control liaison officer. That way, Fontaine will have no idea that you are actually working for me. Then, once we have a clear picture of the doings at Bensonville, Senator Murray will have the Army assign you to Billy Mitchell's staff."

"Where I'll continue to spy for you?"

"Mitchell is a loose cannon who could very well foul up some things I have going. I simply must keep appraised on a daily basis—weekly at the worst—as to what that egotistical nutball is up to. Murray will request your assignment to his committee as a military advisor, for which you would receive your regular Army salary and whatever allowances due you. However, because I'll be asking you for personal services requiring effort above and beyond congressional committee obligations, I will make you a favored shareholder in my private business. You will be like so many of our upper-grade military officers who are privately wealthy, thanks to stocks or other investments."

"Like that cavalry guy? Patton?"

"Exactly."

"So..."

"Let me put it this way: I have a real estate business in private life. It's doing extremely well, so much so, I have people waiting in line to buy shares in it at $100 a share, because my investors routinely triple their money in less than a month. What I'm going to do in your case, for personal services rendered to my company on your own time, is let you buy as many shares as you care to at one dollar a share. You can either sell them at the current rate of

$100 a share to the next applicant in line, or you can hold them and let their value increase exponentially over the coming months. In your case, I recommend that you sell them right away so you can be on your way to becoming a rich man through private investments that have nothing to do with your military status and commitments."

"Is this legal?"

"Of course. The government will continue to pay your salary and allowances as a military officer assigned to my office. I pay you nothing. But with money you have earned as an officer, you invest in my private company. Whatever amount you invest, I can assure you that you will routinely realize a minimum income of at least twenty thousand dollars a year."

Carpenter was doubtful. "I just don't want to get in trouble with the law. I admit how little I know about private investments and the law and the like, but this is—"

"There are, as of today, no laws against such arrangements." Slater took another sip of scotch. "Tip you off, though. There's a movement to expand the modest federal income tax legalized in 1913 under the 16th Amendment to help pay for the war. If you invest in my company now, before Congress swings the hammer, you'll escape any meaningful tax obligations ex post facto. I mean, if you're going to move on this, I'd advise you to move quickly, before it does become illegal or expensive."

Carpenter sat in silence for a time, his eyes filled with astonished disbelief. After draining his glass, he found his voice. "Twenty thousand dollars a year?"

"Mmm."

"That will make me a rich man indeed."

"Mmm."

After relishing the idea a bit, Carpenter's eyes narrowed, wariness and skepticism beginning to take over. "Let me ask an ex-post-facto question, Congressman. Just exactly what does your company do?"

"We deal in large-scale real estate. At present, our focus is on the acquisition and sale of virgin timberland in the northwestern states."

"Ah."

Silence.

"What kind of timber?"

"Ash."

"Ah. My job would be to discourage Fontaine from using anything but ash."

"Not just Fontaine. The industry. The domestic aircraft industry. You do this effectively and your investments will automatically make you wealthy."

"I still admit to some confusion here—"

"I find that hard to believe. Are you holding out for something better, perhaps?" Slater's eyes narrowed.

"No. Not at all. You're most generous—"

"Well, then."

This silence was a long one.

Slater decided to wrap it up. "Agreed?"

"Well, as long as it's not illegal..."

❋❋❋

Dear John:

Your note received, and I'm answering right away because you've been much on my mind lately. As you can imagine, things are pretty hectic here in the nation's capital, and I'm wondering whether I made a mistake welcoming a return stateside. This city is a seducer—whenever decent people come here to work in the public interest, something seems to happen to them, and it isn't too long before they get the idea that all this pomp and circumstance and free-flowing millions are their rightful due, and that they are a kind of chosen people who are above the law and the restrictions of common morality and good sense.

Duty took me to the House Office Building today, and that's one building I hate, I tell you. My old man's office was there. And the last time he had Mother and me there was to show us off at a cocktail party he was throwing in his office for a gaggle of the elite. When we got back to the hotel that night, Mother and Father had a terrible row. I heard them through the connecting door to my room, with her accusing him of flirting with all those god-awful women, and he yelling back at her, saying that it wasn't true, that if she would show even a little bit of interest in him and his work maybe he would get a little more excited about her, but all she did was look down her nose at anything he was and wanted to be. He said she was a freaking jail warden, trying to keep him under lock and key for herself and nobody else, without giving him any reward for being a dutiful husband. He said he had even given her a child in the hope that it would get her off his back a bit, but no, all she did was complain about how the little brat needed the love and guidance of his father, when all the time she was raging at the father who would rather cavort with politicians and hanger-on whores and leave her and little William to gather dust and loneliness or whatever. It came to my father demanding to know if she wanted a divorce, and she said her family had never believed in divorce because they were upstanding, moral Christians and far above hypocritical lip-servers like him, and she was going to stay married to him just to make him as miserable as he was making her. I tell you, John, it was that night I learned that neither one of them wanted me and that I was hopelessly without value to the only two people in the world I gave a damn about.

Lordy, look at me and how I do carry on, eh? I didn't mean to go off on a tangent like that, but I swear I can't go near that rotten building without being all torn up. I remember your asking me that day in Buffalo if I didn't like my father, a question I'd been asking myself for years, and you made me realize that there just wasn't an answer and never would be.

And that's your true value to me, Yo-han. You have a way of making me look at myself, which I've never before been able to do with any honesty.

Those visions or dreams of yours I can't say anything about because I've never experienced anything like that, and I'm pretty much out of my depth when it comes to ghosts and supernatural stuff. But I want you to keep telling me about them, because you need to get all that weird business off your chest, and you can trust me to keep it just between the two of us. Honestly, when it comes right down to it, you are the only friend I have to talk to like this, too. I know a jillion people, but you're the only one I can let my hair down with.

Keep safe, Yo-han. We need each other.

Your friend,

Bill

Chapter 17

Mary Lou had always been vaguely uneasy about the image of unseemly extravagance presented by her family. There were only the four of them—Father, Mother, Uncle Rupert, and herself—and, supported by a regiment of servants, they occupied three huge houses on land tracts which together comprised nearly two thousand acres of some of the most beautiful territory in the eastern United States. Her inborn sense of moderation and balance told her that this was the stuff of imperial lavishness and would someday—in the same cosmic scheme of checks and balances that had called Marie Antoinette to account—come around to bite the Whitings in their nates. But when viewed in the context of the family history, there was a weird logic to it all, a pragmatic, if somewhat gaudy, answer to some very real family problems. Foremost, of course, were Uncle Rupert's incapacities. Rupert was Mother's brother, thirteen years her senior and her only surviving kin. He'd been badly befuddled in the War Between the States, and as an orphaned child and young woman, Mother had endured blue hell to provide for him. She was waiting on tables at a Haverford restaurant and living with Rupert in a livery stable apartment when fate placed Father, one of the country's most wealthy and powerful entrepreneurs, at her table one summer evening. He'd been instantly smitten and so wanted to marry her that he promised to build two houses—one for them and another for Rupert a mile's buggy ride down whatever road—so that they could keep an eye on her ailing brother without smothering his sense of independence and privacy.

The third house, the seaside mansion at Rehoboth Beach they called "The Cottage," had been built in sheer exuberance over Mary Lou's birth in 1896, and it was her hands-down favorite, even over the houses in Paris and Cannes, used as family bases while she was being educated in France. For all its size, The Cottage was informal, rustic, spilling over the high sand cliffs like a giant stone-and-timber growth. But magnificent, sixty-room Farview Manor was so awesome she often found it uncomfortable and intimidating, and at party-time, when it was filled with laughter and music and the happy tinkling of crystal and silver, with the sporadic flashes triggered by *The Bulletin's* society page photographer, she usually found it damned easy to get all creepy over thoughts of the French Revolution.

And somehow it was made worse by the fact that she couldn't take her gaze away from John King.

She examined him from across the garden room.

He seemed quite ordinary: average size; sturdy build; a pleasant, clean-shaven, farm-boy kind of face with that perfect nose; standing alone and awkward now in a corner window bay, where the light of the sinking sun seemed to set him aglow; holding a glass diffidently and trading polite nods with those few passing by who acknowledged his presence. In her acquaintance there were any number of dingleheads who were far more prepossessing than he was. Yet something else, some subtle, indefinable quality, had set him above and beyond the run-of-the-mill Percy. A coolness when facing difficulties? It would seem so. Eyes that spoke of apartness and loneliness? Absolutely. But all of these were surface indicators, easy to read. The subsurface thing—the intimation that when he looked at her he wasn't really seeing her because his mind was on other, more important things—was what really got her goat. She could forgive most sinners anything, except those whose sin was to be uninterested in her.

A hand touched her elbow.

"Is it possible? A garden room aswirl with gorgeous young women and miserably uncomfortable boys in soldier suits and you, alone and long-faced in a corner? Whatever happened to that beautiful belle of the ball I love so much?"

She turned and gave him the obligatory party smile. "Oh, hullo, Lawton. I want to thank you for being here and for putting the Red Cross seal of approval on our little effort."

Lawton Bigelow, one of the dingleheads, was smoothly handsome, almost too much so, like the men in advertisements for automobiles and smoking jackets. His faultless blazer and plus-fours made him appear incredibly dashing and even taller, and his voice was deep and melodious, his presence regal. Unfortunately, he knew these things, which made him insufferably crazy about himself.

He first treated her to his noble profile by pretending to watch the dancers—an angle quickly caught by the photographer—then turned to award her a full-face view, forming his most brilliant smile en route. "My precious Mary Lou, I'm here because I love you, and I want you to marry me."

"Please, Lawton, don't start that again."

"But I do."

She regarded him amiably, as one regards a favorite pet. "You don't love me. You love the idea of me. You want me as one of your accoutrements, another trophy to go with your polo trophies."

He feigned indignation. "Now just what am I supposed to say to that? That's the most outrageous idea—"

"Just stop sputtering and give me this waltz."

He took her lightly and swung her into the current of dancers. "You're impossible, Mary Lou."

"If you insist on talking while we sail the beautiful blue Danube, answer me a question or two, will you?"

"Ask away, dear heart."

"One of your many social gadabout things is the Philadelphia Flying Club—that activity down on the waterfront at Essington, I mean especially. So what do I have to do to join the club and learn to fly one of those contraptions?"

He glanced down at her, openly astonished. "If anyone had

asked me to guess what your question would be, that would be the last guess."

"Stop being coy, Lawton, and answer the question."

"My personal opinion is that flying machines are a fad that will come to nothing. Teddy Roosevelt was enthusiastic about them, seeing possible military applications. President Taft was dismissive, and there's no clue as to the aeronautical opinions of Woodrow Wilson. People I know in the War Department show disgust over his being a shrinking violet, militarily speaking."

"Will you please stop being a snobby poop for a minute? I don't care a fig what the president thinks about them. I want to know how to drive them. I want to know all about them. Who makes them? Who flies them? What's going on in the aero world?"

Lawton sighed. "I must confess, you've caught me unprepared on this. I'm not really involved in the aviating part of the Flying Club. I joined because they thought I might use my influence with the mayor and so on, but all this folderol aside, I, for one, consider flying machines to be rich men's toys."

"I remember you saying the same thing about gasoline automobiles. And this afternoon the driveway outside is packed with them."

"Ha," Lawton said triumphantly, "and every one of them is owned by a rich man."

"That's true, but only because only the daughters of the rich have been invited to this party." She nodded toward the buffet. "I remind you, however, that those goodies over there were delivered by a caterer driving a Ford delivery wagon and leading a convoy of like Fords. So beware of using superior airs, my dear socialite. The automobile is here to stay, and it'll be for everybody. And maybe the flying machine as well."

"I love it when you lecture me like this."

"So what'll you do for me?"

"I'll put you in touch with Avery Saunders. He's a prime mover in Philadelphia-area aeronautics. That's about the best I can do for you. Except, of course, marry you and take your mind off such unfeminine nonsense."

She batted her eyelashes theatrically, like one of those ingenues in the picture shows. "Ooo, Lawton," she gushed, "I love it when you threaten me like this."

※※※

Exasperated, she walked straight up to him and said, "John King, aren't you ever going to ask me to dance?"

He blushed and gave her that lopsided grin. "Truth be known, Miss Whiting, I've been trying to work up enough nerve to ask you."

"Nerve? Why does it take nerve?"

"Well, you seemed to be very busy with that imposing-looking man. And you were flitting about, checking on the buffet and all that."

"I do not flit, John King. Flitting is against my religion. And Lawton Bigelow is an overgrown, puerile, social sycophant whose family owns Maryland and that part of Delaware the du Ponts haven't gotten around to. Lawton is not imposing, he's a misplaced headwaiter."

King laughed outright, and she thought she caught relief in the sound of it. "I'm going to give you that funny little German bow now and ask you if you'll endure my waddling through 'My Blue Heaven.'"

"Waddle away, soldier. I'll be right in front of you."

He took her hand with proper lightness, and off they went into the mainstream. He was really quite good, she found—light on his feet, graceful in the turns, and definitely leading.

"Where did you learn to dance like this, soldier?"

"You probably won't believe it, but my mother taught me. Long wintry nights in Lackawanna, a Victrola, and nothing else to do. We had fun."

"You liked your mother?"

"Sure did. She was a peach."

"I like my mother, too."

"She's a lovely woman. I've been admiring her, the way she sort of presides over the guests, makes them all at ease. The way you do."

In one of their turns, they came elbow to elbow with Captain Bascomb, who appeared to be absolutely radiant, decorated as he was with a stunning brunette.

"Lovely party, Miss Whiting." Nod to King.

"Thank you, Captain. Your men seem to be enjoying themselves."

"I don't see how they possibly could not." He and the brunette smiled again and spun off.

"Your captain seems to be in his element," Mary Lou commented.

"Mmm."

"Obviously he isn't aware that he's in mortal danger."

"Oh? How so?"

"Claire Pinchon. The brunette. She's directly related to Count Dracula. Only she doesn't drain men's blood. She drains their wallets."

King laughed again. "Charming friends you have. Lawton the Snob. Claire the Vampire. Don't you know any regular folks?"

"I'm working on that."

✳✳✳

The moment he dreaded had arrived. It was intermission, and the guys in the small orchestra were out on the side patio, smoking and sipping the god-awful punch, and now he was standing beside the huge black concert grand at the foot of the curving staircase in the main reception hall, and the girls and the soldiers had crowded into an arc and were staring at him. They were all politely silent because the hostess, Mary Lou Whiting, she of the Big Dollars and acid wit, was telling them how they were in for a special treat, "a recital by John King, an accomplished pianist now serving at Whiting Field, who, by the way, just this week had begun the flight course under that charming and very capable commanding officer, Captain Aubrey Bascomb."

She waved her arms grandly. "Let's give them both a real Junior League welcome!"

Bascomb stepped out of the crowd and held his hands high in acknowledgment of the applause. He was actually beaming.

King gave his little German bow and felt the fire in his face. In the ensuing hush, he realized he was expected to say something, so, leaning on the piano, not so much to portray nonchalance as to support his shaking legs, he said, "Good evening. I want to thank Miss Whiting and her beautiful mother for their gracious invitation to join you in this tribute to our troops, here and abroad."

His throat felt as if it were made of cardboard, and his lips seemed entirely unwilling to form the words. Standing there, the focus of all those millions of eyes, he realized that his only escape was by way of whatever language would lead to the keyboard.

"I'm by no means a performer. I play impetuously and usually when I am alone. So whatever I bring out of the piano now is spontaneous and shared with you in the hope that some of it will give some of you the pleasure it gives me. Thank you."

He led off with a few of the standards, starting with an especially dreamy "Clair de Lune," then, fearing he might be putting himself to sleep, he segued into Scott Joplin's "Canadian Capers," played with a rolling, seductive beat. Perking up, he vamped into "Bill Bailey" and was astonished to hear some of the people singing along. When his mood swung to pensive again, he went against what he thought was the flow and played a straightforward "Sweetheart of Sigma Chi." But that proved to be precisely counter to his reach for quiet, because the huge room resounded with the voices of a hundred men and women who had never left their college years and were irretrievably lost to the consequent sentimentalism. The din made him nervous, so with a surge of rebellious deliberation, as if turning a dial, he went impromptu—playing without plan, spontaneously creating great sounds with a softly syncopated series of diminished and augmented sevenths and ninths that he felt making patterns in his gut and leading him into something rather wonderful. The twilit surroundings receded in his mind, and the sounds became everything, taking him into reverie, into ancient side streets with misted cobblestones and leaning chimneys, onto a great sweep of white beach and a flatline azure horizon, into tall green forests redolent of maples and firs and decaying leaves. Taking him around the world and to the moon and into space and back to a smiling Mom at the breakfast table. He played and drifted, and then, oddly, without transition and after a time without dimension, he had run out of soul, and there was a deep silence all around.

He looked up, now aware of this ring of people, and the silence was broken when they erupted in thunderous applause and cheering. Stunned, flustered, and near panic, he sought to direct all this energy away from himself and into something supporting the party's rationale. He plunged into George M. Cohan's "I'm a Yankee Doodle Dandy," and the crowd became even more enthusiastic and boisterous. With the new tune, "Over There," he guessed they could be heard in Miami. Deafened, he finally threw his hands over his head, pushed back the bench with the backs of his knees, and stood up, grinning and signaling surrender.

There was a general happy milling about, and Mary Lou took him by the arm and led him toward the garden room buffet, where she introduced him to a tall patrician with a swirl of gray hair and a long silk gown wrapped in strings of beads. Over the clamor Mary Lou explained that Mrs. Goodman was the darling of Main Line society and a leading patron of the arts, and he tried to acknowledge this and other unintelligible wonders with a polite smile. The piano man from the orchestra came by and shouted into his ear, "Great piano, fella. You gotta put that stuff on paper. No foolin'!"

And then he was gone, leaving King with the realization that Mary Lou was clearing a circle, hands held high, and calling out, "Quiet, everybody! Quiet! I have an announcement that will thrill you all!"

When the obligatory silence settled in, the irrepressible and iconoclastic Mary Lou said, "Among our honored guests is none other than Mrs. Algernon Forsythe-Goodman, known the world around as a titan of the arts, having donated incredible tons of moola to art museums, schools of music, universities, and a huge potful of other big-time cultural things. Not only that, but she is also known for her own marvelous singing voice. And guess what? She has agreed to sing for us here, right now." She waved Mrs. Goodman forward, and the lady was actually wriggling with the pleasure of being photographed and applauded while being thrust into the core of what was proving to be a benchmark social event of the season.

"And putting cream on the cream," Mary Lou enthused, "she will be accompanied by our new musical hero, Aviation Cadet John King!"

This applause was extended, but Mary Lou wasn't finished.

She waved for silence, and when the room settled down she exulted, "And with even more cream on the cream on the cream, I can now disclose that Mr. Fred Regales, sound engineer of the Victor Talking Machine Company of nearby Camden, has been capturing John King's marvelous music on his company's newest gramophone mechanism, having personally agreed to do this as a special favor to Mrs. Forsythe-Goodman, who has been instrumental in getting some of the world's most renowned artists to make recordings for the Victor label. So you see, everybody? We're really hot stuff today!"

More cheers, more applause, and a small man in heavy spectacles and a headset peered around a potted palm to give an acknowledging wave. "Today's record will be a special product available to you all by month's end. Remember, buy Victor: *His Master's Voice!*"

After another round of applause, the room quieted and Mrs. Goodman handed King a scroll of music, then took his arm, preparing to return him to the piano. It wasn't to be, however, because King had taken one quick look at her music and stiffened into shocked immobility.

"Come, Cadet King, and we'll make music together."

"I'm sorry," he stammered, "but I—"

"Come, dear. I won't bite you." Mrs. Goodman chortled.

In the stilted interval that followed, King coughed, cleared his throat, and couldn't decide whether to let his face be ruby red or chalk white. "I'm sorry, Ma'am. But I can't—"

"Can't? Why ever not?"

"I can't read music."

"You can't what?"

"I have no idea what that scroll of music says. I can't even pronounce the title."

This silence was as palpable as a layer of paint, and the assembly appeared to be frozen, like the frieze in an overdone Venetian villa. Drama was unrolling at Farview, where culture was suddenly and outrageously being threatened by the uncouth. Worse, the flashing camera was catching it all.

"Well, I never," Mrs. Goodman rumbled, simultaneously astonished and vexed. "This is absurd. I can't perform without accompaniment. I must have a real pianist. And after all the effort to get Victor records here...I'm speechless..."

King never heard the rest of it. Face afire, he turned on his heel and strode out of the room, onto the patio, and down the stately stairway to the driveway. He walked an eternity in something like blindness, and when he recovered eventually, he found himself following a macadam road in a darkness heavy with fog and drizzle.

A passing milk truck driver invited him aboard and returned him to the airfield.

Chapter 18

The soirées, musicales, debutante cotillions, theater parties, club dinners, and plain-old madcap revelry had left Mary Lou exhausted and generally out of sorts. The feeling was much like the dull aching and the nagging, indefinable disgust she associated with a morning after a night of too much wine.

Thinking about it now, she realized that throughout all the wartime hoopla and pro-forma merrymaking she'd perceived the underlying negativity—a subtle understanding that the merriment had been deliberate, manufactured, a counterfeit in which the laughter came through clenched teeth. The times had seemed to bring a turn in the attitudes of her closest friends. On the surface, the college bunch, debs, and newly marrieds adhered to the old, established pretensions, but she'd felt this undercurrent among them, an unspoken dissatisfaction with things the way they were and a yearning to move on, to throw open the windows, let in some air, and rearrange more to their fancy the furniture of a stuffy, prissy world. She couldn't imagine her mother, that darling, brave, stubborn little square-shooter who had fought the frontier and won, ever for a moment approving, or even tolerating, some of the wild behavior she'd seen and heard in recent weeks. Mother had an earthy streak and understood the pioneer's bawdy sense of humor, to be sure, but she was unwaveringly careful to see that it didn't show in public. And, no doubt about it, she would have been outraged if she'd overheard Bertie Gruber, the perennial frat man, openly commenting on the sexual skills of last year's prom queen. But the new crowd, the constituents of today's Café Society, would most certainly have simply giggled and gasped in simulated shock.

All that aside, her personal imp was the Marie Antoinette thing. It was a recurrent image, too vague to be a vision, too real to be delusion. It came and went, like a mirror's flashing on a distant hill. Yet it lingered in her mind, a view of herself wallowing in undeserved privilege and wealth, with an urgent need to prove that she was more than the pampered doll-baby of a Croesus and his Cinderella. *Unless you do something, something worthwhile,* the inner voice told her, *there will be a reckoning, a dreadful price to pay for the gilded life you lead.*

But which something? She already gave generously and continuously to the poor, had built a church for South Philly ghetto people, supported the local arts and museums, and contributed considerable sums to see that the sick among the homeless and indigent received proper hospital care. And all of this from her personal allowance.

Still, the guilt and uneasiness refused to go away and were especially heavy this morning.

She'd slept late, awaking sluggishly, disdaining the breakfast brought to her suite by Carmella, and making a lengthy business of her bath, as if the mood could be soaked and scrubbed away. When it wasn't, she checked the time and decided to get on with her plan.

✽✽✽

The overcast was low and fast-moving, and the fitful wind was heavy with the promise of rain and approaching autumn. She parked the Packard in the lee of a string of oaks near the airfield bus stop, and when he finally came through the gate she started the motor and drew alongside him.

"Get in the car, John King."

He didn't look at her. "No."

"Get in the damned car."

"I'm on my way to Philly."

"Not yet. First you're going to look at something and advise me about it."

He stopped walking and turned to face her. "What in God's name do I have to do to make you leave me alone? I haven't read your letters, I haven't returned your phone calls, and I sure as hell won't get in your shiny goddamn car."

She felt anger building. "Just what are you so mad about?"

"What am I mad about? Just because you invite me to that art gallery and museum you live in to play nicey-nice with your pompous friends and wheedle me into playing the piano so that I can embarrass the oh-so-marvelous Mrs. Richbitch-Foreskin and get my picture in the *Philadelphia Bulletin* as Wart of the Year, you think I'm mad? How could you have such a silly idea?"

"That's plain drool. Mrs. Goodman is a nice old lady and very understanding of whom she calls 'struggling, uncompleted artists.' You caught her flatfooted and confused and embarrassed before the crowd. Worse, you walked out before she recovered, before hearing the nice things she said about your playing and the potential you show and her regret that she had so clumsily offended you, as she put it. What do you think I was trying to tell you in those letters you wouldn't read? Truth be known, you were the tacky scrub in that little melodrama, not she."

Her accusation hung in the air, and his eyes considered it. What had his mother said, looking up from her sewing, her gaze gentle but uncompromising, unhappy with him? "Remember, John, it's easy to make the other person the bad guy. It's hard to see yourself in the role." The recollection valved off some of his righteousness, and he felt disarmed, relieved of his weapons of sustained attack.

"Well, maybe so," he said. "All I know is how I saw it. It's like I have one of those 'Kick Me' signs hanging on my belt."

"I suggest you cool down first before you decide to kick back."

"I didn't want to kick back. I just wanted out of there."

"When you turn on your heel and prance off from someone like Mrs. Forsythe-Goodman, that's kicking back."

He sighed impatiently and glanced at his wristwatch. "Look,

Mary Lou, I'm more sorry than I can say that it all turned out this way. I think you're a peach, and I was hoping we could be friends, but it doesn't look as if that's going to happen. So let's just leave it at this: I apologize for being such a dud at the party. I apologize to you and Mrs. Goodman, and I apologize to your mother, and I apologize to anyone else I might have offended that day. Meanwhile, I'm off to Philadelphia."

"Just come and look at something I have to show you."

"I'll miss my bus, my train—"

"If you do, I'll drive you to wherever you want to go."

The first drops of rain began to patter on the car's canvas roof, and, after squinting aloft, he swung into the front seat beside her. "I can't afford to get wet. This is my only clean uniform."

"Good thinking." She ground the car into gear, and they lurched off, trailing a shower of gravel.

By now the sky was the color of old metal, with low, sooty clouds racing on the northeast wind. She drove her favorite way, up the state road to the unpaved turn-off, then straight north and up the long hill to the barn.

He finally spoke. "What is this place?"

"My favorite barn."

"Why are we here?"

"You'll see." She shut off the motor, pulled on the brake, and, climbing out, said, "Come on."

She used a skeleton key, then swung open the broad door. "Come on. Inside."

They fell silent for a time, pretending to examine the barn. The wind made soft sounds in the eaves, and somewhere in the shadows a small animal skittered. It was surprisingly calm here behind the stout walls, and the dry, clean smell of old lumber and hay hung in the still air.

"So what's here?"

She pointed upward with her chin. "It's in the loft. I keep it up there because Farview has ten thousand curious eyes, and I don't want anyone there to know what's up. Not yet."

He shrugged, went to the loft ladder, and began climbing. Halfway up, he paused and looked down at her. "Coming?"

She feigned nonchalance, but the pounding in her intensified.

"Of course. I've got to explain it."

She followed him up, and they stood in the dim light, looking about and saying nothing. The roof was sound, the floorboards and uprights had mellowed into silvery gray, and some old tackle hung from one of the rafters. The southeast corner was heaped high with hay that must have been there since the War Between the States, but it had been sheltered well, and its color and dryness made it appear almost fresh.

"So what am I supposed to look at?"

She went to the far corner, pulled aside a sheaf of hay, and drew a wooden box from under a tarp. Opening this, she produced a roll of blueprints and spread them out on the floor. "These are the plans for an airplane I'm having built. You're an aviator. What do you think of it?"

He looked at her as if she had just grown a beard. "Are you out of your mind, woman?"

"I am not. I am having this plane built, and I want you to teach me how to drive it."

"I haven't even learned to fly myself. I'm still in training. Besides, I'm in the Army, and I'm not free to indulge zillionaire birds."

"You will be free when I get finished with Bascomb and some other people around the War Department."

"Don't you understand? I don't want to work with you on this or anything else. I don't want your help, your—intervention—on this or anything else. I want to work out my own destiny. It's important to me that the world sees me as my own success. That can't happen if I'm working with you or for you or, for cripe's sake, even near you. 'Ha,' they'll say, 'he was able to succeed at this, that, or the other because he's Mary Lou Whiting's lap dog.' Hell, don't you see that, by that measure, I can't even be your friend?"

"Oh, just shut the hell up and kiss me."

❋❋❋

When she thought about it later—and she thought about it a lot—it had been very much like an explosion. One moment they were standing in the aromatic gloom, trading angry glares, and then, almost in a millisecond, they were folded in each other's arms, locked in a blind, consuming kiss, weaving back and forth in an erotic struggle, hands clutching.

She remembered sinking into the mow, the gentle combat, the coolness when they fought free of their clothes and the silky warmth that replaced it. Then consciousness blurred, giving way to serial images appearing against the blackness of her closed eyes, some languorous, some rapid and insistent, all of them lewd derivatives of the Gladys Richman and Timmy Randall episode at the Rehoboth Beach house long ago. She strained to see the man she was with in these vignettes, but he was always faceless.

Make it this man. Please make it this man. This boy-man. This lost child. I want to hold him and keep him and protect him and smother him with this huge love that's exploding in me. Let it be, for Christ's sake, let it ...

❋❋❋

She opened her eyes and stared in a mixture of sadness and elation at the stormy sky beyond the window.

Lying on her back, she raised her arms, stretching, and sighed deeply, forcing a joke that might help her thumb her nose at her own perfidy. "So this is what it means."

"What?"

"The old saying, 'a roll in the hay.'"

He continued to stare at the ceiling. "It was a lot more than that."

"Not really," she said, searching for a defense against the anxiety that told her the triumphant fulfillment she had felt was slipping away.

His voice was soft, thoughtful. "You're a grand girl, Mary Lou. You've got more of everything than any girl could rightfully expect, I'd say. Great looks. Easygoing charm. Genuinely nice. Unaffected by the approval people lavish on you. No wonder I can't *not* love you. The world would not be endurable without you. But I have to earn you."

"Love can't be earned. It happens no matter what."

"I've got to make something of myself. Earn some credentials. To feel I'm worthy of you."

"More of the poor boy, rich girl dung, is that it?" She fought against sudden irritability and guilt.

"No. It's this stigma that comes with second-classness and poverty. You can't understand how god-awful wretched it is always to be on the outside looking in, always being denied admittance or acceptance to the human race because you have no money, no credentials, to prove your humanity. Mom was right. She said it's an understanding that you don't belong in this world. You are homesick for the world you came from and love is the only vehicle that can return you there. But love is hard to come by when you're surrounded by, buried by, so much hate and contempt."

"You say your mom was Irish?"

"Spooky Irish. Doted on the metaphysical, mediumistic. Used to drive my father nuts."

"He was the German in your mix, right? The reason your buddies call you 'Kraut'?"

Taken by surprise, King gave her a sharp look. "You know about that?"

"Sure. Your real name is Johann König. Bascomb told me that all the men at your camp call you Kraut behind your back. So what? To me it's just a stupid nickname. You're not a German, you're an American."

Comprehending finally, he said, "Pratt. So that's who he is. He was in the crowd in Lackawanna."

"What are you talking about?"

"Forget it. It's too complicated."

"How did your mother die?"

"She killed herself."

"God..."

"She tidied up the house one day, talking to herself, humming hymns. Then she dressed in her best and told my father and me that she was going out to pay a long visit to someone very important she'd been neglecting too long. We thought that was a bit peculiar, because she never knew anybody who was very important, but she was always being peculiar, and we let it go. It turned out that she went to the square fronting St. Benedict's, laid her purse at the church door, then walked in front of an oncoming truck and stood, arms outstretched and smiling into the eyes of the truck driver. Died instantly, the cops said."

"Oh, God, John. I'm so sorry."

"Well, then, that makes two of us."

How grubby she felt. How far beyond her depth—lured by her inexplicable affection for John King into currents she'd never truly expected to enter.

At first, she had tried to explain her crush on him as mere fascination with the difference he represented: He was more masculine than the fops around her, he was strange and detached and peculiarly Victorian, and she knew with utter certainty that he was too callow, too naïve to plan an assault on Daddy's wealth. When this tactic failed to dampen the heat gathering in her loins, she had turned to cynicism, telling herself that he was just an angst-filled boy, for Christ's sake, and she was an idiot to see him as the man in her life. Just use him as the nice kid next door, addled yet lusty, a dildo without social ambitions, a gauge for plumbing the still-untested depths of her libido. But for all the effort, she'd found that calculated depravity simply couldn't prevail against her innate morality, and now, after this manic, last-gasp, shoot-the-works roll in the hay, she'd been left with nothing but emotional wreckage.

While protecting herself from loving the wrong man, she had fallen in love with the wrong man.

Idiot indeed.

They lay there for a time, listening to the wind and rain. Her terrible sadness eventually merged with sleep. When she awoke, he was gone.

Chapter 19

Tonight the currents flowing into self-pity were especially strong and sly, thanks to the silent oppressiveness of his tent. The others were at the recreation hall, where Lillian Gish's new motion picture, *Souls Triumphant*, was being shown. The tumultuous afternoon, with no apparent reaction from Mary Lou to his emotionally impetuous candor, had left him exhausted, and he lay there on the cot, staring at nothing, trying to fathom the reach and significance of the incident. The revelation that Pratt was a ghost out of Lackawanna left him with no particular surprise or shock. On the contrary, it satisfied his sense of logical order to have Pratt's reason for disliking him so tidily established. But it did nothing to head off the gathering melancholy, so he rose from the cot and went to the field desk, where he wrote a letter to Bill Carpenter. After dropping it into the dayroom mailbox, he wandered down the street to look in on the picture show. He endured the flickering and pasty faces for a time, then, still restless, left for the post exchange and a bottle of soda pop.

The moon was rising over the eastern hills, and he paused to admire the misty beauty of it, when sudden swift motion surged about him, a dark swirling in the darkness. He heard men muttering, low, malevolent, and he tried to turn toward them, his arms upraised in instinctive defense, his frightened eyes searching for forms, faces. But the shadows closed in, and his mind exploded in a roiling of white agony.

※※※

King, alone in the dispensary tent, could only lie there, squinting his swollen eyes against the sunlight that came through the tent flap, taking a pain-by-pain inventory of his body and searching his mind for images of the attack.

Three men. At least three. Striking and kicking and swearing softly. His wallet with its three dollars and the change purse with its two dimes, one nickel, and four pennies had literally been ripped from his pockets. His railroad watch and penknife, too.

He wanted to sigh. But he knew that his bruised chest wouldn't tolerate it. He wanted to cry, but he knew it would be a stupid, unmanly collapse that would not only hurt his ribs but also accomplish nothing. He yearned for a restoring bath, but he knew that it would require an impossible effort to get off the bed and stagger the distance to the latrine.

He was sinking further into misery when he realized that someone was standing beside his bed. "Who is it?" he croaked.

"Captain Bascomb."

Oh, God...

"I want to talk to you, King."

He opened his eyes again and, squinting, managed to see that, as always, Bascomb was a marvel to behold. Tall, lean, resplendent in his uniform, with its crisply pressed olive- drab tunic, its glittering brass insignia, its Sam Browne belt, its tan whipcord riding britches and its glistening cordovan boots. The aroma of bay rum attested to his recently completed shave, and when he removed his cap, his pomaded black hair suggested patent leather.

"Are you all right, King?"

"I am most certainly all right. I've been beaten to a pulp, all my aches have aches, my money's been stolen, and I'll probably be court-martialed for missing two hundred formations. Why should you ask if I'm all right?"

"No need to be snotty, King. If you need anything, I'll see that the orderly brings it."

"Thank you, sir."

"Do you know who did this to you?"

"No," he lied.

"You must tell me if you know. It's a criminal matter."

"Three men. That's all I know."

The captain produced a silver cigarette case. "Root?"

"No thanks."

Carefully—somewhat theatrically, King thought—Bascomb took a cigarette from the case and placed it neatly between his lips. A match flared, and a cloud of smoke rose to the tent ceiling.

"I've noticed all along, King, that you're not very popular among your fellow cadets. Is it the German thing?"

"German thing, sir?"

"The fact that your real name is Johann König."

"I've been keeping mum about that. It's been giving me a lot of trouble since the war began."

"It's in your personnel records."

"I was hoping nobody would mention it."

"Nobody at headquarters did."

"Yeah, I know now how it got around."

"And I know now that you are not a friend of General Pershing." Rueful amusement was in his voice.

"I never said I was—"

Bascomb nodded. "I know. It was my mistake. I heard gossip, I saw a priority cable from London, and I turned into a prime filet of idiot."

"And I continued to mislead you, sir. I'm sorry about that. I should've set you straight right away."

"Yes."

There was a quiet moment as they both thought about that. Then Bascomb said, "You know who attacked you, don't you."

"At least one of them, sir, but I can't prove it."

"I know who all three of them are, King, but I can't prove it, either."

More silence as Bascomb studied the glowing end of his cigarette.

"So where is all this taking us, sir?"

"It takes me back to my office, where I'll sit, crestfallen, feeling every inch the ass-kissing social climber I've become, and wondering if I'll ever be the responsible military leader I've always wanted to be."

King, sympathizing with Bascomb's effort toward penitence, offered helpfully, "You're one helluva good aviator, sir. And one helluva good teacher. That's a good leader in my book."

"Well, that's nice of you, King. But I didn't stop by to make a confession. I stopped by for two military reasons." He took a deep pull at the remaining cigarette then snuffed it out in a butt can on the floor beside him.

"First, I want you to know that I've begun an investigation into the attack on you. I will not tolerate men in my unit who commit violence against a fellow soldier simply because he has an unpopular name. I assure you, King, I'll not stop until I have Pratt, Quincy, and Mogloff in the stockade as proven criminals."

"Sir—"

"Second, I stopped by to inform you, as the finest incipient combat pilot I've had the pleasure of training, that you will be on a ship to Le Havre, France, by the end of next week. And you will go with my congratulations and best wishes."

"Sir—"

But Bascomb had already stood, turned, and marched out the tent door without another word.

❊❊❊

Dear Bill:

I'm moved to write you again because I simply don't have anybody to talk to, and the good part about letters like this is that you don't have to read them or answer me back if you don't want to. You let me know some time ago that you are not one to correspond—that writing letters for social purposes is just not something you do. But in your last letter you said you consider me the only one you can let your hair down with, and I'm using that as my license to bend your ear.

I really made a fool of myself recently. I was among the flying cadets invited to a benefit tea dance at one of the stately mansions near our training field, and I was asked to play the piano during the dance intermission. I did, and it seemed to go pretty well until one of the lady guests asked me to accompany her singing. I was forced to admit that I can't read music, and she and many others were so upset by my "fraud" I actually fled the place, angry and totally mortified.

The worst part is that Mary Lou Whiting, a perfectly lovely lady who was the hostess, came to the airfield to calm me down and reassure me and let me know that she and her friends didn't think I was a fraud—as a matter of fact, she said, they really liked my playing. But I'm so damned thin-skinned, so prideful, so aware of my low station in society, that everything she said sounded condescending, like, "There, there, little boy, you're not really the phony rube everybody thinks you are." So I got mad all over again and, as politely as I could manage, told her to get the hell out of my life, and I could see she was hurt and confused. She's okay, actually, and I think that under other circumstances we could be really close friends.

But the "other circumstances" says it all. She's the only daughter of a stupendously wealthy man, and she lives like a princess in an enormous castle. And I'm what you know me to be — a dumb kid who owns nothing but a mild scattering of acne. It's not likely that we'd ever be able to talk the same language, truth be known. But I still feel the fool, and I'm unspeakably sorry that I can't seem to be nicer to her. There's just something in me, something that keeps me alternately madder than hell and scared witless, and I can't seem to keep it under control. A large part of the problem, I believe, is my resentment of her wealth. Where is the fairness in somebody like me, working his raggedy ass to the bone and getting nothing but contempt in return, and somebody like her, being swathed in satin and draped with jewelry, luxuriating in gigantic homes and legions of sycophants, never having to lift a finger because she was lucky enough to have sprung from the seed of a guy who has made a lot of moola?

You must be laughing about now. You're so worldly, so coolly sophisticated, so ready to stare down and conquer life's inequities, you would have handled this contretemps the way you handled the cops in Lackawanna. Even if he wears a badge, you're any man's equal, and you're not about to take any of his crap. How I envy you that. I often feel that way about myself, but when push comes to shove, I tend to fold and run. God, but I wish I could be like you!

Well, it's late, and I have to be to up, Johnny-on-the-spot, to face the rigors of a morning that seems to be here already.

If you've read this, Bill, my sincerest thanks. And remember, I'd really like to hear from you. But I know that writing letters is not among your strong suits, and so keep your silence if you wish. I'll know that if my letters don't come back to me unopened, you've given me your ear, and for me, that's enough.

With much affection and admiration,

John

Chapter 20

Hobart Fontaine was a fastidious man. He wore a white work smock that appeared to have been starched and steam pressed, and under it, showing at the top, was a white dress shirt with a celluloid collar and a neatly tied maroon cravat. His trousers were black serge, and they reached to a length that was precisely correct, fashion-wise, to show the precisely correct amount of the glittering black leather composing his precisely correct brogans. He moved along the gangway between assembly lines in odd, mincing steps, as if fearing that undue movement would break the brittle smock into a thousand pieces. Carpenter, following behind him, was hoping it would.

"As you see," Fontaine was saying in his professorial way, "we are entirely committed to the construction of the Liberty-powered DH-4, under license from the De Havilland Company. This is the fuselage construction bay, where we have three separate gangs working around the clock, and over there is the main wing construction bay, which, because of the size of the wings themselves, takes up nearly a third of our main building floor area."

Because he thought he'd better show he was still awake, Carpenter said, "I understand wings are also being built at the Eastman Company's Kodak plant in Rochester."

Fontaine stopped, turned slowly, and regarded Carpenter with wry amusement. "True. But it's just another symptom of the madness that surrounds this whole thing of going to war without preparation. When Slater and those other idiots in Congress decided to 'fill the skies with armies of American airplanes,' there were no more than a dozen U.S. companies with only ten thousand workers making up the entire domestic aircraft industry. I was one of the little ones. Glenn Curtiss and the Wright-Martin bunch were the largest—each capitalized at ten million dollars and each solidly in the pockets of automobile manufacturers like Packard and Hudson. Even at best, there was no industry capable of filling the skies with anything but hot air. Then to top things off, Wright went to court claiming that any warping or other in-flight rearrangement of wingtips was under its exclusive patent, and that pulled the rug out from under the rest of us who were using ailerons to control our planes' rolling motions. We're still trying to sort all that out, and meanwhile, the 'armies of American airplanes' amount to only sixty-four out of three hundred and sixty-six ordered from nine factories. Is there any wonder then we're now up to our hips in mud, buying these obsolescent piles of junk from the British and French in which to send young Americans up against Tony Fokker's best?"

The question told Carpenter that it was his turn to say something. And he saw his problem immediately. He was working for Slater, king pimp of the obsolescent-junk-pile whores, but secretly and angrily empathizing with Fontaine. Slater wanted him to slap Fontaine on the back and cheer him on in the agreement to build ash-based shit. But he knew, standing there on the gangway, trading stares in a Damascene reality, that his loyalty belonged not to Slater and his fellow exploiters among the smugly satisfied Brits and Frenchies, but to the discouraged, put-upon Fontaines.

"Well," he hedged, "as Walcott, the White House aviation poobah says, no amount of money will buy time. And that's what you factory guys don't have—time. Either you swallow hard and keep building crap or you pack up and go home to pout. Whichever way, our air crews stand to get kicked in the balls, and the Brits and Frenchies will have to get along without our help."

Fontaine sniffed. "That's another thing that gets my goat. I don't buy into all this hokum about 'saving the world for democracy.' This war, no war, is about high-minded stuff like that. War's about money and power for a handful of megalomaniacs who sell us working stiffs a bill of goods that makes us think we're doing something great and noble by killing each other for the benefit of mankind. You don't think for a minute, do you, that the Brits and the French will actually appreciate our help? That's nonsense. They'll take our fortune and spend our lives and when the heat's finally off them, they'll sneer at us behind our backs for being such gullible rubes."

Carpenter sounded a low whistle. "Boy, you really are a cynic, aren't you?"

"Of course. Why shouldn't I be? My only son leaves Harvard and runs off to join the Lafayette Escadrille and goes down with the ship when the Germans torpedo it off Scotland. He didn't help the French. He didn't help anybody. The only thing he did was break his mother's heart."

Carpenter brushed some sawdust from his uniform sleeve to pretend he didn't see the tear that ran down Fontaine's long nose. "You're right. It's hard to make any sense out of any of it."

"Well," Fontaine said, clearing his throat, "I'm putting you on notice, Major Carpenter. I know that the reason you're here is to do a little spying for Slater, to make sure I'm not going astray. You can assure him I'm not. You can assure him that every penny of federal money he has sent my way is being used here precisely as agreed: to build as many De Havillands as I can in the shortest possible time. But to save you some spying time, I'm also going to tell you straight out, here and now: I'm using my own money and my own free time to design and build an airplane worthy of the kids who'll need it." He pointed out a window to a sizeable, low-lying clapboard shed on the other side of the railroad spur. "It's over there. You're free to look at it any time. And when you tell Slater about it, you can also tell him that if he doesn't like it, he can just take a flying fuck to the moon."

It was the obscenity that pushed Carpenter over the fence. A word like that, uttered by a priggish, pedantical fashion plate, was the hot wax providing the seal of approval to his own incipient rebellion.

He heard himself saying, "You might not believe this, Mr. Fontaine, not yet, maybe, but I'm on your side."

"You're right. I don't believe you."

"I'm not a politician. I'm an American. I'm not a spy. I'm a flyer."

"I'm supposed to go to my knees and kiss your ring?"

"You're supposed to listen to me for a minute."

"Well?"

"I just got back from a tour in England and France. I went over there with the idea that those people would be glad to see me as a symbol of my country's determination to give them a hand in a time of deep shit. To find out what they needed most. To test their equipment and see how we might best spread our millions around to buy some of it—smother them in money in return for their permission to build some of their crappy goddamn airplanes to be used by our guys in the fight to save their national asses.

"And you know what? They weren't glad to see me at all. To my face, the Limeys would grin those shit-eating grins and purr nice little platitudes, but it became pretty clear when I heard one of their high-ranking staff officers refer to me behind my back as," he put on a snooty English accent, "'that rude demmed colonial who's trying to snaffle some of our veddy best machines.' Or when a French technical officer refused to let me try a Spad because 'Spads are for us, Monsewer, Nieuports are for you.' The Nieuport 28 he offered me was like one of those French villages. From a distance, the town is real pretty, with soft colors, snug walls, artsy chimneys, cutesy windows, homey and inviting. But when you get close to it, you see the dingy streets, the filthy walls, the sour, unfriendly faces, and everywhere the stink of manure and cow piss. Likewise, from a distance the 28 looked like a dream, all sleek and pleasantly configured, a real airplaney-looking airplane. But when I looked closely at the one that smug-ass Frenchie showed me, the fuselage between the engine cowling and the cockpit was covered with heavy cardboard—I mean no shit, cardboard—and the tail unit was built of plywood sheet, nothing else, and the cockpit was so small and dark and tight I had to squeeze into it and wear it like my little brother's pants. I told the Frog officer that I'd fly it after he did, but he just shrugged and walked away, muttering about ingrates.

"Take it from me, Mr. Fontaine, we aren't just fighting the kaiser and his collection of horses' asses. We're also fighting a bunch of pricks in London and Paris who see us as butt-ins cluttering up their exclusive playing field. They'll let us fight for them, but only when they say how and when and with what. They'll borrow our money but won't give any guarantees to pay it back. They let us buy them lunch but never take us home for supper with the missus and kids. Well, I'll do what the Army tells me to do, but don't ask me to like it. And believe me, Mr. Fontaine, I'll not say a word to Slater about your new plane, and I'll ask the Army to take me out of his office and your hair, pronto. I can't do any more than that."

They were face to face on the gangway, oblivious to the men pushing past with armloads of blueprints and buckets of bolts and saws and drills. Fontaine was silent for a whole minute, then offered, "Would you like to see my new plane, Major?"

"I thought you'd never ask."

Chapter 21

The shed was even larger than it appeared to be from the window of the fuselage manufacturing bays. Inside it was dim and cool, and with the absence of crews, a hush prevailed.

"Behold, the eighth wonder of the world," Fontaine said, and Carpenter couldn't tell if he was being proud or sarcastic. Perhaps a bit of both.

The airplane stood in the central bay, large, rakish, glittering like polished silver. A monoplane such as Carpenter had never seen before. It stood high on a tricycle landing gear, two wheels amidships at the obvious center of gravity and the third wheel on a stilt-like extension from beneath the nose. The wing, thick at the fuselage junction and tapered to almost razor thinness at the tips, was mounted low and had a pronounced dihedral. Inward from the ailerons were what appeared to be flaps. The fuselage was obviously monocoque, free of protuberances, and constructed of a shiny metal-like substance that overall suggested a long, teardrop-shaped cigar wrapped in a smooth foil. The tail assembly was inverted, with the horizontal fin and elevators flush with the top of the fuselage, and the vertical fin and rudder hanging below, in diametric contradiction to the conventional placement. Not a guy wire, not a turnbuckle, not a single wooden strut was in evidence anywhere.

"Holy Shinola!" Carpenter whispered, his eyes wide and full of awe and disbelief.

"A bit different, wouldn't you say?"

"My aching, government-issued ass..."

"I take that as a 'yes.'"

"Ooooo, yes, yes, *yes*!"

"We'll start with the cockpit."

They mounted a steel-tube scaffolding that had been wheeled close to the fuselage aft of the wing root and stood on the top platform, peering into the crew quarters.

Fontaine's hand swept here and there as he pointed out the features.

"You'll note that the cockpit is a single well with back-to-back seats separated only by a side-mounted instrument cluster for use by the rear gunner-bombardier-photographer if he has to take over the ship in an emergency. The pilot has the standard controls, the standard instrument panel, lighted by hooded spots for nighttime combat operations. The pilot controls twin synchronized 30-caliber light machine guns mounted conventionally inside the forward fuselage and within easy reach, if he has to clear stoppages. But with this lever here," the waving hand designated a special fitting alongside the control stick, "the pilot can also fire the 20-millimeter French rapid-fire cannon whose barrel is mounted inside the engine's crankshaft, with its muzzle in the propeller hub.

"The rear gunner is provided a brace of Lewis air-cooled machine guns mounted on a conventional Scarff ring. As you can see, he commands the maximum field of fire, with no wings or tail surfaces impeding his upper and horizontal aiming arcs."

"That's why you inverted the tail assembly?"

"Mmm. One of my concessions to the Germans. I saw what they did with their Brandenberg seaplane, and I've unapologetically stolen the idea. They were able to do it because their machine sits on the water, elevated by stilt-like pontoon supports. To accomplish the same ends for a land plane, I designed what you see there, a retractable tricycle landing gear."

"Retractable?"

The hand waved again. "That wheel, mounted on the fuselage side just starboard of the pilot's seat: Once airborne, the pilot unlocks that wheel and cranks it. A series of interlocked, highly lubricated gears and chains pulls the three landing wheels into wing and fuselage bays. To lower the gear, he reverses the crank, then locks everything with that handle there."

"But what about the tail skid function? Land planes have tail skids to help drag the plane to a halt, or to keep the plane from rolling too far, too fast, during a landing. With that inverted rudder on this ship, no way can a tail skid—"

"These wheels have brakes. The pilot applies them by pressing his heels against stirrups affixed to the nether side of the rudder pedals."

"Fantastic."

"The idea is to reduce drag. The landing gear and external bracing of conventional aircraft have a pronounced negative influence on the plane's forward speed and overall maneuverability. My machine tucks that stuff away, out of the airflow."

"Sheesh. You're a freaking genius."

Fontaine humphed. "No, just a man who thinks things through. Empathetically. From the aircrew's point of view."

"Question: Monocoque I understand. The French use that a lot. But what's that finish you have on this thing? Metal-like, yet shiny. Real shiny."

"It's duralumin, a relatively new aluminum alloy. Again, developed by the Germans about ten years ago. It's aluminum, alloyed with copper, manganese, and magnesium. In sheet form it's strong and light, and it obviates the need for heavy interior bracing. Couldn't find it here in the States, so I bought a little metallurgy shop and made my own. Its overall reduction in the aircraft's gross weight permits the use of the highest-powered standard aircraft engines we have today. This one is fitted with a twelve-cylinder Liberty engine, but my ideal, because it does away with the need for water-cooling systems, is the new Benoit air-cooled radial, developed by a French company near Nancy. This plane calls for that engine, period, and I'd do most anything to get my hands on one of them. Any way you look at it, though, you get a lot more fighting airplane for your dollar—lighter, faster, more maneuverable, and deadlier than any plane today, even those on drawing boards."

Carpenter shook his head and sighed. "And yet your main plant, your main manufacturing effort, is centered on the DH-4, a great big flying bedspring."

Fontaine gave him a sidelong look. "Might I make a joke?"

"Be my guest."

"I call the DH-4 'Congressman Slater's piece of ash.'"

Carpenter grinned. "Ooo. That's naughty."

"Well, we're both adults."

They stood together for a time, admiring the machine, speculating.

"Have you had this thing flown yet, Mr. Fontaine?"

"Not yet. I don't want to reveal it yet. I want to keep it my secret for awhile."

"Well, all respect, but just because something looks good doesn't mean it'll work good." He winked. "Take that blonde I know down in D.C."

Fontaine's lips showed a faint smile. "Your turn to make a joke, eh?"

"Well, as a guy I know says, 'We're both adults.'"

Much to Carpenter's surprise, Fontaine laughed openly.

"Seriously, Mr. Fontaine, you've got to try this thing out in the air. If it works as well as it looks, you'll make aviation history."

"I don't want to expose it to the public yet. There isn't a place anywhere I could fly this thing without forty tons of press landing on me, without a hundred tons of Slaters slapping me down for misuse of public funds and whatnot."

They stood silent again. Then Fontaine pulled his watch from a pocket, flicked it open, consulted the time, and said, "Class is out. I'm hungry and still have a lot to do before shift change."

They clambered down from the scaffold and headed for the main door.

"Are you going to report all this to Slater, Major?"

"Not on your life, pal. But give me some time. I've got to figure a way to get out from under him without his getting suspicious or causing a stink."

"This Senator Murray, who pulled the strings to get you here, can you get out from under him, too?"

"It's all part of the package I've got to unwrap. Meanwhile, I'm going to chase down an idea I have. I think I know a place where you can fly this baby and not catch a helluva lot of attention."

"You do that, and I'll be forever grateful."

"It can cost you some money."

"So what's different about that? I'll pay you whatever you want."

"Not me. A steamship line."

Chapter 22

The European winter had been an ordeal worthy of Dante. Rain, constant rain, often turning to sleet; snow driven by icy winds; oceans of gummy mud from Brittany to Kiev. King had landed at Le Havre in the middle of it after a dreary passage from Hoboken in a leaky single-stack coal burner assembled of rusting iron and decaying wood. The manifest listed tinned corned beef, No. 1 carpentry nails, 45-caliber pistol ammunition, ash lumber, stewed prunes, hard rubber truck tires, cigarette cartons, laundry soap, canned baked beans, three Presbyterian chaplains, a Catholic priest, two rabbis, and one Air Service pilot.

Since King was traveling alone and unassigned, no one had the slightest notion of what to do with him. The clergy climbed onto a truck and vanished into the dockyard's teeming rain, the cargo remained aboard until the ship's captain sobered sufficiently to sign the pertinent papers, and King somehow ended up on a little train of four-wheeled cars headed east through the storm. His travel orders said only that he was to report to the U.S. Aviation Command in Paris for further assignment at the discretion of the commanding officer there—no delay en route, pay, subsistence, and quarters nearest Signal Corps command. Which meant that until he found the right Signal Corps headquarters, he had no usable money, no ration slips, and no papers authorizing him to rent a room or buy a meal, even if he did have money. He walked through the rainy night from the Gare du Nord to a kiosk where a gendarme, catching a smoke under the cover of a huge black slicker, managed to understand his need to find the American headquarters. For all his condescension, though, there was no way for the policeman to direct him, since a passerby who boasted of great facility with English explained that there had to be "um, how you say eet, um, beeg oodles of, um, teeny headquarters *américain* in ze city, an' maybe...is zat ze word?...ze embassy *américain* can gif' ze assist, *hein*?"

As he walked away, King felt the following stares, full of superiority, suspicion, and contempt. And briefly, as he turned a corner, he thought he glimpsed his mother, standing in the street in the lowering mist, smiling, arms outstretched. He felt no fear, only an abysmal loneliness and a maddening need to weep.

❋❋❋

The Sunday-duty man at the embassy, a fatty named Reese, wanted to be helpful, but he was as much at sea about all this Army stuff as anybody, and he'd been given no instructions from Washington—or anywhere else—on what to do with a man like Lt. King. Perhaps Lt. Ruger, duty officer for the embassy military attaché group, would have some ideas. "I'll connect you with him."

The phone at the other end lifted. "Duty officer. Lieutenant Ruger speaking."

"This is Lieutenant John King, Army Air Service. I came here on solo travel orders assigning me to an unspecified headquarters at the convenience of the C.O. there. Trouble is, I don't know which headquarters, or even where I belong, and I'm here in Paris without any kind of funds."

"So what's your problem?"

"My problem is that I don't have written orders, I don't have quarters or subsistence, I don't have local ground transport, and I don't even have a frigging change of clothes."

"You got a lot of company, buddy. Washington says diplo discretion funds are for local contract service only and can't be transferred to transient military. Congress has to pass a bill or something. Meantime, Washington says that everything purchased by you guys in the field can be obtained by using Signal Corps Form Fifteen, the standard local procurement form for the Corps and its ancillaries."

"So where do I get forms like that?"

"I'll mail you some."

"Peachy. What the hell do I do in the meantime?"

"I regret to say that you'll have to live on your own money until Congress can pass a bill."

"Well, let me tell you something, Ruger, as one of the guys in the field. My second-John's pay's one-twenty-five a month—"

"One-eighty-seven-fifty, counting flight pay."

"—and my next pay isn't due for two whole weeks. If Congress expects me to rent a room, buy my meals, pay bus and trolley fares, get haircuts, and have my pants cleaned and pressed on my own money until it gets around to passing a bill, you can mail that Form Fifteen to me care of Paris Skid Row, because that's where I'll be."

"Don't you have any savings you can draw on?"

"Boy, you're a real comedian, aren't you? The ten bucks in my pocket and the fifty-two bucks in a Buffalo bank, that's what I got. Besides, what does that have to do with it? I'm supposed to use my savings to be in the government's army, to fight the government's war?"

"You're a U.S. Army officer. You ought to be able to get some credit around Paris. Put your necessities on the tab. Hell, if the Frenchies can't trust a U.S. Army officer, who can they trust, right?"

King hung up in disgust and strode for the door.

Reese, sighing and shaking his head, called after him. "Hey, King. Hold your horses." He scribbled something on a pad, tore off the top sheet, and handed it across the counter. "Take this to the transportation foreman in the cellar. I looked up some stuff, and I see that something called the First Pursuit Organization and Training Center is being set up by Signal Corps Aviation at Villeneuve-les-Vertus out near Chalons. Benny, our transport guy, says he'll put you on wheels headed out that way."

King picked up the paper as if it were a crown jewel, his surprise and gratitude a spectacular display. "Hey, thanks. That's right good of you."

"Well, I don't want you cluttering up the embassy. Sleeping on the benches, barracks bag as a pillow. You look like a hobo, and it makes a bad impression on our great French allies."

King grinned. "Makes a bad impression on me, too. Mind if I use the men's room to shave in?"

Reese waved him away. "Just don't let me see it."

❈❈❈

The rain at Villeneuve made the rain in Paris look like milady's flower mister. When King swung down from the truck—which, the driver told him, showing off his Old Hand's savvy, the Frenchies called a *camion*—he literally sank until the gumbo was halfway up his calves. He hung on to one of the camion's grab handles until the vehicle, grinding clear of its own problems, pulled him to more solid footing—a boardwalk leading to a large frame-and-canvas shack bearing the sign, "HQ, First Pursuit."

The office was dry and warm, thanks to a potbellied stove crackling and hissing in a corner.

God, all I ever do anymore is struggle into offices and face off with some nitwit who thinks he's Genghis goddamn Khan and who reminds me that if he has to choose between me and a sty full of pig shit, it's no contest. God, how tired I am of this.

"Close the damned door, will ya?" This one was a master sergeant barricaded behind a tall, boxy typewriter. He had no neck, and his jowls sagged over his tunic collar. He gave King not so much as a glance.

King sighed. "Say 'please, sir.'"

The sergeant looked at him. "What?"

"I said, say 'please, sir.'"

The sergeant finally saw the gold bar on King's collar. He hadn't achieved his rank without learning that it doesn't pay to cross an officer, especially a smart-ass, fuzz-faced second looie. "Oh, sorry, sir. I was busy here, and I thought you were that idiot, Cooch, bringing me my coffee." He stood up. "What can I do to help you?"

"Everything," King said wearily. "Sergeant, I just plain-old need help with everything."

The sergeant's little eyes went up and down King's shivering form, taking in the sodden uniform, the mud slime up to the knees, the blue lips, and the dull stare, and his voice softened. "Yes, sir, I'd say you sure do." He waved at the stove. "Get over there by the heat. I'll bring you a chair." A man in a jerry-rigged poncho came through the door, holding two mugs of steaming coffee so they wouldn't spill. "Cooch, give mine to the lieutenant here. And hand me that GI blanket in the closet."

King settled on the chair next to the stove, wrapped in the blanket, sipping coffee, eyes slit in pleasure. The other two stood by, watching.

"What's your name, Sergeant?"

"Edelmann, sir. Albert Edelmann."

"I'll dance at your wedding, Sergeant."

Edelmann and Cooch traded amused glances.

"Lordy, Lieutenant, don't do that, don't make me go through that again! Three times is enough."

They all laughed together.

"Edelmann, eh? Do you know that your name in German means 'nobleman' or 'honorable guy'?"

"My name with my three ex-wives is Mud."

They laughed again.

Cooch saluted. "Permission to leave, sir. I'm on night KP."

King waved a return salute. "See you around, Cooch. Thanks for the coffee."

When they were alone again, Edelmann asked, "Need anything else, Lieutenant—"

"King. John King. I'm a pilot. I'm supposed to report for duty, but damned if I know where and who with."

Edelmann went to his desk, picked up a folio, and leafed through it. His heavy face creased in a smile. "So, our wandering new pilot has finally surfaced. I'm happy to say that you belong here, Lieutenant King."

"No fooling."

"That's what it says, right here. Cable out of Whiting Field in Pennsylvania and endorsed by Signal Corps in Washington. Chief of the Air Section in Paris advises of your assignment to First Pursuit."

"The least they could have done is advise me."

Edelmann sniffed. "That would be logical, sir. When you've been in the Army as long as I have, you'll see that the Army abhors logic."

"So what do we do here in First Pursuit?"

"We work our asses off. Not at flying, mind you. We don't have any airplanes, and you're one of only four flying officers standing by until we do get some. We have a few engineering officers, but they're in charge of the French and Italian laborers building the hangars, machine shops, guns and ammo sheds, barracks, phone and electric lines—the usual stuff. We'll be grading the field and finishing up the drainage system whenever this damned rain stops."

"No planes at all, eh?"

"Not even a kite. Our C.O., Major Bert Atkinson—I'll introduce you tomorrow when he gets back from Paris—is getting steamed about this and has been raising hell. He's Regular Army and usually gets what he wants. And right now he wants as many planes as he can get, because the Army plans to maintain two tactical squadrons here, and pretty soon we'll be up to our asses in pilots with nothing to fly. The Frenchies keep promising him some Nieuports, but on this, like pretty much everything else, they don't follow through."

King nodded somberly and dropped his coffee mug, which spun on the floor at his feet.

"Hey, you're falling asleep, Lieutenant. Come on. I'll show you to the officers' barracks."

"Lead away, O Honorable Man."

Chapter 23

Slater had a busy day ahead, and he was especially excited about it, since two important aspects of his rise to prominence and wealth were about to converge. He dressed in his favorite banker's gray suit and its vest with white piping, fastened white spats over his glittering black oxfords, and finished the effect with a red and silver four-in-hand tie and a white rose boutonniere. He selected a Homburg and a gold-headed cane from the wardrobe, then admired himself for a moment in the full-length foyer mirror.

Prosperous and in command. Yessiree Bob.

The lunch was being served in a small but elegant townhouse located in a tree-lined courtyard just off Capitol Hill. Slater could rent it by the day and have the luncheon catered, thanks to certain favors he had done for the owner, and it served admirably as a meeting place when confidentiality and convenience were primary considerations. The wait staff was skilled, Continental, and, most important, guaranteed to be discreet, inasmuch as Slater's office safe was the repository for copies of its members' home-country rap sheets.

Mason and Raymond were waiting at the table when he arrived, which irritated Slater somewhat as a lapse in the deference he was due. He settled in the chair held for him by René, nodded when the wine was presented, and gave the others a look that signaled his vague displeasure.

"I hope I haven't kept you waiting too long."

Mason shrugged and made a minimizing sound. Ned Raymond, catching the signal, did a bit of groveling. "We waited in the lounge for a time, but I twisted my ankle yesterday, and this straight-back chair helps."

"I dare say. So, shall we order?"

✱✱✱

After coffee and brandy, Slater gave a concluding touch of the napkin to his lips, eased back in his chair, and lit a cigar. He saw no reason to dally further.

"So then, Mason, just where are we in the ash timber acquisitions? It seems to me you're taking an unduly long time to wrap things up."

Mason, being a lawyer, was not intimidated. "Of course I am. I've got the whole weight of the United States government hovering over me. Plus the fact that you've been fed a bill of goods on ash lumber. Ash was used in the earlier airplanes because it's strong and light in weight, pliable and whatnot. But a couple of years ago, designers discovered that a better job is done by Sitka spruce. Why? Because it's got all the good stuff of ash and is a helluva lot more plentiful and is easier to harvest. Ash is good, but spruce is better."

"So why aren't we nailing down some big swatches of spruce? Why are we messing around with ash?"

Mason didn't so much as blink. "Because the administration is already moving to nail it down as a war-important resource. At least twenty-seven thousand Army officers and men have been assigned to the Aircraft Production Board's Spruce Division and have, in effect, taken over the spruce industry in Washington and Oregon."

Slater's face reddened. "Goddamn that slick-Willie Fontaine. He assured me that ash is it."

"Well, he was right—to a point. But the technology has moved on, so to speak."

"The bastard. He knew, but he didn't tell me."

Mason sipped some brandy, looking smug. "Maybe. But he also put us in an even better position. Instead of selling ash lumber stock to our fat-cat insiders, we sell them high-return, short-term stock in what we call 'secret alternative aircraft resource materials,' emphasizing the idea that if spruce has replaced ash, it won't be long before spruce will be depleted and require replacement by the stuff we're on top of."

"Like what stuff?" Raymond wanted to know.

"I'll think up something."

Slater and Raymond stared at the self-satisfaction dominating Mason's heavy face.

"Tell me about this, Mason. How will this work?"

"In essence, we keep our company, All-Star Realty, operating under a shell fronted by Willis in San Antone. Willis, by the way, is a nincompoop who still, even today, thinks that he's president of a well-funded brokerage, when, in fact, there is no brokerage."

"Does he know about me?"

"He hasn't the slightest clue about you or me or Ned. He thinks he's being bankrolled by rich Canadians. The money he brings in is sent to a postal box in Toronto paid for by a nonexistent corporation. The money is picked up by a runner, then sent to you and Ned and me by way of a cut-out in Chicago. None of that will change. Only the product we're selling will change."

"Do we have to put up any more front-end money?"

"All-Star office overhead only. Not a cent more. We simply send out the word to our greedy, high-rolling friends that they can as much as double their money in a month. We do this by pocketing the money as it comes in and paying off early investors from money put up by the building avalanche of greedy latecomers who keep taking more and bigger risks. Greed keeps all the players playing. And all we do is keep however much we want of the new incoming money and use the remaining sucker money to pay off the suckers."

Ned raised a finger of doubt. "What happens when there isn't any sucker money left to pay off the suckers?"

Mason shrugged. "Willis takes the rap. And he's more surprised than anybody when he discovers there is no corporation in Toronto."

Ned said, "That makes us dirty, rotten crooks."

Mason said, "Correction: That makes us dirty, rotten very wealthy crooks who can't be tied to the scam. And our wealth has come from a handful of other dirty, rotten crooks who, nine times out of ten, have made their money by pulling off other kinds of frauds on other greedy fools. Nobody falls for a scam faster than a scam-artist, and who's he going to complain to?"

They sat in silence for a time, puffing their cigars and watching the birds splashing in the fountain in the garden outside.

Slater stirred. "So where are we in all this?"

Mason grinned. "I've taken the liberty of moving Willis into action." He pulled three large envelopes from the briefcase on the floor beside him, then, keeping one, flipped the others across the table like a blackjack dealer. "Our first take, gentlemen. Forty thousand dollars for each of us."

❊❊❊

For Capitol Hill denizens, one of the most private places to talk was the most public—on one of the benches under the trees in the park across from Union Station. Today everything was responding to the developing springtime, and with the unseasonable warmth of the afternoon and the greening of the grass and trees and shrubbery and the awakening of the scent of flowerbeds, Slater decided the bench was a perfect site for this critical confrontation. Slater knew he made the senator uneasy, simply by virtue of his lack of party affiliation. Murray, the senior senator from Slater's state, was a label-reader. If a man was identified as a member of the opposite party, he was seen by Murray to be an enemy to be treated with diplomatic wariness; anyone from Murray's party was a friend to be trusted categorically. The fact that Slater had run and won three terms as an independent was an entirely mystifying and unnerving phenomenon for a man whose naïveté was exceeded only by his vanity. Murray had been in office for so long solely because he was the only man dumb and manipulable enough to be acceptable to two warring factions in his own party.

But he certainly looked great.

He was coming up the walkway now, tall, leonine, with a

great silvery mane and a jutting jaw and fierce eyebrows. The physical and sartorial embodiment of senatorial power. Political cartoonists loved him.

"Ah, good afternoon, Senator."

Murray nodded haughtily. "Slater."

"Sit down, won't you? I think this thing is big enough to accommodate the two of us."

"I have no more than a moment. A committee meeting awaits. But the governor called and said you have something important to discuss with me, and—"

"I won't keep you long." Slater held out a bag of peanuts. "I've been feeding the pigeons and squirrels. Want to join me?"

"As I say, I have little time."

Slater nodded agreeably. "Actually, that's so. You have very little time left. Hardly any at all. And that's why we're talking."

Murray's deep-set eyes turned to him. "What do you mean by that, Slater?"

"The governor has decided that you must resign and be replaced by gubernatorial appointment. He wants me to replace you. And he wants me to tell you this."

The deep-set eyes blinked, the eagle's beak twitched, the lion's mane seemed to shake with the astonishment and disbelief consuming the overall embodiment.

"I...You...The governor...This is...Well, I simply must say...I was most instrumental in getting him elected...He can't do such a thing to me—"

"Oh, but he can, Francis X. He's throwing you out on your dirty ass—summarily."

"You aren't even in our party."

"That's why I appeal to the governor. I don't belong to anybody. I go with the highest bidder." He threw a peanut to a nearby squirrel that stood on hind legs like a tiny, vigilant soldier.

"You...You're scum—"

"True. But I'm not the kind of scum who diddles little boys."

"Whatever in the world are you talking about?"

Slater reached into his inner jacket pocket and withdrew the sheaf of photographs, which he fanned out on his lap like a hand of playing cards. "The governor finds this kind of thing incredibly repugnant. As do I, of course."

Murray sagged, much like one of those rubber carnival mannequins at day's end. Having been made instantly defenseless, shaken and pale, he offered no argument, sought no discussion. "What would the governor have me do?"

"Call a press conference in your office tomorrow morning at nine and announce that for reasons of health and personal family needs, you are resigning as senator at once."

"Do I have any options?"

"Not unless you consider a pistol bullet to the head to be an option."

Murray sat for a time, head bowed, shoulders sagging. "I'm not really a bad man, you know."

"I understand that. Even the governor understands that." Slater's arm swept the horizon. "But those millions of self-righteous, hypocritical voting idiots out there—they don't and never will understand that."

"I get lonely. Sad. There's no tenderness in my life."

"Same here, Francis X. I know just what you're talking about. But I don't take it out on kids. I take it out on bastards like you and the governor, people who can fight back. You ought to try it sometime. Nothing cures sadness and loneliness like a red hot sunabitchin alley fight."

Chapter 24

The rains continued. The mud became deeper and slimier, and tempers grew shorter. Things worsened when more and more pilots began to show up at Villeneuve, ready to fly for the 95th Pursuit Squadron, only to discover that there were no planes to fly and that their main duty would be to help build barracks and hangars and machine shops. King tried manfully to contain his impatience and, with the connivance of Sergeant Edelmann, who for reasons known only to God and Edelmann had taken a fatherly interest in him, managed to evade the worst of the many onerous work details. But the days became weeks, and the winter refused to admit the likelihood of spring, and the chow got colder and greasier. King was seriously considering an AWOL trip to Paris and a blinding binge when Edelmann poked his bullet head through the tent flap one evening and said, "Ahoy, Herr Leutnant! I got news for you! Good news!"

"I have just been appointed casting director of the Ziegfield Follies?"

"Almost as good. Your records show that you have never had aerial gunnery training. You are officially a pilot without fangs."

"So what's good about that? I've been told I was to get on-the-job training in gunnery. I go up, tangle with some Germans, and watch how they shoot at me."

"The Army is much better organized than that."

"Oh, sure."

"Seriously. Orders have been cut sending you to the aerial gunnery school at Cazaux, out on the coast. The Bay of Biscay."

"You're fooling me, of course."

"Honest to God. The Frenchies are very reluctant to let us good guys learn how to shoot machine guns over the territory they still hold, seeing as how so many naughty Teutons are shooting up so much of their real estate east of here. It is said that the populace takes a dim view of American machine-gun bullets falling out of the sky into their snails au gratin. Thus they have built a special school out on the sand dunes, where falling ammo annoys only the gulls and buoys—that's a pun, by the way."

"Orders have been cut?"

Edelmann waved some papers. "You leave for Paris by camion tomorrow at 0700. You leave by train out of Paris at 1800 hours Sunday. Your gunnery training is to commence Monday. All told, that gives you roughly two days to get drunker'n hell on the Left Bank. Even the Right Bank, if you're so inclined."

"I am about to swoon."

✳✳✳

He never did do the binge thing, although he virtually haunted the bistros in Montmartre, going from one to the other, following the sounds. He looked in on the famous places, the Moulin Rouge and the like, but they were too brassy and filled with raucous soldiers and overdone women and noisy can-cans and were, accordingly, too expensive, so he drifted along the dingy side streets, and when he heard a nice sound he'd enter and invest in a glass of red. The music was so utterly marvelous, so uncontrived, so mellow, and the female singers—*chanteuses* they called them—taught him new things about pauses, suspensions, carrying the melody slightly off the beat, turning whole notes into whispers and segues into plaintive moans, and forming key changes as naturally and effortlessly as snow melting. There was one singer, a middle-aged woman with a face that had been carved by every pain known to humanity, who tore his heart out. Everything about her reminded him of his mother, and yet her voice, deep, resonant, carrying a kind of echo of itself, actually stirred him erotically. And while she never looked at him directly, he had the feeling that she was singing to him alone, through the dim light and tobacco smoke and over the heads of the indifferent clientele, telling him that she understood his lostness, and if times and places had been different, she would have taken him in her arms and stroked his hair.

❈❈❈

Passed by Censor 4320

Capt. William J. Carpenter

c/o General Headquarters

American Expeditionary Forces

Paris (Please forward)

Dear Bill:

Why is it that you must suffer for my lack of anyone to talk to?

I've been having rotten headaches lately, and tonight I have a doozy, and I'm hoping that by writing you I can focus—counteract the confusion that seems to accompany these things.

I have just joined a pursuit squadron in the Zone of Advance, which means I regularly associate with two dozen young officers of fine breeding and excellent education. Beyond them are at least two hundred enlisted men carefully selected by the Army for their skill and good character. Yet there isn't one among them I can call friend and confidant. In the past few weeks, every overture I've made has been met with superficiality, college-boy rah-rah, glib talk about sex and booze and football, and when I fail to respond the way they expect, when I try to talk about more important things, I seem to make them uneasy, and they dismiss me. How can I make friends and find a confidant among pubescent topers and sex maniacs?

That's what's so different about you. You can laugh and joke and say all sorts of outrageous things, and yet underlying them is solid character, intelligence, and good will.

Tomorrow morning I'm scheduled to leave for aircraft gunnery school at Cazaux, on the French west coast. I should have received this training before my assignment to a line squadron, but, as you no doubt know, everything is terribly bollixed up these days, and nothing seems to work the way it's supposed to. A prime example is the fact that although our supply of Nieuport 28s has finally been delivered, there's a bit of a hitch: not one of them is equipped with machine guns! So I'm not the only pilot lacking gunnery training, and there's a line forming for the sea breezes at Cazaux.

And, another weird part of all this is that the 95th Pursuit (part of my squadron's group) actually flew a patrol along the Marne between Epernay and Chalons the other day despite the fact that they weren't packin' shootin' arns. I understand that they stayed on our side of the lines, with the idea of showing the Germans on the other side that there was now an American air presence in the area. But, boy, were they lucky that some bad-tempered Richtenflichtens didn't come bustling across the lines to call their bluff. You can see why I keep wondering if anybody's in charge around here!

Word is that my squadron, along with the rest of the group, is to be located in what's touted as a quiet sector, but one man's quiet can be another man's cacophony, eh?

I didn't mean to make this letter so heavy and dreary, but, damn, my head hurts and I yearn for the feeling that I belong to somebody, that there is somebody who really gives a damn about me. How I long to hear just one word: "pard"!

In any event, I wanted especially at this juncture to let you know how very much I admire you and appreciate the way you have accepted me and my strange ways. I hope that someday we can get together again somewhere for steak and cigars.

Sincerely yours,

John King

Chapter 25

So King had arrived at Cazaux, sober and somber and filled with an aching weariness that no sleep would alter.

He'd tried all of it: shooting at targets towed by creaky old planes, shooting at targets laid against the sand dunes and hauled by boats off shore, and within a week he had gathered considerable confidence in himself and the machinery he commanded.

The school was using Nieuport 28s at the time, which was good, because the 28 was the model the French had agreed to make eventually available to the Americans. It was a single-seat biplane, basically honest for all its limitations and the obvious economies that had been worked into its design and construction, but best of all it gave King plenty of practice at managing the Clerget rotary engine. The rotary created a wicked gyroscopic torque, because its eight cylinders whirled en masse, once around the crankshaft for every turn of the propeller, so there were times when he felt as if he were flying a spinning top. But he gradually became used to the effect and actually learned how to make it an asset by turning on a dime when quick maneuvering was needed.

He wasn't too happy with the cockpit layout, though. It was narrow, cramped, and the fuselage was so narrow and the top wing so low that only one machine gun could be fitted forward of the cockpit. The second gun had to be mounted outboard of the left center-section struts, which, King felt, made aiming a bit awkward and required too much dependence on tracer bullets. He could see why the French were anxious to turn this thing over to the Americans and keep the vastly superior Spad for themselves.

Two days before completing the course he found another overriding reason the French disdained the 28.

His shooting time this day was to be given to the high-speed vertical attack on a target sleeve hauled by a slow-moving Breguet two-seater. Gauchat, the instructor, had been quite specific: the target would be cruising southwest to northeast at fifteen hundred feet over the bay. King was to approach from the northeast at three thousand feet. When passing overhead, he was to roll on his back and commence a dive on the target, opening fire from both guns for the few moments the target was in range.

It was a gray, blustery day, and whitecaps dotted the sea below. King had the wind at his back, and the Breguet came on as instructed, but at a faster rate than he had allowed in his mind. He had just pulled the charge handles to ensure proper seating of the cartridges in the chambers when a glance over the side showed him the Breguet and target slipping quickly past at a kind of side-sliding angle. Realizing that he would have to make his shooting run now or never, he shoved full aileron and rudder and pulled back on the stick. The horizon spun, he felt the pull at his belly, and as the engine wound up in a castor-oil spitting scream, the sea was directly ahead and approaching fast.

The white target floated into his ring sight, and, responding to his squeeze of the trigger on the control stick, his machine guns began their rapid thumping. The tracers flickered slightly to port, and he adjusted, sending them needling through the target in what was an obvious series of hits.

Just as he was feeling satisfaction and had begun his recovery from the dive, everything began to unravel.

There was a loud tearing just over his head, a snapping of wood, a vicious whining of wires exposed to wind, and then an overwhelming sound of fabric flapping—a thousand flags whipped by a gale.

What the living hell...?

A panicky glance showed him that the upper wing had begun to shed its fabric. The top surface was already showing naked wood ribs and stringers and slackening brace wires, and if the lower surface fabric peeled he'd be riding a doomed low-wing monoplane.

He brought the ship into a kind of stable power glide, propeller windmilling, engine throwing a spray of unburnt gasoline and castor oil. In a wild thought he thanked his stars that the 28's ailerons were on the lower wing, not the upper as was standard for most military aircraft. He could still maintain lateral control of his instant-monoplane, and with a fully operating rudder and elevator surface, he might—just might—bring off a fast, if marginally controlled, splashdown.

He did even better.

By heading into the northeast wind under quarter throttle, he felt the 28 seeming to gather itself, a dowager determined to keep her cool despite a torn skirt exposing her bloomers, for a stable descent toward the shoreline.

Atta girl. I love you, darlin'....

The plane wobbled several times, but he corrected with those blessed ailerons, and eventually he was skimming the water, with a wide stretch of sandy beach lying straight ahead.

He held his breath, his eyes on the enlarging shadow fleeting across the sand.

Hold 'er, Newt....

He cut the switch, turned off the fuel cock, tore off and threw away his goggles, and buried his face in his arms.

In his blindness, he felt the 28 settle, yaw wildly as its wheels dug into the sand, and then every bone in his body burst into pain as the machine disintegrated around him.

He lost consciousness.

❋❋❋

"King? Lieutenant King?"

He opened an eye, and somehow his first thought was of Bill Carpenter.

"Nice of you to stop by."

The man's face came into focus. It was Captain Gauchat. "My

God. Are you all right, King?"

"You're not going to charge me for that plane, are you?"

"What?"

"It wasn't my fault."

"What?"

"I did what you told me to do. It wasn't my fault that the plane had other ideas."

He was aware of Gauchat looking away and shouting. "Let's get that goddamn stretcher over here!"

"Why? I can walk."

"Sure you can. Just because you're still strapped in your seat and you're fifty feet away from the wreck and you got a knob on your head the size of Rhode Island and you're drenched in gas and oil and covered with blood and sand doesn't mean you can't walk. No reasonable man would expect you to ride out on a stretcher as well off as you are, for crissake."

❋❋❋

The Army's talent for reverse logic was demonstrated once again when, having been examined and declared fit for return to duty by the chief physician at the Cazaux base infirmary, orders came for King's transfer to the 301st Base Hospital outside Paris for "observation and treatment of wounds received in aviation action." The Cazaux medic, a major named Kruger, suffered puzzlement and hurt feelings.

"What is this?" he murmured, rattling a telegraph flimsy whose origin was something called the 223rd Personnel Administration Detachment, Orly Sector. "I go to college for eight years, do all my internships, serve ten years as staff physician in some of the best hospitals in New England, and when I diagnose a man with cuts and bruises some faceless asshole pencil pusher overrules me and sends the patient to a trauma treatment center with facilities that make Johns Hopkins look like a storefront clinic. How can they do this to me?"

King, standing at attention in front of Kruger's portable desk, sympathized. "I think it's outrageous, sir."

"If I had the time, I'd track this down. Turn it over to the Adjutant General's Office for investigation."

"Don't blame you, sir."

"You realize, don't you, that they may hold you there for a whole damned month, poking your ribs and giving you an enema now and then, when all you got is a bump on the head and a couple of stitches in your ass?"

"Outrageous, sir."

"Makes me wish I'd specialized in gynecology."

"Can't we just ignore all this and return me to duty, sir? I'm only a couple of days away from my aerial gunnery certification."

Kruger readjusted his pince-nez and glared at him. "Are you suggesting that I willfully disobey an order, young man? Do I look like someone who'd do that?"

"Not at all, sir. It just seems so unfair—"

"As a doctor who has seen everything, I can assure you that all of life is unfair." Kruger's lower lip quivered.

"Yes, sir."

"You wouldn't believe the things I've seen."

"I'm sure, sir."

After a silence, Kruger sat up in his chair, squared his shoulders, adjusted his white jacket, and said with ill-disguised self-pity, "So be on your way, soldier."

"But, sir. My gunnery certification—"

"Be gone, I say. Obey your orders."

❊❊❊

The 301st Base Hospital was headquartered in a château with many tile-roof turrets and large, squat stone chimneys, and its auxiliary buildings and all-weather tents covered acres of lush meadows and gentle, manicured hills. The only evidence of war in the neighborhood was the spread of large olive-drab automobiles parked neatly near the entrance and the coming and going of ambulances and motorcycle dispatch riders bearing the Red Cross insignia. The adjacent lawns and gardens and their occasional fountains were dotted with bandaged men in pajamas and robes, some in wheelchairs and some leaning on crutches, looking bored.

King didn't wait. He went directly to the admissions desk in the huge, vaulted entrance hall, where, assuming his most brisk, commanding military hauteur, he demanded of the nurse, "A phone. I must have access to a military phone. One with connections to the base at Villeneuve."

"Well—" She blinked her blue eyes and considered the bandage wrapped about his head.

"This is a war-important matter having to do with an aircraft accident."

"Well, the superintendent's office over there has a phone with theaterwide capabilities. But its use is highly restricted. For hospital administration only—"

"General Pershing will be most grateful."

"Well, the administrator is in the city at the moment. I suppose it'll be all right. But don't take too long, please."

It took him five minutes to get through to First Pursuit, then another two to reach the 95th.

"Sergeant Edelmann speaking."

"This is Lieutenant King."

"Well, hello there, sir. I hear—"

"I want you to stop screwing around in my life."

"*Moi?*"

"You understand? Stop screwing around in my life, or I'll nail your balls to a fence post."

"Whatever do you mean, sir?"

"You know goddamn well what I mean. Phony telegrams to Cazaux. Getting me transferred two days before I get my gunnery rating. Screwing around."

"Sir, I heard you survived a crash and needed hospitalization. I wanted to be sure you got the best."

"I know you're trying to be nice to me, but your trying has just cost me my gunnery certification, goddammit! I want you to stop trying to be nice to me, you hear? I want—"

There was a heavy tapping on his shoulder, and he turned to look into the angry gray eyes of a full-eagle colonel.

"Who the hell are you?" the colonel barked. "What the hell are you doing in my office, using my phone?"

King put down the phone and snapped to attention. "Lieutenant John King, 95th Squadron, First Pursuit Group, sir. I'm trying to get back to my outfit—"

"Well, what you're really going to do, Lieutenant John Smart-Ass King, is get out of my goddamn office and back into hospital garb. Who the hell do you think you are, getting dressed, sneaking into my office, using my phone like you're in a goddamn hotel, trying to leave without proper dismissal papers?"

"Sir—"

The colonel motioned angrily to an orderly standing in the doorway. "Garrity, return this officer to his ward at once. Put him in proper garb and don't even let him go to the latrine without my express permission. Post a guard on him if you have to. Understand?"

❋❋❋

Neither Garrity nor anyone else knew what to do with King, of course, because the hospital had no records on him, no ward assignment had ever been made, and a call to First Pursuit only confirmed that King was not a German spy and that he was needed back there as soon as possible because the outfit was moving up to the Zone of Advance. But Garrity knew his priorities. When a bird colonel tells you to do something, there are no options.

"Come on, Lieutenant, be a good guy and sit there on that bench and don't do anything drastic. We'll work something out."

"I'm just trying to get back to my outfit. Haven't you heard? There's a war on."

"I mean it. I'm on your side. But when Colonel Ramsey gets sore, the ground shakes all the way to Staten Island. So whatever we do, we gotta keep cool and quiet. Wait a day or two. Ramsey has a big ego, a hot temper, but, thank God, one of the worst memories in the history of forgetfulness. To top things off today, he's expecting very important visitors from the States. Lots on what's left of his mind. So hang low for awhile, then just walk out. Okay?"

"Where do I eat? Shave? Sleep?"

Garrity pointed up the curving marble stairway. "See that door up there off the landing? It's a storage room. Has a faucet and a sink. I'll sneak you chow. Bring you a bedpan. Just stay the hell out of sight until nighttime. Ramsey never works nights, seeing as how he has a tootsie in town."

"You're a good guy, Garrity. And I don't want to get you in trouble. But I'm out of here the minute you aren't looking. You know that, don't you?"

Garrity nodded ruefully. "Yeah. Yeah, I know. But give me enough time to think of an alibi in case His Nibs overcomes his memory loss and wants to see you. Okay?"

They shook hands, and King trotted up the stairs to the storage room.

He had been sitting on a crate, staring out the slit window, trying to hurry nightfall along by wishing hard, when a small convoy of American Red Cross cars rolled up the long driveway and pulled to a halt in the paved area below the mezzanine. Officers dressed to the nines swarmed the driveway, leaping to the cars' flanks, bustling about, holding doors open, clicking heels, saluting, and generally making a big fuss. Ramsey, with a spotless white physician's coat over his class A uniform and a stethoscope draped about his neck, hurried down the stone steps, hands held out in greeting, and a tall man in civilian clothes brought forth an elegant woman from the shadows of the largest Cadillac. The introductions were made, and the woman, slipping her arm under his, smiled up radiantly at her escort.

Mary Lou Whiting.

And she was giving an admiring smile to Lawton Bigelow, the Philadelphia Red Cross honcho.

King, sick and shaken, scurried down the stairs, slid out a side service door, and, hitching a ride on the main road, was back at Villeneuve by nightfall.

Damn her. Damn her. Why doesn't she stay out of my life? A whole world away, then here she is. Smiling at that supercilious fop. Damn.

Chapter 26

The leadership of both parties in the Senate, taken aback by the swiftness with which Murray, one of their favorite predictable and somewhat stupid workhorses, had vanished from their ranks, was at first unsure how to handle his replacement, the maverick independent congressman, Thaddeus Slater. However, since Slater had been appointed by a governor whose party was the majority, the decision was to let Slater hold membership in the committees closest in equivalence to those on which he'd served in the House. There was, of course, a lot of grumbling in committee conferences, but Slater was universally recognized to be such a dangerous and treacherous commodity, there was little appetite for open opposition. Simply put, he had fixed too many wagons in both parties. So the consensus was that he be endured until his appointment ran out, and maybe the gods would be just and have him lose his seat in the next general election.

For Slater himself, this idea was highly amusing. Lose an election? Not very damned likely. In fact, after a term or two in the Senate he might even consider a run for the White House. Yet second thought told him that a senator could make more money, get more done, and have more fun than any president ever could, so this area of interest lacked heat. Perhaps when he'd done it all, when he was sated and bored with lack of further challenge, he might permit himself to be drafted into candidacy.

Since he was now a junior member of the Senate Armed Services Committee and chairman of the Military Aviation Subcommittee, he was receiving an incredible number of overtures from interests abroad—primarily aircraft manufacturers and their suppliers and vendors.

"Ned, did you see this letter from the Benoit Moteurs D'Avion in Beauvin-Nancy, France?"

"Of course, Senator. I see all your mail."

"What do you think?"

"It's an interesting invitation that could work to your advantage. Since they want to show you their latest achievement in aircraft engine design, it could provide an excellent rationale for that trip to France you've been contemplating. It would get you over there in the thick of things without having to pull in any of your markers with the De Havilland people, or with the others at the Royal Aircraft Establishment."

"I was thinking the same. Besides, the French have been noticeably cool in their relations with me, and now that I'm in the Senate and the war is really heating up and their needs are intensifying, they may be more, well, friendly."

"Maybe."

"You don't sound convinced."

"I simply don't trust the French."

"Ha. I don't trust anybody."

"You trust me, don't you, Senator?"

"I especially don't trust you. But you're all I've got."

They laughed together.

Raymond glanced at the clock. "Your interviewer is waiting in the anteroom. I told him eleven. It's that now."

"Who is it again?"

"Darrel Montagne, lead editorial writer for the Wilmington evening paper."

"What's he want?"

"Your views on the future of military aviation."

"Why?"

"The Wilmington city council is considering the establishment of an airport large enough to handle all kinds of aircraft, military included."

Slater sighed. "Send him in."

Montagne proved to be a slight, professorial type with thick eyeglasses and a wispy mustache. He carried a briefcase and held his hat to his chest, as if he were saluting a passing flag. Slater stood up and held out his hand. "Ah, Mr. Montana. Delighted to meet you. Looking forward to this. I read your material a lot."

"Montagne."

"What?"

"My name is Montagne, Senator."

"Isn't that what I said?"

"You said Montana."

"Oh. So sorry. Before you arrived I was speaking at length with a gentleman in Helena. Must have been a mental carry-over, eh? Ha-ha." He motioned to a wing chair. "Please sit down. Coffee? Cigar?"

"No, thank you."

"So, then. How can I help you, Mr. Montagne?"

"Well, sir, as you've no doubt been reading, the members of the Wilmington city council have been severely divided over the question of whether the city can afford an airport large enough to accommodate all kinds of aircraft—civilian and military. The bone of contention is basically the fact that no one is able to predict with any precision the future of aviation. There are all kinds of claims, some extravagant, others quite cautionary. I thought that you, as one steeped in the problems of military aviation, might have a few ideas I can work into an article on the subject." He paused, checking his notes. "I'd like to lead off with your personal involvement with aircraft. You are a recognized authority on military aviation, and I think our readers would like to know how often you, yourself, have flown. Are you a pilot, perhaps? If not, how frequently do you go aloft with our flying men? The kind of ironclad credentials a man in your position most certainly must have. I think our readers would really like to know that kind of thing about you."

"Well, first let me say, Mr. Montagne, that I have always had high regard for your newspaper and the community it serves. In fact, with the heavy schedule that's belabored me over the past months, thanks to the war and the recent need to step into the shoes of the very capable Senator Murray, I've been considering a short vacation. You know. Sun, beaches. Sand dunes. Sails on the horizon. I have my eye on Wilmington. Yes, siree. And as soon—"

"Excuse me, Senator. I'm from Wilmington, Delaware. We have no sand or beaches there. Just a rather dirty river."

Slater suddenly seized his head in both hands and slumped, moaning. "Oh, Lord, here it comes again. The aching, the dizziness." His foot pressed the emergency bell button mounted on the floor in the desk well. "Please, Mr. Montagne, would you call in my assistant—I'm quite ill, and he knows what to do." Montagne leaped to his feet and ran to throw open the door. He came face to face with Raymond, who was hurrying to enter. "Quick, someone help, please! The senator has taken ill—"

"Thank you, Mr. Montagne. The senator has headache spells. Dizziness. Loses his train of thought. Nothing serious. I'll take over from here. It would help, though, if you were to give the senator a rain check."

"Of course, of course. I'm so sorry—"

"Thank you for your understanding. I'm sure you won't mention this to anybody before the senator has you back as his guest in the Senate dining room."

"Certainly not. I am not a gossip, Mr. Raymond."

"That's why the senator values you so much. Thank you again. You'll receive his invitation in an early mail."

When they were alone again, Slater leaned across the desk, his face livid. "You son of a bitch! Why didn't you tell me that simple bastard was from Delaware?"

"Slow down, Senator. I reminded you of his visit the first thing this morning. And his letter requesting the interview was on the desk, right in front of you. All you had to do was glance at it. The letterhead is huge."

"I was caught flat-footed, goddammit! Don't ever do that to me again!"

Raymond said evenly, "I try very hard to keep you out of these kinds of things. That's exactly why I had that bell put into my office, the button under your desk. To help you escape when you haven't done your homework. When your mouth runs ahead of your brain."

Slater's eyes slitted, and he shook a forefinger. "Watch it, Neddie-boy. Don't push it. I'll fire your ass."

"That's not possible, Senator."

"Oh, no? Why the hell not?"

"Because I've just quit."

Raymond did an about-face and strode out the door.

※※※

Slater sat, slumped and unmoving. Eventually the rapid heartbeat slowed and the heat in his face dissipated, and when he finally sat up and looked around, the afternoon was already sending long, low shafts of sunlight through the west windows. He opened the lower desk drawer, brought out the scotch and a glass, and had downed a heavy slug when a knocking on the door was followed by Miss Agatha, the Number Two girl, who peered in apologetically.

"Pardon me, Senator, but Major Carpenter is out here. He says that it's important."

"Where's Ned?"

She seemed confused. "Why, ah, he left for the day. He said he'd be back tonight to clear his desk, or something."

"Tell Carpenter I'm busy. Come back tomorrow."

"I can't do that, Senator," Carpenter said airily over Agatha's shoulder. "The war could be lost before tomorrow."

Slater wiped his face with his handkerchief. "I'm not in the mood. I don't feel so good."

"Hey, I invented that process. Best cure is about four more doses of that scotch. For each of us. I don't feel so good, either, and I always feel bad when I don't feel good. Scotch makes bad better. More scotch makes better better."

Slater waved him in. "Oh, all right," he grumped. "The day's already ruined."

Carpenter advanced on the desk, pulled another glass from the drawer, and sloshed it half full of whiskey.

"Easy, dammit," Slater said. "That isn't iced tea you're pouring there."

"Thank God."

"It costs a freaking fortune."

"Worth every cent." Carpenter drank deeply, then, fluttering his eyelids and holding fingers to his chest in a maidenly way, coughed delicately. "My, my. You certainly do make a lovely iced tea, dearie."

Slater shifted irritably in his chair. "So what's so important you gotta break into my afternoon?"

Carpenter sat in the wing chair, swirling what was left in his glass. "As the military aide to a member of the Senate Armed Services Committee, I must have your permission to go to Europe. England, then France, to be more specific."

"Why?"

"I think Fontaine is wheeling and dealing over there. I want to see what he's up to. I can't do that hanging around the Bensonville plant."

"I told you I don't trust that bastard."

"I don't, either. That's why I'm drinking your scotch."

"So what are you on to?"

"I don't know yet. Fontaine's living to the letter of his agreement with you. He's turning out DH-4s like he's running a doughnut shop. Lots and lots of your constituents running around, sawing boards, splashing paint, falling off ladders, feeling great about getting regular pay. Agreement-wise, things couldn't be better. But there's something else. Something I can't quite get a hold on yet."

Slater drank some scotch. "Like what?"

"He's been trading a lot of mail with somebody in London, another somebody in Paris, still another somebody in Epinal. He reads the letters, then either burns them or locks them away in his office safe. And they sure ain't love letters, unless his sweetie wears aircraft dope as perfume."

"You've seen these letters?"

"Only the envelopes, the postmarks, and stamps."

Slater sipped more scotch and sat, thinking. Then he asked, "So what's your plan?"

"First I want to try an end run. Talk to some of our top military guys. General Foulois for rear echelon planning. Billy Mitchell for Zone of Advance combat tactics. Hugh Trenchard about long-distance night bombing. That kind of thing."

"So what good would that do?"

"I'll feed Fontaine's name into all the discussions and see what falls out. I hear the right thing, I tell you, and you pounce."

Slater thought some more, then nodded. "As a matter of fact, I've been invited by Benoit, a French aircraft engine manufacturer, to visit his plant in Beauvin-Epinal this month. You and I can go over on the same boat, split, then keep in touch."

Carpenter grinned. "Bravo. No wonder so many people vote for you."

※※※

Slater returned to the office around nine o'clock that evening.

Raymond was there, hunched over in the lamplight, filling some cardboard boxes with desk items and personal reference books. He looked up, startled. "What are you doing here?"

"I came to say I'm sorry. To ask you not to leave."

Raymond sank into a chair. "I'll be damned. You're apologizing?"

"Yes."

"This is a first."

"Yes. And I hope I won't have to do it again. Ever."

There was a silence.

Raymond spread his hands. "I don't know what to say."

"Say you won't leave."

"Why?"

Slater went to the window and stood there, looking out at the city lights. "I don't know what I'd do without you. I depend on you for so much. You even tell me which tie to wear, for crissake."

"Well—"

"You are the only person I have in the world, the only person who knows all about me and likes me anyhow."

"I never said I like you."

"True. But I can tell."

More silence.

"I don't know what I'd do without you, Ned."

"Know what? You're the only one I have, too."

"So, are we friends again?"

"We're dirty rats. Both of us."

"I don't want to be. But I don't know how not to be."

"Same here."

Raymond crossed to the window and, standing beside him, put an arm around Slater's shoulders. After a time, he said, "Awful lonely out there."

"Yeah. Not so bad now, though."

Chapter 27

The rain had finally stopped, and the morning was soft, clear, redolent of spring. The three Nieuports were sitting in ragged alignment in front of the hangars, their noses pointed east, as if they were already sniffing out the enemy beyond the horizon. Richards, the B Flight commander, would be leading the patrol, which he had described earlier in the mess hut as a familiarization exercise to acquaint King and the other new pilot, Freeman, with some of the Toul Sector and whatever wildlife might be spotted there.

They stood aft of the planes now, tightening helmet straps, resettling the goggles on their foreheads, wiggling fingers in their gloves, and going through the little fussings that always preceded flight.

"The Toul Sector is a relatively quiet part of the battle zone," Richards was saying. "Headquarters has assigned the new, untested Yank units here because there's a lot to be learned without too much of a risk. The Germans also assign their new people here, for the same reason. But we have to remember, the Germans also assign some of their hotshots here for a kind of vacation. So if you see a Kraut plane, be wary. The pilot may be as dumb as we are, or may be a Richthofen catching some R & R. Treat them all with respect." He turned and gave the line chief a wave. "Let's crank 'em up, Fred."

King vaulted into the cockpit of No. 23, his ship for the morning, and watched for the others to acknowledge their readiness. Fred Toomey, the line chief, moved his men to position, and, after the switch off was heard from each pilot, the propellers were pulled through and the cylinders were primed. Richards waved, switches were activated, and the rotary engines barked into a thunderous blatting.

After the handlers pulled away the wheel chocks, Richards led the trio out to the downwind turnaround, the handlers trotting along, tugging or pushing wingtips as needed. Once the position was right, they sat there, engines roaring. Finally Richards nodded and waved a hand forward. The handlers raised their arms high and stepped away, and the Nieuports leaped ahead like startled animals.

King was still not too confident with the rotary engine, and at a time when he should have been feeling the thrill of his first takeoff on his first combat assignment, he was squinting and pursing his lips in the struggle to keep the damn torque from carrying him off to starboard. But once the landing gear stopped its thumping and banging and the ship became buoyant, he was able to keep the trim that allowed him to look around and capture the sense of flying.

They climbed to five thousand feet, and up here the morning was a magnificent panorama, a huge sweep of cerulean blue sky with filmy pink and gold altostratus clouds accenting the horizon to the northeast. Below, the earth was a mosaic of variegated greens and browns, with dashes of purple and gray and magenta, and whatever trace of war lay there wasn't readily apparent. Above it all, their machines rose and fell easily on the hidden currents, and King felt a rush of special kinship with the others, who sat so near yet so far in a universe filled with thunder and the sweet stink of hot oil.

He was glad they were being led by someone who knew the ropes. Richards was a first looie who had cut his teeth flying Camels with the Brits up near Cambrai and had been transferred to the Yank Air Service just before Christmas. He was an easygoing guy with bow legs and a cleft chin, and King liked him because he never put on airs about his two victories confirmed by the Brits.

The first inkling of an attack was when a heavy shadow flashed across King's upper wing, and he was still puzzling over the phenomenon when he heard the tack-tacking of machine guns and felt, rather than saw, a return of the racing shadow. Instinctively he rolled his plane into a hard vertical turn to starboard, feeling that torque helping him along, and then he glanced frantically about, searching for the shadow.

In an almost absurd coincidence, he saw a plane directly ahead and somewhat lower, a dark gray machine with large black and white crosses on its wings. It seemed to be hovering, dangling and yawing, in the very center of his ring sight. His right hand closed on the trigger lever on the control stick, and he leaned forward, heart thumping, eyes wide, as he closed in on the German plane ahead.

But wait. A man was there. A man with a tan leather helmet and goggles that glinted in the sunlight as he turned his head. King suddenly realized that he was about to kill a man.

His hand hesitated.

And then the German machine was gone.

Damn!

Circling wildly, he saw that there were three Germans, the dark gray one, another with white stripes on its fuselage, and a third with a bright red tail. And as he watched, he saw the dark gray machine—his dark gray machine—close with Richards's Nieuport, the one with the big No. 5 on the wing, and rattle off a long burst.

Richards's Nieuport was there, then it wasn't.

What was there was a blossom of yellowish white flame and a fountain of black smoke that threw shredded fabric and torn tin into a cascade that arced down the sky in a mad roiling.

Frozen in shock, unable to breathe, eyes wide in disbelief, King watched until the tumbling smoke and flame disappeared into the mosaic below.

In a sudden return to reality, he was seized by great fear, and he hunched his shoulders and sank into his seat, seeking to make the smallest target possible. But when he finally dared to send frantic glances around, he discovered that he was alone in the sky. No Germans. No trace of Freeman's Nieuport.

Nothing.

Just a huge sweep of blue and the dawning of the worst of thoughts.

He hadn't fired a shot.

And his frozen moment, his aberrant flicker of compassion, had spared an enemy and killed a friend.

❋❋❋

He flew for a time, trying to deal with these things. The shock and shame would simply not let go, and it was a period of idle circling, his mind jammed with self-accusation and contempt. Then came recollected mother's homilies about no failure incapable of correction, no sin beyond ultimate forgiveness, yet the memories did nothing but deepen his guilt. Next he sought redeeming excuses—he'd been caught by surprise; the sun glare had blinded him; the gray plane had been faster, more maneuverable; his panicky hunching in the cockpit wasn't cowardice, it was a boxer's flinching before an oncoming blow. When these anguished fits accomplished nothing, the void in him began to fill with frustration, which became anger, which in turn enlarged into a nova-like explosion of rage—an absolute refusal to accept himself, endure himself, for one moment longer.

Get out of my life, John King! Leave me alone, you miserable freak! I want nothing more to do with you!

❋❋❋

Where was he? In an airplane. High above...where? He looked around, then down.

It was still morning, with the sun in the east, so it followed that home and safety were to starboard, enemy country to port. That river down there, running roughly north to south: the Meuse, perhaps? In his briefing, Richards had shown a chart with the Meuse appearing as a major feature. St. Mihiel that way. Epinal that way. Below, a grayish scar tore across the countryside. A smear of smoke and haze. Trenches? Shell holes? Rubble? It was hard to see detail from this altitude. He must get closer....

He let the Nieuport sink in a fast power glide, setting the nose on what appeared in the distance to be the remains of a village. Just to the left of that was a line of observation balloons, fat, ugly, shaped like swollen genitalia.

Whose balloons?

The answer came quickly. The Nieuport jumped, then staggered when three flashes close by, accompanied by severe concussion, left a series of shrapnel slashes in the starboard lower wing fabric forward of the aileron.

His rage still seething, King threw the ship into a sharp spiral, and the ground came up at an astonishing speed. He flattened out just above a ravaged forest and, banking quickly to port, had a clear, straight run at the first balloon in line. The air around him became a livid tapestry of tracer streaks and light artillery flashes, and he struggled numbly to keep the plane on course.

Defiant anger became a weapon. He heard it in his mind:

Turn-around time, John King! Bye-bye, you goddamn second-frigging-class poor boy, hand-wringing son of a bitch! Hello, you hell-on-wheels, major league Kraut-stomper! Whee-hoo! Yah-hah!

He centered the ring sight on the black cross amidships. When the balloon seemed ready to envelope him, he squeezed the trigger lever, and the Vickers guns broke into a raging duet. Then miraculously he was past, and close behind there was an enormous surge of heat and concussion, and his rearview mirror showed him a tumbling fireball where the balloon had been.

The second balloon was ahead, slightly to port. A tap of rudder, a burst from the Vickers, and he was forced into a virtual ground-level turn to elude the subsequent explosion.

The anger had become a kind of elation.

It's John King, you bastards! The all-new John King, here to see that you lose your worthless, war-lovin' asses!

The third balloon had been reeled in on its cable and was swaying just above its winch truck.

Didn't like that last one? Wait'll you see this!

The Vickers crashed again, and the balloon and its truck and the small knot of men around it disappeared in a welter of flame and smoke.

Hey, you Wiener schnitzels! Yank my doodle, it's a dandy!

He realized suddenly that he was crying.

※※※

The Nieuport was finished.

The engine barely turning, it was clanking, grinding, and leaving a dirty brown oil smudge trailing behind. The fabric on the wings and fuselage was lacy with shrapnel gashes. The portside interplane struts were splintered, and one of them trailed a broken brace wire.

The machine settled quickly, lost its landing gear against a line of sandbags, then slid along on its belly, slewing clockwise through a field of barbed wire, until it rocked to a general collapse in a shell hole.

In an eerie vacuum, King sat in the battered cockpit, staring straight ahead. He was fully conscious, icy cold and trembling violently, yet aware of his sweat-soaked body, so wet it seemed to have turned his flight suit into a grotesque canteen. He raised a hand to tip his goggles so that the tears would run out.

Then other hands were on him, tugging.

"Cut that belt off him," someone said. "And get under his arms and lift slow, easy. We don't know how badly hurt he is."

"He looks okay, Sarge."

"Do what I say, goddammit!"

Chapter 28

The senator and his assistant, Ned Raymond, apparently looked on the voyage as a pleasure cruise, submarines and mines be damned. They'd spend a lot of time leaning on the bow railing and looking out to sea and gabbing, seeming to be oblivious to the fact that the rest of the ship was crammed to the funnels with troops and nurses and artillery horses. That the senatorial party enjoyed sea-gazing, private staterooms, and meals at the officers' mess was a development suiting Carpenter just fine, because, as a member of the party, he was given the isolation he needed to deal with the strange forces at work within him. Strange forces? *Well, not really.* General dissatisfaction, self-disgust? *Close.* A need to amount to something? *Yeah, sort of.*

In all the time he'd been in the Army, Carpenter had never given any passion to an understanding of just who did what, why and where. Devoted as he was to tomfoolery and the impromptu, his military life had been—as had high school and college—a matter of finding out what he needed to know when he needed to know it. As creaky Professor Drummond once said, "If they gave out medals for cramming for tests, Carpenter, you'd be all-star Olympics material." And so when he put on the uniform and mastered the flying machine driver trade, he was satisfied simply to know that, elsewhere in the Army, G-1 had to do with hiring and firing; G-2 was devoted to snooping; G-3 was concerned with getting shooters from here to there at the right time; and G-4 was responsible for groceries, wardrobe, and hardware. Wherever duty took him, he lived each day at a time, and, if he needed to know something gee-whiz specific about G-1 through G-4, he'd look up the pertinent hotshot and ask him all about it. The trick was to find who was pertinent and who was irrelevant.

But that was the peacetime army, when hiring and firing were virtually nonexistent, when intelligence was reading newspapers and detective novels, when troop movements and fighting were sand-table exercises, when chow and clothes and guns and vehicles were invariably antediluvian, and when flying was a matter of launching rubber-band-powered models in the park on Sundays.

When the most fearsome enemy was boredom.

Things were different these days.

One of the oddest differences was this new, indefinable seriousness Carpenter felt creeping into his attitudes.

Chewing his pencil and staring out the porthole, he thought about that now. If he had to choose any one place where it had begun, he'd have to name John King.

King seemed to be an amalgam of scared little boy and ancient esthete, at one moment wide-eyed, ebullient, and guileless, and within an instant, remote and haunted, as if seeing invisible grandeur, hearing inaudible symphonies. His letters, while brief and sparse, would range from deep philosophy to the latest barracks joke within the context of a few paragraphs. A wistfulness was there, a sense of unfulfillment and yearning to belong to something unspeakably important, only to be countered in the next breath by a kind of stiff-legged, purple-faced, egocentric defiance.

King's latest letter, delivered the day before embarkation, was different. Still short, still wistful, but somehow portentous. Carpenter picked it up and read it again. He stood quietly for a time, thinking, then he sighed, shook his head, folded the letter, and returned it to the bulkhead writing desk. After one more look at the sea, he went back to the work table and its maps and volumes of Billy Mitchell's eloquent bitching.

There was a tapping. The senator with another wild-ass idea, probably.

He smoothed his hair, buttoned his shirt, and crossed the little room to open the door.

It was the nurse's aide. Arlene? Maxine?

She giggled. "I told you I'd sneak up here to see you. Didn't think I'd do it, did you?"

He pretended pleasure. "Well, well. You are the sneaky little one, aren't you. How'd you get past the A-Deck guard?"

She made a little moue. "You gotta ask?"

"Well—"

"Aren't you going to ask me in?"

"Oh. Oh, sure. Come on in." *What the hell's her name?*

She went to the porthole, glanced out, then turned to consider the room with mock awe. "All of this, just for you?"

"It is sort of overwhelming, isn't it?"

"You must be important, working for a senator and all."

"Correction. I am a citizen. Citizens elect senators. The senator works for me."

She giggled again. "My, oh, my. You are a caution. You had the whole bunch of us girls laughing to tears down there at the captain's coffee this morning."

"Coffee does that to me."

"A real caution. My friend Deborah said to me, 'Jeannine, did you ever, I mean ever, meet a man who made you laugh like this?' And I said, 'No, he's really and truly a caution.' And I meant it."

"I bet you did, Jeannine."

She made a little pirouette, then sank onto the bunk. "Mmm. Soft. Not like those boards they give us girls to sleep on."

"Want to take a nap? Go ahead. I got a lot of work to do. So make yourself to home." He glanced at his watch. "What time do you want me to wake you up?"

Her uniform was already a small pile on the floor, and, stepping out of her underwear, she moved to him with languid purpose. "On my deck, they take roll call at 1800. That gives us two hours and four minutes," she said.

"I got a lot of work to do—"

"You sure do, buddy-boy."

He took her elbows and pushed her gently away. "How old are you, Jeannine? Sixteen? Seventeen, maybe?"

She made another face. "Hey, I'm twenty-two."

He laughed softly. "Yeah. And I'm eighty."

"What's the matter? You don't like me?"

"I like you too much for what you have in mind. The average age of nurses' aides they're sending to France is what, eighteen? That means a bunch of you is younger. And you're younger."

She pouted, "So what?"

He stooped, picked up her clothes and, pressing them into her arms, said, "Get dressed, kid."

"Lotsa guys'd like to get their hands on me, buddy."

"I'm not lotsa guys. In my time I had so many women and girls I had to keep a score card. I could go down there on your deck right now and have any one of your pals I'd want. But it's too easy. And you're too easy by far. I like classy women. Hard to get women. So put on your clothes and get your little butt downstairs where you belong. Get classy, for cripe's sake."

After she'd left he sat on the bunk and laughed.

Aloud he said, "What the hell's happening to you, William J. Carpenter? You never passed up a piece in your life. And there was never one of them that could in any way be counted as classy."

He couldn't decide if he was laughing or crying.

Passed by Censor 4320

Capt. William J. Carpenter

c/o General Headquarters

American Expeditionary Forces

Paris (Please forward)

Dear Bill:

I was postal duty officer today, and I had to ride a camion to the APO sub office near Villeneuve to pick up the mail for the squadron. It was raining the proverbial cats and dogs, and the camion was ootching along a miserable back-country road. The rain slanted down, insistent and cold for this time of year, and I remember that my loneliness was intense. Around a puddled curve we passed a huge enclosure made of high wooden stakes and barbed wire, and it was totally crammed, so crowded with German prisoners that there was literally no room for them to sit, even in the mud, and they had to stand, shoulder to shoulder, propped against one another, motionless and numb, with their eyes shut against the rotten wind.

In a corner of the compound, near the road, I saw a small soldier squeezed into a corner, sodden and pathetic in his over-large field coat and coal-scuttle helmet. As we lumbered by, I got a good look at him. He was no more than thirteen, maybe fourteen years old, and he was crying his heart out and calling for his Mutti.

He was my <u>enemy</u>?

This sounds mawkish, absurd, but it was all I could do to keep from swinging off the truck and holding that poor kid in my arms.

Oh, God, Bill, where is the sense in all this? What are we trying to prove, and to whom and why?

Your friend,

John

Chapter 29

Captain Bianco, C.O. of the 38th Pursuit Squadron, was unhappy and blunt-speaking. He presided at a tin desk in his office, a cubicle built of rough-hewn boards and tar paper with a jerry-rigged corner window that overlooked a line of tent hangars and elderly Nieuports dozing in the sun.

"This is a brand-new squadron, King," Bianco rasped. "The only one of its members to have any combat experience is you, with a single patrol on your duty file. One patrol and three balloons confirmed destroyed, and that bizarre mix makes you the technical hotshot in this outfit. But I'm the real hotshot. It's my squadron. What I say goes. You have a problem with that?"

"No, sir."

"Well, you should. The only reason you've been assigned to this unit is that nobody else wants you. Except for me, every man-Jack in this outfit is a stumble-bum or an anti-social misfit. I'll leave it to you to decide which category you fit into."

"I'd say a bit of both, sir."

Bianco took the pencil from behind his ear and pointed it at King as if he were leveling a pistol. "Don't get smartsy-fartsy with me, Lieutenant."

"I was trying to answer your suggestion, sir."

"You speak only when I ask you to."

There was a moment of silence.

"Well?"

"Well what, sir?"

"You didn't acknowledge with a 'yes, sir.'"

"You didn't ask me to speak, sir."

Bianco, already tired of the game, decided to move on. He glanced at the sheaf of papers on the desk and cleared his throat, a schoolteacher preparing to review a pupil's list of offenses.

"It says here that you are not a team player, that you have shown no willingness to participate in the give-and-take camaraderie so essential to unit morale. You hold yourself aloof, you address your fellow officers in lofty, supercilious terms, you take offense at the natural ribaldry and exuberance of the young warriors who will win this war for the United States of America. So it says here. Any comment?"

"No, sir."

Bianco squinted. "What do you mean, 'no, sir'?"

"I mean no, sir."

"You don't wish to dispute the charges?"

"Are they charges, sir? Or merely a statement of someone's opinions?"

"Ho. You're trying to go lawyer on me now?"

"No, sir."

"Well, then. What do you have to say about all this?"

"Essentially, I agree with the complaints, sir. I am all that they claim."

"What do you propose to do about it?"

"I see nothing I can do about it. I am what I am."

Bianco leaned forward, elbows on the desk. "So what are you then, Lieutenant?"

"I am a soldier, sir. I will do my duty."

"And what is that?"

"To keep the enemy from killing more of us, sir."

"That's a weird way to put it. Your job is to destroy the enemy."

"All respect, sir: I see it to be my duty to destroy the enemy's ability to kill you and me. I will do everything in my power to destroy German equipment and combat potential. If German people die because they are using that equipment or are involved in that potential, it's a matter of indifference to me. I have nothing against the common German soldier, but I will try to make him militarily impotent. That's my overriding task."

Bianco sank back in his chair, disbelief in his eyes. "My God, you do speak lofty. 'Militarily impotent.' 'Overriding task.' Shee-it."

The tension in the room was tangible.

"You say you have nothing against the German soldier. You don't hate the enemy?"

"He's just another brave, lonely, put-upon fellow who speaks a different language and wears a different uniform. If he gets in my way in my effort to destroy equipment, I'll kill him. But not because I hate him."

"But he's trying to kill you, man..."

"I define that as getting in my way. The same as if you picked up that .45 pistol lying on your desk there and tried to shoot me. I'd kill you first. I don't hate you. I don't care about you one way or the other. But if you tried to shoot me, I'd see that as getting in my way, and I'd make you dead, very fast."

Bianco was silent again. King waited. Outside, toward the hangars, an engine barked into life, snarling and coughing. It rattled, emitted a series of popping sounds, then died. The quiet was even deeper now.

"You're a very, very weird young man."

"That's true, sir."

"How long ago did you develop this, ah, bizarre, ah, philosophy? Do you belong to some kind of sect or something?"

"I belong to nothing, sir. I developed this philosophy, as you call it, two weeks ago, when I was sitting in my wrecked plane. After my compassion for humanity spared a German and killed my flight leader."

Bianco considered that for a time. Finally he sighed. "You're mad."

"In all probability, sir."

Bianco pushed back his chair, glanced at his watch, and arose. "Be that as it may, tomorrow at 0800 I am leading our first patrol over the lines. There'll be you and three other misfits. Since you are the only one with any experience, I expect you to fly cover for me. The squadron needs me. I mustn't be lost yet."

"I'll be following your every move, sir. Any enemy who tries to get at you will be getting in my way."

Bianco paused by the door and looked back at King, a wry smile nudging the corner of his lips. "That's a comforting thought."

"Yes, sir."

※※※

They took off at 0810 hours, the delay due to a local shower that came, obscured the field for seven minutes, then moved on to the south, leaving new puddles, mixed clouds, and a slightly lower temperature. As they climbed for altitude, heading northeast, King noted that the other three pilots, despite the misfit label applied to them by Bianco, handled their machines with obvious skill. Lovelace, Radimer, and Kline. He'd shaken their hands at mess last night, but there had been only the most perfunctory conversation, and he decided that they were all pretty much the way he was when it came to frat house chin-chin. As a matter of fact, the officers' mess, with about half the roster there, picking at bully beef and beans, was like one of those no-talking monasteries. Clattering dishes and clouds of tobacco smoke and an occasional shuffling of chairs, and that was it.

King settled into the business of flying.

They were in a ragged staircase echelon, with Bianco leading from the low step, King next upper right, then Kline, Lovelace, and Radimer. The formation rocked and loosened a bit when it flew through a cluster of rain clouds. But then they were in bright morning sunlight again, leaving trails of evaporating mist. King used his scarf to wipe the water from his face and goggles, grateful that the collar of his flying suit hadn't been penetrated.

They flew to the Meuse, then turned north. Peering down, King had a new sense of the titanic forces in play in the ground mists below. An imaginary line across the woods and fields and hills and valleys. Two multitudes divided by the line, each divided into divisions assembled side by side in a wall designed to attack or repel. The divisions grouped to form army corps, and the corps grouped to form armies, and the armies grouped as expeditionary forces, one sent out in 1914 by the kaiser, the other just arrived at the behest of Woodrow Wilson and the Congress. Divisions in line, divisions behind them in reserve echelons, and, compacted among the divisions, supply groups, depots, motor pools, pack animal pens, and ammo dumps, all designed to arm and feed and clothe and move the twenty-seven thousand men making up the infantry, artillery, engineers, medical units, signal groups, supply elements, transport assemblies, and headquarters contingents of each division. Each host on both sides of the line designed to expand in the attack or contract in defense. Two huge, complex, lethal accordions.

But from here, not a sign of any of it. No movement. No definitive features. Only a matlike spread of smoke and mist.

Two sharp claps sounded behind them, yellow flashes replaced instantly by puffs of black smoke. "Archie," the German anti-aircraft artillery under the haze a mile below, was alerting German fliers in the area that there was an American intrusion.

A brief machine-gun stutter came from Radimer's ship at the top right slot. He was waving and pointing upward and toward the northeast, where King counted seven dark dots cruising in a roughly parallel course just above a line of thin clouds. As he watched, they turned due west, which put them above and ahead on a right-to-left path that would put them in attack position. King glanced at Bianco, who waved an arm and pointed upward in the signal to climb.

Bianco's patrol had gained another five hundred feet by the time the enemy flight began its curving slant downward. King recognized the machines as late-model Albatroses, the D-5 version, each with its top wing and tail painted a gaudy color. They came on in a sliding rush, their guns winking. Bianco pumped a fist, signaling the free-for-all, and the two forces melded in a wheeling, plunging vortex of thundering engines and clattering gunfire.

King followed as Bianco's Nieuport went into a vertical turn and closed on a yellow-tail Albatros. But coming in from the right flank was another with a blue top wing, and it was an easy matter for King to touch in some rudder and give its pilot a brief distracting burst. To his surprise, the "hip shot" of warning had actually connected, and the German machine turned on its back and flashed past no more than fifty yards away, hellfire boiling along its fuselage.

Bianco had scored, too. The Albatros directly ahead of him staggered, then, as it fell into a steep spiral, its starboard wings folded into fluttering trash. In that instant, King's plane moved directly alongside Bianco's, hanging there long enough for him to trade nods with the squadron leader. As they both entered a tight circling to the left, another Albatros, this one in hot pursuit of Lovelace, swept through King's ring sight. Another quick correction, another hip shot, and the German plane fell like a stone, spinning.

"Ladies and gentlemen," King said into the wind and motor roar, "the U.S. Army is proud to present John King and His Magic Machine Guns."

He felt a smile forming.

Bianco pulled up in a gently climbing turn, taking stock. Three Albatroses were in a fast, descending retreat to the east. The other four were history. Bianco raised his right hand and made the circular "form up" signal favored by the old cavalry, and the others sidled into formation to his upper right.

I'm now an ace, King thought. *Three balloons and two planes. And I have yet to unpack my footlocker.*

He tried to decide how he felt about that.

He felt nothing.

❋❋❋❋

King, Radimer, Kline, and Lovelace stood in a little knot in the shade of Hangar A, watching silently as Bianco completed his inspection and made his way through the gang of mechanics and handlers swarming over the five Nieuports. As he approached, his flying boots made soft, squishing sounds in the sodden turf. Instinctively, because they thought he would expect it, they stiffened a bit and threw him a casual salute. He returned it with a small wave of his hand.

"At ease," he said in his rasping way.

They waited.

Bianco pulled off his helmet and goggles, and the breeze stirred his thinning brown hair. "You people," he said, somber, brows knitted in a frown against the noontime glare, "have a lot of work to do."

They waited again.

In the background, ground crews, staff, mess attendants, medics, motor pool personnel, and off-duty pilots began to gather, closing in slowly to hear their commander's assessment of their unit's first combat operation of the war.

Bianco said, "I counted four bullet holes in the rear fuselage of your machine, Radimer. Which means you permitted a Boche to get behind you. You, Kline, have two bullet tears in your right lower wing. Which means you permitted a Boche to get you with a deflection burst. And despite the fact that you shot down an Albatros, Lovelace, your machine shows no damage, which causes me to wonder if you are indeed the timid soul everybody says you are." He paused, took a breath, and centered his gaze on King. "And as for you, King, your assignment was to cover me at all times. This you did in the first attack on me, but in the second attack you destroyed my attacker only after he managed to put six rounds through my plane's upper left wing. This is a sign of sloppy coverage, and improvement is mandatory."

The only sounds were the breeze and the far-off call of a bird. Bianco sighed again and began to unbutton his flight suit.

"To summarize: In an engagement in which we were outnumbered by seven of their first-class pursuit planes to our five decrepit shit heaps, and wherein we destroyed four enemy aircraft and sent three running for the safety of their lines without a loss of our own, all I can say is that I'm so proud of you I could bust. If you people are indeed dimwit misfits, I'm telling headquarters that if they give me a thousand bastards as stupid and inept and gutless as you, we'll have this war over in a week. Tonight the 38th Pursuit Squadron drinks Hennessy cognac, and the drinks are on me."

The crowd stood in frozen disbelief, staring at Bianco as if he had just sung *Rigoletto*.

Bianco threw back his head and laughed in crazy delight, tossing his helmet and goggles into the air and dancing a little jig.

Suddenly the field echoed to the roaring laughter and cheers of the entire squadron.

And John King felt a moment of inner warmth.

It would have been better without the aching and the nagging, far-off sounds behind his forehead.

Passed by Censor 4322

Capt. William J. Carpenter

c/o General Headquarters

American Expeditionary Forces

Paris (Please forward)

Dear Bill:

As you've probably discerned by now, I'm a rather odd duck. I march to a drum very few others seem to hear, and I, myself, am often made aware of this at the least likely of times. I find that I fret about the importance of things that most people consider trivial, or irrelevant, or a pain in the butt. I tend to worry about the things I cannot change and at times lack the courage to change the things I can. I'm struck with the understanding that I'm the polar opposite of men like you—pragmatic, steady, confident, and with the grace to accept yourself without a hint of smugness. I, on the other hand, have become the dreamer, the woolgatherer, the artsy-craftsy dodo my father was.

My weirdness level is most apparent those times I inexplicably experience strange and incredibly realistic visions of what had to be an earlier life. I've told you about the strange, exhilarating visions I had when I was a mere baby, when I was a youngster, and later at Camp Dix, when I was a soldier cleaning garbage cans.

So now I get to the vision I had just yesterday, the one that triggered this idiotic letter. I was sitting on the stoop of a little stone farm building behind Hangar A, polishing my shoes for one of Captain Bianco's silly inspections. I glanced up to stare out across the field, and there, standing arm in arm in the sunlit meadow, watching me somberly from the medium distance, were my Mom and Dad. I stood up, simultaneously shocked and filled with joy, and tried to run to them, but with every step of mine they backed away, so that I knew I could run forever and they would remain out of reach. I tried to call out to them, but I couldn't make my voice work, and

I knew I was crying—feeling tears running down my cheeks. And then, as quickly as it had come, the vision disappeared, and I was sitting on the box, a boot in my hand, my face cool and dry, my heart heavy with sorrow and a dreary homesickness.

Even as I write now, I can't shake the feeling, and I am seriously wondering about my sanity.

Please, Bill, try to find the time to write me, to reassure me, to tell me that you will continue to hold me in high regard even if I do show signs of collapse and failure.

I miss you. I need you.

John

Chapter 30

Slater was pleased. The hotel accommodations simply had to be among the best in Paris. He and Raymond had been assigned a top floor suite, with tall casements and balconies framing splendid views of the Eiffel Tower and parks and an arc of the river that reflected the pastel tints of the adjacent mansions and spires. Fresh-cut flowers scented all the rooms, and the main salon featured a sideboard displaying ranks of wines and silver trays heaped with fruits and sweets.

"R.H.I.P., eh, Senator?" Raymond was grinning.

"What's that?"

"Army talk. 'Rank has its privileges.'"

Slater looked about him, beaming. "Indeed it does. Have you ever seen such a layout?"

"Only in my dreams." Lest he sound too gushy, Raymond made a joke. "Of course, the Freightyard Hotel in East St. Louis comes pretty close."

"Yes, it does, if you mean pretty close to cow plop."

They laughed together, as if this was the funniest of all ideas.

"I don't know about you," Slater said, "but I'm going to have about a gallon of that wine, plunk into a nice warm tub, and then do about ten hours in that big bed in the other room. All this traveling does a real job on me."

"As agendas go, that sounds like a good one. So count me in."

"What's up tomorrow?"

Raymond checked his memo pad. "A meeting at headquarters at eleven with General Foulois and his staff. They will send a car around for us. Subject: the need for congressional action—meaning appropriations, of course—vis-à-vis land acquisition for American facilities in France and Belgium. I've noted a by-the-way here: Foulois is scheduled to become chief of aviation service, 1st Army, at Toul. This will put him over Colonel Billy Mitchell, who, until the move, has been serving as chief of Air Service, First Corps."

"Hoo," Slater said. "Unless I miss my guess, there'll be real fireworks over that one. Mitchell is a gladiatin', egotistical pile driver who thinks he invented military aviation and considers Foulois a West Point diplomat who'll make the Air Service a branch of the State Department. My bet is that Foulois will fire Mitchell's ass in two days."

"Depends on how bad each wants to win the war, Senator. They both need each other, and General Pershing needs both of them. It'll be interesting to watch, all right."

Slater selected a bottle of brandy from the sideboard, popped the cork, and poured a liberal dose into a snifter. "Want one of these?"

"Please."

They took their glasses to the salon and sank into overstuffed chairs facing the city beyond the windows.

"Speaking of Pershing, what's our drill with him again?"

"After our lunch with Foulois, it's off to Chaumont, where Pershing makes his headquarters. The next day a number of meetings, then a banquet in the evening as an occasion to introduce you to the attachés of France, England, and Italy at U.S. headquarters. The following day, Friday, will require you to visit several base hospitals, where you will pin Purple Hearts on some soldiers. The Paris bureau of the *Herald Tribune* will host a press party for you that evening, and this will give you another opportunity to meet and be photographed with more French dignitaries. Great for future election campaigns."

"What'll we do with Carpenter during all this razzmatazz?"

"Let's just keep him out of the way, Senator. Let him do his airplane stuff with the tech people, and so on."

"All right," Slater agreed absently, already on another thought. "You know, I keep feeling that I really should do something about the Benoit invitation. I hate like hell to take the time to run all the way down to the Swiss border just to shake hands and talk airplane engines, but diplomacy is diplomacy, and those people might come in handy someday."

"Good thinking, Senator. Couldn't agree more. So we'll just cut Carpenter loose from our agenda for all of the next five days, providing he lets us know how to get in touch in case we need him. I, for one, will be glad he's not around. He has an annoying way of elbowing into things. Demanding your attention."

Slater gave him a teasing glance. "Jealous, Neddie?"

Raymond blushed, recognizing his own overreach, and was groping for an answer when the tall phone on the desk rattled politely.

"Senator Slater's suite. Raymond speaking."

The voice at the other end was unctuous, heavily accented. "Please excuse the interruption, M'sieur Raymond. This is the main desk reporting that a lady is here, wishing to speak with Senator Slater. Her card says she is Mrs. Algernon Forsythe-Goodman, of Philadelphia. Will the senator receive her?"

Raymond cupped a hand over the mouthpiece and turned. "A very big-named visitor—"

Slater waved testily. "I don't want to see anybody. I told you: I want a long soak, then a long sleep. Visitors can wait."

"This one is the widow of the founder of two major railroads, a steel company, and an international shipping concern. She's Mrs. Algernon Forsythe-Goodman, who, in her own right, is one of the world's leading philanthropists."

"Never heard of her."

"Senator, do me a favor. Never, ever, admit that to anyone but me. Not to have heard of Mrs. Goodman is to place one in the ranks of the imbecilic unwashed and unread. I'm serious. It's like saying one has never heard of George Washington."

"George who?"

"Senator—"

"Ha-ha. Just joking, Neddie."

"Well, dammit, treat her right, and she might slide you a million or two for your campaign kitty."

"She's that big?"

"Last year she gave ten million to just one school of music. Another five to her favorite portraitist."

"Tell the desk you're on your way. You'll personally escort Mrs. Farsight-Washington to my bath, where I'll be awash in suds. She might even join me, if she's in the mood. Or she might prefer to wait until I'm in bed, forthwith, forsooth, forvooom. Hee-hee."

"Senator, sometimes you're the most infuriating, impossibly annoying—"

"Relax, Neddie. I'm just horsing around."

Raymond rolled his eyes, collected himself, then spoke into the phone. "The Senator is absolutely delighted to learn that Mrs. Forsythe-Goodman is in Paris, and he has asked me to join her in the lobby and personally escort her to the senatorial suite."

"Very good, M'sieur."

Chapter 31

The war had taken a nasty turn. On March 16, the Germans had mounted a massive offensive against the British on the Somme Front to the northwest, and in late April, the enemy drive's momentum wheeled to the south, creating a huge V-shaped salient that moved like an arrowhead south-southwest to Château-Thierry, a major town on the Marne only fifty-some miles northeast of Paris. The defending French 6th Army and its air services had been so badly mauled they were incapable of meeting the German thrust, and so Pershing had permitted Marshal Foche, supreme Allied commander, to throw all available American ground and air forces into the gap. In a series of quick moves, the 38th had been among the American squadrons leapfrogged west from the relatively quiet Toul sector to the white-hot Champagne-Marne sector, where Château-Thierry anchored the Allies' last-ditch defense of the capital of France.

The flying had been from before dawn to after dusk and ranged from ground-level strafing runs to dogfights at fourteen thousand feet. The only relief came at night, but most of that was given to airplane repair and payload replenishment. So lack of sleep and a debilitating tension were becoming passengers in every cockpit.

Making things worse was the appearance of virtual clouds of

the new German Fokker D-7, each seemingly manned by a pilot of the most audacious, battle-seasoned kind. The vaunted Baron von Richthofen had died in the assault on the British, but his red *Geschwader* was now spearheading the kaiser's climactic attempt to own the skies over France.

The Fokker D-7 was a thick-winged biplane with a boxy nose, which made it somewhat of an esthetic failure in John King's eye, but he readily admitted that, in terms of performance, it was the best airplane he'd ever encountered on either side of the line. And people had begun to listen to what he thought about airplanes and air fighting, because with nine kills he had kept his lead as the 38th Pursuit's high scorer and was being mentioned now and then in Allied press communiqués.

At the same time, the French had no choice but to ease their hold on the Spad 13, some of which had already replaced the Nieuport 28 in several frontline American squadrons. The 38th Pursuit had received three of them, and Captain Bianco was so thoroughly enamored of his star pupil, whom he had come to call affectionately "Johnny-Kraut," he immediately assigned one to him, kept one for himself, and made the third available as a transition trainer for the remainder of his "misfits."

The Spad, too, was left wanting in the roster of the most beautiful of aircraft, in King's estimation. It was squat and appeared to have everything shoved forward, reminiscent of the English bulldog, with a massive head, jut-jawed snout, bunched-up shoulders, sturdy forelegs, and a body and hind end that tapered off to seeming insignificance. The wings were wide and of roughly equal span, with no dihedral, no stagger, and extensively braced by two bays of interplane struts and a birdcage of turnbuckled wires. The top wing was set very close to the fuselage, forward of the cockpit, which not only impeded visibility but also required an overall cramping of the machine guns, ammo boxes, and their feed and ejection mechanisms. Somebody over at the 94th Pursuit—was it that other "Kraut," Rickenbacker?—had dubbed it "the flying brick," which was not altogether a stretch.

The "Kraut" thing had merely brushed Rickenbacker, who, before the war and his enlistment had been Eddie Richenbacher, a quite famous race car driver, but thanks to Bianco it had clung to King. And he found after a time that he really no longer cared, because his steadily increasing score of destroyed enemy planes and balloons gave no doubt as to where his sympathies lay. It was by now truly a nickname for him and, in any event, no longer very popular as a term for general, national bigotry. Too many "German-Americans" were doing too many great things to have the derision stick.

The weariness and headaches and daytime nightmares were getting to him, though. This he had to admit.

It was the fourth squadron-strength patrol of the day, and he'd begun to fight a stickiness in his eyes, a tendency to yawn. Nine planes cruised in stair-step V at eight thousand feet, four to each flank, with Bianco at the tip. Squadron strength for the 38th, according to the TO&E, was twelve planes and twenty-four pilots. But three planes and pilots had been lost in the past week, with no replacements immediately expected.

It was no time to give in to sleep, especially now that they'd been joined in their slice of evening sky by twenty D-7s, coming fast out of the northeast like a swarm of multi-colored insects.

King decided that the Germans were either hugely overconfident due to their two-to-one odds, or they were rookies with a death wish, because they did no maneuvering, no arranging of forces for the attack. Just a shallow, bunched-up dive, a head-on approach that played precisely into the hand of the wily Captain Bianco, whom each pilot in the V could easily see. On the ground, Bianco was somewhat dotty, playing the martinet at one moment and the baggy-pants vaudeville comic the next. But up here he was a cool Genghis Khan. He always wore gloves, never mittens, and he had taught his pilots to watch his hand signals closely: hand held flat meant maintain this course and altitude; hand held with fingers elevated meant climb together; hand held flat or elevated or tilted down with fingers extended meant maneuver as indicated, but spread out; a pumping fist meant free-for-all, but watch your buddy's ass; a circling forefinger meant reassemble and close up.

In this situation and against these odds, he signaled what he called "the Fokker-fucker"—hand balled into a fist with forefinger pointing straight ahead—which meant "stay together, pick a target, and open fire when I pull in the finger and complete the fist."

Of course, as drawled by "Boots" McKinley of A Flight during a training session, "It's a plain old test of nerves. If neither side's willing to break formation, you're gonna establish the goldangdest, most high-altitudinous smithereen-manufacturing factory known to God and man."

This evening, though, the net effect was as expected. The Germans, seeing no deterioration in the American formation and confronting a mass collision, were themselves forced to break up. And as they did, they were met by a hail of steel—the concentrated fire from eighteen Vickers machine guns.

King's Fokker disappeared in an oily explosion, and the three enemy planes adjacent to it fell away, trailing smoke and debris. Another pair of Fokkers on the right flank actually collided as their pilots chose to make conflicting breaks, and a fourth pair central to the enemy group blossomed into flame.

The odds were now nine to twelve, and Bianco's fist was pumping.

King settled in on a black and white D-7 and managed to get in a few shots before it went into a panicky dive, which, in his new Spad, he could have easily overtaken. But he still saw his main job to be the protection of Bianco, so he pulled up and around, only to find that there were still some very tough nuts among the surviving Germans. One of them, driving a yellow-nosed machine, was perched just aft of his rudder, machine guns hammering. Splinters flew from the left center-section strut, and a neat round hole appeared in the windscreen inches from his head.

"Whoa, Nellie!"

He rolled the Spad onto its back and fell away in a wide-throttle dive, and, although the German appeared to have expected this and tried gamely to follow, he was forced into a diving turn that left him wide open to Bianco's fire-spitting arrival. Bianco didn't score, but the German fled full steam for the darkening east in the wake of his departing comrades.

❋❋❋

It was almost dark when the squadron settled onto the field and taxied up to the hangar line, engines blatting and snorting.

One by one, as mechanics and handlers pushed on wingtips and pulled on tails, the planes waggled into a rough line facing the night—except for Larry Durbin's No. 4, which kept rolling with its propeller windmilling until the ship's left wings crumpled against a camion parked by the little stone house beyond Hangar A. The rotary engine gasped, then quit, and as the wreckage settled, men came running.

"First aid! Bring me some goddamn first-aid stuff, *fast*!" Bianco's voice called from the gathering crowd. "And the ambulance. We gotta get this man to the group surgeon!"

By the time King and the ambulance arrived, Durbin had been lifted from the cockpit and was lying on his back in the grass beside the Nieuport's broken fuselage. In the fading light, his boyish face was chalky. Bianco was kneeling on one side of him, and Simmons, who was said to have left a Johns Hopkins internship to join the Air Service, was kneeling on the other side, opening Durbin's flight suit with one hand and wiping blood from his face with a scarf held in the other.

"Keep back, people," Bianco ordered softly. "Give him space, air."

"I'm cold," Durbin said, his voice clear.

The driver leaned from the ambulance with an armload of blankets. "Here, Captain Bianco. Maybe these'll help."

"Bullet hole in the right lower chest," Simmons said to no one in particular. "Internal hemorrhaging likely. He can't be moved now."

"Get those blankets around him," Bianco said.

"You hear that?" Durbin rasped.

Ken Randall, Durbin's roommate, knelt beside Bianco. "Hear what, Larry?"

"That dog barking. Sounds like my Maxie."

Randall said, "Maxie's home, safe with your mom, Larry."

"Mom? You know my mom?"

"You've told me a lot about her, Larry. How good she cooks, crochets. Sings alto solos for the church choir. Her favorite, 'Just a Closer Walk With Thee.' That kinda stuff."

"Sings it all the time around the house. She's a good egg." Durbin coughed, a shallow, wheezing sound.

King found that he couldn't continue watching this. Detaching himself from the crowd, he went into the little stone house and climbed the narrow inner stairway to the attic, where he opened the creaky casement and stared across the twilit plain beyond the crowd below, looking for something he couldn't define. There was something out there. But what? Sighing, he turned and crossed the small room and went to a corner, where he carefully pulled aside some tarpaulins covering an ancient harpsichord spinet, all age-dulled enamels and scrollings.

"Careful, Johnny-Kraut," he muttered. "This sumbish is at least sixteenth century. Treat it right, and it might still work."

He upended an empty keg, sat down, and, after wriggling and blowing on his fingers, caressed the ancient keys, then eased into "Just a Closer Walk With Thee."

It was eerie. The softly twanging, harplike music drifted through the fallen night, seeming to float over the whole broad plain. And as he played, a voice from the crowd below—a deep, rich, languid baritone—began to sing the lyrics, and when the song ended, it hung in the night, a resonant, haunting echo.

※※※

Later, while having coffee in the orderly room, King felt a tap on his shoulder. It was Ormond, of B Flight.

"You never told me you can play," Ormond said.

"You never told me you can sing."

"Never studied. Have no training."

"Same here."

"Where'd you find the harpsichord?"

"I like old architecture. I was rummaging around one day and found the instrument packed in a corner. It had been there for years. I spent some spare hours tuning it with mechanic's tools."

"Surprised that nobody ever stole it."

"Nobody ever realized its worth, I guess."

"Well, Bianco does. I heard him say he plans to clean it up, take it to Paris, and present it to the Louvre, or something."

"Bianco's a real caution," King said.

"Sure is. That hardcase sumbish was actually holding Larry close in his arms, all teared up, when Larry checked out—at the very moment our duet was finished, no less. Well, to give him his due, as far as I could see, there wasn't a dry eye in the bunch."

"Music does that to people."

Chapter 32

General Pershing's headquarters was in the Caserne de Damremont in the picture-postcard town of Chaumont, a morning's drive southeast of Paris. The building was a large rectangle of several floors, replete with casements and shutters and fussy little balconies, sitting in the center of a formal parade ground. Before the American arrival, the building and its ancillaries had been occupied by the town's French garrison, an aggregation of haughty cavalry officers and dour, unenthusiastic poilus, all of them outraged at having their turf usurped by a gaggle of heathen cowboys playing soldier. The tensions had run rather high as a consequence, but Pershing wisely perceived that the townspeople themselves were just crazy about those crazy Yankees and their readiness to spread around money and affection, commodities that had been woefully scarce in their slice of wartime France. So he had met French military sullenness with the American gift for civic celebrations and block parties, and, even though the French military remained sour and aloof, a kind of amiable civilian tolerance had set in.

Carpenter, thanks to the fact that nobody knew what to do with him due to the gadfly vagueness of his original aviation section orders, was assigned a windowless office in the Caserne's basement. Which was all right with him because he managed almost always to be out of it. This day, though, he happened to be sitting there with his boots on the desk, browsing through a copy of Billy Mitchell's manifesto on air power, when the phone jingled.

"Aviation section, Major Carpenter."

"This is Colonel Oates, aide to General Pershing," the stuffy voice announced. "The general would like you to attend his staff meeting at 1300 hours. But first I suggest you stop in my office so that I might present you with your new orders just in from Washington. They give relevance to your invitation to the meeting. Please be prompt."

The phone clicked, and Carpenter was left to stare at the wall and marvel at his apotheosis. The anonymous waif had been summoned from his subterranean Limbo to sit in with God and the archangels.

"Wow," he said aloud, amused. "When that Slater guy pulls a string the world's pants fall down."

❈❈❈

The meeting was in a salonlike room central to the second floor, and, like the room, everything was central: the huge coffin-shaped table, the orderly row of chairs along the window wall, the flags, the general's chair, the water decanter and glasses, and even the stack of pads and canisters of pencils all gave the impression of centrality. Perhaps this was meant to resonate with the squareness of Pershing himself, who sat in his high, square-backed chair, central to the flag display, gazing levelly into some far corner of the universe, his eyes squarely centered above his square jaws, his square shoulders impeccably graced by the world's most expensive olive drab, and his square-tipped fingers tapping softly on the glittering mahogany before him.

Around the table sat the G-level officers, each pretending nonchalance, and to the general's immediate right, nonchalant without having to pretend, was Billy Mitchell, in some way giving off the air that it was really he who was in charge around here.

Carpenter had been instructed by Oates to take the window wall chair with the card bearing his name. Three chairs had names on them. His was directly to the right of the other two, which were occupied by a colonel and, inexplicably, by a second John wearing a military police brassard. Unfortunately, this placed him directly opposite Mitchell, and they found themselves at once trying to avoid each other's eyes, like strangers sharing a train compartment.

The general cleared his throat and said, "Before we get things under way, I'd like everyone to welcome Major William J. Carpenter, who has just been attached by the War Department to Colonel Mitchell's headquarters as its special liaison on aviation technical matters. I felt it to be important that Major Carpenter be brought up to date on our planning for the impending assault on national Germany. Major Carpenter, welcome."

Carpenter felt all the eyes, particularly the heat emanating from Mitchell's.

"Thank you, sir."

Mitchell's face was, by now, a bright pink, and Carpenter knew that he was in for some bad times. Obviously, in the usual ham-handed Washington way, nobody had thought to inform Mitchell of Carpenter's appointment, and to be broadsided at a G-level conference this way was, for Billy, legitimate cause for Olympian ire.

"So, then," the general said, "to the matter at hand, which is to fill you in on the operations assigned to the American Expeditionary Force. The French and British, as you are aware, have seemed to resign themselves to a separate U.S. military presence and are no longer arguing for piecemeal integration of American troops with their own. The question is, mainly, what is this American force to do, now that the German July offensive has been halted and turned around?"

There was soft stirring around the table. For months this question had been on every mind from the Potomac to Pigalle, and now the Old Boy was going to answer it for his chieftains as casually as if it were teatime chitchat.

"As shown by the red arrow on the wall map, the most direct route into Germany today is from Verdun through Trèves and Koblenz. The AEF will become this arrow, as it were, smashing through to Koblenz behind our 1st Army, whose first job as spearhead is to eliminate the St. Mihiel Salient. It's expected in Paris,

London, and Washington that we will have reached the Rhine River—the German national border—by the end of January 1919. Actual penetration of the German homeland by American troops should result in a quick surrender of the enemy's combat forces. Therefore, the Allied governments expect us to have ended the war by the spring of 1919."

Carpenter could guess what everybody was thinking. Pershing had made it sound as if the Americans were to be the whole show, a point the French and British would be sure to refute. For another thing, the AEF was still a mass of half-trained troops milling about, almost chaotically, winning more by default than design, and if the Allied governments expected this horde of amateurs to conquer Germany before Christmas of 1920 they were out of their freaking minds.

"You all know St. Mihiel," General Pershing continued, "but look at it again on the detailed excerpts. The Allied line is fairly even except at St. Mihiel, where the Germans occupy a wedge fifteen miles deep by thirty-five miles wide. The wedge is anchored at its tip by Montsec, a mountain full of tunnels, dugouts, foxholes, machine-gun nests, and fortified artillery. The approaches to Montsec are girded by miles of east-west defenses six lines deep, one inside the other. The heights are manned by expert observation teams who can see anything we do in the Toul surround. We must take that eminence and the salient it protects. It's absolutely the first requirement if we are to remove the menace to Verdun and to open the way to Koblenz. The St. Mihiel Salient is the cork, gentlemen, and the AEF's 1st Army has been asked to pull that cork."

The silence was deep, contemplative.

"We will begin a secret concentration of our troops beginning next week. The process should take most of August, part of September. On D-Day our main thrust will be against the southern face of the salient, while a secondary drive will be sent against the upper end of the western face. The town of St. Mihiel, just southwest of Montsec, will be under a holding attack. Our main thrust will be anchored at Pont-à-Mousson, on the right flank. From there westward will be the 1st Corps, composed of the 82nd, 90th, 5th, and 2nd Divisions. Between the 2nd Division's left flank and Montsec will be the 4th Corps, made up of the 89th, 42nd, and 1st Divisions. In 1st Corps reserve will be the 78th Division and, as Army reserve for corps, the 35th Division. The 4th Corps will be backed up by the 3rd and 91st Divisions."

Someone whistled low, and someone else muttered, "Sweet Jesus. The Germans will be smothered in the crowd."

The general pretended not to hear this. "The holding action at the tip will be by the French 2nd Colonial Corps, made up of two infantry divisions backed up by the 2nd French Cavalry, dismounted. The western face will be anchored by the 15th French Colonial Division and part of the U.S. 4th Division, and the secondary drive to the southeast will be mounted by the U.S. 26th Division. We expect the main thrust from the south to meet the secondary thrust from the northwest at or near the town of Vigneulles, which sits in the salient's center. The jaws will have closed around Montsec and all other German fortifications of any importance. D-Day and H-Hour are still most secret and will not be disclosed until the last moment, except on a need-to-know basis among G-level officers. By the way, we plan a four-hour hurricane barrage prior to jump-off."

The general cleared his throat again, and, aberrantly, Carpenter remembered the old pun, "he strummed his catarrh." Unaccountably this hit him as extremely funny, and he struggled to keep from laughing openly.

"Which brings us to the airplanes," the general said. "Colonel Mitchell has been urging us to assemble a large number of machines for the St. Mihiel opening phase. And I'd like him now to give us some insight as to what he has in mind. Colonel?"

Mitchell, in the manner of a schoolteacher so familiar with his subject he saw no need for notes, waded right in. "Thank you, General. My plan is basically quite simple in concept but rather tricky to pull off. I propose assembling a massive concentration of aircraft as surreptitiously as possible, by night or under weather cover, so that with H-Hour 1st Army can surprise the Germans defending the St. Mihiel Salient with a virtual overcast made up of Allied bombers and attack machines, protected as much as possible by our pursuit squadrons. The overall mission of this great concentration of air power will be to overpass Montsec and the salient's main fortifications and continue on to attack and destroy the enemy's rearward support mechanisms and to interdict its lines of supply. This should lead to the early weakening and eventual starvation of its frontline combat forces."

The G-3 broke in. "How many planes would you say the 1st Army could have by September first?"

"Round numbers, sir, including aircraft already made available to the plan by the French and British, there should be fourteen hundred airplanes of all categories and twenty-four forward-area support balloons, a total of thirty thousand officers and men operating out of fourteen major airfields and twenty-two secondary installations."

"My God, General," G-3 grumped, staring directly at Pershing, "that's a veritable aerial division. Can such a huge number of planes be handled by a single command?"

The question, of course, was rooted in professional jealousy and irritability over an implicit violation of organizational turf by a mere colonel. All eyes turned to Mitchell.

Pershing remained stony-faced. "Anything to say to that, Colonel Mitchell?"

"Duck soup."

The eyes widened.

"It's duck soup," Mitchell said, just this side of snappishness. "With proper briefing of subcommanders, plus sand table rehearsals and informed guesses by our meteorological branch, I can send our planes to precise targets at precise times with precise payloads of bombs and attack ordnance with an ease that suggests a well-maintained freight railroad or truck line."

G-3 grew more sullen. "The Germans have planes, too, Mitchell. Your little railroad won't be running without considerable harassment."

"To be sure. That's where our pursuit squadrons come in, sir. The Germans will have to fight very hard to get near our bombers. There will be losses, of course. Sometimes heavy, no doubt. But as our pursuits stand off the enemy interceptions, the bombers will forge on, and the Germans—on the ground and in the air—will inevitably wind down for lack of ammo and fuel and food and morale."

There was a pause, and Pershing glanced at the colonel sitting next to Carpenter. "Colonel Ritter, from his written estimate of the situation, I know what G-2 himself thinks about all this. But do you, as G-2's consultant on air intelligence, have any contributions you might add to the discussion?"

Carpenter was intrigued by this. There were forces at work in the room he didn't altogether understand, and this was one of them. Why hadn't Pershing asked G-2 himself to fill in the guys?

Ritter made it pretty clear right off. "I might point out to the staff, sir, that I've been appointed by G-2 to conduct certain counterintelligence efforts to fuel the coals of rebellion we've detected in a number of German cities. A German communist named Liebknecht is organizing an armed uprising designed to oust the kaiser and establish a government of the people. I think this fact, coupled with the massive aerial assault on Germany's national approaches as suggested by Colonel Mitchell, will serve well to unnerve the German Establishment at home and confuse and demoralize the troops in the field. So I am a hearty supporter of Colonel Mitchell's proposal. But I have one thing I would add. I suggest that we show great normality in our aerial operations prior to H-Hour on D-Day. The Germans, of course, know that we are planning to attack the salient, and they have probably figured Koblenz to be our ultimate target. What they don't know is when. We must maximize the surprise element and its attendant shock by seeming to act normally up to the very moment of the hurricane barrage. I therefore respectfully suggest that Colonel Mitchell maintain routine small unit patrols over the salient—"

"My God, Ritter," Mitchell broke in, "what you're suggesting is basic R.O.T.C. stuff taught to cadets in any land grant college back home. And I remind you that all of us in this room have been educated considerably beyond the R.O.T.C. level. What's your point, man?"

Ritter was a cool apple. He didn't even blink at this scorn. "I'll be glad to make my point if Colonel Mitchell will permit me to complete my comment. What I'm suggesting is that Colonel Mitchell change gears a bit in his preoccupation with dropping high-explosive bombs on the German rear. I suggest that the colonel also consider dropping pamphlets that advise both the German combat troops at the front and their support mechanisms in the rear that revolution is brewing in their cities back home. Routine patrols over Montsec, with pamphlets dropped routinely. Bombing raids to the rear, pamphlets dropped, too. If Colonel Mitchell wants to run a railroad, let his aerial choo-choos deliver some mail, as well."

A smothered chuckling rippled, and Mitchell appeared to be ready to slay Ritter with a round from his service pistol.

At this point the sphinx revealed some humanity when Pershing rose regally from his chair and said, "Let's take a latrine break, gentlemen. Reassemble in twenty minutes."

Chapter 33

If Colonel Billy Mitchell was pleased to meet Major William J. Carpenter, newly named by Washington to park at Mitchell's door as a special War Department attaché, he was extremely good at hiding it. In the corridor, standing stiffly beside one of the tall windows, he came right to the point.

"For your information, Major, I insist on choosing those who stay at my house. So who the hell are you to come waltzing in from nowhere, all wrapped up in War Department righteousness, when I haven't asked for you to be here and don't want you to be here?"

Carpenter decided that Mitchell's eyes were like frozen grapes, and his face most surely had to have been quarried. A hard, angry, opinionated man, according to the aggregate evaluations, both official and latrine scuttlebutt, and a man sure as hell destined for either the White House or Cell 13 at Leavenworth, depending on how the dice rolled. But Carpenter's own conclusion, after digesting the tons of information he'd gathered on the colonel, was that all one needed to get along with a cantankerous genius like Mitchell was the schoolyard bully treatment: He yells in your face? You kick him in the balls.

The theory was about to be tested.

"I'm here, Colonel, because nobody topside in Washington likes me or gets along with me. The consensus is that the only thing to be done with a son of a bitch like me is to consign me to slavery under a son of a bitch like you. In short, the official view is that you and I deserve each other."

Mitchell's expression changed not a whit. "So how do you feel about that?"

"I not only agree, but I also see it as the best possible shortcut to winning this frigging war. Sir."

"Oh, really?"

Carpenter took the dry, soft-spoken skepticism as a sign that Mitchell was ready to give him more rope. So he grabbed it. "I've read just about every report you've written, Colonel, and all I can say is that you're one helluva report writer. I've never seen issues described so clearly and arguments made so persuasively. But you've got a problem, and that's where I can help."

Mitchell sniffed. "What's your name again? Major Asstired?"

"That's one of the things they call me. But for your purposes, I'm the man who's going to get Washington to thinking you're the greatest thing since wooden shoes. I've read all your reports and advisories and recommendations and position papers and theories, Colonel, and I think you are one heap big frigging genius. The problem is, you think so, too, and you never tire of telling everybody so. It's time for you to shut up and let me do the talking. It's time for you to emulate Pershing. The less he says, the smarter everybody thinks he is."

"You don't like Pershing?"

"I don't know Pershing well enough to like or dislike him. From what I've seen, from what he's said and written, he's a damned good soldier doing what his bosses expect him to do, which is to personify the United States among a bunch of snobby foreign esthetes and to insist that Americans fight intact, not divvied up in bits and pieces and sent into combat under the command of people who disdain them for their uncouth ways. He's a ramrod officer who demands honesty and has a huge respect for the fighting man, and that's why he likes and supports you, because, for all your faults, you're honest and you're a fighter. And that's why he wouldn't like me, because I can be as cowardly and dishonest as they come. And that, sir, is exactly why you need me. You're a straight-up son of a bitch, and I'm a sneaky son of a bitch who can do things for you that you wouldn't even want to know about, much less do."

Of all things, Mitchell laughed and shook his head, just like a real person. "So that's how you ended up in my headquarters, eh?"

"You're durn tootin'. Sir. Only I suggest that you don't carry me on your table of organization. I suggest you carry me on the duty books as a War Department attaché on temporary duty, top secret War Department business, so that, while I hang my hat in your office, sleep in one of your rooms, and eat some of your chow, you can truthfully claim that you have no knowledge of what I'm doing on behalf of the War Department. This will free me to get under-the-table things done for you without risk to you or your staffers."

Mitchell humphed. "It still sounds dishonest to me." He pointed to a marble bench. "Let's park there for a minute, Carpenter. Let me explain some things to you."

They sat, and Mitchell lowered his voice. "I don't know where you really came from or what's really on your mind. I could make a huge ruckus about this and find out, sure enough. But this is one of those things I don't really want to know about, so for once I'll keep my mouth shut. And this is because you seem to be a benign force, which, after having positively absorbed my literature, is anxious to champion my long-range plea for a strategic, independent air force, equal in standing with the Army and the Navy under a single Department of Defense. For this, you have my gratitude.

"But I'll have to decline your sneakiness, not only because it's not my style, but also because the Germans are already whipped and we're going to wrap up this war by way of all that traditional crap Pershing just laid out. It's both too early and too late to make the big changes I tout—too early for the Establishment to grasp and accept, and too late for enactment in this war even if they did accept. My suggestions will have to wait, have to be formulated and adopted well after this war's done and before the next one starts."

"Next one, sir?"

"You don't really believe that this war will resolve anything, do you, Major Asstired? We'll kick the crap out of the Germans by traditional means, and they'll retire, madder than hell, to lick their wounds and get ready for another go at us, this time by way of Mexico. Meanwhile, their soul mates in the Pacific, the Japs, will get ready for their own go at Hawaii and Alaska. This war's nothing but the opening shot."

Carpenter decided to show some cards. "Damn it, Colonel, I'm saying you needn't be resigned to winding up this war, or getting ready for the next, with the cast-off machinery our Allies deign to release to us. I've got an airplane, ready for mass production as we speak, that will save a lot of our air crews and kick the living shit out of the Germans and anything they have planned for the next twenty years. It's an airplane like nothing you've ever seen, and if I can demonstrate it in actual combat conditions, it'll deal Billy Mitchell a whole new winning hand—without Billy Mitchell having even to open his yap."

Mitchell gave Carpenter a warning glance. "God, but you are truly insufferably presumptuous, Major."

"I know that, sir. But this is my one chance at you, and I can't lose it by being wishy-washy."

Mitchell glanced at the wall clock. "I'll admit that there's enough aviator in me to make me curious about this airplane of yours. But it—"

"I have blueprints in my office and the real article being assembled at a secret hangar just outside the training base at Issoudon."

"By any measure, it's still too late."

"Not for the next war, sir. May I pick you up and drive you out there after this meeting?"

"You are really, truly an itch, Carpenter."

"What time and where, sir?"

"Front of the Caserne here. At 1430."

Chapter 34

Passed by Censor 4335

Capt. William J. Carpenter

c/o General Headquarters

American Expeditionary Forces

Paris (Please forward)

Dear Bill:

I haven't written much lately because I'm always so tired, and my head aches a lot. This flying and shooting stuff isn't exactly a pink tea, I'll tell you, and although I'm getting more confident and expert in the air, it's when I'm on the ground that my miseries seem to increase. I come alive when I'm aloft, with the engine roaring and the wind blasting past, and the huge sky and the distant Earth lure me, like Heine's Lorelei, then close in, enfold me, own me, so to speak.

But when I'm on the ground, things tend to unravel, sort of. I don't know how to explain it, but my ears ring. Well, more than that. I hear music, far off. Voices, too. I can't hear what they're saying, and it may just be a trick of all the infernal noise my poor ears endure in this business, but it sounds as if people are talking, behind my back, just out of eyesight.

And would you believe? The sounds sometimes reach epic proportions. For instance, I was walking down the path to the latrine the other evening when, all of a sudden and behind me, what must have been the entire West Point marching band opened up with "Stars and Stripes Forever." It just about blew me off my feet. The playing soon faded away, but I didn't dare to turn around and look because I knew there was nothing there, nothing behind me on the path. Maybe I'm starting to hallucinate as a result of my weariness and the constant stress I've been under. I can't account for it any other way.

The one reassuring note in all of this is that I can share it with you and know that my privacy remains intact. A couple of the buttinskies in my flight have slyly asked me if I feel okay, and two of them have suggested that I see the wing medical officer. But I told them to go to hell. I'm certainly not going to do that. He might get the wrong idea and put me in the hospital or something, just when I'm clearing the skies of all those freaking Fokkers. I don't hate the Germans, but I sure don't like the way they kill and hurt our people, so all by myself I've begun a program to wipe them out. Shot down forty-seven of them yesterday! Of course, those bastards at headquarters will never acknowledge that fact. They'll credit the victories to all the Fancy Dan college boys.

Your friend,

John

❋❋❋

```
FROM:Maj. William J. Carpenter
Aviation Consultant
U.S. Air Service
c/o General Headquarters
Chaumont


TO:Miss Mary Lou Whiting
American Field Service
c/o Campagne à Val-de-Grâce Hospital

Dear Miss Whiting:
I am a friend of John King, who, I understand, is
a friend of yours. I've read in Stars and Stripes
about your flying supplies to various military
```

hospitals, etc., and I'm hoping that you can somehow find time and opportunity to look in on John, now serving as a pilot with the 38th Pursuit Squadron. His letters to me have me worried. He sounds sick and disconnected, and, as you probably know, he's a very stubborn and prideful sort and might be refusing medical attention. Could you somehow arrange a stop at his location and take a look at him? Maybe you can persuade him to see a doctor. I certainly know I can't. Appreciate anything you can do to help.

Respectfully, and with many thanks,

WJC, Major

Chapter 35

Weather was building in the western twilight. Towering cauliflowers of soot-colored rain clouds took on golden traceries and an inner glowing as they rolled across the setting sun. Below, the terrain was already in deep dusk, and straining to see landmarks was becoming more tiring by the minute. The modified DH-4 itself was part of the problem, thanks to its built-in tail-heaviness and its wretched exhaust stack layout that further obscured the dimness ahead with the flaring at its ports. Worse, the fuel gauge, almost invisible in the cockpit's interior darkness, was flirting with empty, and unless she found a proper flying field, she would soon be faced with a blind, nighttime dead-stick landing.

Mary Lou raised her goggles and, using her scarf, dabbed at the burning in her eyes. She knew now that she should have heeded the transport director's advice not to try for Lassigny this late in the day, but she'd have done almost anything to escape the dull oppressiveness of the hospital ambience, even if it hadn't been the letter from that Major Carpenter and its understated urgency. The charts had shown Lassigny to be at the confluence of an east-west canal and a minor river whose name eluded her now, and it was this landmark she needed badly. But she must have wandered off course, because all that appeared below was a great dark platter of scarred landscape and occasional unlit villages.

Ha.

There.

What was that?

A canal, by God.

But where was the "minor river"? And where was the town of Lassigny?

Tension and anxiety had joined her in the cockpit, and she felt the clamminess in her gloves, the dryness of her mouth, the knot in her belly.

Oh, boy.

A flash of relief, a thrilling in her chest.

Over there.

A line of hangars, a scattering of planes. Barely discernible in the settling gloom.

Heart pounding, she let the DH-4 sink into a gliding turn and lined up the nose with the area just east of the planes. She cut the throttle to idle and waited while the ground came up slowly. A bit of power, back a little on the stick to clear a line of trees, and then back to idle. The big plane dropped heavily onto the turf, its undercarriage squeaking and rumbling, its wings waggling as the machine coasted across ruts and weed patches. Rollout complete, she used the rudder and bursts of power to taxi to the flight line, where a small knot of men had gathered to watch her approach and several handlers came running to guide her through the final turnaround.

She cut the switches, and when the engine had gasped into silence, she flipped off her seat belt, swung onto the wing, and dropped to the ground, calling out, "Can you gentlemen direct me to the ladies' loo? There's a matter of some urgency here."

Somebody said, "My God, it's a woman."

Another somebody said in elaborate disbelief, "It's that rotten cognac. We gotta get a better batch."

❋❋❋

It was a wonderful change from the antiseptic gloom of hospitals. She was surrounded by young men, as always, but these were fully alive, exuberant, and competing for her attention. No sorrow here, no sounds of suffering, only the happy-go-lucky, tipsy humor of college boys on a weekend romp. Even the jokes were clean, some of them actually funny, but each received its share of hooting laughter, and an attempt to launch a barbershop quartet was doused by boos and a spate of amiable roughhousing. She sat at a small table in the midst of all this, warm with brandy and friendship and lost to the luxury of not having to think, to console, to hold trembling hands, to read heartbreaking letters, to listen to deathbed confessions, then to load her plane with mail and medicines and surgical supplies and fly to another place, another hospital, for more of the same. All that was required of her here, on this rainy evening in the middle of Nowhere, was to wait for John, to laugh, to wink, to play the coquette, and to enjoy the beauty of all the healthy young faces.

A car drove up and squeaked to a halt outside the shack, and there was a slamming of doors and some voices. A chill wind and a misty swirling came through the blackout flaps with the two men who entered, stamping their feet and shaking water from their raincoats. Someone called attention, and the taller of the arrivals said at ease, carry on, but an odd pause followed, a kind of noisy silence, which was broken when Mary Lou stood up, feeling an odd thrill. "John! John, it's me!"

King stared. "Mary Lou?"

They stood, locked in an awkward confrontation, the center of the great curiosity and amused silence of the pilots, who seemed to sense that this, whatever it was, was something to write home about.

As usual, Captain Bianco broke the impasse. "Well, now, who have we here? Johnny-Kraut, if you are a friend of this beautiful vision in the nurse's uniform, I insist that you introduce me at once."

King overcame his confusion sufficiently to mumble, "Oh, yes. Sorry. Miss Whiting, may I present the commanding officer of the 38th Pursuit Squadron, Captain Bianco. Captain, this is Mary Lou Whiting of Philadelphia. We met when I was in primary flight training near her home, and now, obviously, she's here in France with the Red Cross."

Bianco beamed. "So, then, that explains the DH-4 outside, emblazoned with huge red crosses. I had no idea that the Red Cross had lady pilots. What a wonderful idea!"

She had assembled her inner self and felt ready to deal with the rest of it. "No, Captain, I'm not with the Red Cross. I am carried officially as an ambulance driver for the American Field Service, but when Hélène Dutrieu—the famous Belgian aviatrix who now serves as director of Campagne à Val-de-Grâce military hospital—learned that I am a licensed American flier, she decided I might serve more effectively by flying medical support missions between the many hospitals spread across the country here. I got lost in tonight's terrible weather and made an emergency landing on your field. And your men have been absolutely marvelous at making me feel at home."

Bianco's grin widened. "As well they should have. I'd be thoroughly disappointed and ashamed if they'd done anything less. We're delighted to have you here, aren't we, men?"

The uproar and milling about resumed, and in another awkwardness, King took her elbow and led her to the tarpaper-and-frame corridor connecting the dayroom with the ramshackle administrative offices. "It's a little quieter here," he said stiffly.

She stood back, her face serious. "Let me look at you, John."

"I'd rather you didn't." He tried to make light of it. "I'm pretty...disheveled. A long day, and all that."

A long day? A long year, it had been. Disheveled didn't do it, either. Haggard. Empty. Unspeakably weary. Disconnected. Any one of them would be more apt. His face was still young, boyish in configuration, and that nose retained its perfection. But overall there seemed to be a subtle veneer of pallor, itself an amalgamation of exhaustion and weary resignation. The months had worn heavily on him, and she felt a wave of sadness.

"I've been reading about you," she said. "You're becoming quite famous. All those aerial duels. The victories."

"There are no victories, Mary Lou," he said slowly. "Just those who survive and those who die. There's not much difference between the two, after all's said."

A swelling in the party's uproar caused her to send an exasperated glance down the corridor. "Isn't there some place out of the rain we could go? Some place where we can hear what we're saying?"

He thought about that. The hangars and auxiliary sheds were filled with planes and crews making them ready for tomorrow. The orderly room was the province of late-working pencil pushers. He hated his own messy hut, so how could he take her into that filth?

Only one place, really.

He took her hand. "This way."

❋❋

She knew at once it was a place very special to him, this tiny room on the upper floor of a small stone building behind the hangar line. It smelled of eons, and, after King exchanged his flashlight for a pair of candles mounted on an upturned nail keg, its plaster walls took on the color of those she'd seen in so many ancient village churches during her childhood hikes through the Tyrol. They seemed to retain an afterglow following each lightning flash beyond the casement window.

They stood in the center of the room, looking around.

"What is this place?"

"I don't know. Just an old farm building, I guess. I come here now and then, when I want to be alone and do some thinking."

"It's sort of cozy, even with that roaring rain outside. And yet there's something, well, eerie about it, too."

"You notice that?"

"I'll say." She smiled. "Think it's haunted?"

"Every place on earth is haunted in some way. Lives don't just stop. They...linger. Some for quite a while."

"You think that's true?"

"I know it for fact."

"How can you say that?"

"None of the other guys will come up here. Bianco wanted to use it as a private office. He spent one day and one night here, then ordered a crew to take his furniture back to the orderly room hut. The squadron clerk wanted to use it as a file room. Same thing. The place ended up mine because I'm the only one in the whole damned outfit who can put up with its weirdness. And that's because I'm the only one who had a mother like mine, I guess."

She hugged herself and looked around in the candlelight. "You're scaring me."

He shrugged.

To change the subject, she pointed with her chin. "What's that in the corner, under the blankets?"

He seemed glad that she'd given him something specific to talk about. "A medieval harpsichord," he said, watching her carefully. "I found it the first time I came here. Captain Bianco plans to turn it over to some French museum."

"May I see it?"

"Of course."

He removed the army blankets, folding each as he went, then placed the lot in the far corner. When the instrument stood finally exposed to the candlelight, she said softly, "It's beautiful. Absolutely beautiful."

"Mmm. I've cleaned it up some."

"Have you played it?"

"Once."

"Why only once?"

"It was a special occasion."

"This is a special occasion. Will you play it for me?"

"No." He turned and gave her one of those peculiar, off-center stares. "Mary Lou, this place is haunted, sure enough. Right now by you and me. We're a pair of ghosts. We can see each other, hear each other. But we can't connect. Our lives were a long time ago. There's no reaching across the gap. What little we had is gone forever. Whatever lies ahead can't be shared."

She was unable to resist it. She reached out and touched his cheek. "I love you, John. I can't not love you."

He looked away. "The last time I heard those words was a long time ago. In Lackawanna. Tillie Connell, a neighborhood chum. A schoolmate. I loved her like I love you. A dear sister. She wanted more. So I'll have to tell you what I told her: No you don't. You're just being sentimental. Please don't sell yourself on anything more. I'm too risky for anything more."

"John, darling—"

"You're a splendid girl with a wonderful lifetime ahead. I have nothing ahead. You love the idea of me, but your idea doesn't accept the fact that I'm doomed. There's something in me, eating at me, and if that doesn't get me first, the Germans will. When I was a kid, I was a pretty good egg, and I liked most everybody and most everybody liked me. But then I started changing inside. An up-and-down thing, then sounds in my head and daytime nightmares. I'm doomed, dear girl. And it's only getting worse. Meanwhile, I'm just a One-Purpose Johnny. I'm a killing machine."

She stepped close to him. "John, hold me."

"No."

"Please. I'm so lonely and frightened. Can't you see? We're alike. You're no longer a decent, loving, creative man, you're a machine that kills. I'm no longer a decent, loving little girl who wants to hug the world, I'm a slot machine—pull my arm the right way and I'll build you another college, or finance your business, or underwrite your museum. The world tolerates you because you do its dirty work so well. The world indulges me because I'm an easy touch. You and me as people? Nobody gives a damn about you and me as people."

She broke off, a catch in her voice, hating herself for the self-pity that she had allowed to wash through her.

Slowly, silently, he reached out, pulled her to him, folded his arms around her, and held her close. When he spoke she sensed that he wasn't talking to her, but to himself, and she felt a deeper chill.

"We're not alike at all," he said. "In no way are we alike. You have a lifetime ahead of you. You'll do great things. I'm already dead. I was dead the moment I was born. And—you can believe this—I'm ready to move on now. I've done my time here. I'm ready for something new."

She pulled back, giving him an intense look, and she realized that, for the first time in memory, he was gazing directly, warmly into her eyes. No fear. No reluctance. No indirection. No shadows.

"Don't fret," he said. "You'll find what you're looking for." After a moment he added, "Be grateful that I wasn't it."

"I wish I could have done more for you, John."

"So do I."

They held each other a moment longer.

"Well," he said finally, "the war's waiting. Bianco will probably put you up in the medical hut. You'll be fine there. Me, I have the dawn patrol, so I probably won't see you again."

She hated the tears that wanted to form. So she made a teasing face to go with her macabre joke. "Don't be so sure. Maybe it'll be right here, in this room, in the next life, eh?"

He laughed softly. Actually laughed.

Chapter 36

They almost didn't see each other in the dawn light. He had somehow been separated from the patrol when they passed through a clump of altostratus, and while trying to find the others, cruising at three thousand feet, his landing gear surfing through a broad swath of morning fog, there it was, a malevolent insect on the edge of the brightening day. It was one of those Hannoveranner two-seat recon machines the Germans used for photography and ground support missions. An ugly airplane, if there ever was one: a brutish nose, a fat belly, a biplane tail—everything squat and mottled in green and purple. There it was, thrashing along on a southwesterly course, alone and somehow defiant and arrogant in its solitude. King had tangled with this type several times, and none of them had been easy going.

He began to stalk, just beyond the range of the rear gunner, who stood high in the humpbacked fuselage and tracked him warily with one of those wicked, long-barreled Parabellum machine guns. Then, for no apparent reason, King's thoughts went to Mary Lou and their awkward, ambivalent reunion of the night just passed, and he felt a return of the old anger. He'd fallen asleep on his cot, oddly gratified by the forgiveness he'd been able to grant her, but alone in the melancholy dawn, old resentments had begun to intrude, and once again he was the man on the outside looking in and growing self-righteous and bitter about anything and everything. She could be so sweet and pretty and la-de-goddamn-da, and she could talk the talk, but somewhere down in his gut the forgiveness gave way to an ember of anger that insisted on flaring into hatred and just wouldn't give up. Now, in this instant of impending violence in the heavens, he could see her as an imp from hell, on earth for one mission: to torment him.

Bitch!

The word rang.

Was it a thought? Or had he actually said it?

Was he talking to himself now, for crissake?

There was so much noise. Noise everywhere.

The Hannoveranner made a gentle turn due south over Montsec and the 1st Army staging area there, and King could see the pilot eyeing him as the man at the rear-gunner station turned from the Parabellum and began concentrating on shooting pictures.

Well, we can't have that, can we.

He waded right in.

Nothing fancy.

Simply a direct, shallow dive from the German's left front quarter, positioned just so, keeping the enemy's top wing between him and that Parabellum. It was almost head-on, so they closed fast, and King's machine guns began to pound as the ugly bruiser grew fatter and uglier in his ring sight.

They passed with no more than ten feet of clearance, and the Spad bounced in the German's prop-wash. King rolled out and dropped, recovering quickly and pulling up and around below and to the rear of the Hannoveranner. He fired a short burst, and there was a flaring and an unfurling of white-hot fire, and as he zoomed for altitude, he glimpsed the German rear gunner, twisting in his cockpit, beating madly at the flames that ate at his chest and head. Then the man and the airplane around him dissolved in a starburst of heat and smoke, and the wreckage scattered in individual burnings that tumbled down the sky and disappeared in the mists.

A series of cracklings and splinters erupted from the center section about him.

Holy shit!

He rolled out and down, and as the Spad dropped he saw the Fokker behind him.

Where'd you come from, you bastard?

There was a loud snap beside his head, and he felt the heat of the passing bullet. But once again, luck was with him. His fast vertical turn was too much for the over-confident German, and the black and red Fokker seemed to hover as it entered a futile attempt to follow. It was enough for King to get into position for a deflection shot, and his brief burst caught the enemy amidships. Another flaring and another cascade of fire and wreckage, but this time with a difference. As the burning Fokker tumbled, its pilot fell free, turning in a weird slowness behind it until a white parasol flowered.

Well, well. Lookee here. One of them there newfangled parachutes. Target practice comin' up, Pumper Von Nickel!

King went into a wide turn and came back. The German pilot, clear and close in the Spad's sights, dangled like a doll at the end of a string. A long burst from the Vickers guns blew him apart, and he fell free of the harness, leaving the parachute to drift and roll in a downward fluttering.

Auf wiedersehen, dickhead!

❋❋❋

Bianco had just signed all the dailies to Wing and was sitting with his boots propped on the desk when Osborne came through the office door and threw a preoccupied salute.

"Got a mo', Captain?"

"Sure. What's up?"

Osborne's face showed worry. "I'm not sure how to approach this...matter, I guess you'd call it, but I think something's wrong with King."

"Wrong? What kind of wrong?"

"As you see from the report he filed, he led me and the others in A Flight over the Montsec sector but got detached from the rest of us, and while trying to relocate us he ran into some enemy and shot down a Hannoveranner and a Fokker. He requests confirmation from 1st Army arty, which he says was directly below."

"So what's the problem?"

Osborne took a deep breath and blinked twice. "The problem is, it didn't happen."

"What?"

"His report is just plain horseshit."

Bianco swung his feet from the desk and leaned forward, his eyes filled with incredulity. "Say again?"

"The patrol was proceeding normally. We were between three and four thousand feet and climbing, with King at the point and me as assistant flight leader riding above and behind him to the right. The other guys stacked behind me. You know. Normal. All of a sudden, King peeled off to starboard and dived into a pretty sizeable cloud patch. He didn't get separated. He plain old took off.

"We were all looking around like crazy for the threat he must have seen, but there was nothing. He just disappeared on us. I supposed he'd developed engine trouble or something, so I took over and we completed the patrol without incident. When we came back to the field, King's ship was sitting on the line, and I assumed he was in here writing his report. I came looking for him to find out what happened, but he wasn't around, so I read his report, which he'd put on the adjutant's spike, like always. As I say, it ain't true. He didn't get separated. He ran. The four of us watched him do it."

Bianco was nearing apoplexy. "My aching government ass! Are you sure he didn't see those two Kraut planes and went into the attack, expecting you guys to follow?"

"I don't know what the hell he saw, if anything, Captain. All I know is it didn't happen the way he said it did, and I'm sort of worried about him."

Bianco pushed back his chair and stood up. "Where the hell is King now? Get him in here. Toot sweet!"

"Somebody mention my name?" King stood in the doorway, smiling affably.

Bianco and Osborne traded quick, astonished, and somehow guilty glances.

"Damn right we did," Bianco said. "Your report says you got

separated from the flight. Osborne says you didn't get separated, you just dropped off into a cloud bank. Now who the hell's right in all this shit?"

King laughed softly. "I'd say we're both right. To Osborne and the other guys, it must have looked as if I just took off on my own. I did, but only for the couple of minutes it took to investigate what I thought was a pair of enemy planes below, tracking us in the clouds. When I found it to be a false alarm, I climbed back to join the flight, but I couldn't find them."

"Goddammit, Johnny-Kraut, you know that was a violation of procedure! You, a frigging flight leader, should know that best of all! What the hell were you thinking of?"

"Hey, back off, Captain. I thought I saw an enemy threat. My job is to find the enemy and kill him. Which I later did, by the way. On my own, while the rest of the flight was going home, leaving me in the lurch."

Osborne bristled. "Whoa, John. We didn't leave you. You left us."

Bianco threw up his hands in angry frustration. "All right, all right, all right! Enough of this he-says-I-says-you-says crap! So there's room for debate on this flight-leader's report. We'll let it stand for now, and we'll wait for 1st Army arty's confirmation reports on King's victories. In the meantime, let's everybody calm down and get the hell out of my office."

Osborne shook his head and stomped out, but King lingered.

"Well, what is it, John? Something else?"

"I want to remind you, Captain, that I'm under a Foulois command to fly to Paris this afternoon to meet with somebody important from the States."

"All right, all right. It's already on the report. So get the hell out of here and see me first thing you get back." Bianco ran his hands through his patch of hair and asked the ceiling, "Oh, Lord, is there no relief?"

※※※

King strode anxiously down the flight line, squinting in the noonday sun and assuring himself that the ringing in his ears would go away once he'd caught a catnap. Noise from aviating and combating was one of Satan's most diabolical curses. There were times when the roaring and the screeching came through so loudly it would awaken him in the middle of a night's sleep.

But it was no more than a ringing now, and a quick nap usually took care of it.

The main source of his current worry was the condition of his Spad. If he was to fly it to Paris-Vigneulles, he wanted it to be in acceptable shape. The burst of fire from that Fokker had hit the center section pretty good, and the fact he'd returned from the patrol with no mechanical difficulties was no guarantee that there was no damage that had to be fixed.

The Spad sat serene in the noon. He put his foot in the stirrup and swung up for a close look at the cockpit, the machine-gun mounts, the windscreen, the forward sheet metal, the upper wing auxiliary wing tank, the fabric around it.

The shock took him close to nausea.

There was no damage.

Not a single bullet hole. Not a dent. No splintered strut. No violated fabric. No sagging wires. Not even a paint scratch. The entire machine looked as if it had just arrived from the factory.

Chapter 37

He was in the air again within fifteen minutes, alone and climbing swiftly east by northeast. Up here he could gather himself, deal with the acidic panic that had congealed in his chest. Up here lurked reassurance.

He leveled off at four thousand feet, set the throttle at cruising, and struggled to reconstruct details of the morning patrol. The panic was joined by exasperation when the images remained jumbled and just beyond precise focus.

How can this be? How can I have seen and yet not done?

The feeling in his throat was now like bile, just this side of retching, and to counter it, subdue it, master it, he concentrated on the specifics around him—that cloud pattern over there, the shadow it made on the landscape below, the trembling of the taut fabric on the left lower wing, the way the sunlight turned the dirty snaking of the river over there to a muted sparkling, the feel of cold air blasting his face below the goggles. The realities. The things of life and substance.

And there, plying a lazy, side-sliding course a thousand feet below was a black airplane with a yellow tail and tidy black crosses outlined in white. A Pfalz—one of those new D-12 types that looked somewhat like the Fokker—appeared to be serenely oblivious to his presence up here.

Awash in a mixture of hope and fear, he kicked the Spad into a wingover, followed by a fast, slanting dive that brought the enemy plane into a position just above the outer ring of his gunsight. He made a quick adjustment to set up the proper lead, and at a hundred yards he opened fire. The hammering, the smell of cordite, the coppery rush of spent cartridges, the trembling of the cockpit coaming were utter reality, and he watched, his breath suspended, as his tracer bullets flickered about the Pfalz's fore-section.

There was no combat. The German machine leaped and wallowed to port, its smashed propeller coming to a halt, its engine obscured by a welter of trailing steam. The pilot's goggles sent out a flash of reflected sunlight as he twisted and turned in his cockpit, searching out the source of his sudden calamity.

It was a brief business.

King brought the Spad alongside the Pfalz and stared across the void at the German, who, struggling for control of his powerless, rapidly descending machine, nodded his understanding of King's hand signal to land at once and surrender.

Circling a hundred feet above, King watched the German plane sidle into a belly landing on a strip of green forming the river bank, where it slewed into a cartwheeling pile of junk that came to rest against some broken trees.

He said aloud, "Stay there, Heinrich. I'll be right down."

He managed to settle the Spad in a relatively tidy landing in a meadow on the other side of the tree line. Switching off the engine, he swung out of the cockpit and loped toward the river bank, his service pistol in hand.

The German was a boy, lying entangled and helpless in the wreckage around him. His face was suety with fear and pain. "Do not shoot me, please, dear sir," he choked in thick English.

King holstered his pistol and asked, "Now why would I want to shoot you, pal? You're not going anywhere."

Surprise and a kind of relief showed in the youngster's eyes. "You speak German?"

"Why not? You think you have a patent on it?"

"But it's such good German. Bavarian, but good."

"Are you badly hurt?"

"No. But I can't stand up to defend myself."

"Against what?"

"My Jasta adjutant has assured us that Americans are not taking prisoners anymore. They are shooting the wounded, the helpless. It is their red Indian heritage."

"Your adjutant's full of shit, pal."

"But—"

King knelt and began to tug at the wreckage. "If you promise not to defend yourself, I'll try to pull you out of this junk and make you comfortable until the medics get here."

"You would do this?"

"Sure. It's my hobby—pulling aviators out of wrecked airplanes. I'm well known for this."

"Hobby?"

"What's your name?"

"Leutnant Siegfried Bauer. You want my papers?"

"No," King said, "you'll give them to those American soldiers running toward us over there. They'll get you out of this tangle, treat your cuts and bruises, and put you safely into the prisoner of war process. One thing you can do for me, however."

"What is it, sir?"

"Let me have your helmet and goggles. As a souvenir."

Bauer swept them from his head, revealing his close-cropped, whitish blond hair. He managed a smile that revealed a narrow gap between his front teeth. "I thank you, sir, for your kindness. Perhaps we will meet again."

"Perhaps, Bauer. Perhaps."

King checked his watch.

Next up, a return to the field, refreshed with this token of his grasp on reality, then a shower, shave, and the flight to Paris, as ordered.

He glanced aloft. The light was still good and would remain so.

Still on schedule.

But, boy, the helmet and goggles sure felt good in his hand....

Chapter 38

Senator Slater and Ned Raymond were enjoying the morning sun at one of the tonier sidewalk cafés on the Rue de la Paix. It was still relatively cool, and a gentle breeze rustled the leaves of the potted trees and gave special sway to the long skirts of the women passing by. Even the traffic seemed quieter and slower paced, with only an occasional honking from a china-closet cab and the grinding of camion gears to signal the Parisian pulse.

Slater sipped some coffee, returned the cup to its saucer, dabbed his lips with a napkin, and sighed contentedly. "I suppose I should feel guilty for missing so much of the 65th Congress, but I don't."

Raymond looked up from his copy of the *Herald Trib*. "You shouldn't. You're on a legitimate fact-finding tour on behalf of your committee. Besides, the only business of any note is the wrangling in the House over that proposed resurvey of western public lands."

"It's about time. Most of the towns and farms and outhouses west of Kansas City have been built on turf nobody's sure who owns. Hell, even when I was selling guns to cowboys, I'd now and then have to kick out customers who got into fistfights about property lines."

Raymond humphed. "And look at you now—up to your

galluses in history's biggest fistfight over property lines. You've come up in the world."

Slater laughed softly. "You really do have a way of getting the slant on things, Neddie my boy."

After another period of people-watching, Slater said, "All that aside, Neddie, something's stirring in the House that tightens my buns. Got a note from Porky Beane on the Commerce Committee. He's prepping a bill that would outlaw pyramid schemes and lay heavy financial and jail penalties on those who run them. He asks for my support."

"Pyramid schemes?"

"Yeah. Like that thing we've got Mason to set up with Willis in San Antone."

"Uh-oh."

"Yeah."

"So what's your point?"

"I want you to tell George Mason to liquidate All-Star Realty. Give Willis twenty-five thousand as a good-bye bonus and keep a hundred thousand for himself. Whatever's left goes anonymously to the Salvation Army."

Raymond's eyes were wide with disbelief and astonishment. "You've got to be joking. That's a bloody cash cow you're killing, Senator."

"It's already too old. These things wear out fast. I want All-Star shut down without a trace before any whisper of it gets to the government. I just hope we're not too late."

"What is all this? You're getting ethical all of a sudden?"

"I'm getting practical. I'm building a pretty good image for a long run in the Senate. I don't want to be blindsided by some stupid outburst of Porky Beane righteousness that makes a felony out of our San Antone take. I don't want Porky or somebody doing to me what I did to Senator Murray, know what I mean? Besides, there's tons of money to be made legally just by pretending to listen to the right lobbyists. You think All-Star made money? Wait'll you see the moola we can lift from the Amalgamated Peanut Butter Corporation when they want the government to subsidize the forty-lebben grape jelly factories they plan to build."

"Well," Raymond said resignedly, "whatever you want."

"Start the process this morning. And keep me the hell out of it."

Raymond pretended to return to his reading, but after a time he said without looking up, "I noticed you had trouble sleeping last night. You did a lot of tossing and blanket-stealing. Was it the All-Star thing?"

"Partly. But I also kept thinking about that yokel columnist from Wilmington, Delaware."

"Now that is a cause for insomnia, sure enough. Here you are, trying to dump a scam, plus trying to save the world for democracy, and you lose sleep over a nobody newspaper guy whose name you got wrong. Sheesh."

"It wasn't him. It was what he asked."

"And what was that?"

"He wanted to know how much I've flown in airplanes. Me, heading up a committee trying to build an air force, he assumed I knew a lot about planes, had done a bunch of flying."

"You don't have to be an auto mechanic to order a set of tires. You know that. I know that. Even people in Wilmington, Delaware, know that. What's your point?"

"I want to pee in my pants when I hear myself saying this, but I think I ought to go for an airplane ride. Maybe two or three, if I can find the nerve."

With slow deliberation, Raymond folded his newspaper and used it as a sun screen for the incredulous stare he sent Slater's way. "Airplane ride? You? Are you out of your freaking senatorial freaking mind?"

"It would look good in publicity handouts. On campaign posters. Mailers. Me, in helmet and goggles, waving from an airplane seat."

"Well, hell. We could get the same effect by just having you sit in an airplane. You don't have to go buzzing around in one."

"Yes, I do. I gotta be able to look a guy in the eye and say, sure, I've been up in a plane. Quite often."

Raymond sighed and shook his head in that way of his. "Who are you kidding? The only time you look somebody in the eye is when you're lying."

"Whatever."

As always, Raymond's mind, sensitive to any hint of political advantage, went immediately into gear, and he began to use the ensuing lull to consider ways and means of turning this current asininity into a practical plus. He pulled his watch from its vest pocket and snapped open its glittering gold lid. After staring at it, playing its reading against the idea that had begun to form, he closed the lid—absently enjoying the solid click—and said, "Mrs. Forsythe-Goodman's meeting with John King is set for two this afternoon. Your appearance at the Italian Embassy reception is set for six. That gives you the time to make John King's acquaintance, preferably after his meeting with the lady, and arrange for him to take you on, ah, let's call it an orientation flight at a date and time still to be established."

"John King. You mean the ace? The young man from Lackawanna who is becoming one of our premier airmen?"

"Damn, Senator, your mind is getting to be a sieve. We went to a huge amount of trouble to pull King off the front to come here and meet with the lady. And you have to be reminded who he is?"

"Oh, don't make such a big thing of it, Neddie. I meet a zillion people a day, I attend another zillion thingies a day, and I have to remember this and that and whatever every twenty-four hours a day. Cut me some slack, for cripe's sake."

"But this young man is one of our leading war heroes, and he's on his way to becoming a freaking aerial legend. And they tell me he's a terrible iconoclast who refuses to kiss ass and make nice for cameras and the Brass. From now on, Senator, you forget his name at your peril. A news guy from Wilmington, Delaware, he ain't, goddammit."

Slater delivered a teasing, sidelong glance. "All right, all right, Freddie."

Raymond, on the edge of apoplexy, caught the tease, and he exploded into relieving laughter. So did Slater, and the surrounding coffee sippers gave them quick, disapproving glances.

"I just love to get your goat, Neddie."

"You're a sadistic wretch. You'll give me a heart attack yet." Raymond touched his napkin to his brow. "Seriously, what better choice for the chauffeur on your aerial debut? What better chance for a great photo, showing you with a famous American warrior and one of the world's leading philanthropists?"

"Right."

"I'll call Clancy at the *Trib*. And the *Stars and Stripes* and, yeah, that AP guy."

"If that Wilmington fellah is still around, be sure to call him, too. I owe him."

❈❈❈

Since the night before, when the staff car had met his plane at Villeneuve and dropped him off at the entrance to the hotel, King had struggled with his rising puzzlement, confusion, and curiosity, ending up with an irritability that wouldn't go away. He'd been in the armorer's shed, hand-selecting machine-gun cartridges for the next day's business when Bianco had come in, as breathless as a ditzy debutante, to announce that none other than General Foulois, AEF boss of everything airplaney, would be pleased if 2nd Lt. John NMI King, serial number O-545169, A Flight commander, 38th Pursuit Squadron, were to report Sunday afternoon at 1400 hours to the mezzanine salon of the Hotel Imperiale, Paris, to meet personally with a civilian visitor who preferred temporarily to remain anonymous.

"My God, Johnny-Kraut, you're turning into a frigging celebrity. May I have the men line up so you can autograph their dinguses?"

"Blow it out your barracks bag, Captain."

"Ah, that's the Johnny-Kraut I know and love." Bianco lowered his brows severely. "Be there, goddammit, or I'll have you on KP until the Army is issued submarines."

"Officers don't get KP."

"You wanna freakin' bet?"

"So how do I get to this fancy hotel?"

"Fly your patrol as scheduled. Then give me your paperwork, get into proper uniform, pack a bag for an overnight, then fly your Spad to the Paris maintenance field at Villeneuve. You'll be met there by a staff car."

"Come on, Captain. How do I know you're not just setting me up for some kind of joke?"

Bianco stared at him in disbelief. Then, clasping his hands together and holding them to his breast, he fluttered his eyelashes and moaned, "Oh, please, dear Johnny-Kraut, believe me. Tell me that you believe me, lest my poor heart breaks."

"What a pain in the ass."

"You should see it from here, pal."

※※※

For the entire flight to the capital, he'd brooded about the mysterious absence of damage on his ship. How could he have heard the shots, seen the splinters fly, and then find no damage? This was the stuff of major hallucinations. He had heard about overworked, fatigued combat pilots claiming to have done things that never really happened, but there had been nothing illusory about the vicious fight he'd been in. The Hannoveranner collapsing in flames and the Fokker pilot falling free of his parachute were sights still so vivid in his mind, his mouth would run with the juices preceding nausea, and he would awaken on his cot, drenched in sweat and pressed by an urgent need to defecate. You don't just dream up stuff that specific, damn it. Especially when you have a set of square-lensed goggles and a black leather helmet whose lining was inscribed "Lt. S. Bauer" to prove the reality of that very same day.

Suddenly tired and annoyed by all this spooky-dooky psychological stuff, he sought to will it away with deliberate speculations on what this trip was all about.

Still...

The beautiful furniture-like finish on the struts about him, the satiny, unbroken sheen of the cowling, continued to mock him.

So he was not in the best of moods by the time he followed the unctuous hotel manager to his digs, a modest little hovel comprising two bedrooms, a full bathroom, a drawing room, a dining room, a kitchenette, and a balcony overlooking Forever. An in-room haircut and an hour-long tub bath, followed by dinner served by a pair of maids who could have been borrowed from the *Folies Bergère*, did little to improve things.

He called the desk.

"Lieutenant King here. Who's paying for my stay here?"

"I'm sorry, sir, but I am not permitted to say."

"You're not going to charge it to me, I hope."

There was a polite chuckle. "Oh, no, sir."

"Well, all right then." He hung up.

But now, ascending the marble steps to the mezzanine in his shiny boots and squeaky-clean uniform, made thus by the overnight crew in the hotel's bowels, his mood had risen all the way to grumpy.

❈❈❈

A doorman bowed him into the salon where, standing regally before the filigreed fireplace, Mrs. Forsythe-Goodman held out her gloved right hand and said solemnly, "Yes, Lieutenant King, it is I, and I am more grateful for your being here than I can possibly say."

In the past year, King had met and dealt with about every shade of surprise to be found in the universe, but this one really, truly, in the total spirit of the cliché, rendered him speechless. Innate good manners and reflex habit compelled him to stand at attention and bow slightly in deference to age and dignity. He was even able to open his mouth. But, try as he might, he was entirely unable to send a word through the astonishment that had congealed there.

"Please, Lieutenant, come and have a seat." She designated an ornate two-seater adjacent to a small but lavish buffet. "May I pour you tea?"

Good manners again came to help by breaking through the speechlessness. "No thank you," he managed. "What's this all about, ma'am?"

"Please, have a seat. There are some things it's absolutely necessary for me to tell you."

"You and I are hardly friends after I caused you so much embarrassment in front of all Philadelphia society. What could there be for us to talk about?"

Her watery old eyes went to the ceiling, as if searching there for language that eluded her. "I've written to you any number of times. Either there's been no answer or the letters have been returned unopened. So, with no other option, I've traveled halfway around the world and, with Senatorial help, into a major war zone to find you and plead for your forgiveness."

"I don't understand, ma'am. What is there for me to forgive? It should be the other way around."

It was as if she were delivering a memorized speech. "I ask you to forgive me for the unintentional hurt and humiliation I caused you at Mary Lou Whiting's party last year."

He stared. "You mean you came all this way just to apologize to me?"

"I was so thrown off balance when I learned I had no accompanist, my sputtering made it seem that I considered you inept and at fault. That wasn't the case at all, but unfortunately—"

"I still don't see why what I think and feel mean so much to you, ma'am. I really don't get it."

"I think you are a natural musician. A splendid, but not fully developed musician. I don't want to lose you. At the very moment I picked up on you, I fumbled and dropped you. I want you back."

He shook his head, confused. "Back? To what? For what?"

She examined the jewels on her bracelet, as if guidance or words might be found there. "I'm an enabler, Lieutenant. I've spent most of my life and much of my fortune enabling handicapped, abused, disenfranchised, and disadvantaged individuals and groups to find the power within themselves to attain worthy goals. I don't do it for them. I support them while they discover how to do it themselves. It's the only thing, frankly, that makes me feel that I, myself, am a worthy person, that my life has purpose and meaning."

"So—"

"I was entranced by your music. I decided then and there, at the party, that I'd enable you to climb to whatever zenith you set for yourself."

"That still sounds like charity to me."

"It is. But the charity is for me."

He went to the buffet and selected a gold-trimmed cup, filled it with tea, and, after carefully placing it on its gold-trimmed saucer, carried it to her. "Won't you sit down, ma'am?"

When they had settled on the two-seater, he gave her a direct, probing stare. "All of this is a bit more than I can sort out, Mrs. Goodman. You say that you liked my piano, and, because I wasn't formally trained, you decided that I'm a logical target for your enabling thing. Then, due to a moment of confusion and misread signals, I walked out and you lost me. Is that right?"

"Essentially."

"But you had no idea at the time as to whether I needed your help. I might have been pretty well off. I might have been the heir to big bucks. Or I might have been the world's laziest, most unambitious oaf. Why did you automatically assume I'd need or welcome your help?"

She took a thoughtful sip of tea, her eyes on the distance and, oddly, her cheeks hinting a blush. She said nothing.

"Why, ma'am?" he pressed. "Why me? There are a lot of talented piano players out there, a lot of them needing help. Why and how did you decide so quickly that I was the helpee du jour?"

She sighed, and her face registered a mixture of annoyance and resignation. "You're even smarter than I thought."

"Probably. But that's no answer."

She gave him a quick look. "The answer is light on logic and heavy on emotion."

He waited.

"I had a son. You remind me of him. I loved him very much. He was perfect, but I wanted him to be more perfect. I was forever refining him, polishing him, admonishing him when he was less than I expected. And one day, after I'd scolded him for some lack of perfection, he turned on his heel and ran down the front steps and hopped on his bicycle and rode off. Ten minutes later he was dead, run over on the highway, without my ever having told him how sorry I was for being such a demanding wretch, for trying to make him over into some impossible image in my egotistical mind. And that day, when I seemed to react to your music so negatively, awkwardly, stupidly, you got that same look on your face, and you turned and fled the same way, and I saw that, for all my years of shame and pain, I hadn't changed a whit, that I was still the same pompous busybody. And I vowed, then and there, that I wouldn't rest until I'd searched you out and told you directly how very sorry, how very ashamed, I am for hurting you so desperately. Something I'd failed to do for my own son. And how very much I want to make it up to you in his name. To make things right. To guarantee that you get the best musical education the world has to offer." She touched the tip of her nose with a lace handkerchief.

There was a long pause, and the silence between them seemed to enrich the soft music rising from the lobby below.

"Well," King said eventually, "I've got a better picture of this now, and it appears that I'm the one who owes an apology. If I hadn't been so touchy and so ready to pull on my hair shirt, you would've been spared an ocean trip and all this expensive tea. We could've kissed and made up right there, on the spot."

She laughed chokingly through her bleariness. "Oh, my, you are a dear boy."

"And you're a very gracious, generous lady. Your son was lucky to have such a great mom, even for a short time, and I don't doubt he'd say that right now if he could. But let me tell you something, too. There was a time when I'd have been so glad to get the recognition and support you have in mind, I'd have tap-danced all the way to Mars. If it were up to me now, I'd get that great education. I'd have suffered for my art, I'd have walked the streets and rung the doorbells looking for jobs, and I wouldn't have stopped until I got to the top. But I'm of a different mind now. A career in music isn't to be, I'm afraid."

"Why ever not?" she asked, surprised, alarmed.

"I'm unraveling. I'm a nervous wreck. I can't eat or sleep. And I have these god-awful headaches and nightmares, even when I'm awake. My hands are starting to shake, and my vision blurs now and then. I wouldn't advise anybody to bet on my surviving the war."

She was truly appalled, he could see.

"There are doctors, medicines—"

"It's beyond that now. But don't be upset, ma'am. It's really all right with me. I'm not the least bit worried."

"You mean," she asked, faltering, "you're religious?"

He smiled. "I wouldn't say so. Not really. Religion is for organization men. I believe in things that aren't organizable. Whatever, I'll be okay." He patted her hand, glanced at his watch, and stood up. "Time to get along."

Another pause, another exchange of slight smiles.

"Are you all right now, ma'am?"

"Yes, dear, I am. I'll always be grateful to you."

"So we're friends. So let's write each other now and then."

"That's a promise, John. You'll always be in my heart."

He kissed her cheek, turned, and strode out to the mezzanine, his heels clicking on the polished marble.

Chapter 39

"Ah, Lieutenant King," Raymond crooned, rising from a marble bench, holding out a hand of greeting, and waving his other hand at Slater, who was standing at the mezzanine balustrade like a wedding usher in his swallowtail coat and striped trousers. "How fortunate that we meet this way. I'm Ned Raymond, and it's my honor to introduce you to United States Senator Thaddeus Slater."

"Oh, yes. I saw you both in Buffalo once."

Raymond's eyes rapidly went into fast-memory gear. "Really?"

"You were having lunch with Fontaine at that fancy restaurant on Delaware Avenue. Before we went to war."

Raymond quickly changed the subject. "Senator Slater is chairman of the Senate Committee on Military Aviation, and he's long been an admirer of yours."

"That's nice."

Slater came forward and pumped King's hand. "Absolutely delighted, Lieutenant King. Yes, indeed. I must tell you how very proud and impressed we of the Committee are regarding your extraordinary exploits. Of your twenty victories in aerial battles–"

"Twelve. Twelve victories. You must be thinking of Frank Luke."

Raymond was openly flustered now. "But only today I read in *Stars and Stripes* that you've shot down twenty German aircraft–"

"Not so. I've actually shot down twenty-four planes and seven balloons, but only twelve of the lot have been confirmed. The people in the Confirmation Office are very happy with Luke and Rickenbacker, but they aren't all that crazy about me."

Slater saw an opportunity. "Well, now, if that's the case, maybe we can do something about it, eh? There's no room for playing favorites in something so important, so vital, is there now, mmm?" He took King's arm and led him toward the staircase. "Let's go down to the dining room and catch a snack. There are many things I'd like to talk over with you, Lieutenant, and this seems a very good time for it. All right?"

"Well, as long as we're here."

※※※

They ordered wine and cheese, fresh sliced fruit with hard-crusted rolls, then sat for a time, pretending interest in the small orchestra as it fussed its way through some operetta tunes.

"Tell me, Lieutenant," Slater said, disassembling a roll, "as a pursuit pilot, which plane do you consider the best?"

"The Fokker D-7."

Raymond said, "Ah, that's a German plane, isn't it?"

"He asked which plane. That's my pick."

Slater chuckled. "I meant which of the Allied planes do you consider the best."

"The Spad 13, with the 220 Hisso engine and squared-off, equal-span wings. It's best because it has fewer faults and liabilities than any of the others. It isn't best because it's best, if you follow me."

"Mmm. Yes." Slater sipped some wine and rolled the glass stem in his fingers, thoughtful. "I realize you're a pursuit pilot, Lieutenant, but have you ever flown a two-seat plane? The DH-4, for instance?"

"Learned to fly on a Jenny. I've flown the DH-4 twice, once on a familiarization thing at Issoudon, the other time when it had to be ferried from a depot to Toul. Why do you ask?"

"I'm just wondering if you're qualified to fly anything but a single-seater."

King laughed. "Senator, I'm qualified to fly anything. Period. You put some wings on a locomotive, and I'll get it into the air and do loops."

Slater and Raymond joined in his laughter.

"Well, then," Slater asked, becoming serious, "would you be kind enough to take me for an airplane ride? Nothing special. Just a ride in an airplane."

King's amusement faded as he considered this. *So now I'm a frigging chauffeur. What is it with people? One minute they treat you like you are something, the next minute it's as if you're some kind of lackey.*

"Well, I don't know, Senator. For me it would be an honor. I'm truly flattered that you've asked me. But for those sourpuss bosses of mine, they might not think it's such a great idea for somebody as important as you to be using a military plane for a sightseeing gadabout in a war zone."

Slater smiled a cat's smile. "You let me handle those sourpuss bosses of yours."

"Sure. But they may want to assign you another pilot. They're pretty down on me these days. They used to like me, but it seems they don't anymore. They might resent my getting this kind of privilege."

"I couldn't care less if Black Jack Pershing doesn't like you. I like you. All of Congress likes you. The press likes you. Millions of Americans like you. Nobody's going to fly my plane but you, the fastest rising star in the American aerial combat universe. Your bosses can go whistle."

"Well, you put it that way, just tell me when you want to go and arrange to have a plane assigned. I'll be your chauffeur. Okay?"

"Splendid!"

"Meantime, I have to go now. I shot down three planes the day before yesterday, and I want to check in with the 1st Army Air Service office to see if confirmations have come in. Excuse me?"

Slater tried to be unruffled by this abrupt dismissal, but it wasn't easy. King was proving to be an unpredictable, boorish sort, no matter how many assurances he'd received to the contrary. Well, what the hell, all they had to do was meet somewhere for a good photo session, take a short ride around the field, pause for more pix, and then the arrogant little nincompoop could go back to his squadron and bore the hell out of others. *God, what I won't do for publicity. Shee-it-oh-dear.*

Raymond, knowing that Slater would be impossible to live with after a brush-off like this, developed a quick, self-protective delaying tactic. "Hold on, Lieutenant. Before you go, would you please explain for the Senator and me just how aerial combat victories are confirmed? From what I've seen and heard, it seems to be a rather catch-as-catch-can process."

The question caught King at a moment of sudden lucidity. Just as a haze of inexplicable panic had moved in, an urgent need to prove that the action of two days ago had indeed taken place, his mind intervened, as if it had moved from a siding onto the main track, and he saw the hotel and its busy people, the senator and his aide, the ornate marble surroundings, the potted plants, with a kind of relieving clarity.

"Well, Mr. Raymond, you're right. The confirmation process is dependent on a number of basically unreliable or imperfect elements. Take those planes I just shot down as a case in point. I engaged them one at a time, not by plan but by happenstance, in a partly cloudy morning sky over territory occupied by American forces. As in all aerial combat, the action was fast, intense, with impressions and images and visuals fleeting and basically imprecise. In the first fight, since there were only two enemy planes involved, and since they both fell in flames only a few moments apart, I can safely claim that they were destroyed, and they were destroyed by me, because I was the only Allied plane in the adjacency. If competent observers on the ground—and by that I mean military people who are trained in observation of military involvements, like balloon crews, artillery spotters, and so on—also saw those planes fall, and they saw a solitary American Spad as the victor, they'll advise the appropriate office of 1st Army Air Service, and, by comparing my report with theirs, credit will be given. Anything less will be put down as unconfirmed, or maybe possible, and I'll have to accept that. The third plane I shot down is a definite—the pilot was captured by U.S. troops, and I was identified by those same people.

"The largest problem is when large groups of planes join a battle, when things aren't so easy to determine. The pilots are so busy flying, both aggressively and defensively, so fast and reflexively, it's hard to find the time to place some well-aimed shots at a clearly identifiable enemy. And it's just as easy to place those same shots, by accident, into a friendly plane passing by. And when planes blow up, or fall in flames, it's obviously somebody's victory, but whose? The sky is so crisscrossed by tracers and solids flying every which way, it's hard to tell."

"So that's why you say you've shot down twenty-four aircraft but have been given credit for only twelve."

"That's right."

"And you say bias and personal prejudice sometimes enter the picture?"

"Yep. Some pilots are darlings, some are shits. You're looking at one of the latter. If race-car hero Rickenbacker or any of the Ivy League rich-kid snobs claimed those two planes I shot down the day before yesterday, do you think for a minute the Air Service would hesitate to give them credit? Nosiree. But Luke, a hairy-ass cowboy, or me, a colorless boob out of the slums? 'Well, let's see, we'll take it under advisement.'"

A lengthy pause followed while they each considered the inequities in their worlds.

King stood up. "I really do have to go now, gentlemen. Sorry to break this up, but leave I must. I just remembered something urgent, and, since it will take me back to my field, I'll wait until the confirmations come down through regular channels."

Raymond managed a shrug and a weak smile. "So be it." Glancing at Slater's cloudy face, he added, "The basic agreement has been made, and I'm sure you'll be ready when we get back to you with the details."

King nodded. "I appreciate your patience with this. But as busy as he is, I'm sure the Senator knows what it's like to have urgent duties that take precedence over pleasure."

Slater waved a dismissing hand. "Of course, of course. You run along, and we'll get final details to you at your squadron."

King came to attention, clicked his heels, and saluted. "Thank you, sir. You're most kind."

After he'd left, Slater said, "Now there is one truly peculiar young man."

Raymond nodded, not out of habit but out of fervent agreement. "He sure is. One minute an arrogant, snotty know-it-all, the next a quiet, well-mannered gentleman. He can't seem to make up his mind which he is."

"Like a lot of our friends in the Congress, eh?"

Raymond was relieved to hear the senator's joking, so he laughed especially loudly.

※※※

The senator wasn't fond of tobacco, but he liked to wave a cigar around at important functions, because he saw it to be a ritual of the rich and important, and, naturally, he was always ready to use any prop that might signal his membership in that fraternity. So it was with no little irritation that Raymond received Slater's instructions to go back to the hotel suite and pick up the silver cigar case, which the senator had left lying on the coffee table, then bring it to him at the Italian embassy. After helping Slater into a cab, Raymond took the elevator, his mind filled with rebellious thoughts. *God, sometimes I hate this job. I've got to be one of the highest-priced errand boys in the whole freaking world. Next thing you know he'll have me doing his laundry and baking him pies. I'm going to start looking around.*

He knew something was wrong the moment he stepped from the elevator car. The huge hotel security guard, known to Raymond only as "Pierre," was not at his post. The gilded chair at the end of the tiled corridor from which he could keep an eye on both doors to the senatorial suite—the main entrance and the service entry, the latter used primarily by maids and maintenance people—was empty. Raymond understood that Pierre and Rudolf, the equally enormous night-shift replacement, would leave the post, even for bathroom trips, only after the desk sent up a temporary replacement from the hotel cadre.

An empty chair? Bad news.

Raymond moved quietly along the corridor and, finding the

service door slightly ajar, eased into the vestibule. Moving silently to the inner door, he peeked through the gap between the door and its jamb. The living room mirror showed Pierre holding up a bottle of the senator's favorite scotch in his gloved hands. He then returned the half-filled bottle to the bar top and fished a vial from his jacket's side pocket. He was about to pour the vial's contents into the whiskey bottle when Raymond stepped behind him and swung the fireplace poker. *Ba-a-lam! And Rag-ass Raymond, all-time leading slugger for the Buffalo Bellyachers, drives a long, sizzling liner just clear of the left field fence to win the 1918 Wurld Serious!*

Pierre went down, a grizzly bear bouncing on Oriental carpeting, and when he tried to rise, eyes rolling and nape bleeding, Raymond hit him again across the knees. When Pierre passed out, Raymond seized the drapery cords from the closest window and, jerking them free, used them to tie Pierre's hands behind him and bind his ankles together. He took a moment to sniff the vial, then shoved it between Pierre's slack jaws.

Sitting on the sofa, Raymond prodded the half-conscious Pierre with the poker. "If you ever get out of jail, Monsewer Pee-err, tell your German Intelligence bosses that if they ever try this again, I'll have Paul von Hindenburg gelded at high noon on Unter den Linden. In the meantime, I suggest you don't swallow, because there's likely to be some strychnine residue dripping from that vial."

He reached for the phone and called the main desk.

"May I help you, Senator?"

"This is Ned Raymond. Please send some gendarmes to the suite here. I've captured an assassin. He's tied up and woozy. You better hurry, because he has some poison in his mouth, too. Meanwhile, I'm off to join the senator at the Italian embassy. I want no word of this incident made public. I mainly don't want the senator to hear of it. Otherwise you and your hotel will be caught up in a nightmare of law suits and bad publicity. Understand?"

"Of course, Monsieur Raymond. We will take care of it at once. Is there anything else we might do?"

"Yeah. Have a cab waiting for me when I come down."

He handed the cigar case to Slater.

"Damn it, Neddie, what took you so long?"

"Sorry, Senator. I had to tie up a few things while I was in the suite."

"Do you realize that I've been standing around here, surrounded by ten thousand stuffed shirts and an equal number of horse-faced hoity-toity women, without a single cigar to show? What was so important that you couldn't come right away?"

"I remembered you said you'd stiffed the Germans for a lot of money and a mortgage. I was costing out a bodyguard service. Never know when they might send some payback."

"Bah. The Germans are too busy losing a war, too low in the old cash box, to bother with revenge against one man."

"You're not just one man. You're a world-famous celebrity."

Slater rolled a cigar under his nose, the way he'd seen tycoons do. "Well, I can't deny that. But it just isn't likely that the Germans would go to that kind of trouble."

"Whatever you say."

"But cost it out anyhow. Might add to the old image to have my personal bodyguard, eh?"

"Good point."

Chapter 40

The battle to retake the St. Mihiel Salient had been a success, and the Germans, despite their incredibly complex defenses and large numbers of skilled combat troops, had retreated with astonishing speed under the pummeling of the 1st Army and the other hell-for-leather components of the pincers designed by Pershing and his staff. Montsec and its defenders had simply had enough, and the German High Command decided to withdraw what was left to a new line along the Meuse and in the Argonne. The going was tougher there, thanks to German tenacity and the hellish tangle of forests and gullies and swamps that gave them maximum natural cover.

Carpenter's success at winning over Billy Mitchell's heart to the new Fontaine fighter-bomber was somewhat less than overwhelming. They'd gone together to the secret assembly hangar at Issoudon, and Mitchell's reaction was, predictably, that this was one hell of an airplane and he wished he could have at least a thousand by Friday. So it wasn't the plane that gave him problems, it was what would go with it.

"I don't think you fully appreciate the complex nature of the problems I must deal with," Mitchell had said, running a reverent hand along the airplane's fuselage. "First of all, Congress—and

I'm thinking of your boss, Slater, right now—doesn't give a rat's ass about airplanes, of whatever age or whatever design. Congress doesn't care about quality; it wants volume. Congress keeps talking about how we're going to darken the skies over Germany with American-built planes, because that's what the vengeance-minded citizen demands: 'Hey, Kraut, you sink our ships and kill our people and make plans to give Texas to the Mexicalis, so we're gonna bomb every one of your wieners into schnitzels.' Scads of American planes by tomorrow, that's what the voters want, and the only way Congress can get those votes is to deliver scads of airplanes—quality and efficiency be damned. But guess what? No factories, no plans, no experience. So we buy the rights to build European rejects and leftovers in whatever factory space we can find, knowing damned well that the young American men who'll be ordered to fly them have less than one chance in eight of living to tell about it.

"It would take at least a year, maybe two, to get this gorgeous Fontaine thing into the production numbers we need, and the public and the Congress and the big business types are not about to wait a year. Nor are the Germans, who are making their planes better all the time. This Fontaine thing is perfect for what we need now, but there's no way we can get it now.

"And then there's me. Every traditionalist in the industrial-military-political infrastructure will do anything he can to make me shut up and disappear, because I'm preaching a sermon that threatens his various empires. I could get up and yell my head off tomorrow morning about the virtues of Fontaine's plane and its potential role in strategic mass air warfare, and that alone would be sure to get Fontaine's plane relegated to limbo. If Mitchell likes it, wants it, forget it."

Carpenter was irritated, and he let it show. "You mean you're just gonna give up? Go along with this nuttiness?"

"No, Major, I'm not going to give up. I'll keep plugging. But sooner or later the Philistines will prevail, and they will run me out of town on a rail. That's why I'd like to keep you aboard. To help take over when I'm put out on the farm."

✳✳✳

In recognition of Mitchell's great performance in arranging and directing the St. Mihiel Salient air armada, and to demonstrate their lack of malice toward him, the Brass gave him a temporary promotion to brigadier general, with "temporary" understood to mean that if he didn't behave himself and keep his mouth shut, he'd be back to yard bird in nothing flat.

Carpenter dealt with all this ambivalence in his new-found determination to reform and make something of himself. He now had a cause, a rallying point offering a focus for the energy emanating from the absolute need to rid himself of self-disgust and, for lack of any other definition, to become closer to what that little know-it-all John King said he was, to live one day at a time, and to make each day count for something.

Thanks to his unblinking acceptance of Mitchell's turn-down of the Fontaine fighter-bomber and his own often-repeated paeans for air power and its amalgamation under one department, Carpenter received Mitchell's VOCO permission to observe the continuing aviation action in relative independence. To make that possible, he'd been authorized the use of a new Spad 13, a billet and temporary administrative attachment to the 38th Pursuit Squadron, as well as attendance at whatever group or wing tactical meetings he chose to look in on. Mitchell worried about him a bit, though, specifying that whenever he flew over the lines or any other tactical combat area, he should always be in the proximity of scheduled 38th Squadron operations. "After all," Mitchell had grumped, "it won't look very good on my record if it shows that I let the special aide to a U.S. senator get his butt shot off while tooling around on his own."

"Well, General," Carpenter had twitted, "will the record look any better if the special aide to a U.S. senator gets his butt shot off while flying in the company of some of your great aces?"

"That I can handle. There aren't many at Chaumont or the War Department, for that matter, who would be particularly upset over a unit's loss of a spy sent out by some U.S. senator."

"You'll be giving me a complex, General."

"Good. I'd like that. But what I'm saying is, don't, under any circumstances, get involved in any actions. You are to be an observer at all times, not a participant. Watch. Don't intervene. Got it?"

"Yes, sir."

"I want your written observations, opinions, your commentaries supporting my air power convictions. I do not want you getting in the way of my working airmen. You aren't experienced enough to be of real help, and you could be a distraction that could get somebody hurt."

"I understand, sir."

"Stay by yourself. And if a German happens to come at you, run like hell. We're now up against the Richthofen conglomeration, a bunch of squadrons flying Fokker D-7s led by a hotshot named Göring and featuring the likes of Udet and Gabriel—none of them rookies and all of them mean sonsabitches."

"If running isn't an option, am I allowed to defend myself? I mean, I won't get demerits or KP duty if I blow the hell out of Göring while he's got me cornered, will I?"

Mitchell gave him a look. "Get out of my office. I'm a busy man."

One of the most bizarre aspects of this arrangement was the coincidental presence of John King, whose hut was down the muddy road no more than a hundred yards from his own. He found this out on arrival at the 38th's field near Rembercourt. He was filling out forms in the adjutant's office when King came in to pick up a combat report sheet. The reunion had been stilted and disturbing. King's general appearance was a shocking confirmation of the mail-inspired misgivings that had caused him to write Mary Lou Whiting. King was thinner than ever, and his already short stature was accented by a slump in his shoulders, akin to that which characterizes the elderly veterans who stump through town parks on the Fourth of July. They'd shaken hands and slapped each other's back and made all the appropriate noises, but King's natural reserve had seemed to have deepened, and there were moments in which he came across as being slightly retarded. Then, just as this melancholy impression was forming, there would be a change, so swift it seemed as if he'd never been anything but affable, alert, and, as he'd been back in Buffalo, one smart kid.

He was proving to be one gutsy kid, too.

Carpenter, cruising about a mile away and around a thousand feet higher, was watching him now. Flying at the apex of a

V widening into a rank suggesting a cavalry charge, King appeared to be literally at ground level, skittering down the chalky ribbon that was the highway close to the Meuse between Stengy and Mouzon, rising and falling with the wooded terrain, raking German positions with machine-gun fire and the small Cooper bombs that had been fitted to the 38th's ground-support flights. To his flanks, the other Spads in his flight were working just as low, just as hard, just as dangerously.

When the low-level run had been completed and A Flight was climbing over the smoking rubble of Mouzon, the Spad second to King's left wobbled, rolled onto its back and plunged into a patch of woods, creating a streak of fire and smoke and a welter of wreckage. It was unclear to Carpenter whether the Spad had been the victim of ground fire or fire from the wedge of wildly painted Fokkers that suddenly appeared out of the haze. Whichever, a mad, swirling dogfight at treetop level ensued, and two more Spads fell, followed by a Fokker.

What the hell am I doing up here with all that going on, goddammit?

Carpenter felt his heart pounding from anger and frustration, and he was close to defying Mitchell's order when coincidence made a play. A Fokker with red wings and a blue fuselage, plying a parallel course, drifted in just below and to his starboard, and it was obvious that it was flown by some kind of flight commander so busy overseeing the low-level action that he had remained entirely unaware of Carpenter's presence.

"This'll never appear in my reports, General. Scout's honor."

His words were lost in the blattering slipstream as he eased back on the throttle and allowed the Spad to sink directly behind the Fokker.

Shit-oh-dear! Are my guns loaded? Cocked? Off safe?

Of course they are, you dumb bastard. What's with the panic? You're not some wet-pants recruit! He's filling your ring sight. So shoot the sumbish!

He fired a burst of no more than ten shots—five from each gun.

The Fokker stood on its tail as if it were actually writhing in sudden pain, and then it mushed off on its right wing and fell into a tight, flat spin that never ended until it became a smear of flame and smoke on the Meuse River bank.

Well, well, whatcha know? Four more and I'll be an ace.

Chapter 41

Twilight settled over the valley, laying a wash of gold and pink on the foothills of the Vosges and a deepening indigo across the lake they flanked. In the village on the shore below, dots of light winked on, suggesting a tiny galaxy coming to life in some distant sweep of the cosmos.

Mary Lou sat at a table beside the balustrade of the hospital's eastern piazza, considering this analogy, putting her mind to it in the hope that it would provide an antidote to her inexplicable anxiety. The effort was wasted. The uneasiness prevailed.

Suddenly testy, she sighed and shook her head. One of the most beautiful views in the world, an extravaganza of vastness and color and serenity and sweet breezes, and from it she was getting gloom and doom. The incongruity between the grandeur she was seeing and the apprehension she felt was annoying in itself, but worse was the understanding that she was suffering a relapse, an eruption of what she called her "Wordsworth Curse," born that day in her late teens when she first read—or rather, understood—the poet's broodings on immortality.

The suspicion that she had been here before, seen it all before, experienced life before, in another context and somewhere ever so much more compelling, had resonated with the poet's words so fully that she had not since, over all the intervening years, been able to shake it. It had become a kind of imp on her shoulder that dispensed, with seeming whimsicality, both blessing and curse. As a girl, it had worked to her special advantage in surviving the shock and confusion that followed the deaths of beloved friends, but as she grew older and more worldly, it became a source of this nagging discomfort she now felt.

Like Wordsworth, who preceded her by a hundred-some years, she'd been pestered by hints of immortality early on. He devoted much of his poet's lifetime to scratching the itch. Still young, she'd nonetheless done the same. And both Wordsworth and she seemed to have perceived the same tantalizing intimations along the highly dissimilar roads they had traveled.

Her road, she was convinced, was a paradigm, a representative, microcosmic view of humanity's experience with this strange, compelling, and overall moving phenomenon. But who was she? Certainly not a poet. And definitely not a religionist. In fact, much of her life had involved a bitter antagonism with "Churchianity," that current of organized religion that presumed to serve God yet in reality served only itself. Personally, she'd done or considered most of the rotten things the world had to offer. But along the way, she'd also had unexplainable encounters and had risen in mystifying rebellions that spoke of the cosmic reach of that thing within—that force—the religionists of all persuasions liked to call the soul.

And now, John King.

She'd offered him everything. As she saw it now, she had deliberately rebelled against her own immortal soul by giving her mind and body to a man who had long since lost his.

"So why the hell am I here?" she asked aloud, bitter.

"I'm sorry. You said something?"

She turned and looked up, startled. It was Dr. Stevenson, looking splendid in the evening light, with his thick white hair, his trim white mustache, and his Class A uniform and boots providing incontrovertible evidence that here was a man of regal authority and very little time for nonsense.

She pushed back her chair and prepared to rise. "Oh, Doctor—Colonel Stevenson—I didn't realize you—"

He held out a hand. "Mary Lou, my dear. Don't get up. How good it is to see you. I didn't know you were in France until recently when I read that splendid *Stars and Stripes* article on your medical transport flights." He sat in the chair across the small table from her and, smiling, examined her face in that manner of physicians.

"It's been a long time," she said. "I last saw you at my parents' party at the Rehoboth Beach house. At least two years ago, wasn't it?"

"Yes. When you were a lovely girl surrounded by all kinds of muscular, handsome beaux. And now here you are, a lovely young woman in uniform, with a face that has been seasoned by what goes with it."

She smiled and reflexively patted her hair. "I know I'm a dreadful sight, but *c'est la guerre*, as the saying goes."

He sank back in his chair and crossed his legs. "So how are your parents?"

"Fine. Just fine."

"Small talk dealt with, the more important question right now is how you are. How I can help you."

"I'm really reluctant to bother you with this, but you're the leading psychiatrist in the AEF medical corps, and when I want to learn something I always go to the best source."

He laughed. "And it doesn't hurt to have a longtime friend of the family as the best source, eh?"

"Touché."

"Seriously, dear, what's up? How can I help?"

"A year or so ago, I befriended a young flying officer who's now serving here in France. A nice young man, not altogether sure of himself, but good and worthy in many ways. I happened to see him here recently when one of my flights took me to his base. I hardly recognized him. He'd changed."

"In what way?"

"Both physically and in attitude. Very thin, worn down. And haunted, so to speak. Spoke of nightmares, headaches. Hinted at having hallucinations."

Stevenson sighed, feeling the weight of a hundred thousand such conversations, the tonnage of unrelieved puzzlement as to why people were so compelled to beat around the bush, even when their own survival was at stake.

"You and this flier: Are you lovers?"

The heat in her cheeks intensified, seeming to become incandescent. "Well, no, not in the usual sense. We had a couple of intimate moments, but in each he made it clear he really didn't want to have a continuing association with me."

"How did you react to that?"

"Hurt. Angry. Puzzled. I'm used to having men chase me, turn themselves inside out to get my attention. I'd never before had anyone reject me out of hand—even my riding horses at home like to nuzzle me, for Pete's sake. But this was something new, and it got my nanny."

"I see."

"Understand, I wasn't really too deeply upset—in a romantic way, so to speak. I think the idea of him touched me most. Young man, family gone, no resources but an extraordinary, unrequited musical talent. All that and his winsome manner, his shyness, his need for approval, his plain old masculinity. I like masculine men, but all my life I've attracted the self-adoring puffballs."

Stevenson smiled faintly. "That's why you gave into these intimate moments?"

She nodded.

"Did he say why he didn't want more?"

"Yes, but it's a kind of complicated yes. The old rags and riches story: He's a first-generation American, born and raised in poverty, I'm from a long line of plutocratic Americans, and he thinks that leaves us with nothing in common. He's a self-taught piano virtuoso, a gigantic natural musical talent, but the fact that he's self-taught gives him a sense of unworthiness, of implicit fraud and the guilt that goes with it. He describes himself as a man full of dark contradictions. When he was a kid he was smart, capable, and easygoing. He pretty much liked everybody and was liked in return, had kindly thoughts about most everybody, was even-tempered, sympathetic, and generally ambitious. Then, as I get it, somewhere along the line he lost the joy of life, became lonely and gloomy, increasingly pessimistic, and it's my guess that in an effort to run from himself he enlisted in the Army. When I last saw him, during a visit to his airdrome, he pretty much described himself as a basket case, a disaster, and claims that I'm lucky that he doesn't feel any passion for me."

Colonel Stevenson gave all this some thought. "Well," he said eventually, "from the detail you've just given me, I suspect that your relationship was a lot more...intimate... than I'd thought. And if I were truly a guessing man, I'd guess that the young man is right. You are lucky. A man showing those symptoms is almost sure to be a roller-coaster ride, and a dangerous one to boot."

"Symptoms, you say. You mean he's ill?"

The doctor struggled to maintain his impassive expression. "Well, my dear girl, I dare say even you would have to admit he hardly shows signs of vigorous health."

She laughed. "That was stupid of me. What I mean is, does he show signs of a specific illness?"

"I'd say so, yes. Again, if I were asked to venture a guess, I'd guess that, in addition to the extreme fatigue and stress popularly known as incipient shell shock, he's suffering from the early stages of paranoid schizophrenia—a mental illness found most commonly among young men. Girls can be afflicted by it, of course, but its beginnings are more noticeable among males in their teens and early twenties."

"What causes it?"

"No one can say for sure. There are many theories, but the one that's increasingly accepted is that a chemical imbalance develops in the brain and a kind of short circuit evolves. You know how a lightbulb often flickers on and off before it fails altogether? So with the schizophrenic brain."

"There's no cure?"

"None that we know of. It can be treated with medicines and its social impact mitigated, but a cure? Not yet."

They sat quietly and watched the descending twilight for a time. Muted sounds came from the hospital behind them, and a smell of cooking was on the breeze.

"What can we expect from this man, Doctor?"

"Anything and nothing. Someone in this condition, even in civilian life, unthreatened by the kind of terror and anxiety combat brings, suffers from an acute sense of rejection, which triggers an increasingly intolerable lack of self-respect. People with this thing often show anger, aloofness, anxiety, and argumentativeness. What's even more troubling is the fact that he's a combat aviator, daily facing incredible stress. It's possible he's lost some comrades in battle, and he feels that he caused their deaths. This builds, and between self-recrimination and the need to assuage his guilt, he begins to fantasize, to relive the action, or, through visual and auditory hallucinations, to suffer the fate he delivered to others. He's almost sure to sleep fitfully, have nightmares."

"Poor dear."

"Yes. We can only hope that he unravels to the point his commanding officer sends him to a hospital before he hurts himself or others. Short of that, there's little to be done." He consulted his watch again. "Well, I'm due at a staff meeting in five minutes."

She put her hand on his. "Thank you, Doctor. I'm very grateful for the time you've given me."

He stood and took both of her hands in his. "You're most welcome." Then, giving her a gaze filled with gentle sympathy, he said, "You've no idea how I wish I could help you more. For all your efforts to have me see otherwise, you're simply a brave young woman who's fighting to save the man she loves, and my heart goes out to you. But in a way your beloved is luckier than most of us. His torment has a name. War leaves no one untouched, so you, I—none of us—will ever be the same again. The America we left no longer exists. When we go home, people and places will be the same, but different somehow. People will see something different in us, too, and because there's no name for its cause, we'll back away from each other, and we who have been here will eventually feel at home only with those who have also been here, who've shared the cruelties we've delivered and received."

"You've seen through me, Doctor," she murmured. "I do love him so very much. It's all so bleak."

He straightened, pulled his elegant tunic into proper alignment, and nodded unhappily. "Indeed. Accept the fact that you've already lost him, and after a time of healing you'll find that your capacity for love remains unimpaired. You'll find someone to lavish it on. Not in the same way, of course, but in a way that's every bit as fulfilling."

Struggling to stifle her need to cry, she turned outward. "Doctor Stevenson," she asked through a constricted throat, "is there anything I can do to help you?"

He gave her a lingering stare, then smiled most beautifully. "Not really. But do you have any idea how long it's been since anyone has asked me that? Thank you so much."

He strode off into the night.

Chapter 42

"Hi, pard."

King, busy at his hut's table washing a pair of socks in a tin pan, looked up. "Hello, Bill. Didn't hear you come in."

"That was one helluva show you put on yesterday along the Mouzon Road."

"Got a bit sticky." King wrung out the socks, hung them on a tent rope, then dried his hands on a scrap of toweling. "Perkins and Zorn, two of my guys, say they saw you nail a Kraut, too. Nice going, pal."

"Well, for God's sake, tell them not to mention it in their reports. Billy Mitchell made me promise not to treat the enemy roughly."

"Too late. I already put in a confirmation of your kill. It's on its way to Chaumont."

"Shee-it."

"Don't worry. Mitchell never reads reports anyway."

"Wanna bet?"

King sank onto a chair and waved at the cot. "Sit down. How are you making out with Mitchell? Is he the SOB everybody says he is?"

"Not by a long shot. Pretty much all business, but a nice guy underneath."

"Damn. Nice guys never win wars."

"He ain't that nice, pard."

There was a pause while King lit a cigarette with a shaking hand. After blowing a stream of smoke at the tar paper ceiling, he asked, "Something on your mind?"

"As a matter of fact, yes. I want you to do me a favor. A two-step favor."

"Name it."

"I understand you've agreed to take Senator Slater for an airplane ride."

King gave him a waggish look. "Something wrong there. How could I fit that fat little ward-heeler into my Spad? There's hardly enough room in it for me."

Carpenter remained serious. "That's the second part of the favor. I want you to take Slater for his ride in a very special two-seater. A new fighter-bomber designed and built by Fontaine."

They exchanged stares for almost a full minute. It struck Carpenter that King was having difficulty thinking this through.

"Isn't that sort of risky, Bill? Putting a U.S. senator into a new, experimental airplane? In France? Near the front?"

"Maybe. But a helluva lot is riding on it."

"Slater wants publicity for himself, and you want publicity for Fontaine."

"It's a lot more complicated than that, but, well, yes."

"What's in it for me?"

"My gratitude."

"What are you grateful for?"

"If you fly this revolutionary new airplane, it will get a lot of attention. And if it gets a lot of attention, the powers that be might just go ahead and order some. And down the road, it could keep more of our guys alive. And if that happens, I'll be grateful. That's what I mean by complicated."

"Has Mitchell seen this plane?"

"He says he'd like to have a thousand of them by Friday."

"So why doesn't he order me to fly Slater in it?"

"He wants to keep a low profile in all of this. He thinks that if it's known he favors the plane, the powers that be will kill it on the spot. He wants to pretend he doesn't know about it, and that the Slater flight will be Slater's idea, not the Air Service's."

"Has Slater seen this plane?"

"No. You'll be showing it to him."

"God, the world's so full of phony shit."

"Ain't it, though."

King's eyes narrowed, and he leaned forward like one preparing to share a secret. "Know what I think, Bill? I think we're already in Hell. This world is really Hell, and it's our job to figure out how we can get out of here. We're condemned to stay here in Hell until we find the secret way out. When we die, and we haven't found the secret yet, we're sent back to try again in another life. And we keep dying and getting sent back until we finally get the picture, and then we're allowed to move on to another plateau of existence."

Carpenter felt a wave of something like apprehension. But he went along. "You mean you aren't afraid of dying?"

"Of course I am. All of us are. But I finally got the picture. What we're afraid of is the idea of coming back as somebody or something we don't want to be. Like the poet Dryden said, 'Death in itself is nothing. We fear to be we know not what, we know not where.'"

"Christ, John. That's creepy. Where are you getting all this creepy stuff? What's coming over you?"

King laughed an abrupt, odd little laugh. "Yeah. Well. Forget it. So where is this wonder plane of Fontaine's?"

"Issoudon."

"What's the drill?"

"You and I fly there tomorrow in our Spads. We fly together in the new Fontaine to Beauvin, the town in Vosges where Benoit Industries has its factory and flying field. Slater will be waiting there. He's visiting the Benoit people. We think this is ideal because Beauvin is in a very quiet corner of southeastern France, and there's little if any military action within miles."

"Meaning Slater won't be exposed to any real danger," King said.

"Right. There was an item in the *Paris Herald* yesterday about his visit to Benoit, but G-2 tells me the nearest German troops are forty miles away from there, and they're all conscripts in training, so it isn't likely they'll cause trouble."

"To play it safe, I'll fly Slater even farther south. He won't know the difference. He just wants a quick ride and a photo session, if I know politicians."

"You got it, pard."

King stowed his wash pan, then, sinking back in his camp chair, he gave Carpenter an unblinking appraisal. "There's something else, isn't there, Bill. Something's bothering you."

"Well, not really—"

"Come on, what is it? Have I offended you in some way?"

Carpenter shook his head and waved a hand of denial. "No. No kidding. You haven't done anything except—" His gaze wandered out to the brilliant day, seeking a way to complete the thought.

"Except what?"

"Except make me think of things I hate to think about."

"I can't recall making you think about anything."

"That's not what I meant. Just you, being you, makes me think. Bianco told me about that night when some kid was dying beside the wreck of his plane and you played his mother's favorite hymn while he was checking out. That, pard, was a classy thing to do, and it was a kind of legacy, because every guy who was there will remember you and what you did for the rest of his life, and he'll tell his pals, his girl, his wife, his family about it, and they'll never get you out of their minds, either. And when I think about it, I realize that there's nothing I've done or possibly will do that anybody will remember. I make a lot of noise and move fast, but class I ain't got. There's nothing in me or about me that means anything. You not only do great, human things, but you also are a famous ace, a top scorer in battle. The only score I've run up is women, and I haven't even done so hot at that, seeing as how most of them were playing me for money or some advantage."

King sighed, exasperated. "Bill, for crissake, all I did was play a hymn for a kid who was hurting. It wasn't the concert of the century."

"It was the right music at the right time coming out of a guy who feels and cares. Even if I played music, that would never have occurred to me. It was classy. The kind of classy I don't have. When I look at you I see how shallow I am, and I feel bad about myself." He stared thoughtfully at the sunlight beyond the tent flap. "Our friendship began when you pulled me out of the wreckage of a Jenny. And in a way, it's been the same all along. Ever since, you've been pulling me out of the wreckage of my life."

King stubbed out his cigarette. "Well," he said, "let me tell you something, Bill. First, I'd be as rich as Croesus if I had a dollar for every time I wished I could be like you. But it's more than just a mutual admiration thing. The one part of me that's still intact is my intuition. I have one hell of an intuition. I know things. Just know them, sometimes before they happen. And I know about you. You've got great stuff in you. Intelligence. Guts. Kindness. It's like cream. It just hasn't risen to the top yet. Give it time, Bill. You'll achieve wonderful things someday. It's written all over you."

"God, but that's hard to believe. I put on a big front, but underneath I'm a real prick."

"Underneath everybody's a prick. Not one human being escapes prickdom. But everybody's got cream in them, too, and the need is to harness the prick so that the cream can rise."

Carpenter made a testy noise. "You're mixing the hell out of your metaphors, pard."

"And you just delivered a massive non sequitur."

"Well, hell, if I know what a mixed metaphor is, and you know what a non sequitur is, we all of a sudden got a bit of cream bubbling up."

They both laughed at this relieving silliness.

❊❊❊

That afternoon, King took his Spad to five thousand feet and set up a cruise south by southeast. He'd been hearing a strange rattle in the cockpit well that seemed to come and go with medium-range throttle settings, never during ground tests but always when aloft. It was as if something were loose, swinging back and forth on a hinged mounting. But there was no such fitting anywhere, and yet today the sound was loud and insistent, clearly audible over the cruising engine sounds.

He raised his goggles and leaned forward to peer into the cockpit shadows. And then he saw it.

A white garden gate, swinging on its hinges, creaking loudly. Beyond it, a terrible darkness. A complete blackness. A total absence of light.

As he stared, eyes wide in a grotesque, unbelieving gaping, the blackness exploded into white-hot flame, and in an instant the cockpit was an oven filled with roaring, stinking fire. He screamed and beat wildly at the seething heat that ate at his coveralls and dissolved his helmet and turned his hair into a swirling of sparks. Somehow he worked free and flung himself over the side of the disintegrating fuselage and into the wide blue sky. He was tumbling and twirling, with the earth below a madly flipping platter of gray-green. The clouds were around him then gone, around him then gone, and all the while the flames raged at his agonized arms and legs and tore away his boots, miraculously sparing his eyes in an outrageous, sadistic irony that allowed him to witness it all.

And he went down and down and down, screaming through the blue chasms, through the mountains of mist, and toward another, oncoming blackness.

※※※

"Lieutenant? Lieutenant King? "Yo, Lieutenant. Wake up. It's me, Barney."

"Barney?"

"You told me to break up your nap when I had your plane ready. Well, it's ready. All ready to try out."

"Ready?"

"Jeez, Lieutenant, you don't look so good. Gray an' shaky. You okay?"

"I saw through the gate, and it's all black over there."

"Tell you what, Lieutenant. You just lay there like that for a while. I'll get Rooney the medic to come by and give you somethin'. We'll find that rattle tomorrow."

Chapter 43

Slater was impressed with the Benoit establishment. It was centered in a generally rural area in the foothills of the southern reaches of the Vosges range, and, for all its broad stretches of flying field and its orderly ranks of industrial architecture, it had an odd compatibility with its beautiful pastoral surroundings. There were many trees and winding, hedge-lined drives. A tributary of the Rhine wandered in from the east like a glittering ribbon, and the low-elevation factory and office buildings seemed somehow to be natural growth along its banks.

"Quite a spread, wouldn't you say, Neddie?"

Raymond, surveying the valley from the guest chalet's balcony, took a deep breath of mountain air and nodded in obvious pleasure. "It sure ain't Buffalo."

Feeling a slight chill in the morning breeze, Slater pulled his bathrobe closer about him. "I hope we can do business with the Benoits, if for no other reason than the need to make frequent visits here."

"We can do business with them, Senator. That plant tour led by Mademoiselle Benoit yesterday revealed more than just a lot of airplane engines and shiny tile floors. This outfit needs money. You can smell it. They want a fat American contract so bad they're ready to lift that robe of yours and kiss what's under it."

Slater laughed his hissing laugh. "Neddie, you've really come a long way since I hired you two hundred years ago. From awkward college kid to a beady-eyed money machine."

"I've had an excellent tutor."

"We play things right, you and I can stay in the Senate for the rest of our lives."

"Speaking of which, we have a busy day ahead of us." Raymond glanced at his watch. "And it begins two hours from now with the arrival of the new Fontaine airplane carrying our boy Carpenter and your aerial chauffeur, John King. The Benoit airfield manager told me last night that they're due to land around eleven, and after the photo session Carpenter and King will see to the flight preparations, and you and I will have lunch with Mademoiselle Benoit and her management team at the Benoit mansion at noon. More press stuff from one to two p.m., then your flight with King at two-thirty. Dinner with Mademoiselle and a gaggle of French politicos will wrap up our day at seven. You and I catch the Paris train tomorrow morning at eight-thirty."

"Okay. So we still have time for that nice long bath." Slater made quickly for the door to the suite. "Last one in is a horse's ass."

Raymond turned quickly and, throwing off his robe, raced after the senator, laughing like a schoolboy.

CHAPTER 44

Carpenter simply couldn't rid himself of the sense of foreboding. It was not helped at all by John King's worsening appearance, nor by the apologetic suggestion of Sergeant Barney Deakins, the 38th's line chief, when leaning into the Spad's cockpit just before their takeoff for Issoudon.

"Ain't my place to play medic or to give ya advice about an officer pal a yours, Major," Deakins had said in a conspiratorial tone. "But Lieutenant King just plain looks sicker'n a dog, and I think somebody ought to rassle him into a hospital. Maybe you can say or do somethin' that'll turn the trick."

"I think you're right, Barney. When we get back from this trip I'll talk to Captain Bianco about it. And I appreciate your concern."

"Lieutenant King's a good guy and a helluva airplane driver, and I want him to stay that way."

"Me, too, Sarge."

The strange thing about it, Carpenter thought now, staring at the back of King's helmeted head from the rear cockpit, King seemed to be as chipper as all hell up here in a bright blue sky, four thousand feet above one of the most beautiful stretches of all French real estate. He'd looked pretty wan when they'd swung aboard the Fontaine back at Issoudon, but they hadn't been aloft very long when his voice came over the intercom, announcing cheerily, "This here is one piss-cutter of a flyin' machine, Bill."

"I told you you'd like it."

"Like it? Hell, man, it gives me a hard-on." King's laughter was loud in the earphones. "Watch this."

King threw the plane into a snap roll to the right, followed immediately by another to the left. Then he stood it on its tail and pushed it to its limit, allowing it at the zenith to fall into a lazy three-revolution spin. Recovering, he went into a pair of tight figure eights followed by a conclusive loop.

"Wanna try it, Bill?" He raised his hands above his head, laughing.

"Hold on and grit your teeth, pard. I'm gonna show you how this thing really works."

Carpenter unlocked the rear seat controls, resettled his goggles, and shoved the machine into a whistling, 45-degree power dive, holding the nose steady on a village below. He recovered at steeple-tip level and flew down the main street at full throttle, wingtips barely clearing the flanking rows of sleepy houses. When out of the town, he followed the country road, making its turns, nearly kissing its straightaways, roaring tilt-winged between trees, rising and falling with hills and gullies, stampeding sheep and exploding flocks of birds.

"Ratta-tatta-ratta-tatta, boom bam boom! Take that, you naughty Germans!" he yelled into his mike.

"Whee-oo!" King exulted. "Holy shit-oh-dear!"

After five minutes of this, Carpenter took them back to four thousand feet. "Okay, young sojer, you just had a lesson in angrified, ass-kickin' aviatin'. This flyin' machine is now yours again to take us where we're goin'."

"Yes, Master. Ha-ha."

As they circled the Benoit field at Beauvin, King said quietly, "God, Bill. Can you imagine what our guys could do if they all had this thing to use?"

"Don't ask me, pard. Ask Senator Slater."

❈❈❈

At lunch, a lavish affair featuring splendid food, splendidly served to the strains of a truly splendid ensemble, Slater learned just how badly the Benoit company wanted an American contract. Mademoiselle Benoit, a willowy fashion plate with a large pile of carefully arranged hair, a long, slim nose, arched eyebrows and a dimpled smile that revealed two rows of glistening, orderly teeth, sat at the head of the table. Immediately to her right was a beautiful blonde she introduced as Maxine Dumont, her administrative secretary, and it was apparent from their giggling asides that the two were not only coworkers but also great pals.

Slater was flanked by two young women who had trouble keeping their lungs from popping out of their elegant bodices and their hands off the senatorial thighs underneath the exquisitely decorated table. At first he thought the ladies—one was Mitzi, the other Carmella—had made inadvertent contact, but after the contact had become continuing, insistent squeezes, he began to get the idea. He thought about this momentarily, then decided that, on behalf of Mademoiselle Benoit, they were simply administering a Gallic afternoon libido-orientation test.

He leaned over Carmella to his left, where Raymond sat toying with some paté, and murmured, "This broad wants to get laid."

"Well, don't look at me," Raymond murmured back. "I've signed a chastity pledge."

They traded grins, and Slater turned to their hostess. "This is such a lovely home, Ma'mselle. How long have you lived here?"

Fortunately, the lady spoke faultless English-English, and Slater had therefore been benignly disposed toward her since their meeting. Foreigners and their absurd accents had always been a terrible bore.

"Benoits have occupied this estate since the days of Charlemagne, Senator. I, personally, have lived here since birth."

He attempted a joke. "Oh? You mean for twenty-two whole years?"

It worked. She laughed heartily, showing her dimples and her splendid teeth. "Tell me, Senator, do you live in one of those gorgeous white marble buildings in Washington? I've seen photographs, and it appears to be such a lovely city."

"You mean you've never visited Washington?"

"Not once. My parents, for all their expansive world views and industrial diversity, never took me or allowed me, their only child, overseas. They were determined to make me a scholar, and while they were living they saw to it that I attended the Sorbonne and Heidelberg, where I eventually established myself as one of Europe's few women historians. I have an enormous love of history, both ancient and modern, and there was talk of my assumption of a full professorship. But my elders died in a motoring accident and left me to run the company, so today I remain hopelessly parochial and pragmatic, committing body and soul to the Church of the Higher Power—horsepower, that is."

Slater laughed. "Hey, you can make jokes, even in English."

She winked. "I can do many things, in any language, my dear Senator."

"So where did you learn such excellent English?"

"I had a governess, imported from London by my father. She would spank me every time I used English correctly." She winked again. "For me that was a great incentive."

Slater laughed again. "Ma'mselle, you are indeed one of the most amusing and interesting women I have ever met."

"More seriously, I studied English for the ten years I was in the universities, and three years ago I hired an American tutor to help me master business English and American idiom."

"Good move. I'm looking forward to your visits to Washington."

"Why should I visit Washington?"

"To sign the many contracts I expect to arrange between you and the American government on behalf of our country's aviation industry and its suppliers."

"You can do this?"

He winked. "I can do many things, in any language, my dear Ma'mselle."

They laughed again.

※※※

Later, in the evening on the broad veranda overlooking the river and the magenta mountains beyond, the senator and

Raymond, Mademoiselle Benoit and Maxine, lounged in a quartet of fatly stuffed piazza chairs and, nursing brandy, chatted idly of this and that.

"I'm sorry, Senator, that your flying officers couldn't join us this evening."

"Me, too. But King is apparently a bit under the weather—bad headache or something—so he's resting up, and Carpenter is seeing to the airplane I'm supposed to ride in. He says he thinks you'll understand."

"Of course."

After a silence, Mademoiselle Benoit murmured, "I'm truly looking forward to visiting your country."

"Mmm. It's a pretty nice place, all in all," said Slater. "A lot of rough spots, but nice, in the main."

"We should all rejoice that our ages will allow us to enjoy it while it's in its prime. Before it withers and dies."

Slater gave her a sidelong glance. "What do you mean by that?"

"Today it's already halfway through its cycle. As a democracy, it will be dead, or at least dying, before this century is out. Meanwhile, a more ailing Europe is already careening into another dark age of tyranny. Take my word for it. By the beginning of the next century the world as we know it today will be beyond recognition. It will be destroyed by tyrants waging wars many times larger than the one we're now enduring."

"You can't be serious."

"Oh, but I am. History proves it. No democracy—no democratic civilization—has ever lived longer than two hundred years. I can give you chapter and verse and all the reasons, but I'm not going to ruin this delightful evening."

Slater and Raymond traded uneasy stares.

"What do you think the next tyranny will be like?" Slater was genuinely curious.

She finessed. "Tyranny is in the eye of the beholder, Senator. The religionists, for example, speak of 'paradise,' a place of unending peace and contentment. The supreme tyranny would be eternal life, in which all our needs and all of our hopes and pleasures are fulfilled with no effort on our part. Can you imagine even considering an escape from such bliss?"

"Sure. The boredom would drive me nutsy."

They all laughed, and she added, "Ah, yes, the human dilemma. The yearning for perfection in all things, and when all is perfect, the craving for change."

"Well," Slater said, "at least we Americans have another fifty years of good stuff, eh?"

"If you are lucky."

They laughed again. Nervously.

Chapter 45

The Fontaine fighter-bomber sat on the flight line, glistening and haughty in the afternoon sunlight and surrounded by the small crowd of mechanics, handlers, and newspeople with their array of cameras and gear. Senator Slater looked very much the aerial warrior in his helmet and goggles and flight coveralls and white silk scarf. He stood in the rear-gunner's cockpit, blinking as photography lights flared and listening politely while John King, kneeling on the front seat and facing the rear, explained things.

"When we're flying, Senator, I think you'll get the most realistic impression of the rear-gunner's view if you were to fold back that seat there and stand, feet firmly on the floorboards and body secured by those two waist belts toggled to the fuselage longerons. There. You will be more comfortable if you adopt the position favored by most gunners, resting your forearms on the gun ring, there, and keeping the twin Lewis machine guns locked in an elevated position with that toggle, there. If you wish to move the guns to another attitude, flip that toggle, unlock the gun ring, and simply shove the guns to where you want them."

Slater interrupted. "I used to sell guns out west, and I'm pretty familiar with them. You know, six-shooters, rifles, shotguns. But I never saw a Lewis gun up close like this."

"They're a pretty good aircraft weapon, Senator. Lightweight, flexible, air-cooled, gas-operated."

"How many rounds are in those drums?"

"Ninety-seven each. Thirty caliber. When a drum is expended, you unlock it like this, then slap on a fresh drum and secure it like this."

"This is the safety here, right?"

"Yes, sir. Loading handle there. The sights on this rig are of the vane type, but, believe me, sir, when action breaks out most gunners forget the sights and start shooting by tracer, moving the stream and leading the target as if they're squirting a garden hose."

"I'm familiar with leading the target, too. Did a lot of upland game hunting, duck pond shooting. That kind of thing."

"Then you know exactly what the rear gunner must do. The major difference is that in duck shooting, the gunner is stationary, and only the target moves. But in aerial combat, everything is moving. The gunner's plane, the enemy plane. Leading the target can get pretty tricky under those circumstances."

"I'll bet."

King shifted his position and rose to point at something else in the rear cockpit, when suddenly the air resounded to an insane crackling and snapping, and the chest area of King's coveralls fluttered, and blood splashed in all directions. He fell over backward into the front cockpit well, amid an eruption of splinters and flying glass.

Slater stood, frozen, gaping in disbelief, as the thunder and shadows of five low-flying planes flashed over him and went on down the field. He became aware of many people running, the billowing of smoke, shouting, a turmoil of motion and sounds and smells. Hands were pulling at him, and he looked down into the frantic face of Major Carpenter, who stood in the fuselage stirrup and shouted, "Get the hell out of there, Senator! We have an enemy attack. Get out! Drop to the frigging ground! Now!"

And then Carpenter, too, spun around, blood smearing his face as he tumbled away amidst the crackling.

The fabric covering Slater's upper right arm and shoulder magically puckered and fluttered as two shots tore through, and it was then that he broke free of his paralysis of fear and plunged into mad anger. He shook his head like a stunned prize fighter, then slammed his fist against the gun ring lock and, with the other hand, freed the Lewis guns.

"Senator! Senator, for God's sake, get out of there and grab my hand! We'll make a run for it!" It was Raymond reaching up from below, tears running down his face.

"Get the hell out of here, Neddie! I don't want to lose you. Goddammit, get out! Run!"

"I won't leave you! I'll never leave you!"

"Then get your ass up here, grab hold of King, and pull him out of the fucking plane! Hear me? The poor bastard's hurt—bad!"

Slater threw a wild glance around, and he glimpsed people running, soldiers shooting, and smoke rising from a broken plane near the hangar line. He heard a humming, and he saw a cluster of five low-flying planes, dark and malevolent, skimming across the field to the north, coming in angry swiftness for another run at the Fontaine.

"All right, you sonsabitches, come on! I'm turning you into campaign material!"

He flipped off the safeties, jerked the loading handles, and set up a lead.

"Steady, Slats. Easy does it. Get the red one in front and the others'll scatter. Easy. *Now!*"

The pair of Lewis guns rattled and thumped madly, and for a moment he was startled by the sheer power he had unleashed. But then he settled and watched his tracers.

"There. That's it. Good go, Slats."

The red plane suddenly rolled belly up and plunged to the ground, throwing debris and flame and smoke, a spinning fountain of fire that bounded across the field. And, sure enough, the other four machines roared into climbing turns, scattering, and he was on the blue and yellow one, giving it a long burst as it climbed away.

"Hot damn!"

The blue and yellow one seemed to pause, hanging on its propeller, before it turned lazily and plunged through the roof of a warehouse beside the river.

"It's okay now, Senator!" Raymond shouted. "King's out of

the plane and on the ground!"

"Good go, Neddie! I'm proudaya! Now drag him the hell outa here before I lose both of you!"

"We got help now! Medics! Firemen!"

"Okay, but watch out! Here they come again!"

The three remaining German planes came low and fast, their guns winking, and suddenly the Fontaine sagged, and flames erupted in seething white and yellow runnels trailed by sooty smoke.

"Senator! Get out! The plane's about to blow!"

"I accept your invitation," Slater said, unbuckling his belts and rolling over the cockpit rim.

※※※

Slater and Raymond sat in the grass, watching the Fontaine's embers crackle and snap amidst plumes of stinking smoke.

Raymond said dully, "German Intelligence must have picked up on your visiting here today. Why else would they send planes to blow the hell out of this nowhere place?"

"How many did we lose, do you know, Neddie?"

"King's been hit bad, but still hanging on. Bill Carpenter got a bad scalp wound, but he's okay, from all the cussing I heard coming out of him. A Benoit engineer and two mechanics were killed. Ma'mselle Benoit took a shot in her rump while she was pulling the engineer out of a burning camion. That's all I know now."

"She's something special, that Benoit dame."

"Sure is. And so are you," Raymond said.

"Hell, it was just like shootin' ducks."

"Yeah, but ducks don't shoot back at you."

Slater looked around at the sound of a small army of reporters and photographers jumping out of cars and trotting across the grass toward them.

"You do the talking, Neddie. I just don't feel up to it. I just killed a couple of guys, and I don't feel so hot about it."

"They were trying to kill you and me, don't forget."

"And you know what? Damned if I know why."

"The war. It's the war."

"Know something? I'm tired as all hell of this war."

"Well, Senator, it just got you some publicity and votes that just ain't ever gonna end."

"Know something else, Neddie? I don't give a good goddamn."

Chapter 46

Carpenter eased into the hospital room and peered down at the bed where King lay, looking like a mummified small boy what with all his bandages. His eyes were open and oddly bright.

"Hi, Bill."

"What say, pard."

"They nailed me good."

"Looks as if. But you'll be okay."

"That's crap, and you know it."

Carpenter shrugged, not knowing what to say.

"Eighty gazillion dogfights, and the bastards nail me on the ground. Wouldn't you know. I'm even a failure at getting killed."

"Aw, cut it out, pard—"

"It's all right. I never belonged here anyhow. I never really left the other side—I always had one foot on the other side. Like Mom..."

Carpenter could only nod.

"How come your head's bandaged, Bill? Did they get you, too?"

"A little bit. Made my ears ring."

After a silent interval, King said, "Guess what, Bill?"

"What's up?"

"I just saw through the gate. It's not all black in there. A real pretty light. A kind of music. Piano music."

"That's good, pard. Real good."

King sighed lightly. "I'm sure glad it's over." His eyes, glassy now, turned to regard Carpenter with something resembling great fondness. His voice was a whisper. "You make like a blustering horse's patoot, Bill, but that's crap. You're really a great guy, and it's been an honor to be your friend."

"Aw, hell—"

"Tell Mary Lou I really did love her."

"She knows that."

A spasm ran along King's body, and he coughed gently. "I'll save you a place, Bill."

"I'm holding you to that, pard."

King gave him that lopsided smile, closed his eyes, and died.

And Carpenter closed his eyes and wept.

Chapter 47

She cleared the high dunes and rode straight south, the stallion's hooves making rhythmic thuds in the sand. To her left, the sea was a lead-hued infinity, and above the languid surf, close in, a file of seabirds lazed along a parallel course, elegantly precise, as if keeping her under a wary surveillance. To her right, the slopes of sea oats and myrtle arced upward from the beach to form a high horizon against the somber winter sky. Ahead lay thousands of miles of sugar-white beach, and then the Caribbean and Cuba and South America and Antarctica and then all the way around again. The image simultaneously amused and depressed her: a tiny horse and a tiny rider, trotting an endless road through a boundless nowhere, only to end up behind themselves.

She said it aloud. "That's me, all right—running so hard I bump into my own backside."

The afternoon light told her that she could give no more than an hour to the ride if she were to return to The Cottage in time to dress for the reception. She was estimating distances and turn-around points when the air began to throb—a faint drumming that quickly crescendoed into thunderous clattering, popping, rattling, and hissing. The horse wanted to bolt, but she held him in with a hard rein and threw a startled glance upward.

Leaping over the landward crest and slanting overhead like some prehistoric bird on the attack, a Jenny—all dirty green and spidery wires, its propeller thrashing, its motor belching oily smoke—settled to the beach ahead, bounced violently, then veered to the left and cartwheeled into the sea some twenty yards out.

Holding her snorting mount tightly, the harness creaking as she stood in the stirrups for a better view, she stared in disbelief. As the eruption of foam and spray subsided, she could see the plane, now a heap of rags and splintered sticks, settling onto the sandy bottom.

In the subsequent quiet, a voice called across the water. "Hey, kid! Walk that horse out here and pull me out, will you?"

She saw the man then, a helmeted head, a waving arm.

With this confirmation of the pilot's survival, her stunned silence gave way to a mixture of annoyance and relief. "What for? You got yourself into that fix, now get yourself out. I'm not about to get soaked when all you have to do is wade ashore."

"Not possible."

"The water's only hip deep where you are. And my horse is spooked enough without me asking him to sink into sea bottom. So just stand up and wade."

"I can't stand up. My legs are caught, and I can't get a grip on anything with my hands. And the tide's coming in fast."

She glanced at her lapel watch. He was right. The wreck would be under water in less than an hour.

"Damn."

She coaxed the stallion across the beach to a gnarled stump at the base of the slope. After tethering him there, she jogged back to the sea, shedding her denim jacket and shirt as she went. She sat at water's edge and tugged off her boots and trousers, thinking in a crazy divergence how lucky it was that this ridiculous situation was occurring in Delaware. If it had been Cannes, she'd have been gussied up in all the high-fashion trappings for sidesaddle. Here was virtual wilderness, with the nearest society tongue-cluckers some ninety miles north in Wilmington. The saddle was western, and she was togged out in Levis and jackboots, with cowboy long johns underneath. But for all their practical comfort on horseback, the duds would weigh like armor plate in the running tide, so the Levis would have to come off and the man would just have to put up with her immodesty.

She splashed through the shore wash and was immediately up to her chest and beyond effective wading. But she was a good swimmer, and her strong crawl put her beside the wreck in short order.

"You all right, mister?"

The man's nose and mouth were at waterline. His eyes were steel gray, and she saw the beginning of panic in them. "As a matter of fact," he sputtered, "I'd rather be playing croquet right now."

Despite her irritability, she felt a smile forming. He had the stuff, all right. He knew what to do about panic. "Don't go away. I'm going down to see what's up."

The water was cold and murky with roiled sand and spilled fuel, and the afternoon light faded quickly below the surface. Still, she saw the problem at once: the man's legs were crossed and his booted feet were jammed into a V formed by broken spars. She rolled on her back, placed her feet against one of the spars and pulled hard on the other. Lucky again. The wooden vise parted easily, and she was able to tug the man's legs free. When she surfaced, gasping, they were bobbing nearly face to face.

"Can you swim, mister?"

"I'm pretty good at the belly-flop and dog-paddle."

"Get serious, man."

"You get serious. Who can swim with numb legs and all this leather? Right now all I'm good at is sinking."

"Roll on your back and I'll tow you in."

Somehow they reached shore, and they lay on the beach for what seemed to be a long time, faces to the sky, regaining their breath. Eventually he turned his head and gave her a methodical examination.

"You're a girl," he said.

"You noticed that, eh?"

"I thought you were a cowboy at first."

"I'm not one to worry much about fashion."

"Good thing. You're a looker, all right, but long johns won't win you any Easter parade prizes."

Her hair was sopping with oil and silt. The underwear was caked with sand, stank of gasoline, and clung to her like a filthy skin. And he was calling her a looker? "Come on, mister. I look like a pan-fried banana. You must've been in a monastery for a year or so."

"Pan-fried's one thing. A great face, perfect titties, and an arse to die for are something else."

Should she laugh or cuss? There was no surprise in being the target of rude male appraisal. In her time, she'd parried a thousand suggestive sallies from a thousand men, most often those who lusted not for her but for her daddy's wealth. But whatever the motive, none had ever dared to be so outrageously blunt as this one. She knew she should be scandalized—convention demanded it. But that was hard to bring about when what she really wanted to do was guffaw. The mirror told her daily—hourly?—that she was a nice-looking girl, which was enough to immunize her from the lances of female rivals and give her the self-confidence she needed to encourage those few men she'd found interesting. But, dammit, few they were. Men were mostly overgrown, randy, self-enamored brats, the only unqualified exception being her father, a mountain of attractive virility and loving generosity she admired to the point of occasional—and undeniably shameful—daydreams. And this was what had thrown her into this weird struggle between amusement and anger: The aviator's unapologetic, clinical evaluation had had something of her father in it. So she lay, staring at the sky, breathing deeply, fearing that if she spoke at all she would end up cackling and sounding the fool. After a time she got a grip and asked, "What's your name?"

"Bill Carpenter."

She sat up and gave him an astonished look. "*The* Bill Carpenter? The letter writer? John King's pal?"

"Yep. But letter writer—what means that?"

"I'm Mary Lou Whiting."

"You're kidding. John's photos say Mary Lou's a knockout. You're a pan-fried banana."

They laughed together.

"I was flying down from Philly to bring you some of John's

mail. Letters he never mailed. Some pictures of you. I flew over your house and was looking for a place to sit down when the Jenny did its Jenny thing. Thank God you were doing your horse thing, or I'd be a coral reef by now."

"You liked John, did you?"

"Liked? Hell, I loved that nutty kid."

"That makes two of us."

"Closest I ever came to having a brother."

"He's becoming a very big star in Victrola records these days. A legend, they say. Right up there with Scott Joplin and Jelly Roll Morton. Nobody seems to remember he was a war hero."

Carpenter laughed softly. "No, that's been handed to Senator Slater. He shoots down two enemy planes, and everybody in the whole damned country, from Congress down to Twiddledorp, Tennessee, calls him 'The Ace.' Where the hell's the justice in that?" He laughed again and shook his head.

"I think it's sad."

They said nothing for a time, considering this. To break the melancholy creeping in, she cleared her throat and asked, "Is that what you do for a living—crash airplanes?"

"No, that's just a hobby. I've been working to start up a little flight service. A between-cities delivery and passenger service, sort of. Got the money together now, and I'm about to open shop."

"I hope you'll have better equipment than your recently expired Jenny."

"That was just my runabout. Didn't owe me anything. Up in Mineola I've got a pair of new Eaglerocks and a Waco, and I'm already deep into angling for licensing and the various government these-es and that-ses."

"Sounds good."

He sighed and managed to get to his feet, a towering mass of oil and wet sand, and folded his arms against a shuddering. She saw that he was close to suet-gray shock.

"We'd better get you to some warmth, Mr. Carpenter. I'll help you to the horse."

"Bill."

She took his hand and shook it. "Mary Lou."

His chattering teeth showed in a tight grin. "I hope that nag's big enough to handle the two of us."

She pulled his arm around her shoulders and steadied him as they made for the stallion. "I hope the world's big enough to handle the two of us," she muttered.

"Are you flirting with me, Mary Lou Whiting?"

"You're durn tootin' I am, William J. Carpenter."